The Second Amendment Killer

a novel by

Mark Everett Hall

D1445601

To Cathie, for always as always

Chapter One
Seventeen

I

Six million times last year Americans got into car wrecks. I was one. Unlike the thirty-odd thousand unlucky souls who perished in their crashes, I was only injured slightly. But, in the end, I was another casualty.

While driving past the Costco in town two weeks before Christmas, I was t-boned by an over-eager shopper anxious to save a bundle on 30-packs of Charmin for the holidays. He was going slow. I was too. Still, his RAM-tough truck crushed my Mini Cooper. I sustained a minor injury and took an ambulance to the hospital. My insurance company wanted to cover every possible angle for inevitable litigation. So I was sent off to a series of doctors and diagnosticians for weeks after the accident. If I got a new pimple, my insurance sharks intended to make sure it would become part of a lawsuit.

When I was called in for my second CT scan in mid-January I didn't give it much thought. Smoking Lauren, my virtual admin, had to remind me of the appointment three times that day and I still barely made it on time.

I stripped. Laid on the hard table. Put up with the machin e's whirring noise and the humiliation of being half-naked amidst strangers. Got dressed when the ordeal was done and returned to my job.

My precious job.

Chapter One
Seventeen

I

Six million times last year Americans got into car wrecks. I was one. Unlike the thirty-odd thousand unlucky souls who perished in their crashes, I was only injured slightly. But, in the end, I was another casualty.

While driving past the Costco in town two weeks before Christmas, I was t-boned by an over-eager shopper anxious to save a bundle on 30-packs of Charmin for the holidays. He was going slow. I was too. Still, his RAM-tough truck crushed my Mini Cooper. I sustained a minor injury and took an ambulance to the hospital. My insurance company wanted to cover every possible angle for inevitable litigation. So I was sent off to a series of doctors and diagnosticians for weeks after the accident. If I got a new pimple, my insurance sharks intended to make sure it would become part of a lawsuit.

When I was called in for my second CT scan in mid-January I didn't give it much thought. Smoking Lauren, my virtual admin, had to remind me of the appointment three times that day and I still barely made it on time.

I stripped. Laid on the hard table. Put up with the machine's whirring noise and the humiliation of being half-naked amidst strangers. Got dressed when the ordeal was done and returned to my job.

My precious job.

It was everything for me. It was my lifeline. My had job saved me. After my daughter was murdered and my wife left me, I had nothing else to embrace. Nothing but my job.

You might remember me from news reports. Jefferson Fitzgerald Black. Does that ring a bell? I was the father of Jessica Fitzgerald Black, one of the seventeen victims of Walter Riggs, who rampaged through the pews of Saint Hubertus in Wilkes Barre. That's in Pennsylvania. You've undoubtedly forgotten. There are too many mass shootings too often to keep track of where they happen, or who the dead are, or let alone the grieving. But the grieving never forget.

Jessie and her mother, my now ex-wife Loren, had taken the five hour drive from our house outside Pittsburgh to visit my wife's mom. Like the good kid she was, Jessie had volunteered to attend early morning mass with her grandmother. Loren had declined and slept in, intending to dream on until they returned. She didn't wake up until the police called a couple hours after mass should have ended to tell her that there had been a shooting.

Jessica was the ninth victim that Sunday morning. The FBI reported that specific detail to the local police who later told me and Loren. Three bullets. Two in her back, severing her spine and one through the nape of her neck and into her brain where it bounced around before exiting out her left eye. No one voluntarily told us that fact. I demanded to see the complete autopsy report. It was all there. Loren refused to look.

The police did tell us that she had died instantly. I think they said it to make us feel better. It didn't work.

My mother-in-law was Riggs's tenth victim. It's irrational, I know, but to this day I cannot forgive her for not stopping the bullets that took Jessie's life. She should have shielded her granddaughter. Instead, she took one round to the heart and died clutching her rosary beads.

To the relief of most Americans, certainly our politicians, Riggs was not deemed a domestic terrorist by the FBI. He was a common mass murderer. The most recent one with a respectable kill-count; big enough to make the top of the evening news on your TV set.

I was just another grieving parent. You've seen us. Every week. Some cowardly dickhead with a gun shoots as many unarmed strangers as he can. He either shoots himself afterwards or forces the cops to kill him. It's the same story every time. Only the kill count and the zip code changes.

Riggs was the rare exception. He was caught and arrested. After his broadcast perp walk to the courthouse, the wrecked next of kin took stage and melted down on camera. Jaded journalists put microphones in the faces of newly shattered human beings and asked, for them, routine questions. The day after I had arrived in Wilkes Barre, it happened to me. A reporter asked one such question outside the courthouse where Riggs was being arraigned. It was something about gun control. My answer made the rounds on the TV news.

"There will never be gun control until someone kills the daughter of the head of the ARI! If you really want gun control, that's what has to happen!"

The American Rifle Institute had spearheaded the drive to make noise suppressors legal for gun owners. Riggs had used a silencer so that hardly anyone realized there was a shooting at first; those who heard pops didn't immediately recognize it as gunfire. Life-saving panic seeped in slowly throughout the congregation, leaving more people as easy targets for the fiend. The ARI had also thwarted efforts to make the semi-automatic assault rifle and high-capacity magazines used by Riggs illegal. In my mind then and now, the ARI was as guilty as the shooter.

The same day I was interviewed the same intrepid journalist, always seeking the cover of balanced reporting, tracked down the ARI's telegenic boss, Wayne Laskey, Jr., via Zoom. His interview ran in time for the evening news alongside mine. Laskey gave the camera a well-practiced, serious, square-jawed look and said I ought to be arrested for making such threats. The media played it up like they do on slow news days. Later, in fact, the police did come and talk to me about my wrong-footed, though understandable remarks. Nothing ultimately happened to me with public sentiment clearly on the side of the grieving parent and not ARI's slick CEO. The incident passed.

Riggs had never popped up on anyone's database of potential mass killers because he had purchased his entire armory legally like they all do. The ARI makes sure of that. But unlike other mass murderers, he stood trial, and was sent to prison to be executed for simple murder.

He had entered the church only to kill his ex-wife and her new husband. He had stalked them for weeks, discovering which pew they favored so he could enter on the side they sat; the same side my mother-in-law preferred. His ex and her beau were the first people he shot, but, as he told the police after his arrest, he saw no reason to stop until he ran out of ammunition. He had brought two 30-round magazines and used them up before the cops could get there.

Riggs was killed by the state last year. The first death row inmate in Pennsylvania to be executed since 1999. Naturally, yet another heartless t-crossing, i-dotting journalist tracked me down over FaceTime to my new home in Oregon. She asked me if I thought justice had been done.

"Incomplete justice." I spoke directly into my smartphone's camera.

"What do you mean?" the reporter asked.

"How many mass shootings have there been in this country since Riggs murdered my daughter and sixteen other innocent people that awful day? Do you know how many? One every single day in this country. Seven-point-three shootings each week. More than a thousand victims. Every year. Those are the simple facts. And what's the common denominator behind all those killings? The ARI and all the politicians who support it. Their actions and inaction are implicated in every mass killing in America. I believe Wayne Laskey personally is complicit in thousands of crimes. Yet, he has not faced justice. So, yes, I'd say killing Riggs is only incomplete justice."

That quote made the rounds, too. This time ARI's leadership declined to debate or threaten me on camera, issuing instead a lackluster statement about the sacredness of the Second Amendment.

It's been seven years since the St. Hubertus massacre. Jessie would have turned eighteen this year. I should be writing her first college tuition checks and worrying about her being away from home. Instead, every day I wake before dawn after fitful sleep, get into the shower, and weep. Then, as every morning so far, I decide not to kill myself and go to work.

II

Smoking Lauren texted me. Again. I had ignored the first message. The second one persisted until I read it.

"Doctor Reese's office called for a follow-up on your CT scans. You see her at 3:00 this afternoon. I cleared your calendar."

I share a human admin, a Haitian man, Jameson Dese, with a dozen other sales engineers. I'd met him once back at the Pittsburgh HQ. Great guy. Overworked as hell. So I mostly rely on my digital assistant, Smoking Lauren. She's artificial intelligence software that manages my schedule, everything from business trips and customer meetings to vacation travel and social engagements, though I seldom need it for anything but work. For my virtual assistant's image I had chosen an animated emoji of Lauren Bacall lighting a cigarette in the film *To Have and Have Not*. Smoking Lauren was almost always the interface between me and the company's enterprise sales software. When I thought of the ESS, I saw Smoking Lauren. She was with me everywhere.

I worked from my car, my home, airplanes, terminals, hotels, Ubers, Lyfts, and once in a blue moon my office. Even throughout the surges and waves of the Covid pandemic, I was on the move and depended on Smoking Lauren and the ESS.

She, it, connected me to everyone who mattered at work: bosses, customers, coworkers, industry analysts, trade journalists, and even the baristas in the company-owned buildings. Outside the company, my friends knew to contact me through Smoking Lauren if they wanted to be sure I would get the message, not my personal cell or email, which I looked at sporadically. With few exceptions, if anyone needed a sliver of my time, they got it through Smoking Lauren. Appointments got made and prompts sent. That's how the doctor got a slot. But once in a while I rebelled and told smoking Lauren "no."

I'd never asked to see Doctor Reese. I'd never heard of the person. I shot an "I'm busy" comment in reply.

Smoking Lauren fired back instantly.

"No you're not. Go to the appointment. I'll have an Uber meet you outside the office at 2:40. Traffic is projected to be heavy, so the ride will take a full eighteen and a half minutes. I will have plenty of new files ready for you to review during your ride."

So that was that. I was going.

As promised, at the appointed time Smoking Lauren sent me a series of files with new integration ideas related to my latest project for the Uber ride to the doctor's office. I'm always open to anything that improves a project's chance for success, something never guaranteed in the software-installation business. In fact, more times than you'd think, giant software installations crashed and burned, wasting millions of dollars and often embarrassingly and regularly shared online at *Computerworld* and even the *New York Times.*

To my ever-popular credit, none of my projects have ever shown up unexpectedly in the media. I'm lucky but also extremely careful. Measure twice, cut once, an uncle told me as a kid while showing me how he hand-built his elaborate kite frames. With software integration I follow a similar maxim: test twenty times, run forever.

If I didn't I wouldn't be the database god people call me behind my back. But I'm not a miracle worker; rather, a patient and detailed one. I install my company's flagship software for the biggest organizations in the world. Government. Manufacturing. Communications. Transportation. Tech. Science. Anyone who's anyone runs it in their data centers. It's mostly used to figure out how to make a buck; but a few apply it to help reverse climate change; how to parse a search request on the Internet; how to track and reverse a pandemic; how to secure data; but frankly, its primary purpose is to learn how to sell stuff to suckers with more money or credit than brains.

I'm in demand from our best customers because I do things right. I travel the world on the company's dime, staying in posh hotels and flying first, or worst case, business class. In the distant past, I took Loren and Jessie on junkets to Asia and New Zealand. The company happily picked up the tab. Anything to make me happy, productive, and indifferent to the time I spent away from home on the job. Wherever home was. They moved me around a lot.

Loren and I talked about our twenty-year plan with me working my ass off while we stashed cash in IRAs, 401k's, and old-fashion savings accounts. Like Stalin's true believers, we were gonna make ourselves a personal worker's paradise after a few years of suffering, all for the good of the family.

It did not work out that way. Ironically, after Jessie died and Loren left, it was the company that stayed with me, keeping me, if not happy, at least alive and, I'm not completely naive, productive. Work let me forget life. I could distract myself by breaking down an abstract problem: getting one bit of software to work with another. Hard to do, but I was good at it. Some scripting, some coding, a hard drive full of patience and hacks. That's what it took. That's what I had. It's all I had.

Our analytics software product works with the industry's biggest, fastest, most complex databases like SAP HANA,

Oracle, Teradata, IBM DB2, and the rest. If you know anything about software these days, you know that getting different apps to work right together is the trickiest part. And the trickiest part of the tricky part is the database. The more complex the software, the more difficult it is to play nice with the database. Big-ass software databases are messy, impenetrable tarpits of incompatibility.

Except for people like me. I don't see their complexity. I see patterns that I can link together with a few keystrokes. I see shortcuts to information and pathways to insight. It's not hard, if you have a part of your brain that can't not figure those things out. Or at least it will try to whether I want it to or not. Once I've gotten a whiff of an integration problem, my mind shapeshifts into a ferret-sniffing terrier's brain, deep in the burrow, digging to the end, until I snag my prey. I can't help myself.

My company pays me a hefty six-figure salary and piles on glittering benefits because I can do what for most people looks like sheer magic: I bend software to my will. Among mere mortals, precious few people actually understand how their home PC or the Internet works let alone database-driven places like Google, Facebook, Baidu, PornHub, the IRS, NSA, CIA, and the rest. I am one of them. Not only do I grasp it conceptually, I do it; make them work together and work properly.

Half of your Web searches and most of your thumbs ups and downs around the Internet are tucked into our analytics somewhere. It predicts where you'll eat, what you'll watch, how you'll shop. You may think you have a mind of your own while you're online or out and about with your cellphone and smart watch. Think again. Like everyone, you're another victim of the wisdom of the crowds, the whimsy of an algorithm, the lure of social media. Everyone's got their own rathole to descend. Damn near every bit of it is predictable. At least with my company's product. That's why every major organization with a big enough IT budget wants it. With the right data our software can forecast just about anything anyone might do, when they'll do it, and how much they're willing to pay for the experience.

Don't think you can avoid it. It's everywhere. I know. I configured a lot of it. A whole lot of it.

I didn't write the code that collected and sorted the data. I didn't write the code that probed the data. They're very different things. I did the work that connected the collecting with the analyzing. The nerdy go-between, making and keeping the connections alive and fluid while hiding the complexity of those connections from users.

My work invigorates a part of my brain that can't not solve puzzles. No matter the problem's intricacy, I persist in working it through. When the rest of me wanted to succumb to personal despair after the murder of my daughter, in the corner of my mind I would detect a pattern in one integration project or another; I'd see connections. I couldn't let them go. I'd take them to the end, pulling all the strings together into a nice, tight bow.

I can't help myself. I fix things. And the rest of my life, my wretched life, ebbs for a while as I dive deep into the puzzle. Whatever it might be. Don't really care. I'm happy, lost in the digital dilemma of the day.

Whatever that doggedness is in me, it continues to lift me up each morning to make it into work. Against my best instincts, I don't swallow a bullet. I don't give up. I rise from my bed and, for the last seven years, check to see what Smoking Lauren has for me to do that morning. It's more than a habit or even a ritual. It's a commitment to meeting the expectations imposed by a schedule; to making it through one more day not being toted up as another suicide stat for the evening news. For good or ill, Smoking Lauren kept me alive. Not surprisingly, I liked my virtual assistant. Combined with its Haitian master, it was extremely helpful. Beyond efficient. I would not be the successful software sales engineer that I am without it.

So, as commanded by Smoking Lauren, I shrugged, accepted my meeting with Dr. Reese, and, once prompted with the tingling on my smartwatch, walked out to the curb at 2:39, adjusted my company-logoed Covid mask, and met the Uber car as instructed.

It only took seventeen minutes to reach Reese's clinic. The driver took a shortcut she knew. I tipped her double the rate on the corporate app.

I stepped to the curb, walked inside the medical building, and approached the information kiosk.

An old guy with a volunteer vest and a badge that ID'd him as Norm sat next to it.

"Looking for Doctor Reese. Suite eight seventeen."

"Don't know any Doctor Reese. They come and go," he told me. "But eight one seven is down the hall to the left. Third door."

I thanked him and moved along as an elderly lady in a walker approached behind me. Since the accident I've been going to one of the Kaiser-Permanente clinics in town. KP is the health insurance my company buys. The company pays for everything, so I don't need to worry about co-pays or anything. I like it. You show up with your member number and you're good to go. Once in a while, KP sends patients to specialists. As I looked up and saw I was not at a KP clinic, it struck me that this was one of those times.

Reese's office was located in a low-slung building across the creek from Salem Hospital. A short bridge let doctors move between their surgeries, patient rounds, and office appointments only a few hundred steps away. Two men and a woman populated her waiting room. I approached the frosted glass panel that closed off the receptionist from the waiting sick. It opened as soon as I reached it.

"Mr. Black?" the receptionist asked, wearing the standard blue surgical mask.

"Yes."

"Please go right in," she said, gesturing toward the lone door. "The doctor is ready for you."

I glanced at the waiting trio of patients, but they did not seem perturbed by my jumping to the head of the queue. I walked through the entry. There was a small vestibule with a nurse's station stocked the usual gear: two chairs and a small table; blood pressure cuff on the wall; scale; sink with a box of hygienic gloves next to it; a mask dispenser; posters illustrating how to wash your hands. I walked through it into a larger, less medically obvious room. It was a standard office any executive might have. Big desk. Plush chairs. Matching credenza with side table with chairs. Diplomas and such hung on the walls.

In the back, a stoic doctor sat behind her uncluttered desk. She set down an iPad as I walked in. Dr. Reese apparently had popped over from the hospital and was still in her green surgical scrubs. She gestured toward a straight-back chair with leather upholstery. It was surprisingly comfortable.

She rose and came over to the chair after I had sat. Her dazzling dark brown eyes held mine for a heartbeat or two and she took my hand, holding it for a moment without shaking. Her face pleasant and neutral.

"Jefferson Black, it's a pleasure to meet you."

Tongue-tied for some reason, I nodded. She returned behind her desk.

Beyond her notable eyes, she had a small nose, a row of perfect white teeth, and clear skin under a curly mop of red hair, fading to white. She looked to be in her fifties with a fleshy body that suggested she spent her late evenings reading rather than her early mornings running.

"You're a specialist."

"Yes, I contract with Kaiser when they have a serious case like yours."

"'Serious case,'" I repeated, bewildered.

"Yes, I'm sorry to tell you that you have a cancer."

"Oh, Jesus!" I not been prepared for that news, nor delivered in such an abrupt method. I felt hit by a bullet. My mind raced in confusion and fear. "Are you sure it's me? Jefferson Fitzgerald Black. Has to be a mix up. How could I have cancer? I feel fine. Great even."

"I'm sorry to be so blunt. And, yes, it's you, without a doubt. I'm so sorry. In my experience...," she trailed off

"But how? What?" I managed to mumble.

"Of course, it's hard to hear," she said and offered a sympathetic nod. "We weren't looking for it. The scan of your spine after the car accident revealed an anomaly. But that imaging was not targeting your tumor. That's why we took a second scan."

"What kind of cancer?" I whispered.

"Heart cancer."

"Heart cancer!" I nearly shouted. "What the...!"

"I'm saddened to tell you, the image shows you have an angiosarcoma that presents itself as a primary malignant cardiac tumor."

"A malignant tumor?" I hung my head shaking it back and forth in disbelief. "I just rode my bike forty miles on Saturday and another thirty on Sunday. Lots of hill climbing. I had no trouble at all."

"I understand. This kind of cancer is usually caught after some symptoms are experienced. It was only, as I said, because the radiologist saw the anomaly in the first image after your car accident that we are here now."

The part of my brain that liked to solve puzzles fired up. There had to be medical protocols to learn and follow to beat back the cancer.

"So how are we going to treat it?" I asked looking her in the eyes. "Cut it out?"

She took a deep breath and said, "The worse news is that it's inoperable and chemo in that part of the heart will kill you faster than the tumor."

"Transplant?"

"You will automatically be put on a list. It's a long list. And you're AB-negative, no smaller pool of blood type exists, meaning the smallest possible number of organ donors. To be frank, it's not something I'd pin my hopes on."

"Artificial heart?"

"Nothing approved."

My heart, my stupid, fucking traitorous heart, raced. I felt flush.

"You've just given me a death sentence."

She fetched me a bottle of water from a desk drawer cooler, unscrewed its cap and passed it across the desk. It was cold to the touch. A couple swallows of icy water calmed me.

To fill the silence, I said, "This is not the first time you have had to deliver this kind of news, is it?"

I set the perspiring plastic bottle on the edge of her desk. Droplets pooled at the bottom and began to slowly bleed over the side.

"Sadly, no. But it is the first time I've had to tell a perfectly healthy person such news; one with no symptoms like you. Even the most obtuse people have more than an inkling, a clue that they're ill when they come here. That's why they see me.

That's why they're sitting in that chair." She nodded in my direction, her eyes boring into mine. "You? I blind-sided you. I can't imagine how you feel. But I am so, so very sorry."

I could see that she was. We sat in companionable silence staring at each other for nearly a minute. It never felt weird. Empathy wafted from her like a subtle fragrance.

"I hate to sound so cliche, doctor, but how long do I have? Do you know on average how long I have to live?"

"Nothing's for certain, of course. Most people diagnosed with angiosarcoma like yours already have shortness of breath or angina."

"But I feel great."

"I know, that's what should give you hope for longer life."

"But…?"

"But," she said, shaking her head, her soft eyes linked to mine, "honestly, once detected, less than fifty percent of people with your condition are alive after twelve months. Most everyone else dies in the year after."

"Shit."

"Exactly." She offered a wan smile as she continued. "However, you are outside the normative demographics. Most cancers like yours are discovered later, as I said. People are already in decline. You're not. Still. We, I, don't really know how long you might have. I'm hopeful that because you present no symptoms, absolutely none, that you may have well more than two years of good life ahead of you."

"You think that long?" I asked sarcastically.

"I hope. I really do hope," she replied softly and stepped around her desk. She handed me a USB stick. "This has all your files, imaging, and test results. The data is there. You'll see."

I took the stick, numb.

She said, "Come with me, please."

The doctor took me by her warm hands and ushered me into an office down the hall from hers where another medical professional sat. His walls were decorated with Monet and Cassatt prints along with a requisite half-dozen framed diplomas. I noticed Stanford and Heidelberg universities among them. His combined medical degree came from Johns Hopkins. It was issued to Javier J. Charcot.

Reese introduced us. He rose and eased his way around the desk. He took my right hand in both of his and, like her, sought my eyes with his. He was a couple inches shorter than me and more than a few pounds heavier.

"Dr. Charcot is a psychiatrist." She pronounced it *shar'ko*. "He's also trained as a grief counsellor. I thought maybe you'd like to chat with him."

Having his office nearby had its advantages for the kind of news Reese dispensed to her patients. Charcot and I shook hands for a long time; his softer than mine. He had a round, almost flat face with bright dark skin and close-cropped black hair. His large, clear brown eyes radiated sympathy. He wore a gray wool suit; he'd draped the jacket over his chair and loosened the knot in his forest green tie with its vague yellow flower pattern.

Reese made the standard social movements to leave, stepping backwards, gesturing with both hands toward Charcot. She assured me I could call her office anytime with questions or concerns. She pressed a business card into my hand and slipped out the door, preparing, I supposed, to give another unlucky soul their health report.

I took the chair Charcot indicated. He studied me for a few seconds.

"May I," he said in a quiet slightly nasal tone as if he were fighting off a cold or had allergies, "offer you my sincere sorrow at what you must be feeling now. I can't imagine. It must be the worst day in your life."

I stared at him for a full five seconds.

"No," I said at last. "Not even close."

He blinked a few times, confused.

I said, "My daughter was murdered. That's the worst thing that ever happened in my life. This is nothing."

He nodded as if to himself. He spoke for a while about the nature of grief, which he believed I was experiencing, or would soon. I pretended to listen. This went on for a while before I simply shrugged.

"Doc, really, thanks a lot, but I gotta get going."

"Yes, yes, yes, I understand, Jefferson. I understand. Completely. Completely."

He moved from behind the desk to stand over me in the chair where I sat. I got up. We shook hands again as if we were concluding a business deal.

He stared at me with his kind eyes and said, "Jefferson, I want you to think carefully about your next few days, your next few hours. Don't let anxious thoughts overwhelm you. Don't be rash. Be thoughtful. You might become angry or mournfully depressed. I can prescribe...."

"Not yet, doc. I'll let you or Doctor Reese know if I need anything."

"Yes, yes, of course." Pausing for a breath, he palmed a card into my hand, leaned in close, and whispered, "Know you're not alone, Jefferson. We can be part of the strength you need in the time ahead."

I stuffed his card into my pocket along with his sorry platitudes and Reese's card, nodded my farewell, and left.

III

The over-tipped Uber driver had returned for me and took me back to my office. Unlike the journey to Dr. Reese's clinic, I never once looked at the files Smoking Lauren had sent to my phone. Instead I listened to and felt my back-stabbing heartbeats. Despite my medical news, nothing sounded amiss. Just the quiet, steady thump, thump, thump in my chest.

A persistent buzz became a shrill voice that startled me.

"Sir? Sir? We're here. Mr. Black? We've arrived!"

I literally shook my head vigorously to wake myself. I had no idea how long we had sat at the curb outside my building. I mumbled an apology and tipped double the maximum again before stepping out. The Uber whisked away.

Nodding to the building's security guard and blinking at the iris scanner while passing my smartwatch ID by the electronic detector in front of the elevator, I acted as I always did, but inside I felt like an alien presence fresh from its pod. I was no longer the person who had left the place little more than an hour earlier. Despite my face, my biometric identification, even my DNA that said I was who everyone thought I was, I had been transformed from the living to the practically dead. I was no longer me. I was now possessed by a mortal enemy, one that will slay billions of us in the end, cancer. My turn.

By instinct I arrived at my desk. My computer flashed on the moment it detected my presence via the Bluetooth smartwatch. On the screen's left side a series of recent banners scrolled upwards; the newest alerts rising from the bottom, the oldest rolling off the top. Most were snippets of the latest email or text that had arrived from colleagues and customers while I was at the doctors'. It also included breaking news from the *New York*

Times, BBC, CNN, *Deutsche Welle, WSJ,* and a few other news sites. A lot of our customers made headlines regularly, so I made an effort to stay apprised of current events. They were market research for me.

One message was from my primary physician at KP. She let me know she'd reviewed both the radiologist's and specialist reports on my sudden and surprise diagnosis. She expressed sympathy. She cc'd her assistant to set an appointment up with me through Smoking Lauren. I couldn't think of anything to say, so I closed the message unanswered.

I still held the USB stick Reese had given me. Curious about the details, ready to search for cures, I slipped the stick into my laptop. The security software sniffed the device before connecting. Within a few seconds it opened. All my insurance information right on top, of course, but the doctors notes and imaging data looked complete and overwhelming.

While I was reading about my condition, a horizontal window dead center on my screen appeared with a single question from Smoking Lauren.

"Will there be any change to your schedule tomorrow, Jefferson?"

Adding my given name at the end of the question expressed a level of intimacy I did not know my virtual assistant possessed. It almost made me cry. Of course I was reading some inchoate emotion into the message. Everyone, except Smoking Lauren and total strangers, called me Jeff.

I squelched the impulse to call my ex, Loren, and reap her pity. I wanted a portion of her sorrow, but restrained myself. Nothing could have been more selfish than calling her. My voice would only resurrect Jessie's ghost between us, even if I was phoning to tell her that I would soon be a ghost myself.

Any thought of Jessie, no matter how tangential, brought on her unbearable guilt. She blamed herself for taking Jessie to see her grandmother, a woman our daughter adored. She blamed herself for skipping mass, believing she would have done what her mother couldn't: save Jessie. She even blamed herself for sleeping in, as if by being awake she somehow could have kept her daughter alive.

"I remember my dreams that morning to this day," she'd once told me. "They were horribly banal and pleasant. The endless nightmare only began when I woke up."

If I ever tried to soothe her, she'd curse me. I remember one outburst a few Christmas's ago when she yelled at me over the phone, "Goddamn you, Jeff, she died on my watch! You don't fucking understand. She died on my watch. I was fucking asleep while she was being slaughtered! Goddamn you, Jeff!"

No. Calling her would be a mistake. It wouldn't help me and it would only make her feel bad, but not for the selfish reasons I would have wanted.

I thought about calling my boss and chatting with her about my prognosis. I ruled that out in less time it took to think the thought. Like me, she was a problem solver, but with a heart. Her well-intended empathy and subsequent intrusion into my life to make it better was not what I wanted now.

I considered Dr. Charcot's card and Dr. Reese's. I wasn't sure how complete strangers, even professionals, could help me now. Again, I felt my total isolation as if I were the only person standing in a closet while the door was closing me into darkness.

Smoking Lauren's question about my schedule gnawed at my orderly, well-behaved, everyday self. Its answer might somehow turn me back into me again, to escape the darkening closet, and to slip out of my breathing deathtrap of a body.

Then something caught my attention in between the business emails and texts in the digital bubbles floating up my computer screen. It was the number that caught my eye.

Seventeen. A very unlucky number.

It marched up the left side of my display in a half dozen alerts interspersed with my texts notifications and emails. They steadily rolled up until disappearing at the top of the screen.

My hand trembled as I touched one of the scrolling banners. A CNN headline burst into a window on my display. I clicked on it.

Seventeen dead in armed massacre

I switched to *USA Today*.

Seventeen confirmed killed

The BBC was more scolding.

Another US mass shooting kills 17

It happened in Ohio. Or Iowa. The geography did not matter. I don't remember whether it was an irate boyfriend or a psychotic teenager whose finger was on the trigger. It was only the number that mattered.

Seventeen.

I read more and more reports. They're never-ending after such a massacre. Every major news agency files at least one original report, which means quotes from everyone and anyone who happened to survive or be passing by the latest monument of slaughter to the Second Amendment.

In time, the office emptied. People left me alone staring at my screen as they filed out, mumbling their goodnights while I waved absently, presumably rapt in my work as always. Soon, I was alone.

I amped up my search and hopscotched between the constantly updated headlines, looking for the one that's always there. The one that tears me apart every time. I wasn't disappointed.

Not surprisingly, Fox News carried it first and prominently, happy to be on the cutting edge of bloodthirsty journalism.

ARI Defends Second Amendment Against Elitest, Freedom-Hating Politicians

Fox regularly interspersed it in the crawl on the bottom of the screen all day. The head of the American Rifle Institute issued it as a statement. No full press release. Just a headline. Later the ARI flushed out their screaming headline response with a longer version, though no less hyperbolic. According to the ARI, anyone against guns was against America. People against guns were practically traitors, said the ARI chief.

My cursor passed over his face. The cursor changed its icon to a live link. I clicked and found myself into another story. According to Fox's stellar stenographic reporting, the gun lobby's CEO regretted that the fake news media insisted on turning a singular tragedy into a political issue with the backing of out-of-touch urban politicians. He urged prayers and sympathy as the only meaningful way to help victims heal and move on. One evil man, he said, cannot tarnish the freedom America cherishes and enjoys because of its God-given Second Amendment.

Next to the story was the square-jawed, look-you-in-the-eyes file photo of the ARI's leader: Wayne Laskey Jr. Seven years after Jessie was murdered, the same man with the same title was still spewing the same unadulterated, hypocritical crap. He had so much blood on his hands he might as well work at an abattoir.

The man deserved to suffer, just as countless families had suffered because of him. Nothing was truer or clearer in my mind. Whatever caused him anguish was good. What gave him pain was blessed. If I could play a part in anything that inflicted suffering on Wayne Laskey Jr., I would do so, joyfully.

I was about to close the screen when it came to me in an instant. Ideas do. An entire plan unfolded in my mind. I knew how to make it happen. Make him suffer in equal measures as he had done to countless others.

I glanced at the list of meetings for tomorrow that Smoking Lauren had confirmed for me. Pointless encounters now. Each and every one a waste of my limited time.

I clicked into the message window and typed back a simple reply to the avatar's question about changing my schedule.

"Cancel everything. I quit."

My mind was racing so fast with my fantastic idea as I hit return, got up, and, grabbed my jacket and briefcase, and left the office for the last time. I never looked back.

IV

True inspiration overwhelms you; so much so that you miss some important details. Like, in my case, the difficulty of cashing out from the company and pursuing my mission. Let me explain.

Embedded in my inspiration was the fact that I had no one to live for but me. I had few friends, mostly work companions; no one I'd call a best friend. I'd never actually had one in my youth either. Not that I'm a loner. I bought people drinks and dinner and received a decent share of invitations. Long after Loren and I divorced I had had a girlfriend or two; nothing serious. I wasn't seeing seeing anyone now. As for people I loved unconditionally and who loved me, there wasn't a soul. Not even a cat. I was, am, alone.

My parents were dead to cancer, five years apart. My younger brother was killed during the 2006 Battle of Ramadi in Iraq. My dad's older sister has Alzheimer's and is currently institutionalized in Florida. My mom was an only child. Jessie was dead; Loren gone and remarried, presumably happy-ever-after, I sincerely hoped.

I was, am, alone.

From the moment I exited the Uber car it struck me hard that I would find no comfort in shared love. It hurt deeply knowing this. I was unanchored, my emotions hurtling in an empty world. As I had staggered into my office, the image hit me of George Clooney in that space disaster movie where he lets go and drifts away in silence, leaving a distraught Sandra Bullock to weep for him. Maybe self-pity was sucking me in, but I felt worse than Clooney's heroic astronaut could ever feel. I didn't have a back-story family on Earth to miss me and I certainly did not have an Oscar-winning actress to fake tears for me. I was, am, much more alone.

Then sitting at my desk, in a flash, as the number seventeen had cracked through my desperate thoughts, I realized that revenge not love would give me the greatest solace for my condition. Instantly, a plan to exact vengeance revealed itself like a parachute opening with a jolt before guiding me to solid ground.

The next day, after I had given Smoking Lauren my resignation, I took about a dozen phone calls from my boss, her boss, colleagues, and even a honcho from human resources, all pleading with me to stay. Each offered me more than the previous caller; whatever they thought would entice me to remain; money, more vacation, less travel, more travel, a new office, even an actual personal assistant to replace Smoking Lauren. I said no to everything and eventually the calls ceased.

Given Dr. Reese's death sentence, a fact I kept to myself, I was in a hurry to sell my house for its equity, sell my vested stock options back to the company, and cash in my 401k and two IRAs. I was willing to incur paper losses in my haste and pay a ton of taxes. Money in hand was worth much more to me than investments for my non-existent future retirement. Even with my indifference to profit, the process shuffled along for six weeks. When finally paid out in full, my cash horde hit $667,761, a tidy little war chest. And war it was.

I quickly began to spend my funds with serious intent, starting with my arsenal. For about the price of the latest 27-inch iMac, I bought a Sig Sauer semi-automatic with a 16-inch barrel. It came with 30-plus rounds of NATO-class 5.56 x 45 mm cartridges, which cost about twenty-five cents apiece when you buy in bulk. I did. The rifle took after-market bumps that turned it into an automatic rifle and it could be fitted with a silencer. I added a Tango6 tactical riflescope that cost as much as the gun itself. I now owned a perfect ARI-approved, street-legal, open-carry, human-killing product. I couldn't wait to use it.

I added a handgun, of course. No ARI-sanctioned mass shooter goes into battle with only one weapon. The Glock 40 had a six-inch barrel and fired 10mm bullets, fifteen in a clip. When I practiced with it I thought it well-balanced, accurate, and lethal. It cost less than the newest iPhone. However, I broke the bank with a pair of Glock 60-ec extended capacity handguns. Twenty-round magazines. Minimal kick. Beautiful killing machines.

My arsenal included my dad's old Remington 30:06 and my own Marlin 336 from occasional high school hunting days. I bought a couple hundred rounds for them, too.

While waiting for escrow on my house and the cashing-out 401k/IRA rigamarole, I reacquainted myself with guns. Like my brother, I was touched by a pang of patriotism after 9/11 and joined the Army. Unsurprisingly, that's where I got a heavy dose of gun wisdom and culture.

Unlike my younger brother, when I had enlisted I already had demonstrated my tech-savvy nature in community college. We were four years apart. I was trained by the military to deliver computer and communications support to units in Afghanistan, my brother, fresh out of high school, was trained as a fearless infantryman and got himself KIA in Iraq.

Like a lot of Americans sent to Afghanistan, I was based in Bagram's lousy wooden B-huts or, even worse for a time, the frigid canvas tents clamped to the flimsy soil. It wasn't much of a step down in accommodations when I got sent out on field operations. I helped set up data collection and comm systems between remote units engaged with the enemy and central command centers. Headquarters expected information-rich reports from operational units to feed into their central databases for analysis, which told the brass in the Pentagon how fast we were not winning the war.

Usually I was sent in after a remote territory had been deemed secure. Most of the time it was tense, but not dangerous because the area was under American control. Sometimes, though, cocky officers looking for quick promotions prematurely called for enhanced information-gathering systems to be brought in, which was to say, me. So I'd arrive with my half-million dollars worth of gear and software, then be forced to join a firefight to defned the position against the Taliban or remnants of al-Qaeda because some dumb-ass hotshot lieutenant from West Point overestimated his command of perimeter security.

But I was good with a rifle. My brother and I had successfully hunted deer as kids and during training at Ft. Bragg I hit thirty-five of forty targets in the Army Weapons Qualification Course, giving me a sharpshooter-level grade, one below the top. I know I'm bragging, but in fact, I was credited with two kills during Operation Redwing in 2005. I got a medal for those killings. I do not think I'll be given one for my next ones.

I'm telling you all this so you know that my inspiration, while murderous, was not fanciful or, for that matter, odds nothwithstanding, blatantly suicidal. I had the shooting skills to pull off becoming the first civilian serial mass-murderer in history. And I bet I'll be the only one with a specific anti-gun agenda. Yes, I appreciated the irony.

There are plenty of military and political serial mass murderers in the past, present, and future. Governments kill at scale, at will. Nothing new about that. Civilian mass murderers, though, only get one moment in the sun before, per usual, they're thrown in jail, killed by cops or by themselves. Civilians, until me, did not have the skillset and the motivation to leave a slippery red trail of multiple events in their wake. They were one and done. Not me. I was determined to join the murderous elite, killing my enemies in numbers deemed large enough by the FBI to be considered a mass murderer. In the purest sense I was a government of one, invading enemy territory like a latter-day Henry Thoreau packing major heat.

While cooling my jets waiting for my big payout, I had spent lots of time at a quarry between Philomath, Oregon and the coast. The landowner was happy to take a hundred bucks from a stranger to let him shoot there for a day. I went every weekend until all my accounts finally liquidated. I now had the scratch to fund my itch.

By then I had my eye and trigger finger back in form. Even in cross winds, with the sun in my eyes, and through shadows, I was hitting my honeydew melon targets at five hundred meters thirty-six out of forty times. I'd take those odds.

Probably more important, I spent extra time working through the details of how to become the most successful mass murder in American history; not one who killed at random, but with purpose, with sweet revenge, with a righteous message of eye-for-an-eye suffering. I couldn't think of a more challenging and rewarding project for myself before my heart crapped out. Of course, the risks of my plan meant I might not live that long. Not that such a detail mattered to a man like me. I was doomed either way.

I was anxious to begin. If it weren't going to be so gruesome, it might even be fun.

V

In between my weekend target practice, I dived deep into the backgrounds of all my victims, downloading an endless amount of data. I slipped into the computer networks and data centers of dozens of companies and government agencies, federal, state, and local that had collected data on Laskey's family and others. Any entity storing information on those I hunted, I pulled down gigabytes about them. I normalized the data, a tedious process that eliminates redundancy and improves the accuracy of the analysis. Next I fed the normalized data into a ghost version of my former company's analytical software.

Analytics is what my old company's type of computer software is called these days. But it's had different monikers over the decades: decision support systems, knowledge management, expert systems, enterprise decision management, and more. The idea is always the same: computers do the heavy lifting of thinking. It's core to the emerging dubious age of machine learning and artificial intelligence.

Today these advanced, lightning quick systems have what they've always lacked to make them useful: data. Big Data, to be precise. Every transaction. Every measurement. Every event. Every utterance. Every fact, true or fake or in-between, is currently available for analysis. Everything can be poured into one algorithmic model of probability or another and answers will result. It's an exciting time in the field.

I don't care about any of that. Not anymore. I am using analytics simply to hunt my prey.

Let's say you were my target. Maybe you live in Indianapolis or Spokane. I don't care. With analytics I don't even need to know your address to find you, but, of course, I do know. That plus your credit rating, bank account number, Visa, Social Security, and ATM pin numbers. I can follow your behavior by, say, tracking your credit and debit transactions over any length of time. I use the data to find your most favorable behavioral pattern for me to kill you. Maybe it'll be at the gas station you use every six-point-two days or, possibly, your morning visit to the ATM or Starbucks. I'd evaluate the various angles for my shot, using analytics for variables like the whereabouts of nearby video cameras, passing police cruisers, and possible witnesses, not to mention the average crosswind velocity for the kill site. Ultimately I'd have to decide where to pull the trigger. But with analytics and my shooting skill, I would have a better than ninety-seven percent chance of hitting your head on my first shot. Anyone in America. Anytime.

Boom. You're dead.

Actually, it's not a boom at all, more of a puff of wind with the legal silencer the ARI lobbied for and that I've attached to my weapon. No one will hear a gunshot. Out of the blue your head would explode and your body would fall to the ground like a tossed rag doll. But by that time I'd be gone, off tracking my next unsuspecting victim. It would be that easy.

You see, though, I don't want to be known as just another successful serial killer. Someone who picks people off one at a time. I'm no Jack the Ripper, Son of Sam, or Night Stalker. First, I'm a *mass* murderer. That means I have to follow the FBI definition of killing at least four people in one place or in a limited geographical area in a short time frame. Otherwise I'm merely a run-of-the-mill murderer, serial or otherwise. Not their concern.

In my case, I will not only murder a quartet or more in each instance, my victims won't be any random four individuals who just happened to be where I showed up to do my despicable deed. They will be specific individuals killed with specific intent. Each event will be a premeditated crime of passion. My mission is to exact vengeance on every strata of America's gun run society until I reach the very top. No one is safe for a killer with the right data. No one.

Chapter Two
Grieving Parent

Celeste Youngblood

I

The state police had wrapped crime-scene tape like yellow and black bunting around dozens of trees, each yards apart, draping them together into a sprawling geometrical perimeter. Three narrow equestrian paths in Maryland's T. Howard Ducket Watershed Park converged along the slumping hills in a thick wood of elm, maple, and oak coated in moss, lichen, and shadows. An isolated, but tamed and pretty corner of the natural world, she thought. An insulated, deserted place. Perfect for an assassination. Special Agent-in-Charge Celeste Youngblood saw that possibility immediately. Great camouflage, yet with excellent sight-lines for a shooter.

Coincidently, it was not her first visit to these woods. As part of the intermittent rich-suburban-white-folk outreach to the inner city, the then teenage Celeste Youngblood had visited the Runnymede Equestrian Club and ridden ponies along these exact paths with other city-wise middle school girls from Baltimore twenty-four years earlier. The dark forest seemed unreal and scary to her at the time, like a place where Tolkein's Orcs lurked; that was her memory of it.

Not much had changed. It was still a scary and, now, deadly place. Undergrowth on the shady hillsides made it impossible to see more than twenty feet beyond the paths into the silent woods. The place absorbed sound, too. She couldn't hear traffic, neither in the air nor on the nearby roads and highways. The pervasive silence was more unnerving to a city girl like her than the corpses strewn on the path like twisted fallen limbs after a storm.

At the nexus of the three horse trails two women in matching beige jodhpurs with identical lavender contrast stitching lay dead; their lifeless, expertly made-up faces looking up into the sun-dappled leafy canopy. A third victim, a man in too-tight blue jeans and a black leather jacket, was spread-eagled face down on the path a few yards away. The women's bodyguard. From her vantage point striding toward the bodies alongside her superior, Assistant Director Richard Lakes, Youngblood saw that they all had been shot in the head.

Based on the splayed and random positions of the bodies, Youngblood knew they'd each been hit from long range. The man in the leather jacket went down first, his revolver holstered tight. He was followed by the two women. One, two seconds max between shots, no more. The killer was a marksman and smart. That narrowed the pool of possible suspects by plenty. She knew most smart people were lousy shots and most marksmen were idiots. Statistically speaking, of course.

A trio of horses and a large pony grazed further down one leafy path. Their expensive English saddles shone from care and wear in the shimmering sunlight. A fifth animal stood uneasily near the victims. Youngblood saw that it had been hobbled with clear postal tape.

"Remove that tape from the horse's legs," she ordered a uniform standing by. He hesitated only a second before her hard look sent him to his knees near the horse where he pulled his tactical knife and sliced through the tape. She added, "Carefully, it's evidence."

At that moment, out of the foliage a uniform ran in their direction, carrying a young girl in his arms, alive, dressed in the same beige jodhpurs with the matching stitching as the female victims. The girl did not look conscious.

"Explains the pony," Youngblood said to no one in particular.

The uniform, suddenly realizing that he was carrying a traumatized victim back to the scene of the crime or possibly that he was contaminating the scene, turned and high-tailed it back up one of the paths deeper into the forest. Almost comic, except for the tragic circumstances. The child, whose arms were loosely clasped around the officer's neck, never seemed to notice anything. Youngblood got the immediate impression the kid was not unconscious but drugged.

"Get her story," Lakes barked.

Youngblood trotted off. Lakes, as head of the Major Crimes Division, had investigated more than his share of mass murderers doing what they do: slaughter lots of people with guns. Without those kinds of sick killers, he wouldn't have his job. But she knew he'd have given up his position in a heartbeat, if it were at all possible. She admired his indignation after all these years, all those bodies. He never got jaded by the horror.

Lakes had recruited Youngblood four years earlier. Like every FBI newbie with promise, once hired she had been diverted into the agency's insatiable anti-terrorism budget. But in a couple of years she saw that the ocean of agents fighting the puny tide of terrorism did not meet her ambition. She did not think of herself as a small fish among many. She also felt queasy about the racial profiling and the entrapping of gullible Muslim boys and dumb-ass hillbillies into FBI-fabricated plots.

She wanted to remove criminals from the streets, not be part of a force dedicated to defeating what was largely a politically-convenient shibboleth. Twenty-first century terrorism, even the domestic variety, was not an existential threat to the United Staes, but it was the best show in town and everyone wanted to be there. Except her. So she was ready the instant Lakes called her; despite his warranted reputation as a crap boss, he was also known as a great detective, someone she could learn from.

Lakes was the fourth and longest lasting Assistant Director in charge of the FBI's work on mass shootings. One of his predecessors was dead, one retired, and a third in prison. But that was for tax evasion; something Lakes had overlooked because he admired the man as a crime solver, despite his criminal record. Given the workload of Lakes's division, closing a mass-murder case was paramount and anyone, tax shirker or not, who could do that was first rate in his book.

That he chose Youngblood for his group spoke volumes about his belief she was a crime solver not a butt kisser. It was how she saw herself. So Youngblood gave her boss wide latitude when he flew off the handle. After all, like his predecessors, he was a busy man.

There was no shortage of mass killings to investigate, even after the killer's been dead and buried. More than sixty from the last decade remained open. Twelve last year alone. Seventeen so far this year. Hundreds of victims. In every case the shooter had been locked up or, most likely, dead at the scene. For most homicides that would be enough to finish the file and move on to the next tragedy.

Not for Lakes or the Bureau. Closing a case meant sweating out every detail as to why and how the killer acted, which meant uncovering every facet of the bastard's life, and filling in the database with every verifiable fact about the mass murderer. Because, like every AD of the division, Lakes's goal was to build the perfect profile of mass killers so his agents could find them before they shoot their victims.

"Pun intended," Lakes would say once or twice a year, "we need to discover the psychological triggers for a mass murderer before he puts his physical finger on the trigger."

A good line, Youngblood thought, but not realistic. The FBI can never prove it stopped a mass shooting by a lone gunman in advance. It has arrested men with scary arsenals and freakish politics, but it could never say with any degree of certainty that this or that guy was hours or days away from creating another American bloodbath. They didn't live in a Philip K. Dick novel. She knew that, but believed, like her boss, the more they knew about past mass killers would, in some way, help prevent future ones.

"We don't read the minds of evil men," Lakes would say on occasion. "Yet."

Given the impossibility of his job, Youngblood did not begrudge Lakes's outbursts, his anger, his digs at staff. He was fully aware of his reputation and tried to contain it. She wondered if in this case he'd be able to hold his temper.

That's because this killing was different for obvious reasons. It was a political mass shooting, at the very least, and possibly one of revenge. That became clear once the victims were ID'd. Daughter and mother-in-law of Wayne Laskey, Jr., CEO of the American Rifle Institute.

Four victims, making it an FBI case. The first, a middle-aged equestrian named Darien Fornby, who rode his horse, Nada Nada, regularly in the park. His body was found a hundred yards down a trail, partially covered in bramble, leaves, and dirt. Nada Nada, they learned, was the horse hobbled at the three horse paths' meeting place.

"The killer wanted the cops to immediately find his fourth victim so they'd call us in," she'd said to Lakes when they had arrived at the scene. "He wants to be chased."

"That makes him either very stupid or very dangerous."

"Let's assume the latter."

Neither Lakes nor Youngblood doubted the local cops theory that the shooter had taken out Fornby first, hid the victim's body, and hobbled his horse to capture the attention of the horsewomen. By getting them to stop in a particular place, he could pick off the women and their bodyguard one by one.

The how question was pretty obvious and the why question already partially answered by who the victims were related to: Wayne Laskey, Jr., a man who gets multiple death threats in every imaginable form every day. The only important question for Youngblood was who.

Perhaps the young girl in the retreating cop's arms might offer something. She shouted to the medical examiner to follow her. The ME had been standing over the second victim, the bodyguard, her arms akimbo.

Youngblood knew that Lakes would be hollering for the ME to give him a report on the victims, so she bellowed first.

"Doc, we've got a live one over here! The dead won't be leaving anytime soon!"

The ME glanced up from examining the victim, shrugged, grabbed her bag, and headed in Youngblood's direction. They ran to catch up with the state trooper. He had laid the girl on the ground atop a thermal blanket another uniform had pulled from an emergency kit. The second cop also folded his leather jacket into a pillow for her head. The girl looked about ten years old to Youngblood. Hard to tell with thin, blond, blue-eyed kids of a certain class. They all look and act alike. The kid's pupils were dilated to the max and they floated from object to object like blue-black butterflies skitting across flowered meadow where she lay.

The trooper said he had found the girl bound at her ankles and wrists to a tree a couple hundred yards further into the woods. The killer had bound her heavy elastic bands popular with physical therapists. He said he wore gloves when he untied her and left the bonds at the tree. He said the girl never spoke a word or made a sound.

The ME quickly located a puncture mark where the girl had been injected with something that made her awake but not alert. The ME did a few more rudimentary tests flashing a light in the kid's eyes and checking her vitals.

"I'm guessing she's been shot up with something like propofol; won't know for sure until we run a tox panel," the ME said. "She may not remember a thing. She may remember everything. For now, let's get this girl to ER and stat."

"An ambulance has been called. She'll be on it," Youngblood said.

She then ran her gloved hands over the girl's clothing's pockets. She was surprised not to find a smartphone, but figured it was on the pony's custom saddlebag. The jodhpurs were skin tight, but in a rear pocket she found a worn card that identified the child as having a severe peanut allergy. Youngblood figured they'd also find an Epipen in the saddlebag. The card also gave the girl's name. She was Laskey's granddaughter.

While they waited, Youngblood squatted down on a knee next to where the girl lay wrapped in the trooper's thermal blankets, her head resting on the gallant uniform's jacket.

The kid's wrists and ankles were ringed with shallow welts from the restraints. After the killings the shooter took the girl into the forest and tied her up. For what purpose?

Bending to the ME's ear, she whispered, "We'll need to have her checked for sexual assault."

The doctor nodded, but said, "I agree. But a quick look at her appearance," she lifted the blanket slightly and gestured to the fully dressed girl, complete with knee-high riding boots, ready for dressage and Freudian stereotyping, "suggests, thankfully, it will come up negative."

Youngblood studied the girl. Her eyes were open, but dull and not taking hold on anything. Youngblood gently brushed aside some errant bangs on the girl's forehead. She smiled at the child and pulled a strand from her unseeing eyes to behind the young girl's delicately diamond-stud pierced ear.

Suddenly, the girl's irises steadied. For a moment her gaze latched onto Youngblood's unwavering look.

"Pappy's a killer," she mumbled. "Pappy is a mean killer. And there will be more to come. There will always be more to come. More to come...."

Just as quickly her eyes began their incessant dance again and she fell silent. No one spoke for a few minutes in case she spoke again. But there was nothing else. The stretcher from the ambulance arrived. She was loaded on it and taken away. Children's services was called to meet the ambulance at the hospital.

Youngblood ordered two of the uniforms to follow with code blue and to stay with the kid. One inside, one outside of wherever the doctors treated the kid.

"Stay with her. Highest priority," she directed them tersely. "She's a witness to a mass murder. Our only one. Keep her alive."

The cops took off after the ambulance with more purpose in their jobs than they'd had in years. Given that the killer had not murdered the girl initially, Youngblood was not unduly concerned for her life. But it didn't hurt to be overly cautious.

"Who's Pappy?" the ME asked her. "Did he kill those people?"

"Can't say," Youngblood replied before she turned on her heel toward AD Lakes and the murder scene. "But we'll find out."

II

Lakes ordered one of the troopers to show him the dead bodyguard's horse, which he'd identified quickly by the longer stirrups and the less well-cared for saddle. After the techs had cleared the scene, just before the medics were to remove the body, Lakes spread out his six-foot frame on his back next to the male victim, below the looming horse, a chestnut gelding with infinite patience. His head as close as possible to the dead man's shattered skull.

Prone on the ground, Lakes was staring up toward the forest canopy. Youngblood knew enough to watch, learn, and keep her mouth shut. She had seen him do this kind of thing before, so she wasn't concerned by his actions. Rather, she took a moment to study his face. Clean-shaven. Generous cheekbones. Close-cropped hair. Smooth, pale skin. From her angle, his narrow nose with nostrils so thin she wondered how he breathed through it. His watery blue eyes glared at everything and everyone in constant assessment. He rarely smiled, but she knew from memory that his gleaming teeth, when bared, could be a fearful sight; what you'd see on a predator whose lunch has sauntered by.

Eventually, Lakes jumped up and mounted the compliant horse gracefully in one fluid motion. Youngblood had never seen him on a horse before. Never heard him mention horses or any animal besides his cat, Cat, which Lakes swore was in honor of Cat Stevens, a singer the AD never listened to, as far as she knew. With a couple nudges of his knees and clicks from his mouth, he coaxed the animal slowly in ever widening circles around the body as he studied the surrounding dark forest. Youngblood knew he was estimating potential bullet trajectories and then ruling them out until he made a decision. When he located the killer's position he jumped off the horse and directed a forensic team to the area, while handing the reins to a bewildered state trooper.

Youngblood had seen her boss use eccentric methods to pinpoint shooting angles before the techs could, although never from horseback. No one read a crime scene better than he did, so it didn't surprise her. But it did the homicide detective from the state troopers.

He asked her boss skeptically, "I can understand how you might be able to see where the shots came from being up on the horse, but what the hell does getting on the ground have to do with figuring out where the perp fired from?"

Lakes answered indifferently, as if he thought anyone with a brain would understand.

"Before I could determine the trajectory of the bullet, I needed to see the trajectory of the body falling from the horse. You can't have one event without the other."

"But what if the horse twisted and flung the guy off, it would change your perception of the angle the shooter took and, therefore, his location," the detective persisted.

"'What if' did not happen, detective. What happened, happened. Never speculate. Don't invent possibilities when the probabilities are readily observable," Lakes continued. "He was shot and gravity took over. He fell, propelled in a particular direction by the impact of the bullet to his cranium. He wasn't flung by the horse or any other force than gravity, which is obvious from the position of the body. He crumpled and, as I said, submitted to gravity." Lakes switched his gaze. "The older woman, who turned to look, was shot next and fell in a similar fashion. The young woman, who barely had time to register the horror of what she saw, was hit with the third and final rifle bullet. Three stationary targets taken down in short order by an expert marksman at less than fifty yards."

Within minutes a shout came from the dense spring foliage. Lakes phone rang. He listened, then said that they'd located the sniper's nest, confirming his directions. They had begun processing the scene.

He turned her way while pocketing his phone.

"One other thing," he added. "They said the killer left his rifle behind."

"That's one hell of a calling card," Youngblood said.

"It is, indeed. Well, we'll find out more on that later," he said. "What's with the girl, Celeste?"

He used the first name of anyone who worked for him, though none dared to reciprocate.

"Alive, sir. Drugged. Possibly propofol. I've ID'd her as Wayne Laskey Jr.'s granddaughter. She was tied to a tree before the uniform freed her. She's off to the ER now. Techs are processing the abduction site. The girl will be thoroughly checked for external DNA. Probably not molested, thank Christ. But doctors will check. I ordered police protection, though it's probably not necessary. If the killer wanted her dead, she'd be dead now."

"Exactly, Celeste. Did she speak?"

"In fact, she did, sir."

He moved closer and edged her away from the scrum of state troopers and investigators. He bent his head and lowered his voice.

"What did she say, Celeste?"

She kept her voice a notch below a whisper, knowing Lakes hearing was acute.

"She'd just come out of her stupor for a moment. A few seconds. The kid said, 'Pappy's a killer. Pappy's a mean killer.' She said there would be more killings. Then she faded out again. I can't make sense of it."

"Oh, I know what it means, Celeste."

"Yes, sir," she said, waiting.

"Pappy is her grandfather."

"She thinks Wayne Laskey killed her mother and grandmother?"

Lakes thought for a moment, then shook his head.

"No," he said softly. "Someone, the killer most likely, put the idea in her head after he drugged her."

"Why?"

"To make her hate her grandfather. To send a message to 'Pappy.' To sow confusion in our investigation. The possibilities are manifold, Celeste. That's why we investigate, isn't it?"

"Yes, sir. But it also brings Wayne Laskey Junior closer to our investigation and it means we need to talk to him."

"I agree, Celeste. One hundred percent. Let's go do that. We'll set up a meeting ASAP."

He gave her his rare, hungry smile.

III

"Do you know what Zillow is, Celeste?" Lakes asked as she navigated a big, black GMC Suburban through the exclusive, leafy Maryland zip code to the Laskey estate.

His head was bent over his phone while she drove. He was using one of the Bureau's encrypted units communicating over a secret FBI virtual private cell network. For Zillow? Youngblood wondered. Really?

She was still slightly peeved at being held at arm's length by Laskey's playing buddy-buddy with the Director. It had taken more than two days to get a meeting with the ARI's CEO. Sixty hours to be exact. Sixty lost hours.

Laskey's "good friend," the FBI Director, had called Lakes and told him to respect the man's sorrow and give him time before interviewing him, even though they had seen Laskey on television a half dozen times since the killings, decrying the rise of "the Second Amendment Killer," shedding real tears on every occasion, calling the dead "martyrs for freedom" in between sobs, making the killings about him and the ARI before the FBI publicly had made any such definitive connection. In Laskey's most recent interview, on Breitbart, he said his daughter was a casualty in the leftist war against guns. Again, he wept on camera for the streaming audience.

The Director, Lakes had told her with an unnatural calm, told him he had interviewed his friend and Laskey had assured him he knew nothing about the killings when he felt "psychologically ready the official Q&A," as if it were a red-carpet celebrity chat before an awards show.

The national politics involved were well above Youngblood's pay grade. She ignored them as much as possible. But this nonsense pissed her off. She briefly wondered whether a more politically savvy FBI squad might take over the investigation.

Lakes had spent to many hours locked in his office on the phone with the Director, Otis LeBlair, a stooge of the Vice President, and other higher ups.

The building media frenzy about the murders meant that neither the Director nor even the President could take the investigation away from Lakes's team. If they tried, it would appear as if they were meddling. The AD had designated Youngblood as the internal SAC of the investigation, that was that. LeBlair insisted he be the FBI's public face. That was perfect for her. She hated standing in front of microphones listening to stupid questions from journalists trying to disrupt investigations.

Even better, internally Lakes filtered most of the actual meddling from internal management. Still, her visibility within the Bureau meant she'd shoulder the blame if the FBI failed, that is, she failed, to bring in the Laskey murderer. Soon. Bureau politics she understood and knew she shouldered that risk to her career by being the front-line SAC on this case.

Letting Laskey stall bothered Youngblood a little less than she complained to Lakes. His tactic deluded the ARI boss into thinking that he had control over the situation; that he was pulling strings from above; that he had an advantage.

Nothing could be further from the truth to Youngblood. Showing his power at the start of the investigation made him weak, and not completely innocent in most agents' eyes. What kind of father would want to slow down the pace of his daughter's murder investigation? One who needed to get his story straight with his lawyers and the media before helping the good guys. Why?

Nor had her team of agents been idle during the interval. What they had found amazed her.

Not surprisingly, forensics confirmed that the bullets in the Laskey victims matched those remaining in the rifle left behind in the sniper's nest. The recoveed bullet from the first victim, forgotten by the media because he was not connected to the ARI and its media-drenched CEO, also matched the weapon.

Laskey, with no appreciation for hypocrisy, had no trouble giving permission for investigators to speak to his granddaughter when first asked. That told Youngblood that he was the worst kind of coward; the kind who battled women and children for a seat on a lifeboat.

She watched the girl's interview through a camera feed. A pair of highly trained and empathetic child trauma experts talked the girl through her experiences. Her father, recently divorced from her deceased mom, sat through the sessions, mostly in stunned silence, holding his kid's hand; Youngblood thought, for his comfort as much as hers. The brave young lady offered her impressions of the killer's likeness to a sketch artist. Not much to go on. He wore a mask.

But she was able to describe his voice.

"Calm. Slow. Deep. Like on a pickup truck commercial."

Then she passably mimicked the Dodge RAM truck ad's voiceover. "RAM tough!" Although she was not trying to be funny, the girl's earnest portrayal brought a smile to Youngblood's lips.

But the most explosive data they learned leading to the Laskey interview came from the murder weapon. It linked Laskey to the gun.

Yesterday morning AD Lakes had visited her office.

"A moment, Celeste?"

He had phrased his words like a question, but she knew it was an order. She immediately closed her call with an agent in the field and followed her boss down the hallway at a brisk pace. He stepped into an open conference room, closed the door, took out his phone, tapped the screen, and handed it to her. She was looking at an image of form FD-258, which the FBI and other agencies used to track fingerprints for everyone from the millions of incarcerated criminals to the millions of job-seeking civilians wanting a security clearance. The name and signature on the form was Wayne Howard Laskey Jr. The Social Security number matched his, too.

Lakes had said, "His 258 form from when he was in the Navy came up for the prints on the weapon found at Duckett Watershed. And ballistics confirm that was the weapon used to kill our victims. They were the only prints on the gun."

"Shit," she whispered and immediately apologized. "Sorry, sir."

Not that he was a prude, but Lakes, in an effort to curb his swearing, had set up an on-your-honor empty aquarium as a swear jar in his office. At New Years the sizable funds were totaled and the potty-mouthed department would throw themselves a party, usually lavish with the funds they had collected. She made a mental note to drop a buck in the jar later.

"No, it's true shit, Celeste. Deep, stinking shit."

She had smiled. The AD would be making a rare addition to the jar as well. Not long after she'd joined his team he'd explained the swear jar to her. "I want my staff to be efficient communicators, not lazy speakers. English is such a rich language with almost infinite alternatives to the ubiquitous and uncommonly vague fuck and such," he'd said, then reached into his wallet and tossed a dollar bill into the aquarium.

She had told Lakes in the conference room that her agents had confirmed with video evidence that Laskey couldn't have been there. He was giving a speech onstage in Oklahoma City at the same time of the shooting. Witnesses by the score.

"He simply was not at the scene," she concluded. "It's more likely he could have given the gun to the shooter or it was stolen."

"His prints on the gun have to be falsified, we'll find out how," Lakes said.

"And yet…"

"The killer had the chops to transfer Laskey's latents to the weapon while keeping his prints off of it. What's that make him?"

"A sophisticated shooter."

"More dangerous than we originally thought. Much more."

"If we ever get to interview Laskey, maybe we'll get some answers."

That's when he had told her that they'd secured the Laskey interview.

Now they were almost there.

She glanced at Lakes from behind the Suburban's wheel and asked, "Zillow, sir? What about it?"

He ignored her question, asking, instead, "Do you think Laskey's a suspect in the crime we're investigating, Celeste?"

"I keep an open mind. Why? You don't believe it possible for Laskey to be a suspect?"

"It's not that he's above the law. It simply makes no sense that he'd stage such a symbolic and ironic killing that hits a bullseye on the Second Amendment. Why hurt your own cause, even in the abstract? Makes no sense. And he's not a stupid man. He wouldn't leave prints on a murder weapon. My guess: weapon was stolen and somehow unaccounted for by Laskey. You can imagine the guy has a lot of them."

"With all due respect, I doubt it," she said. "You've seen the report. Although it's a used gun, the AR-15 has never been registered to Laskey and it's never been reported stolen or missing. Its most recent provenance is from Oregon. Purchased by a Jefferson Fitzgerald Black back in March, 13 March. We're running that down now. I may need to fly to, uh, Salem, Oregon and check this guy out."

"Do it."

"The revelation of the fingerprints throws a monkey-wrench into the investigation," she said, pausing for a moment. "Did he know? Was that why Laskey stalled us? Did he know he was connected to the weapon?"

"It's going to need explaining," Lakes agreed.

"Yet," she let out a frustrated breath and said, "He didn't do it. Couldn't have done it. He simply wasn't there."

"Absolutely not. We know where he was at the time of the killings. And even the head of the ARI can't shoot people in Maryland from a podium in Oklahoma."

"A hired gunman?" she had asked in a low voice.

"Motive?"

"TBD."

"That's a stretch, one best left unspoken until..."

"Yes, yes, I know," she said. "Until all the facts are in."

Some of the facts were already pouring in, none of them pointing to Laskey. Most critical, it hadn't taken long for the agency to zero in on a plausible suspect, the said Jefferson Fitzgerald Black. The man who first purchased the rifle found at the scene. He appeared prominently in the threat matrix she had developed around Laskey. JFB, as the FBI agents referred to Black, had made a specific threat against Laskey's daughter and in-law a few years ago. JFB had lost his daughter and mother-in-law to a mass murderer in a church using an AR-15. In the aftermath, JFB in a TV interview had wished a similar fate on Laskey.

At the agency's request the local police visited the man at his then home in Pittsburgh. They filed a report concluding that JFB posed no real threat. He did not own a weapon of any kind and had zero history of run-ins with the law. He was a decorated vet. He was pegged as a grieving father snapping at a journalist's rude question. Filed and forgotten. Until the Laskey killings.

Initially, Youngblood had thought JFB's threat merely a coincidence, but she still dispatched agents from the Portland office to his current Oregon residence. Their report alarmed her. JFB had recently and unexpectedly quit his job, sold his house, cashed out his company stock and 401ks. He had also bought an AR-15, the one found in the Duckett Watershed. After that, he disappeared. Co-workers, neighbors, and his ex-wife were questioned. No one had heard from him in a couple months. He'd vanished.

One field agent discovered that soon after leaving his job JFB had purchased a small arsenal, in addition to the weapon that had been used in the Laskey killings. All the purchases completely legal. Another agent had unearthed the owner of a quarry who had rented it to JFB for target practice. The agent's email quoted the owner saying, "Sometimes I'd watch him for a while. He didn't seem to mind. He practiced a bunch. Same size targets. Over and over. I could tell he was one of them what you call perfectionists. He was good, too. Real good."

His military record gave her pause as well. Despite working as a warfare software specialist, he did so on the front lines. And he'd proven himself an expert marksman and courageous soldier with the medals to prove it.

Then there was the fact that his only brother had been killed in Iraq; his only child was murdered. Both his parents were dead and he had no siblings. All he had was an ex-wife, whom he seldom talked to. A man with nothing to lose.

It was no longer a coincidence for Youngblood. JFB was connected to the crime. Likely did the crime.

It was time to put out an APB on him as a person of interest. Five-foot eleven. One hundred-eighty pounds. Fit. No visible scars, tattoos, or deformities. Brown hair. Brown eyes. Usually clean shaven. His military records flagged little of notice, except he was a bit braver than other fighting men and a better shot. While he'd lost a brother in the endless Middle East wars, he did not get besmirched as being bitter in his psych reports. No PTSD detected. Went immediately to work in tech land, after the government spent thousands to train him, easily snagging the highest security clearances along the way.

That worried her, too.

When her eyes had raced over his curriculum vitae it sent a shiver down her spine. The list of blue chip companies and government agencies around the globe that JFB had helped connect their databases to the internet was frighteningly long. It was wise to assume he retained access to some, most, or all of every project he had ever worked on. Some or all of them would have personal information on anyone JFB wanted to kill. Not only could he hack into systems and steal identities, JFB's knowledge of his targets would be comprehensive, culled in excruciating detail from the piles of information people load into corporate and government systems. He could learn every aspect of a target's life and pick and choose the perfect moment for their murder.

"In truth, JFB looks good for it," she said without preamble. "Still too early to officially call him a suspect. But I'm putting out an APB on him has a POI."

"Right move," Lakes acknowledged.

"Then there's the Laskey connections."

"The killer left us damn obvious clues to follow," he muttered. "Even Inspector Clouseau could suss them out. In fact he'd spin his wheels on them, just as the killer wants for us. If we could be assured of a complete media blackout,…"

"Which we can't."

"…we could ignore this bait. But enough people, especially local police, will get wind of some things pointing to Laskey or everything about him, especially the fingerprints on the weapon, and if they don't see us talking to Laskey about it, it will be in the news, slanted as the agency protecting a politically powerful person."

"Should we get a search warrant after our talk?"

Lakes nodded.

"Yes, calling out his home and work computers and smartphones in particular. But we may not even have to execute it, if we can explain to him and his pack of lawyers why we need to search his personal files with his permission."

"Why's that, sir? Why should he let us do it voluntarily?"

"We're not looking for evidence to convict Laskey. We know he's innocent. It's safe to say JFB hacked into Laskey's and his family's digital lives. We're looking for the intentional and unintentional clues JFB left behind. We're looking for dots that could connect us to him. Maybe those dots will help us find him and take him down quickly."

"Will Laskey acquiesce?"

"Probably. If we execute the warrant, it has to be filed in court and becomes public record. If he lets us search his stuff without invoking it, odds are much better we can keep what we find unrelated to the investigation under wraps. Fewer people in the loop reduces the likelihood of JFB's planted evidence going viral, a top priority for the grieving father. And the Director."

She nodded and said, "If anyone understands the equation of information containment equals peace of mind, it's the head of the ARI. Facts in the open aren't his strong preference."

SAC Lakes's eyes scrunched closed when he said, "You're such a cynic, Celeste."

She jerked the steering wheel of the SUV to avoid a stupid squirrel intent on suicide.

"Back to my question, Celeste. Do you know?"

"Do I know what, sir?"

"Zillow."

"Of course, sir."

"Do you know what it says about Laskey's property?"

"No."

"It says he bought the place for seven and half million dollars nine years ago. Zillow estimates his place is worth eighteen million now."

"Some people are lucky, sir."

"Except when your family gets murdered."

"Certainly if it's something random. Horrible and random, which is what we deal with all the time. Yes, that's unlucky. But if it's because of who he is, what then? Is it payback or karma?"

"No luck being him then."

"I'd say less luck being them, his kin. He's still breathing, though through no fault of his own."

"I guess you're right," he conceded after a second or two.

After seeing Laskey perform on the news for years, it took all Youngblood's will power to contain her disdain for the man. Like most members of law enforcement, she was bewildered by the work of the modern ARI. Back when it was an organization designed to promote gun hunting, marksmanship sports, and weapons safety, it was a great institution. But since it became a tool of gun and ammunition makers and the unhinged Second Amendment ideologues of the dominant right-wing party, the ARI had become the most dangerous organization confronting local police, state, and federal officers. Its advocacy put more law enforcement personnel in harm's way than all the immigrant gangs and Middle East terrorists combined. Like most rational cops, she kept the ARI and what it stood for at arm's length.

As they got closer to Laskey's estate she asked if Lakes had seen the man on TV.

"I have, indeed, seen the man," he said keeping his eye on his Zillow app. "Many think he's a patriot. Of course, he has his critics. Anyone of his stature would. Do you have an opinion of the man?"

She shrugged as she pulled into the estate's meandering, shaded, out-of-a-1930s-movie dynastic driveway.

"He's controversial, that's for certain," she said, keeping her true thoughts to herself.

"No one doing that kind of high-profile work isn't," her boss replied, possibly abiding by her cautious comments. "Which isn't to say he's doing good or bad. Only time and God can make that call."

"Have you ever met him?"

Lakes paused before answering. "Yes, I have actually."

He didn't elaborate, put his phone down, and gazed wordlessly out the window. She pulled the car to a smooth stop along the circular cobblestone parking area by the home's polished limestone facade. At the center of the circle was a fountain with a Revolutionary War soldier rushing off into battle. The barrel of his musket sprayed water above the man's head so that he was perpetually fighting in the rain. Three other cars, two Mercedes and a Lexus were already parked. A man in actual butler's livery stood by the imposing oak front door, his hand ready on the brass latch, expecting their arrival.

She remarked on the butler.

"My God, a black butler. In Maryland."

"Would a white one be better, Celeste?"

"Certainly more unusual here south of the Mason-Dixon line, sir. It makes the Laskey's household come across as a cliche and not in a good way."

"Are you suggesting Laskey is a racist?"

"No, just a man who's trying hard to fit into his neighborhood," she said shutting off the engine and pocketing the keyfob.

He turned and gave her his vampire smile.

"You're not seeing the whole picture, Celeste," he said softly. "Out here in Elitesville, having a butler of any race makes no sense. No one comes here without an invitation. No one gets through the front gates without an invitation. No one gets beyond security without an invitation. We didn't get through without an invitation. And we're the FBI, for God's sake. The last place you need a butler is out here where everyone is expected and arrives precisely on time. If you need a butler to answer your door out here, you're all about presentation and tradition. He wants the privileged few who are invited to feel even more special than they already feel, extra special just to be here."

"Is that your general relativity theory on butlers, sir?"

"It is." He gave a short bark of a laugh as they mounted the steps, then whispered, "You take the lead, Celeste. I'm window dressing."

Even before he became AD, that's the way Lakes approached most on-site interviews: his number two looking like number one. In the agency's many different interrogation facilities, Lakes always relished the Grand Inquisitor's role. But in the field he often passed the torch to an underling. It served dual purposes. First, it groomed his staff as leaders, including thinking on their feet and not being intimidated by powerful people. Second, he liked watching, not being watched. Every FBI interviewee and their attendant lawyers kept their eyes glued on whomever asked the questions, not the goons in the background in dull suits with their wrists crossed classically at their crotch. Lakes loved standing in the background while his eyes spun around a room, taking in details that no one else could see, places where the guilty hid their secrets, places with answers to questions yet to be asked.

She had expected his deferring to her for the interview. Youngblood relished being the point person on an interrogation. Asking uncomfortable questions was her specialty. Just ask any of her old boyfriends.

Lakes's mobile burbled a customized ringtone she'd only heard a couple of times on his phone. It was set for the Director.

He glanced at the screen.

"Text from LeBlair," he said. "Seems Laskey got two messsages from the purported killer. One three months ago and one early yesterday. He didn't report it because he gets so many threats. That's what he told LeBlair. They're in the same riding club, you know. The Director says we're not to press Laskey too hard. He's a grieving parent. And a powerful one, the Director reminded me. Just collect the evidence and interview him and anyone else we want. Then move on."

"He's the victim," she said flatly.

"Exactly. Whatever you think of him, that's the situation as seen from above."

She tried to put her mind to the coming interview. Given her job, she had perfected a solemn approach to those reeling in the wake violent death. She'd never questioned a grieving relative or friend, even one she suspected of the crime, with anything other than sympathy and sorrow in her words and tone. And in her eyes. Her delicate, deep brown eyes radiated sympathy and concern at its warmest. She could easily sit with someone for an hour or longer, head bent, honest tears in her soft eyes; calmly, slowly, whispering, prodding, ultimately revealing whatever the person knew. It was an art reaching inside torn apart hearts and minds of those suffering from an appalling crime, one in which they likely had the key to solving if someone would only listen. She did.

Much of what she knew about peeling away the truth from the innocent and guilty alike, Lakes had taught her. It was his core principle of criminology. Some of us are born empathetic, he'd preach, the rest of us can be taught, adding that agents' empathy solved more crimes than their government issued 9mm handguns.

He was the agency's best at getting the recalcitrant to reveal things that, in times when emotions were tattered, might not otherwise come to light, things that often could resolve a case. Solving a crime quickly, he'd say often enough, depended on the living to tell what they know of the dead, everything they know; which was not always in the dead's or the living's best interest.

Three additional agents from the following car met them at the door. Their phalanx of three men and two women in dark clothing were led by the butler into a large wood-paneled study with floor-to-ceiling polished bookshelves filled with expense bric-a-brac and framed, signed photos of the famous, the rich, the powerful, all with Laskey in the picture. No books were in view.

Laskey sat behind his desk, an ornately carved mahogany boat that dwarfed him and the other furniture in the room. A trio of well-dressed women and one man stood off to Laskey's right. They looked like lawyers, professionally downcast, not sorrowful family members. Youngblood thought the two sides were evenly matched.

Introductions were made. Neither Laskey nor Lakes indicated they knew each other. She took one of the two chairs in front of the desk, pulled out her phone, turned on the recorder, got their acknowledgement and permission, then leaned back and crossed her legs demurely. The other agents remained standing behind her; arms crossed at their wrists protecting their groins, even the female agent. She glanced at her opulent surroundings briefly before speaking.

"Mr. Laskey, let me extend the deepest sympathies of the Bureau, the FBI Director personally, and all of us here. We are shocked and appalled by this savage act. And we will bring you justice, sir. We will."

She dropped her voice to a whisper and lowered its register, giving it a warmth and sincerity she did not feel. But it worked. Laskey's lawyers visibly relaxed and the man himself seemed briefly touched.

"Thank you, er, agent, I'm sorry, I forgot...."

"Special Agent in Charge Celeste Youngblood."

"Yes, thank you for your sympathy, Miss, uh, Agent Youngston..., I mean, Youngblood. Forgive me," he stammered.

"No, please, this must be an impossible time. We can step out for a minute, if you'd like a moment."

"No, no, that's not necessary. I'm fine. I'm ready. I want to help."

"Of course you do, sir," she said, locking her eyes with his. "Do you think you can answer some questions we have after our initial investigation. We...."

One of the ARI lawyers stopped her.

"Mr. Laskey has been shocked by this horrific event, we want to be clear that anything he says...."

Youngblood nodded curtly, then cut her off.

"We completely understand. We are not looking for testimony, only leads that can help us capture the killer or killers quickly. We do not expect, under these conditions, for Mr. Laskey's comments to be either complete or completely accurate. He's been through a terrible ordeal. Memories are imperfect. But it's possible, even likely," her eyes still linked with his, "that what he says now will help resolve this case and bring the killer to justice swiftly. Perhaps he even has information in his possession that will help expedite justice."

She could tell he liked the sound of her words. They put him at the core of the story, not his child or grandchild. Him. For men like Wayne Laskey Jr., there was only one center of one universe. He was it. She gleaned that about Laskey from not just his file she'd read, but the room itself. Originally designed as a library for someone's books, the shelves were filled with images of the man behind the desk. In between the framed pictures were endless trophies, plaques, engraved goblets, and a veritable arsenal of handguns and rifles in glass and wood cases with elaborate inscriptions etched into the glass. All for him. All about him.

Reading in between the lines of the Bureau's official file on Laskey, she concluded he was an asshole. "The subject is known for angry outbursts but responds well to flattery," was one line in the analysis she remembered. Walking into this shrine to himself added to the evidence that the man was an asshole.

But he was an asshole to be reckoned with. The framed images of Laskey with dozens of corporate captains, religious leaders, senators, presidents, prime ministers, and rock stars; anyone important who he could fit into a photograph. Most were autographed and dated, going back into late in the last century. The room was a Laskey time machine of still shots that shrieked, "I am important. Listen to me." Subtle he wasn't.

"Can you tell me about that day, sir, from your perspective?"

When he started to talk to her it was more like a formal presentation, as if he needed PowerPoint to discuss his daughter's murder. He made it clear that he was in Oklahoma, tapping his left forefinger to his right palm when he said it. He had hired the bodyguard because of long time threats, while tapping two fingers on his right. He added that he didn't know the other man killed.

"Never heard of him," he said, tapping three fingers one by one as if they were bullet points to be memorized.

Youngblood thought that he'd been running the words through his head over and over, practicing his performance with his legal team before law enforcement. He sounded as if he were dictating a press release.

"This is a tragic event, devastating for my family and anyone who cherishes what it is to be an American. Of course, personally, I am crushed," he exclaimed. "Crushed! Devastated. My heart is ripped out. My sweet child and her dear mom were the sweetest people on earth, thrust into becoming heroes for freedom through no fault of their own. There was no reason...."

He stopped to cry. She thought the tears genuine, but insincere, or, at least, about him and not his family. His suffering mattered more than the reason for his misery.

She waited.

One of the women behind Laskey took a package out of her handbag. She set it on Laskey's desk and nudged it across in Youngblood's direction.

"This might be evidence," she said in perfect understatement. "It came to Mr. Laskey's attention only recently."

Youngblood nodded, ignoring the lawyer's intentional obfuscation. She reached across the desk for the package with her left hand and handed it to an agent behind her.

Nodding vigorously to himself, Laskey said to no one in particular, "But I cannot be anything other than convinced that these despicable murders happened for political reasons. It's the cold-hearted haters who conspire against freedom and took my daughter and her mother to score points in an election or some other awful trade-off. But I will not let whoever did this to stop me from protecting the Second Amendment. With my life, if I have to."

She waited again.

He seemed done. He had stepped off his soapbox. Speechifying over. He went quiet. So she began.

"Let's start at the beginning, Mr. Laskey. It's always the best place. When did you first hear from who you think is your daughter's killer?"

There was a long pause before he spoke, his voice low, like an admonished child.

"The song. He sent the song."

"What song, Mr. Laskey?"

"The murder song," he replied, crying once more. "The song that killed my daughter."

Chapter Three
A Brutal Song

Excerpt from the memoir of Jefferson Fitzgerald
Black
Q-Level Access
Eyes Only

I

I liked the 1960s frenetic version of "Hey Joe" recorded by
The Leaves, a rock group whose only talent was to play
someone else's music loud and fast. Their guitar work was
shabby and their voices nasal and irritating, but the band's
"Hey Joe" was an unappreciated classic. I overdubbed the lyrics
slightly on the mp4 file I had sent to Laskey for his and,
presumably, law enforcement's listening pleasure. I wanted to
get the obvious message across that he's a murderer, too. Like
me.

Worse than me, really. My murders are precise and purposeful;
his random and merciless. My targets are chosen for their
complicity directly or indirectly in the nation's perpetual mass
killing orgy sponsored by greedy gunmakers, pliant politicians,
jaded journalists, and selfish, stupid citizens. Revenge is my
straightforward message.

Laskey and his ilk talk platitudinously, ideologically,
constitutionally, and, above all, convolutedly to mask the
essence of their message: money trumps murder, so shut up and
buy a gun. Elementary and high school children, concert and
church goers, college kids and office geeks: none of them matter
one iota compared to the sacred sale of another semi-automatic
weapon of war to anyone with a Visa card. Theirs is a sickness
to snuff out, not an idea to propagate.

Truth be told, my mission hews closer to the core fantasies of
America's gun culture than any slogan or soundbite from the
ARI. Every card-carrying member of the ARI would cheer my
actions, if they knew about them. Countless pro-gun movies

have glorified the vigilante, the angel of vengeance, defender of the weak. My work validates the lurid fetish of gun nuts: I kill those who kill innocents. I exact justice, when law has failed. I am, along with Charles Bronson, Clint Eastwood, and Luke Fucking Skywalker, not just absolved of the death and mayhem I leave in my wake, I am honored for it. Or should be.

Laskey's hands are bloody from his bullet-and-bullshit-laden message that celebrates the slaughter implicit in every over-the-counter purchase of every AR-15. Oh, I freely admit that like him I have innocent blood on my hands from my store-bought AR-15. My you-reap-what-you-sow message makes my murders of his family inevitable. They had to die for the arc of justice to bend its way toward truth. That Laskey's vile ideas have come seeping back onto his doorstep should be no surprise to him or anyone else. Though, I suspect, he didn't anticipate karma to knock so hard.

"Hey Joe" is part of the payback. It's typical in the extreme of the misogynist music that Laskey grew up tapping his toes to Top Forty radio back in the day. I know he likes it because when I hacked his PC I saw that he had listened to Jimi Hendrix's more famous version three hundred and sixty-two times on iTunes. So, I do hope he enjoyed hearing my rendition of "Hey Wayne" as much as I did making it.

Hey Wayne where you goin' with that gun of yours?
Hey Wayne, I said where you goin' with that gun in your hand?

Oh I'm goin' down to shoot my young lady
You know I got me some life insurance on her
I'm goin' down to shoot my young lady
You know I got me some life insurance on her
And that ain't too cool

Huh, hey Wayne, I heard you shot your in-law down
You shot her down now
Hey Wayne, I heard you shot your in-law down
You shot her down in the ground, yeah
Yeah

Yes, I did, I shot her
You know I caught her messin' round, askin for gun control
Yes I did, I shot her
You know I caught my in-law askin for gun control
And I gave her the gun
And I shot her
Alright
Shoot her one more time again, baby
Yeah
Oh, dig it
Oh, alright

Hey Wayne
Where you gonna run to now, where you gonna go?
Hey Wayne, I said
Where you gonna run to now, where you gonna go?

I'm goin' way down south
Way down to Mexico way
Alright
I'm goin' way down South
Way down where I can be free
Ain't no one gonna find me
Ain't no hang-man gonna
He ain't gonna put a rope around me
You better believe it right now

It's a brutal song in the original, especially in the excitable and altered version I had sent to Laskey sung by *The Leaves*. The music glories in the shooting of a woman for a man's ego. That ego alone makes it justifiable and the gun makes it easy. Honor killing on the hit parade in the U.S. of A., just as Laskey's evangelical God had intended.

Since his tenure at ARI, Laskey has flaunted his Christianity together with guns as if they were inseparable. He had been "saved" in the 1990s and claimed Jesus directed him to lead the gun group. "God inspires ARI leadership" is an actual Laskey quote you can buy on the ARI website stitched on a t-shirt or hoodie. "Jesus would be packin' heat" coffee mugs are the most popular items the ARI sells online.

When I was pawing around his computer I had intended to load it with some dodgy pornography. Unsurprisingly, there was no need. He had plenty, should any minion of the law care to look.

I intended that they would, too. My revision of the lyrics had the virtue of being salted with obvious clues the FBI would need to verify. They'd discover that Laskey had recently took out a substantial life insurance policy on his daughter before receiving the threat/song I had sent him more than two months earlier. I know because I took it out in his name with his existing Allstate broker. I had put a meeting between them in their respective calendars at their favorite Starbuck's, noting the purpose of buying a policy for his daughter. I arranged for direct billing to his domestic checking account with his other insurance premiums. A deep forensic analysis would eventually reveal that neither man had been where I had put them, but it would take days, if not weeks to prove it wrong. Hopefully making Laskey's life a little more hellish, a little while longer.

The lyrics about Laskey's daughter's mother-in-law were public knowledge. She had voiced support to journalists for tighter gun restrictions after Sandy Hook and Parkland, which infuriated Laskey. He had remarked about her "plus-size mouth matches her figure" at a fund-raiser that resulted in a kerfuffle that showed up in the society pages of the *Washington Post*'s website for a few days. I also peppered his digital and real lives with little Easter Eggs for the FBI and the police to find, ones that, with any luck, would continue to cause him more pain and anguish in the days ahead. Couldn't happen to a nicer guy.

In the meantime, Laskey was receding in my bloody new calling's rear-view mirror. My ambition reached beyond his miserable life. I was already working on my next hit. Well along, actually. Something connected, but not necessarily as personal. My revenge on Laskey was only my first strike against the profound ignorance and selfishness of American gun culture and laws.

I needed to do Laskey. I wanted to do everyone else on my mental list.

After shooting four relative innocents—Laskey's daughter, her mother, their guard, and the random equestrian—I knew without a doubt that continuing with my bloody project would not be a problem. For one thing, I was not revulsed by my action even though my victims were completely without blame, just like my daughter. My conscience remained spectacularly clear. No regrets. By comparison the rest of my prey would be more directly responsible for the continuing carnage in our country. They would be a cinch, a joy to kill.

Not that I wrestled much with killing Laskey's family. The moment I used my ARI-approved silenced rifle to shoot the passerby on his horse, I knew I was cut out for my mission. I felt nothing but a sense of accomplishment in my task, as if I had just solved an integration issue between two incompatible databases.

I had shot and killed a living man. I took his life with one bullet, probably less painfully than had he suffered from cancer or heart infarctions. Still, I took it. In one sense, perhaps I cut short his life's inevitable gruesome pain. The guy looked over sixty years old and statistically would be suffering from something soon, if not already. Of course, he could have lived on hearty and happy to one hundred years old. You never really know about such things and I never bothered to find out anything about him. He was truly arbitrary; the proverbial wrong place/wrong time scenario for the fellow. I needed a fourth victim to qualify for minimum requirements to be a mass murderer in the official FBI rulebook. I wasn't about to shirk on standards that our law enforcement bureaucracy set for society. Four dead you need. Four dead you get. This guy just happened along. And I nailed him. Mission accomplished.

I wonder, though, whether, had I botched the man's execution, perhaps I might not have carried out the rest of the murders. If I had needed two shots to kill him, would I have been horrified and quit? Perhaps had I felt the slightest exhilaration, panic, or, worse, guilt after shooting the anonymous horse rider, I might have gone no further. It didn't happen.

Instead, I felt a familiar satisfaction, giving myself high marks for a job well done as I would have after any work assignment in my career. Step one's success made it easy to proceed with step two, three, four, and the rest of the planned protocol in precise order: set the dead man's horse as bait, go to my nest, wait, and shoot. Three shots. Three more blameless, luckless people down and dead.

The only difficult part of the assignment was Laskey's granddaughter. Not surprisingly, she was a mess of a twelve-year-old girl, crying hysterically, flaying purposelessly at the air. Her genuine sorrow and shock was sad to behold.

It didn't interfere with the protocol I had designed. I grabbed her, frog-marched her into the woods, and drugged her. All the while I kept repeating a wicked little mantra about her Pappy, her pet name for Laskey, that hopefully will scar their relationship for life. I told her that her Pappy was responsible for the death of her mom and grandma. He was to blame. He's the killer.

I bound her to a tree and left her. That was hard, too. It would have been easier on me psychologically, I know now, to have killed her. I could have easily made her the fourth victim to make the FBI's mass murderer cut. But I wanted to leave a survivor to send a clear message. Like Laskey, I was all about staying on message.

I won't pretend that I am proud of what I did, but I am pleased with how I got away with my mid-morning ambush. My methodology, the protocol, was simple. I rode a dull gray Bianchi Denali mountain bike to my sniper position. It blended into the forest shadows and is an excellent escape vehicle, cruising along on either asphalt or dirt, both of which weaved through the Duckett Watershed.

Even though Maryland allows people to carry rifles and shotguns in public, I disassembled my gun put the parts and the ammunition into a handlebar bag that I carried to the killing zone. In my backpack, I had multiple changes of clothes and a few Clif and Kind energy bars plus an apple, with two bottles of water attached to the frame.

I knew the trail my victims had chosen to ride because I had hacked into their text apps and followed their messages about their equestrian plans. I knew exactly when they would be arriving at the kill zone because I had linked the GPS apps in the women's smartphones to mine. I knew exactly where they were as they meandered on their ride directly to me. I had taken no chances on missing my quarry.

My next mission would be equally thorough. Just as targeting Laskey's kin, I had spent hours every day gathering data on my upcoming victims. I broke into their personal computers, tablets, and phones. It was easy for me since I had installed so many connected databases on the internet in my previous career. Tracing my victims data down in detail was no more difficult than looking up a word in a dictionary.

During every software installation process in my career, I was always given root-level administrator privileges on the operating systems and databases to get the job done. I was proven and trusted and given complete access to every computer I touched. I had the most powerful rights and access credentials for some of the most used and powerful databases in the world. I also controlled their operating systems: Windows, Linux, AIX, the works. I had total access to individual profiles on hundreds of databases that I had worked on. What's so amazing is that there are hundreds, if not thousands of tech experts just like me. Not all of us are trustworthy; more's the pity, most of us are.

Rarely were my administrator profiles deleted after I had wrapped up an assignment. Even if they were, I knew my company's product so well, I could hack my way into any system that used the software. In short, I had the credentials to access the keys to the digital kingdoms around the world; I wore the crown jewels of content; I flew the mothership flag of information pirate for anyone I chose to investigate. Pick your overwrought metaphor. That's it's true scares even me. Almost everyone's life online was at my fingertips.

The Laskeys had been at the top of my list, but they were far from the only lives I'd ransacked. With ease I scoured the databases of cable providers, banks, telcos, doctors, retailers, DMVs, and so many other organizations I had done work for as a systems integrator. I vacuumed terabytes of data on all my targets. To be cliche, I knew more about them than they did about themselves.

I was careful when backing out of these databases not to leave a trace. But after so many embarrassing data breach episodes, some of these organizations had hired a few smart data security gurus to actually defend and fight back against endless hacking. I did not assume the backdoor I had used would not be discovered and shut after I had used it, so I grabbed more information than I would probably need during each hack, not only stealing data on the Laskey family but everyone in their computer and smartphone contact lists as well.

In the process I learned that Laskey's granddaughter, daughter, and her mother rode together often in the Duckett Watershed. I scoped it out, found it lush with an abundance of snipers's nests, and waited and watched their texts until they set a date.

It took me about a month to set up the ambush. The women led complicated, busy lives. They didn't exclusively use the equestrian paths in the Duckett Watershed. They rode elsewhere, but it was Duckett that offered me the best line of sight for the kill shots and the least likelihood of encountering a witness. That's why I set up the shoot there. Complicated, to be sure, but with manageable risk and the satisfying reward of vengeance well served.

As I said, the shooting went well. Clean kills. Easy, quick escape on the bike. No witnesses. Little suffering, except the girl, of course. But as Laskey once remarked to a rally of gun supporters, "We all need to be comfortable with a certain level of violence in our lives, physical and psychological. Gun owners accept that fact. They embrace it."

Back atcha, Wayne.

With my personal revenge satisfied, I moved on to make certain my point would not be lost on even the dimmest bulb in society. My next mass murder would not be as complex. I'd simply walk up to my victims and shoot them down. But these targets also would be armed to the teeth and as angry as a sack of rattlesnakes. Luckily for me, they were also as dumb as posts.

II

Georgetown, Texas is a long way from the Duckett Watershed. But it's a fine place to be a new person, to blend in, to disappear while remaining in plain sight. It's a growing community. Housing developments and apartment complexes rise at a steady clip inside the city limits. It courts business like sports agents swarming urban high school basketball tournaments. It's the conservative rump to the body politic of the People's Republic of Austin. Lots of churches and ARI stickers on Dodge RAM pickups.

I drove a generic SUV. White, beige interior. Nothing flashy. No stickers. I rented a townhouse not far from the San Gabriel River that slithered through the city. Kept my little patch of lawn watered and trimmed. Knew all my neighbors after only six weeks living there. Texans truly are friendly. I had moved in a week before my little massacre in the Duckett Watershed hit the news. I met a few folks, seeded the story that I was a chemical salesman who traveled a lot. I knew enough about phosphates and nitrogen to bore my listeners into changing the subject soon enough in a normal conversation.

When I came back from D.C. my new neighbors greeted me with open arms as they would any other business road warrior, a Bud in hand. Like them, I was another GenXer in the battle to make money and survive, maybe even thrive. I got invited out to barbecues. I invited people over and grilled burgers. We drank beer and kept conversations away from politics but argued sports endlessly. Lots of laughs and good-natured fun. I could have stayed there for the rest of my life, short as my cancerous heart would allow.

When I killed the Laskey clan, I left behind the AR-15 I had used, extra ammunition, and the rifle sight. Not my bike, though. I kept the bike with me the entire trip. When I fled the scene in Maryland, I had changed into clothes that hinted at eco-conscious government worker, lots of khaki, Gore Tex, and attitude. Then I carried the Denali nearly a mile through the underbrush to a paved path that led me to endless paved country, suburban, and city roads that eventually took me to Silver Springs. I hopped a bus with a bike rack up front that took me to Baltimore, where I changed to the Brunswick line on a MARC train to Washington.

After making it to D.C., I spent two days under an assumed name as a tourist in the nation's capital. I kept up on my murders in the local and national news. There was a lot of breathless reporting, though not much information. The murders stayed atop of the headlines for a full day and might have run longer had there not been that plane crash in St. Louis, the suicide of the popular rock star, and, of course, a different, bigger mass shooting, involving dead children later that week. Little ones, always tug the hearts and grab the headlines. For a little while, anyway.

Made my mission easier, my message all the more vital.

Not long after I had returned to my Georgetown townhouse I came down with Covid-19. Add me to the millions on earth, but not the hundreds of thousand unlucky souls who have died from it in the United States. My neighbors knew I was quarantined. We exchanged upbeat e-mails and a couple good-hearted people left casseroles on my front porch. As I said, Texans are friendly folk.

I remained in self-isolation for three weeks and skid through the disease with a mid-grade fever and a chest thick with fluid. Breathing was difficult, but I had arranged for the nearby American Medical Supply to deliver a couple of oxygen tanks, which helped tremendously. Had I gone to the hospital there was a chance my true identity would be revealed, something I wasn't about to risk.

Once I recovered I accelerated researching my next victims. They lived nearby. I wanted five future dead men and one survivor to carry the message live, instead of through Laskey's granddaughter, an inefficient method, I admit. But, hey, I'm new at this killing quest.

First, I needed to devise a new killing methodology for a new environment. What I did in Maryland did not apply to Texas. Eventually, I worked it out, step-by-step, the new killing protocol: the how of getting six armed men to let me shoot them dead one-by-one. My plan would only work if everything went in a precise sequence. Any variability and I'd likely turn out dead, not them. But, as with sequencing the integration of software, if you write clean scripts and execute your programs in precise order, any complex issue becomes another problem solved.

What that meant in real life was to practice my moves over and over for the encounter. Like a choreographer, I would engineer an infallible script between me and "the boys," as I dubbed my upcoming targets, that left them dead, while delivering a clear message to a wide audience, and me escaping. It would take more than good code and execution. Like a dancer hoping to perform Balanchine, it would take a lot of practice.

Once again I found an idle gravel pit with an owner happy to pocket undeclared cash to rent it for weekends; this one far into the Texas Hill Country. I set my props and targets and ran my routines repeatedly until the shooting became a ballet that my legs, arms, and fingers memorized. I studied it until I was as confident as a talented twelve-year-old ballerina before her tenth public recital. Ready, but wisely nervous. Unlike Laskey, I was still a tyro at this mass murder business.

Chapter Four
Limousine Driver

Celeste Youngblood

I

Until the Laskey killings, in all her thirteen years of service, Youngblood had never flown in one of the FBI's small fleet of comfortable Gulfstream jets. Like most agents she traveled coach on the cheapest airline available; rarely even a direct flight. But she had taken one of the agency's G600 planes direct to Salem, Oregon from Reagan Airport. She went to look over JFB's old residence and to talk with his coworkers. After easily getting permission from the current, cooperative, and very curious homeowners, she learned almost nothing from looking at her prime suspect's former residence. Almost, because she learned that whatever she observed was not part of who JFB was any longer. His dial had been reset. He was a new, more dangerous man.

His co-workers offered little insight on the man they'd worked with for years. Great guy. Fun to be around. Neither quiet nor loud. Smart. Helpful. Worked like a beaver. A genius when it came to database integration and analytic software installation. Polite. Strong. Had been in a recent car accident. Injured, from what everyone heard. Never complained. Continued his hard work. A Boy Scout by all accounts, as he actually was in his youth.

Youngblood noticed that JFB's office had no secretaries, personal assistants, admins, whatever they were called. The Hoover Building was crawling with them. Instead, the company used a virtual avatar administration system that was managed remotely. JFB's digital helper was called Smoking Lauren.

JFB's employer, which got tens of millions in revenue from government contracts, did not ask for a search warrant to give Youngblood complete access to Smoking Lauren. The first thing she asked the avatar to show her was his schedule the day he quit.

There it was: a doctor appointment.

She found the heart specialist without any problem. Smoking Lauren instantly connected her to the doctor's office. The M.D., however, needed a warrant to cooperate, which took a couple of hours to procure. Satisfied with the paperwork, over Zoom the doctor told Youngblood that on the day in question she had "informed" JFB that he had terminal heart cancer. That was her word, informed. Like she was giving him a personal weather forecast.

He took the news as well as could be expected, she said. Better than so many other of her patients, she added. But the specialist made certain that JFB talked to an on-call trauma therapist, just in case he had "issues." Again, her word, issues.

Youngblood's conversation with the psychiatrist, after yet another wait until early the next morning for the search warrant, had yielded nothing more during that video conference. The clinician barely remembered the encounter with JFB, constantly looking down and referring to his notes from the day of the meeting, which were minimal at best when Youngblood reviewed them.

```
Patient: Jefferson F. Black
White male.
47 years old.
Single.
Primary insurance: 100% NW Mutual
Secondary policy: 100% Washington Health & Life
Billing Rate: 1
Pre-billing for co-pay: Complete ($70.00)
Payment: Received: $70.00
Time scheduled: 28 mins
Time used: 16 mins
Pre-billing for consultation: Complete ($325)
Payment: Received $325
```

Consultation notes: Patient referred by Reese
diagnosed with terminal heart cancer.
Interviewed patient after being given diagnosis
and dismal prognosis. Patient calm. No
prescriptions written.

Neither doctor had heard from JFB since his diagnosis, nor had
either of their offices attempted to contact their newly terminal
patient. The best medical care in America did not get you a
whiff of real care, Youngblood decided.

II

The comfortable flight back in the G600 was scheduled to
touchdown at DCA in four hours after take off from K7M9,
Salem's quaint runway. After take off she talked with AD Lakes
about their suspect.

"Not only does JFB have motive and capability, given the
murder of his daughter and his military credentials, he has
nothing to lose. Absolutely nothing. No family. No future.
Literally, no life in front of him. He bought the gun, despite the
registration. It's his. Plus, he threatened Laskey in the past. It's
him. We need to find him fast, sir," she concluded. "He may go
after Laskey or, more likely, other ARI-affiliated targets."

"Agreed,' Lakes said. "Still, we need to dot the I's and cross the
T's on the evidence pointing to Laskey. If it gets out that we
skipped over it, the media will chew us up. After we, after *you*
do that CYA mission with the Laskey alibi, we'll turn all our
attention on JFB unless something extraordinary happens. Tell
the pilot to alter your flight plan and pull into OKC. I'll pull
together an impromptu meeting of local cops. I'll tell you where
before you land. Once you're there, you talk to the locals about
what they know about Laskey's visit there. Flash your SAC title
and let them know we appreciate their help. Yada yada. You
know the drill. Then get back here ASAP and find the real killer,
Celeste. That's Jefferson Fitzgerald Black. We know what he
looks like. We've got his photograph. We've got his personal
history down to the last six-pack he bought. We will find him
and we will nail him fast."

His pep talk charged her up and she went into action. It took only her word to the pilot and the jet smoothly shifted direction toward an Oklahoma City tarmac. With luck the G600 would get her back to D.C. after her gladhanding in OKC in plenty of time to stop at home, eat an over-the-sink dinner, grab a few sundries, and toss another change of clothes in her gym bag before diving into a series of twenty-four hour shifts that she knew lay ahead of her. Day after day after day until she brought down JFB.

III

The Stillwater Regional Airport's watery and tepid coffee sat unsipped in its Styrofoam container on the conference room table in front of her. The Bureau had secured the windowless room on short notice and brought in locals to run down their eyewitness reports of Laskey's speech on the day his daughter was murdered. Except for Youngblood, the table was populated by a baker's dozen of uniformed middle-aged or older men. Most wore buzzcuts and carried paunches. And white. Save three. The handsomest man in the room, a black police chief three chairs down from her left. A burly Latino from the State Marshalls. And a watchful Indian in plain clothes. Cherokee, she guessed.

The Latino and the Cherokee were standing against the wall with the other junior white guys. Because of social distancing, the table could only accommodate eight folding chairs. Like so many times before, she was the only woman in the room. She strolled the space, making the occasional and awkward elbow-to-elbow tap with men who'd rather break your hand while shaking it, but succumbed to reason and the new convention among strangers. Most of the guys were probably nervous about being in the same room together, but kept their anxiety to themselves. At least it was big enough for social distancing. Everyone wore masks.

The gathering was feel-good theater for interagency politics and, maybe, an evening news cycle. There was a van from

KOKO, an ABC affiliate, parked illegally near the terminal's entrance. She guessed one of the men at the table leaked the news to a friendly reporter. It hadn't come from her side she was certain. The less said, the fewer people in the loop, the better, was her mantra. Like Lakes, though, she understood that the dynamics of local law enforcement were different from hers. Most of these men were either beholden to elected officials or elected themselves. Notoriety, if not popularity, mattered a lot.

She hated the limelight. And the spotlight of this meeting was on her. Her rules for herself in situations like this were simple. Be concise. Never lie. But mostly shut up and smile with her eyes.

She recognized her keep-it-to-yourself rules didn't apply too far beyond her office cubicle and tried not to get upset when those outside her control did stupid stuff. And yakking to the press about the Laskey killings was stupid. She understood that in these cops' minds Laskey was a famous celebrity. Being seen as hot on the trail of his child's murderer would not hurt a local's career. The temptation to brag was too great for some. For others, it was the simple *quid pro quo* between the police and the press in every town in America.

The Bureau had called the airport meeting simply to stroke the local cops, who otherwise would snipe to one journalist or another if they felt ignored or their supposed evidence overlooked by the agency. Nothing new would be revealed during the gathering. She'd listen attentively. Ask questions. Consider their theories. Build camaraderie. Give them her text number. It was part of managing an investigation. Half of what agents did during one was soothe the locals' feathers. Whatever they told her she already knew from written and oral reports that had already been vetted by members of her team. Her visit was the final phase of the charm offensive.

As they went around the table, each of the badged dignitaries confirmed the obvious: Laskey had been under their jurisdiction when 1,300 miles to the east his daughter and others were shot dead. He was here. She was there. No connection. An iron-clad alibi, if there ever was one. Not that any of them even mentioned the word alibi.

As she already knew, Laskey was informed that his daughter had been shot dead during a social event after his breakfast speech. Witnesses said he nearly collapsed. Per usual, stories varied. Some recalled that he raised his hands over his head. Many said he bent his head down to his knees. His hands covered his face or clutched at his own shoulders, depending on whom you talked to. Some witnesses said he moaned. Others said he cursed, taking the Lord's name in vain. "Oh, Goddamnit," he had whispered, many heard. One was adamant, however, Laskey muttered "Oh, God, not now." Laskey either sat down after or stood up straight after his outburst. However, everyone agreed, ARI's CEO instantly changed his plans and announced his return to Maryland immediately.

"He was gone from the hotel in minutes," more than one cop at the table reported.

"He was a grieving father. He raced outta here to be with his family like anyone woulda done," the handsome black man said to nods all around the table. "Syd Peltry there," he nodded toward the Cherokee at the back, "from hotel security drove him right to the airport."

Not much later, seventy-two minutes from the start, the meeting concluded with another long round of rowdy elbow tapping and promises of continued cooperation in the investigation. She joined the locals to stand before a couple cameras from local stations joined by a half dozen bloggers with their iPhones asking urgent questions that were vaguely unanswered by every cop who took to the podium. The press conference lasted a grueling fifteen minutes, until the final uniform got in his soundbite. She left immediately.

Minutes later, as she hustled her way back to the plane, her thumb-print-locked Caseva black leather briefcase swung back and forth with every step. An airport employee with a passkey to let her exit onto the tarmac jogged behind her to keep pace.

When they reached the armed, locked doors someone shouted her name a couple of times.

"Agent Youngblood! Agent Youngblood!"

It was one of the men she'd seen standing at the back of the room. The Cherokee. Syd Peltry. He wore blue jeans, an Oxford collar shirt, and a linen sport coat. He was the point man for hotel security the day of Laskey's speech. He had wrangled an invitation to the meeting and Youngblood, who had approved the attendee list before landing, saw no reason to exclude him. He hadn't spoken while he stood in the background during the group meeting nor had he attended the press event, which is how he got to the airport ahead of her.

"Yes?"

"I'm Syd Peltry. Security manager at the hotel. The guy who drove Laskey to the airport."

A faint slur in his voice softened hard consonants. His wide-brimmed hat, while smaller than most of the cops she'd just met, shaded much of his sun-lined face. He had a wide nose and deep-set gray eyes under medium wide black eyebrows. He wore his hair stylishly long to cover his ears, which had seen a surgeon's knife more than once. Peltry was not tall, maybe five feet nine. But you could see he was a strong man, with a thick neck and a broad chest and narrow waist. His fists were big. Huge, even. He had an intensity about him. His dark eyes never wavered from her face.

"I saw your name on the list of attendees," she answered. "And, of course, you were mentioned during the meeting."

"Yes. That's why I stopped you, Agent Youngblood. I wanted to tell you something. Clarify it."

"But not in front of the others?"

"Right."

"Okay, let's move and get some privacy."

She turned to the employee with the passkey.

"You stay here," she ordered.

He looked aggrieved, but didn't move.

They shifted a few dozen steps away. Satisfied they were out of earshot, she said in a low voice, "Okay, Mr. Peltry, what have you got?"

Despite his minor speech impediment, he spoke quickly, but concisely, while keeping his eyes on her face.

"I drove Mr. Laskey from the hotel to the airport after the event, just as you were told. During a social hour sometime after his speech he'd learned that his daughter and the others had been shot. Had been killed. Once he'd been told, the hotel went into action; maids packed up his room, and I helped them load the car with his stuff. We got him out in record time. Then I drove Mister Laskey here, to the airport. He had a private jet like you."

"Not mine, actually," she said with a smile.

Peltry stopped as if waiting for a question. She kept quiet and he continued. His eyes glued to her.

"When I met Mr. Laskey at the curb outside the hotel he was on his phone and he was never not on his phone when he was with me. It wasn't his first trip hereabouts. He always carried a few phones when he was with me. I even saw one in his sock once. Anyway, I held the door open for him."

She obliged him with a question.

"What kind of car?"

His eyes lit merrily for a moment.

"The hotel runs a 1958 Chrysler Ghia Imperial limousine. Very impressive machine. Rare. It's old, but in mint condition; exquisitely comfortable. We keep it running like a top. Inside it's modern. Wifi. Beer on a nitro tap. Chilled wines. Big screen TV. Big for a car, I mean. Also, we got a button that turns the car into a secure communications center so no one can eavesdrop on what's going on. Totally secure. Oilmen, who are the bulk of the hotel's paying customers, like it. But the outside is equipped with cameras to keep an eye on curbs and pedestrians and such. They're mostly to keep the car safe. They're not standard and you can't see them. Most riders never notice. There's a small video screen in the dash above the speedometer. Nothing big or fancy. But as the hotel security chief, I can also get video feeds from the car's cameras sent to my iPhone."

He took a breath and went on.

"So, Mr. Laskey he approaches the car and he never stops talking on his phone and he gets in the limo without looking at me and the first thing he does is turn on that security button then he closes the door. The second thing he does is close the soundproof glass between him and me in the driver's seat. I don't think much of it right then. But when I'm driving him to the airport Mr. Laskey pushes the comm button so he can talk to me, the driver, and he says *not* to take him to the airport right away. He told me to make a stop first."

"Where was that, Mr. Peltry?"

"Deerfield." He paused, watching her carefully, as if waiting for her reaction to the word. She didn't have one. So he explained. "It's where the rich around here live. The really rich. People like Ivy and Garland Tock. That's whose place he had me drive him to."

Although Youngblood had not heard of the hoity-toity Deerfield neighborhood, she did recognize the names Ivy and Garland Tock, two of the wealthiest people on *terra firma*. They owned the privately held Tock Corp., which controlled massive tracts of timber land in the American West and South, sprawling oil fields throughout the Anadarko Basin in the Sooner state and the Permian Basin in West Texas. They mined coal in huge open pit mines in Chile, Borneo, Congo, and West Virginia. They refined lithium from Ecuadorian lake beds and extracted gold from Australian hillsides. They had majority interests in African cobalt, Indian sapphire, and Canadian oil shale extraction businesses. They owned a shipping line to ferry their raw materials around the globe. They employed more than three hundred thousand people in sixty-four countries who scratched at the earth day and night, taking one thing in one place and turning it into something else in a different place to be bought and sold somewhere else; all making the Tocks two of the richest individuals who had ever lived. Combined, they were the richest.

It didn't surprise her that Laskey knew the Tocks. Power sucks up to wealth and wealth clings to power. Youngblood had read a blurb online in the *Stillwater News Press* while in-flight that Laskey had dined with Ivy Tock at the Ranchers Club Steakhouse the night before his speech, the night before the murder of his daughter and the others. For Laskey, going to see Garland Tock was not, in the broad picture, particularly notable.

Then Syd Peltry said something very interesting.

"I'm mostly deaf. Eighty-eight percent since birth. But I read lips. Really well. I read them very well."

Immediately her lawyer-self raised red flags about the admissibility of lip readers in court. Her detective-self ignored the warnings, knowing at this state of the investigation any lead had possibilities.

"That good?"

"Most people can't tell. Can't tell I'm practically deaf, that is. Some can, but they have to spend a fair amount of time with me to catch on."

"Spend much time with Laskey or Tock?"

He smiled and shook his head.

"We run in different social circles. However, once a year or so, the Tocks will fly me and the '58 Imperial, the limo, to an event somewhere stateside; where they want to make a splash, I suppose. Also, they already know how to work its secure comm system, which they trust, and, I forgot to mention, it's completely bullet proof. The car. As good as what the President rides in. Better even, but don't tell the White House. It could run through a chain link fence while taking heat from AK-47s on all sides."

"That's some car. They choose you for the driver?"

"They choose a security guy they recognize who drives a particular limo, that's me," he said in a matter-of-fact way, as if being trusted by two of the planet's richest humans was no big deal. "They also bring along their own personal guard."

"But the Tocks know your name?"

"Garland does. Not sure about Ivy. She's the quiet one."

"Do they pay you well for the travel?"

"Yes, ma'am. I get seven hundred dollars a day plus all expenses paid. And, the hotel, knowing where its bread is buttered, continues to pay my salary while I'm gone and I don't get docked for vacation. It's a sweet deal for me."

"Would the Tocks approve of your contacting me, Mr. Peltry?"

"I doubt it."

She tucked his answer into her memory and switched her line of questioning to the evidence at hand.

"So, after you brought Laskey to Tock's place, did they know you were observing them?" her voice a question.

"Oh, yeah, they knew I was watching them occasionally in the rear-view mirror because I was waiting for them to signal me when to pull back up to the walkway and pick up Mr. Laskey where I had left him."

"Describe the situation for me."

"Huge spread," Peltry said of the Tocks' estate. "Curved, smooth cobblestone driveway goes for nearly a mile, shaded with huge, old Shumard oaks. Beautiful, big mansion at the end of the driveway. Well, truth be told, I'm not much on architecture, but I can say it was massive and modern, maybe not beautiful. I've brought more than a few important people there. The Tocks have places around the world—New York, Rome, Moscow, Dubai, Singapore, and Aspen, I think. But they spend most of their time here. They're from here and proud of their roots. They're local heroes. Everyone here knows about them. Truth be told, we're proud of them. Anyway, if you want to talk to the Tocks, you need to come to OKC and most likely stay at our hotel and, if you're important enough, most likely to be driven by me to the Tock's place."

"Happens often?"

"Regularly."

"So, nothing out of the ordinary when you took Laskey there. That's something you do. So, why are we talking?"

"I'm getting to it," he said. "Slowly, I know, but bear with me. The Tocks' place is an impressive fortress. I know. I'm in the business. It has massive steel-reinforced oak doors on silent electronically-controlled pneumatic hinges. All the locks are modern, high tech, bulletproof, literally. Stainless steel. Titanium. Biometric sensors made from palladium. Cool stuff.

"Anyway, I pulled up with Laskey to the Tock's front walkway. It's gorgeous, made with beautiful blue, white, and gray paving stones in a geometric pattern you'll never see anywhere else. Right away, out comes Garland Tock. No butler. No valet. No maid. Those were the people who usually greeted my car's riders, including Laskey every time before. Not this time. Tock himself."

"How many times have you dropped off Laskey at the Tocks place?"

"I checked my logs. Four times. This was the fifth."

"As I said, this time it was just him. Tock. That tipped me off that this wasn't just an ordinary meeting. He never greeted anyone, anytime. Not before. Always had the help do it. Recognized him right away. Comes into the hotel once in a while to eat with his sister. She's a regular.

"Anyway, Laskey nodded for me to move on ahead, so I parked the Imperial up about twenty yards, stopped, took out my iPhone, and watched in the rearview mirror for them to give me a signal to return and get him. While on the phone I followed the stream from the camera inside the right rear bumper."

"Okay, so tell me, are you saying you were lip reading while the two men were talking?" she asked.

"Yes, ma'am."

"Okay, so now you're going to tell me what they said that's so interesting that it brought you here."

"Sure, I can tell you," he said agreeable, while pulling out a four year old iPhone in a battered leather case. "But I can also let you listen. I recorded what I saw in the Voice Memo app while I was seeing them talk."

"Real-time transcription?"

"Yes, ma'am. Time-stamped and everything." He handed her the device and said, "Just tap the screen and listen."

She did so and lifted the device to her ear. She heard Peltry's distinctive voice. He began with the date, time, and location of his recording even though the iPhone automatically did so. His voice was identical to the man speaking in front of her.

"Tock speaks: 'Wayne. Wayne. Wayne. Our sorrow is so deep for your loss, your sacrifice, your daughter. For Christ's sake, she's a martyr, a hero for her generation. For all time. We will not let her memory die. I swear to God Almighty.'"

There was a notable pause before Peltry's voice returned.

"Tock: 'I know. I know. I know. But her death was swift, painless. Think of that. Unfair to you, your loss, but painless for her. Remember that. Wayne. Wayne, Wayne, you know that. And you know, we take care of ours. Here take this.'

"Laskey speaks: 'What's this, Garland?'

"Tock: 'A USB stick. It has a few hundred Bitcoins on it for you, Wayne. Just you, Wayne. To help you grieve and to heal. Nothing more. Ivy and I are overwhelmed with sorrow by the sacrifice of your daughter to the haters of freedom. We will not forget you.'"

"Laskey: 'I am grateful for this, Garland. Thank you so much. But...'"

"Tock: 'Yes, Wayne? But? But what? What do you need to know, Wayne?'"

"Laskey: 'Is there something else going on with the Plan that I need to know about?'"

"Tock: Absolutely not. Everything is as we agreed. The Plan is working. If there is anything good that can come from your personal tragedy, Wayne, it's that we win sooner. The Plan will triumph. Hold to that. Hold to that."

Peltry's voice memo ended.

"Anything else?" Youngblood said. "What happened?"

"Right," he answered. "Tock, he's a tall fella, he leaned in and grabbed Mr. Laskey into a bear hug. He whispered in his ear for quite a while. I could see his jaw moving. Finally, when they let go of each other, Mr. Laskey was wiping away tears. He walked Tock back to the front door, they shook hands, and he turned around and gave me a sign to pick him up. By the time I parked, got out and opened the door, Mr. Laskey was on his phone again."

"Then what happened?"

"Only one thing. We pulled into the hangar. His plane was still being refueled and the pilot was just beginning his inspection of it. I popped the trunk and one of the plane's attendants was johnny-on-the-spot getting out his luggage, so I jumped to open Mr. Laskey's door. As I opened it for him, he was the phone, but I could see his lips clear as day. He said, 'No, honey, no. Garland said the little shit is setting me up. He's gonna try and tie me to it. It's gonna be awful for a while.'"

"'Garland said the little shit is setting me up,'" she repeated. "You're certain?"

"Yes, ma'am. Is that significant?"

She gave him a smile, but ignored the question. She handed him a business card and held up his phone.

"The FBI will need to take your phone. I will send you a form you can use to reclaim it once the investigation is over."

Peltry waved her off and pulled out the latest large-screen iPhone from his jacket.

"Don't bother. I expected you to take it. I cleaned it of anything personal and made the passcode 0-0-0-0-0-0. I suspect I won't see it for a while," he shrugged. "Besides, it gave me an excuse to upgrade."

She used her thumbprint to open her leather case, put the phone in an evidence bag, labeled it, and slipped it into the case's inside pocket, before snapping it shut. She extended her hand, then retracted it self-consciously, and twisted her body so they could tap elbows. He smiled at the gesture.

She said, "Thank you, Mr. Peltry. You did the right thing by coming to see me this way. This is sensitive information and we would prefer that you keep this to yourself. But I suspect you know that, which is why you approached me here in the first place. I appreciate your trust in me and I will return that trust. You may hear from me in the future. But feel free to call the number on the card I gave you, should anything else come to mind."

"On Laskey? Doubt it. I can't think of a single thing I haven't told you, Agent Youngblood." he said. "But do me a favor and catch that young lady's murderer. I saw a picture of her in the paper afterwards. She looked like a nice young woman with a long future ahead. Can't help the sins of her father, if that's the way this crime plays out. Anyway, not right to take her future away."

She nodded.

"You," she called to the airport worker waiting patiently. "Open that door. I've got a plane to catch."

Chapter Five
The Plan

Excerpt from the memoir of Jefferson Fitzgerald
Black
Q-Level Access
Eyes Only

I t's trite, but true: follow the money, find the truth.

How the ARI and even weirder fringe groups, like my
upcoming Texan targets, got funded baffled me. What was their
appeal? Demographics weighed against them. Baby Boomers
and the Greatest Generation, the bulk of the ARI's paying
members, were dying like flies. Getting replacements posed
problems.

Women became the biggest obvious member replacement
market the ARI went after. Despite the heavy promoting of
sleek, fashion-conscious pistols and flattering conceal-carry
clothing to housewives, the effort bombed. Most suburban
moms hated guns. They saw the common-sense danger firearms
posed to their kids. Educated women and their obliging
husbands especially eschewed them for all the smart reasons.

Licking their wounds after that marketing fiasco, the ARI next
attempted to lure younger generations to embrace sacred
Second Amendment extremism. Laskey directed his group to
spend millions of dollars in advertising at major events
attended by the nearly-eighteen crowd. X-Games lovers,
especially skateboarders, became the focus. He bragged in an
email that the endorsements from rock and hip-hop artists like
Ned Sargent and Wyldmun would "be a game changer." Didn't
happen. Millennials and Generation Z had almost no interest in
hunting or marksmanship. The politics of the geezers pushing
guns appalled younger women and men. They were the ones
who survived Columbine, Parkland, Newtown, and all the rest.
Guns, to say the least, were not their thing. For the most part,
they disdained shooting anything other than virtual weapons in
digital games. Besides, who could afford a weapon during such
precarious times? The debate between a used iPhone and a new

Glock was a non-starter. In the real world, the younger generations worried more about surviving pandemics and unemployment than their rights to buy a semi-automatic rifle. The macho allure of guns escaped them.

For being such a powerful force in society, in truth, most people gave little thought and zero care about the right to bear arms. The Second Amendment didn't really intrude into their daily lives; and when it did, it was usually anxiety over another mass shooting. If anything, most citizens wisely considered guns dangerous and in need of stricter regulation. Weapons were not designed for polite company. They're built for thugs and terrorists, soldiers and cops. Sure, in many paranoid pockets of the country people kept handguns for security, but nearly two-thirds of Americans lived a gun-free existence. And they were way safer than those with guns. You're seven times more likely to die accidentally in a home with a gun than in one without a weapon. Seven times!

Okay, I apologize, I'm getting preachy.

But I did not understand the appeal of guns *über alles*. Why were gun special interests so powerful, if the thing they represent was so unpopular and dangerous? Yet the money was always there to fund even the most obscure Second Amendment fanatics. Indifferent and declining importance of weapons among the general population did not affect the financial support gun groups enjoyed. How could that be? I became obsessed with getting to the bottom it. When I delved deep enough, the answer surprised me.

It's not about guns. It's never been about guns.

The money propping up Laskey's 501(c)(3) tax dodge and other fake non-profit organizations like his comes from people with an abiding personal indifference to gun ownership. The Second Amendment is hardly their favorite paragraph in the Constitution. In fact, precious few of them actually own weapons of any kind. They're rich enough to buy protection from trained professionals; far less dangerous to the household than keeping a handgun under the mattress or a shotgun in the closet.

While following the money, I spent many hours burrowing through the ARI's virtual private network, chasing down purchase orders inside the organization's enterprise management system, the software that tracked all income and expense data. An EMS processed anything that had to do with money, from membership dues received to paper clips purchased. If you know how to read an EMS, you'll learn where the corporate bodies are buried; where money is being spent and misspent; where it's flowing and where it's foundering. I can read EMS reports as easily as teenagers peruse texts.

The ARI used its EMS comprehensively for every department. Outgoing dollars were tracked to the penny. Income likewise. Any transaction in ARI's history lived somewhere in the log files of the EMS. It was the Dead Sea Scrolls to understanding the fraud behind the ARI's power. I needed access.

Not surprisingly, ARI's EMS included my former company's software. Although I did not work on the gun lobby's installation back four years ago, it did not take me long to snake my way through the common security procedures my ex-colleagues used to set it up. Once inside the database I focused on where the ARI's money was counted: the Accounts Receivable department. Like I said, the EMS sniffed out every nickel that made its way into the American Rifle Institute Limited Liability Corporation's coffers. Dues. Big bequests; small ones, too. Logo licensing. Tchotchkes sold. Speaker fees. It was gratifying, but not shocking to learn that Laskey produced less revenue giving his overpriced talks than his inflated salary. Any possible angle to con a nickel out of a sucker was charted in the EMS data. It was all there in black and white.

From what I could see, the ARI was a dying business. Literally. Despite steady hikes in annual subscription rates, membership revenue was down by at least six percent year over year for five straight fiscal cycles. The ARI inflated enrollment numbers by including people it called "emeritus," which was anyone who had paid three consecutive years of dues before quitting the organization; more than a few thousand deceased remained emeritus for years. Gone were the days when people aspired to be ARI members; being expired was often rnough to get you membership.

Added to subscription woes, corporate donations were way down. Personal ones were flat, including the revenue from bequests left by the quickly departing oldster members. The ARI's online store offered T-shirts, ashtrays, and knick-knacks stamped with its logo, commemorating Colt .45s and AK-47s and everything in-between. The shop barely broke even. Long ago the organization had shut down its once profitable gun-safety program since most current ARI members cared little for the subject. Halfway through construction, the long-planned National Museum of the Second Amendment teetered on the edge of insolvency from a lack of anticipated tax-deductible donations from the public. The entire organization was an unholy mess.

However, the ARI's over all balance sheet looked as black as ever. A steady growth in what the gun group called "Product Development" more than covered the troubles in every other category. Product Development turned out to be an under-the-table collaboration between the ARI and the Plan, a dark-money group led by Ivy and Garland Tock, the fraternal twin billionaires. They secretly directed tens of millions of dollars to Laskey and the ARI to keep pushing a core segment of Americans further and further to the right. Their goal was to radicalize the righteous to assure that only the most extreme candidates in both parties succeeded to become candidates, driving a wedge in the nation and creating the conditions for a hard right political revolution. Audacious, but simple.

The Plan laid out who won revolutions. The side with the guns. Who had the guns? Besides the army and the cops, both conservative by nature, right-wing citizens were the ones armed and ready for the ramparts. The Plan plotted against democracy because it shackled raw power to the will of the people, the common good, and the law. The Plan could not stand for that. Revolution was called for to set things right.

I know. I sound like a conspiracy nut. A rich cabal pulling strings behind the scenes to seize control of the nation. So very hokey and Qanonsensical.

Surely, if true, the FBI would have uncovered something by now; or certainly the mainstream media would have splashed investigative stories in every way shape or form to their mass audiences. If not the Feds nor the press, that vast conspiracy petri dish, the internet, would have uncovered the truth about the Plan, its revelations percolating from one end of the Web to the other. We would know about it by now. Wouldn't we?

No. Not if the Plan works. And it does.

The best way to deflect conspiracy investigations, let alone charges, is to fund the biggest conspiracy machine in world history. Well before the internet made the Plan's work so much easier, it had backed the most extreme, kooky, right-wing ideologies throughout the United States. Fervent evangelicals were the easiest to imbue with outlandish conspiracies. This was an audience primed for apocalyptic scenarios painted by their ministers. The Plan made certain over the decades that the vanilla middle of well-mannered Protestantism, Catholicism, and Judaism lost tithes to the firebrand preachers. Only radical right, conspiracy-minded congregations of the mainstream religions thrived to compete with their even more paranoid theological competition.

The Plan brought religions together that were normally at each other's throats. They rallied around abortion and fighting against gender equality. Nattering men in pulpits agreed that women were incapable of controlling their own bodies, so railed against the right to choose. On the sly, however, thousands of conservative politicians, preachers, priests, mullahs, and ministers sent their fluke pregnancies to be terminated as discreetly as shame and money made possible. These righteous men chose for their women just as their God had intended. And they got paid by the Plan, knowingly or not, for the pleasure of it.

The Plan also underwrote secular writers, editors, movie directors, journalists, TV producers, almost anyone who contributed wild theories about the Roosevelts, the Kennedys, the Clintons, the Obamas, and beyond. They had a penchant for documentarians with only fleeting grasp of evidence, fact-gathering, verification, basic research, analytic thinking, and, of course, the truth. That mattered least of all. What mattered was promulgation of an endless litany of conspiracies that would turn your hair white with fear.

The Plan's work succeeded because they made it personal. They did not win over allies with facts about issues. They won because they made their supporters fear and hate the other side. The Plan's backing of Second Amendment fanatics was simply another string to pull. The Tocks' consortium invested widely in gun culture, even though neither they nor their peers seriously embraced the guns-equal-freedom mentality themselves. The Plan's only goal was to keep the interests of those in power the first and foremost policy of the United States government.

One part of the Plan targeted gun rights. Make firearms available to as many poor people as possible. Disadvantaged folks were led to believe that their guns made them special, made them free, made them special. It was a lie, of course. The more guns that flooded their communities, the more violence they experienced; the more violence, the more fear; the more afraid they became, and the more likely that they'd use their weapons, mostly in suicides or against each other.

From urban ghettos to Appalachian hollows, the Plan's Second Amendment strategy was an unmitigated success. "Let them eat lead," was a phrase used often by the Plan's leaders. All the while once sedate, one segment of rationale suburbanites succombed to the anxieties fostered by the if-it-bleeds-it-leads journalism, and bought guns by the bucketful and voted for anyone who promised to keep them safe. Another, larger segment, recoiled at the thought of guns and voted the other way in the extreme. Polarizing people was the Plan's purpose. And, as I say, it worked.

Despite the cult of the Second Amendment they engendered, the Tock siblings detested guns. Their mother had killed herself using their stepfather's stainless steel .45 Remington just after the twins finished college. Her death tarnished their view of personal gun ownership. Political ownership was another thing. For them, and billionaires like them, guns were merely a means to an end, a tool in the Plan's very large toolshed.

Keeping the ARI and other American radical gun groups afloat in the face of increasing unpopularity of guns themselves was easy. The ARI's revenues poured in from the sale of so-called "intellectual property" created by Product Development. A maze of a revolving handful of obscure 501(c)(3) groups and evaporating business LLCs backed by the Plan purchased millions of dollars worth of this bogus intellectual property. The way overpriced IP amounted to nothing more than tedious PowerPoint decks and unwatchable turgid videos. Without the Plan purchasing the shit in bulk through dozens of these ephemeral non-profit groups and sham small businesses, most of the hard right gun groups would evaporate like cordite from a fired bullet.

All Product Development transactions happened online. Buyers got a special code to gain access whatever overpriced IP was sold. The ARI's EMS would duly record the incoming dollars and automatically release the access code to the buyer. In the scheme, buyers used PayPal accounts to transfer funds and only identified themselves with a throwaway gmail address. Naturally, the ARI took BitCoin and other shady currencies. Automatically, probably unbeknownst to ARI's IT workers or certainly to Laskey and the board, in the background the EMS would track how many times the ARI's expensive IP was being accessed through each access code. Ninety-seven percent of all access codes, representing close to seventy-million dollars, were never used. Never. Not once. Of the three percent that were accidentally legitimate purchases, half the buyers asked for and got refunds.

"This is utter crap," one complaint read.

No argument from the ARI. They immediately refunded a member's money and extended her membership for another five years for free.

The laundered cash from the Plan weaved its way into the ARI's pocket through a variety of channels, but they invariably originated from a Houston law office that I also had in my sights. It specialized in massaging funds through a fibrous web of real and unreal organizations while at the same time being courtroom heroes of the gun lobby, successfully defending the most outrageous mass killing weapons, including one that led to the death of my daughter. Turns out Second Amendment radicals were half right: guns don't kill people, billable hours do.

But, as I said, ultimately, the Plan is not about guns. It's about power and keeping it in as few hands as possible. Not just a few hands, but the select few. The best way to accomplish the Plan was to prop up small, controllable but loud and outrageous organizations, ones that made headlines and reveled in controversy. The ones whose leaders have no shame. The obvious choice were radical right-wing groups, whose causes ranged from sanctimonious never-taxers, pious right-to-life folks, and, my *bête noire,* the rabid shoot-to-kill goons of the gun lobby. By fanning the flames of the incandescent extremists in those factions, the Plan assured that a cowed political establishment would happily hand over the levers of power to the likes of the Tocks to operate behind the scenes in hopes of keeping the extremists happy.

What levers of power? A sane person asks skeptically. Simply put, the laws of the land: those bulky one thousand-page-plus pieces of legislation that roll through government committees and passed by city, state, and federal bodies year after year. They get written by somebody. Nine times out of ten, if that legislation's important like, say, a Congressional spending bill, that somebody is beholden to the Plan through one means or another. They can be elected politicians, trained bureaucrats, or rapacious lobbyists, the writers of our laws know where their bread is buttered. They weave the views the anti-abortion people, the anti-tax people, the anti-science people, the anti-gun-laws people, and all the rest of the fringe thinkers of our time into the fabric of the rule of law.

It's anything but democracy and it happens every day in cities and counties and states and in Congress. Groups like the ARI, with no intellectual credibility and no true grassroots support, not only get heard by our governments, they are deferred to when statutes are written and signed into law.

No matter what side of the political football you line up on, you believe the will of the people has failed. Special interests rule. You blame the other side. They blame you.

The Plan is working.

People of the Plan want us to believe that power in the world is a complex web of political and economic factions vying for control. It's not. People of the Plan rule. They employ politicians, media, academia, and more lawyers than citizens in a good-size city.

Through the Plan, the Tocks and their ilk secretly pour major dollars into all three corners of the right-wing's hardcore supporters. They marginalize opponents by carving up their ideas into buckets that can easily be vilified and opposed by one faction or another.

All the while the Plan keeps constant pressure on world governments to encourage rapacious and profitable environmental regulations, or the lack thereof. It applies technology solely to oppress labor. It fosters religious and racial animosity to encourage violence and wars and fat defense contracts. It enflames cultural differences to atomize communities into me-versus-you loudmouths.

I learned all of this by reading the ARI's Enterprise Management System reports. Data don't lie.

Chapter Six
Creepy and Compelling

Celeste Youngblood

She finished her report long before the Gulfstream touched down at Reagan International. A waiting driver whisked her to Bureau headquarters, where she immediately headed to the small, team-only conference room and its stand-alone, off-the-grid server that kept the agency's files on the JFB manhunt. She sat at one of the five dedicated terminals connected to the server. Two other agents were working on their own terminals.

As SAC, Youngblood had concluded that while JFB was on the loose and a foremost expert on the powerful database software widely used inside the Bureau, it was best to keep her investigators' files off the FBI's virtual private network and make certain the shared computer was not linked to the internet. She ordered the set up, so any workstation with access to the server was hardwired to the isolated server.

Her IT specialist, a gray-haired security analyst who'd seen it all, assured her that the only thing coming in from the outside was electricity. And even that was being conditioned through a Universal Power Supply.

"Safe as houses, that's you," he'd said.

She plugged a USB stick with her report into a slot on the server. She dropped the Word doc into her unit's mandatory-read lists. In addition to her summary of the meeting with local law enforcement in Oklahoma, the top-secret memo included details of her discussion with Syd Peltry and the linking of Ivy and Garland Tock to a person of interest, Wayne Laskey Jr., on the day of the mass shooting in the Ducket Watershed. She mentioned Peltry's lip reading about the Plan. She knew her information would raise some eyebrows. So she wasn't surprised to see AD Lakes trooping to her desk ten minutes after she'd posted the report.

"Welcome back, Celeste," he said casually. "We've already received five unsolicited comments from participants in Oklahoma about your smarts and your smoothing of the waters we Feds churn up in any local fracas we're called to. You made them feel engaged and important and actually involved in the Laskey-related murder investigation. You were, in short, Celeste, a big hit in OKC."

She accepted his praise with a nod. Then asked, "What about the detail about the Tocks? Is that something we move ahead on?"

"Not yet, obviously," Lakes replied. "I prefer to put my fist into one hornets' nest at a time. We haven't even fully pissed off the people involved with the Laskey angle yet."

"I believe 'pissed off' qualifies for a dollar in the swear jar, sir," she said laconically.

He shrugged.

She said, "You know, sir, our JFB is far more calculated, far more dangerous than an average mass shooter."

"You should know," Lakes said. "You're the expert."

She huffed away his comment. Anyone inside the D.C. zip code knew Lakes was the renowned expert on mass shooters. By comparison, she thought herself a rookie.

Still, Youngblood had enough credibility that Lakes had hired her. After a couple of the initial interviews for the job, he'd told her admiringly, "You get these sickos at their core. It's the quickest way to track them down and stop them, if they get away. Good thing they rarely do because once they start, they never stop. Killing becomes what they do, who they are. Like a pathogen, they live solely to bring death."

Sadly, she grasped the dark interior of mass murderers. Before she joined the Bureau, while writing her thesis at Georgetown on the lack of federal prosecution of mass killers in the second half of 20th century, she had been a consultant to Xbox designers of mass shooter games so they could get an accurate behind-the-gun action pattern of a real killer. Well before that, as a student at Baltimore City Community College, Youngblood privately scouted obvious public venues for mass shootings. She looked at likely shooting angles and calculated the number of victims. The places were compelling when seen through the eyes of a shooter and, unsurprisingly, creepy at the same time. Malls. Churches. Auditoriums. Ballparks. Anywhere people gathered to celebrate shopping, God, music, and sports was a ripe target for the demented man, always a man, with an automatic weapon. That's what mass shooters did. They went for the obvious. The big. The bloody. The noisy breaking news. The bold headlines. She knew that before she joined the FBI.

Like most Native Americans she understood that a frighteningly high number of white male Americans were primed to be mass shooters. They had it in their genes. White men have been slaughtering tribe after tribe in North America since the pious Puritans landed at Plymouth Rock. The Mystic Massacre. The Great Swamp Massacre. The Hillabee Massacre. The Sacramento Massacre. The Chetco River Massacre. Lots and lots of massacres going back hundreds and hundreds of years. Youngblood knew most of them. She'd studied mass killers going back to the Romans, but focused on the U.S., the modern global leader in mass shootings.

Mass shootings were simply today's manifestation of Indian massacres long-baked into the white American male psyche. Instead of slaughtering villages of women and children it was killing the innocent in concert halls, shopping centers, synagogues, workplaces, and a never-ending list of schools. They were the tribal villages now. For the most part, she thought, today's crop of mass killers simply were carrying on a long tradition in the bloody history of the nation.

But something in her mind told her that JFB wasn't in that mold. Your everyday mass shooter would have taken out the girl and continued on the rampage until stopped. JFB shot a precise number of people, just enough to bring in the Bureau officially; although it likely would have had a hand in the investigation anyway because of the victims' high-profile relative. Still, JFB wasn't seeking undue attention. He did it in a remote area, quiet, away from prying eyes and headline-grabbing journalists. He didn't want the biggest number. The biggest headline. His revenge wasn't driven by an abuse he suffered from family or schoolmates or lovers. He wasn't haunted by demons or a rage that could not be contained. In short, he wasn't crazy. His vengeance had meaning beyond the headlines and the body count. His killings had purpose. They signaled he would do it again.

"So, what do you think, Celeste?"

"Well, sir, I think JFB is planning his next operation as we speak."

"Me, too, Celeste. Me, too."

Chapter Seven
@ReadyFireAim

Excerpt from the memoir of Jefferson Fitzgerald
Black
Q-Level Access
Eyes Only

I

It was an additional risk stealing the pickup. I knew that. Risk aversion and management were, after all, essential to every successful database integration project I had ever worked on. I had written more than one memo for my old company on the subject. On the other hand, shooting a half dozen well-armed men on their home turf by myself and expecting to survive unscathed already carried its own inherent risks. So, what the hell? I went for it. Took the truck.

In the pre-dawn, still dark Sunday morning, I had set out on my Bianchi mountain bike, the same gray Denali with its 27-gear Shimano derailleur I had used for my first killing. Worked great then. In my handlebar bag I carried two brand new Glock 60-ec semi-automatic revolvers sporting the coveted bigger capacity magazines, each with twenty 10mm-shells. Gun fetishists, like tech geeks, wanted the latest and greatest toy available. They had total hard-ons for the 60-ec because it could empty its twenty rounds five milliseconds faster than the best-selling, already deadly Glock 40s, with their puny fifteen round magazines and pokey firing. More bullets, less time, more bodies. That was the trifecta for shooters, making the 60-ec irresistible to them.

Banned in most states, even gun-friendly ones like Texas, the 60-ec was hard to come by. Lusted after specifically by my targets, which they freely admitted to on social media. In fact, the truck's owner posted three days earlier that he "wuld luv to hv 1 of thez LibTard poplation control mashines!! 60-ec rocks!!! Go Glock!"

It had nineteen hundred and seventeen likes. One of them mine, or the identity I used for the gun crowd, @ReadyFireAim. They embraced my handle without irony. I planned to seduce my targets with one of the 60-ec pistols and killing them with the other one. It was a straightforward plan that would succeed because, first, they'd be confused as to why I was driving one of their trucks; baffled further when I'd tell them I was their biggest fan, @ReadyFireAim; dazzled completely when I showed them the porn-perfect 60-ec hardware; and, finally, these boys were as stupid as a sack of hammers but not as useful, making them my perfect victims.

One of the Glocks in my bag included all twenty lethal 10mm bullets in its magazine. There is only one purpose for such a weapon. It's not to hunt or target shoot or defend your suburban manse. It's to slaughter the enemy on the battlefield. Or, to massacre as many unarmed people as possible as quickly as possible. There is no other purpose. In my hands, the weapon will under perform. I will only obliterate a handful of victims.

The other Glock in the bike bag had only four live rounds and sixteen blanks. I could tell the difference by the slight weight difference, but to make no mistake I dabbed the bottom of the full magazine with pink paint. I did not trust myself getting distracted by the unplanned, the unexpected.

The added weight of the weapons slowed my pedaling down a tad. I'm a strong cyclist and average a hundred miles a week on a road bike. Sure, my heart may be about to shut down from cancer in the near future, but my legs and lungs feel tip-top for someone in their forties. Mountain bikes are harder to propel than road bicycles, even when optimized for streets like my Denali. So I gave myself extra time to ride the mostly flat thirty-one miles between my place in Georgetown and Thrall, Texas, where my next crime would occur: grand theft auto.

I did not hesitate when I got to Thrall. I stopped the bicycle next to Lucas Pine's pride and joy, his bright white 2017 Dodge RAM 1500 crew cab perched in his front yard. He flew two huge Confederate flags on seven-foot poles bracing the tailgate.

Brightly colored bumper and window stickers praising guns and God dotted the backside of the pickup like pimples.

I listened for less than a minute and didn't hear a sound beyond distant dogs barking and the hooting of a barn owl. I quietly lifted my bike onto the truck bed. In a single motion I opened the driver's side door, slipped behind the wheel, reached above the visor, and pulled down the keys. I was surprised at the number. No wonder Pine didn't carry his keys with him. There were at least thirty, many of them fitting vehicles of all sorts. I guessed every key he'd ever had in his life hung on the large tarnished brass ring like some pathetic war bracelet. I sorted through them as fast as I could.

I didn't need to steal Pine's rolling billboard of barely suppressed violence to complete my project. But it felt right. The added risk was that someone would see me do it and call Pine or the police. My guess was that he was such an asshole that even in the off chance that someone saw me, they wouldn't care. Still, I was careful.

Sheriffs had been called to this address on at least five occasions in the past 18 months, I'd learned. No shots had been fired. No arrests made. But Pine was known to authorities as a troublemaker, who kept his toes inside legal limits, while dealing weed and beer to high schoolers on the side. He was a big fella, more than six-foot-two and closer to two-fifty than two hundred pounds. He'd intimidate people without touching them, picking his threatening words carefully, lawfully, but menacingly. If he'd been a black man he'd have been in jail years ago. Or killed.

Pine and Jimmy TJ Polton shared a clapboard house down near the railroad track off West Tayler St. They were friends with Edgar Flynn, who lived in town on Eckhart Rd. Flynn's cousin, Billy J, had inherited a mobile home on forty acres, without the mule, surrounded by thousands of Big Agra acres of wheat, sorghum, and corn. Billy J's homestead straddled a wash that meandered in the wet season through a tunnel of honey locust, red mulberry, and Texas oak trees. At one time it was probably a lovely spread.

Billy J's old school mates, Timbo and Elam, lived with him and Flynn on the property. On the east side of the wash Billy J had set up a sprawling shooting gallery. Hundreds of shattered truck tires, splintered telephone poles, bullet-scarred 14-inch horizontal load-bearing beams propped on concrete barriers, sagging moldy haystacks, shredded plastic cans, beer cans, Coke cans, shattered bottles by the thousands, hundreds of wounded manikins, and concrete walls plastered with bullet-ridden posters of every prominent liberal in the United States. One of their props was a stretch Lincoln limo. Years ago someone had painted "Lemozine Liberal" in red paint. But it was beyond legible now and the car itself barely recognizable as something that once ferried people, liberal or not, around a city somewhere, sometime ago.

Billy J and his friends had been shooting there for years, blasting at anything they could find as a target. Nothing remained recognizable for long after their furious fusillades had rained down on it by the hour until the boys got bored and moved on to the next target. But they never stopped shooting.

In the low early morning stark Texas sunrise, which they seldom saw, brass casings blanketed the ground of Billy J's property, shimmering like Dorothy's yellow brick road. When they bothered to clean the glittering mess of shells they used snow shovels, otherwise pointless tools in their part of the state.

I knew all of this because @ReadyFireAim was one of the most ardent followers of the American Free Patriot Movement, the brainchild of the six men who comprise the entire movement. My persona is one of a demented demographic that pursue the AFPM on Facebook, Reddit, Twitter, 4Chan, and a couple of even less savory places in the gun-toting dark corners of the internet. AFPM publishes tedious and loud videos of the group's drunken, wild, cacophonous, free-fire fun at Flynn's place out on County Road 424.

"It's about our freedom," one or all of them said in every video.

I had been monitoring each AFPM member's private digital and voice communications for some months now. So I knew that on Saturday afternoon Edgar had given Pine and Jimmy TJ a ride to his cousin's place, leaving Pine's truck for the taking, for which I availed myself.

The Second Amendment sextet had spent the previous day downing Bud Lite like always and shooting the hell out of images of the current Democratic Party contenders in the upcoming primaries. They constantly filmed their shooting parties, but Facebook and even YouTube had standards, and would not let them post all of their Go Pro video contributions to social media culture. Other places would. They always garnered at least a smattering of comments by lonely boys and scary men, who clicked their approval while offering their coarse, inane, inarticulate, but supportive observations. Those words and retweets spurred my targets on to greater lengths in their glorification of the gun.

A little over a year ago *Guns&Ammo Illustrated* ran a special issue on "gun rights" celebrities and included the AFPM in a long list of notable online "Second Amendment Influencer"organizations.

After that mention, Pine had texted Edgar Flynn, "we r f@ckin influences, man, just like fully loaded kardashians."

As with the Laskeys, I saw whatever they texted, emailed, Instagrammed, Facebooked, Skyped, Zoomed, wrote, searched on Google. I also snagged photographs they took with their smartphones as well as wherever they surfed the internet, mostly porn; and whatever they bought online, mostly guns and ammo. I had it all. Once I had penetrated their home laptops and phones, I mirrored everything they did on those devices onto servers I was renting from Amazon Web Services in its computing cloud. I could review their documented antics at my leisure. I did it for weeks.

In that time I confirmed a hypothesis before I had even moved to the Lone Star state to stalk my targets: these young men, while certainly dangerous, were, like so many gun nuts, predictable and stupid. Creatures of habit and feeble-minded creatures at that.

Their predictable characters improved my odds against them immeasurably. These were paintball boychiks, playing with real guns, real bullets, but in a pretend world, a delusion they shared, apparently, with a large gaggle of subscribers to their social media channels.

Not surprisingly, they were fakes. They were out of their league when it came to actual killing. They were not true killers like me. Or Laskey. As far as I could tell, none of them had been directly responsible for a single death by gunfire. By judicial standards practiced in the courts, they were as innocent as my daughter. But in my eyes, they were guilty in the first degree. They had everything coming to them because they fostered the fantasy among gun fetishists that they are the good guys, society's protectors. They're not. They're the zombied enemy, brainlessly marching to the ARI's drumbeat. If they prevail, humanity loses. For civilization to endure, those zombies need to be stopped. I'm only doing my part.

Every other Friday after working hours, though not all of them were employed, the entire AFPM would pile into Pine's truck and drive down state highway 79, connect to Interstate 35 into Austin. Rebel flags flying, they were off to mindlessly invade civilization. I followed them multiple times, but it was easier to watch their antics online by tracking their smartphones' GPS signals and watching their posted videos later. They'd roll through the capital of not just Texas, they'd explain to their audience, but also ground zero for all of the weak-assed gun-haters in the state.

They'd hoot and holler, sucking their vapes, reefer, and Bud Lite as they drove loudly along quiet city streets. When they knew it was safe, they'd brandish their weapons at solitary old black men, because they didn't fear them, and young white women, because it made them feel powerful, masculine, and desirable, not the repulsive fools they were.

They were all single, though Jimmy TJ and Elam had fathered children out of wedlock. From what I had learned, neither woman even bothered to keep in contact with the father. Among their peers the young women's choice not to get an abortion gave them cred as Christians, but it was far more Christian of the young women to exclude the fathers from their child's existence. The young women knew instinctively such a relationship would subtract from the kid's life. Both mothers were living with their own mothers; both working as sales clerks, one at Wal-Mart, the other at a gas station mini-mart. Their Facebook pages were chock full of kids' photos in various stages of happiness. I liked them. That's why I had taken out paid-in-full life insurance policies on both men with their biological children as beneficiaries. Like stealing the truck, it seemed like the right thing to do.

Those women had had a hard row to hoe. Take Elam. Although no charges were ever filed, police came to break up fights between him and his girlfriend at least twice. Once pregnant, she filed a restraining order against him. But she was smart. She had a lawyer send him an agreement. So long as he abided by the court order, she wouldn't ask him for a dime in child support. His lawyer told him it was a great deal. That's why he forever after boasted to his shooting buddies and whomever was watching online that her getting pregnant had been his ticket to freedom. No way he wanted a "rug rat" to screw up his life. He was proud to have abandoned her and the child.

"Men need to be free like birds," he'd say, inspired by Lynyrd Skynyrd lyrics playing in the background of the video. "Women need babies."

Jimmy TJ's lady had simply packed up and moved north, all the way to Michigan. Once in a while Jimmy TJ liked to brag that he was a dad, but he always had to lie with his answer to the inevitable follow-up question about whether he had a son or a daughter. Why did that matter? he'd always ask. Then he'd say, "boy," which was wrong.

Despite their obvious odiousness as people, the six young men actually had standing among fervid gun lovers. Heroes to some, even. They were, after all, a full-fledged militia, complete with a cool logo.

They initially had dubbed themselves the Free American Patriot Movement. But when Timbo had returned from Georgetown with really cool-looking red and black t-shirts with the name wrong, they opted for the t-shirt that read American Free Patriot Movement.

Though not without some grousing.

"Only free Americans can become patriots. American free patriots makes no sense," Jimmy TJ, who with his high school diploma considered himself the group's intellectual, had complained in a text to the group about the name change. "But the shirt is cool enough to change it."

The polyester XXL black shirts depicted a rippling Betsy Ross flag with thirteen red 9mm bullets circling inside a blue corner square on a black landscape of red and white stripes of high-calibre ammunition clips. In a gaudy, glitter and gold Synchro font the words "American Free Patriot Movement" embraced the flag top to bottom on the t-shirt. On either side of those words, pointing to the wearer's neck, were stark white AR-15s bracing the flag. On the back a screaming eagle dived through a ball of flames and clutching an Uzi in each claw. Minimalists they weren't.

But it was the number one best seller on the AFPM website. They had sold five hundred and sixty-six of the t-shirts at $17.95 plus tax, shipping, and handling.

For a few months late last year, after the *Guns&Ammo* piece, the AFPM was an ARI-affiliated group. They defended the Second Amendment by hiking around the streets of Austin toting their semi-automatic rifles out in the open. An ARI-contracted film crew followed them walking into random grocery stores and Starbucks, hoping to normalize the behavior of being armed to the teeth while shopping for beef jerky and Venti lattes. In a country obsessed with guns it seemed like a good idea. Instead, local news stations showed the camo-clad trolls frightening customers and ruining everyone's day.

The exploit backfired. Seems casually sipping coffee next to a dick brandishing his Smith & Wesson is not a preferred customer experience, in marketing parlance. In the real world, it's creepy.

Injunctions were filed against the AFPM and the ARI. Businesses by the dozens posted No Guns Allowed signs. Some wag with Photoshop created a Wild West-like "Not Wanted" poster, with a photograph of the Jimmy TJ and his buddies walking in town brandishing the AFPM plus ARI logos, overlaid by a red circle and slash. Common sense citizens were horrified. The police harassed the AFPM by visiting Billy J's property more than once. Bad press doused the idea almost faster than the ARI publicly abandoned the Thrall boys, backpedaling quicker than Republican politicians in Miami Beach during high tide.

But the internet did not toss aside the AFPM so easily. In more than a few virtual territories they were beloved citizens, treated as brave souls, fighting the good fight to keep white men armed and free. Their six thousand gun-obsessed YouTube followers made them feel obliged to continue producing their provocative videos from Flynn's farm. Their fans demanded it. It didn't hurt that they had been getting money every month from the Google AdWords' links for gun shops and gun makers who advertised with them.

"People are clicking and buying shit, I guess," Jimmy TJ had texted his comrades in the AFPM, explaining the substantial quarterly payment to the group from Google. They spent the extra money for ammunition at GunsGunsGuns.com, getting a swell discount, according to Jimmy TJ, because that website was an advertiser.

Money was never a problem for the AFPM. Most of its income was funneled through a law firm, Wythe, Braxton, Wolcott, Rutledge, & Adams, with an office in Houston. Not from the lawyers themselves, of course. They set up bogus gun shop and swap meet advertisers that sent free money to the AFPM, laundered through Google. Wythe, Braxton was the conduit for a registered 501c non-profit operation called The American Century Victory Fund, which funneled money to a motley selection of gun-rights groups through the law firm. I traced the ultimate source to the Tocks, to the Plan.

For all its follies, unprofessionalism, and pure stupidity, the AFPM was successful, if notoriety was the Victory Fund's goal. The bulk of the Fund's largesse went to tenured losers in academia who professed to read the minds of the Founding Fathers when it came to approving American citizens' easy access to automatic weapons and large-capacity magazines.

The Victory Fund fronted these fringe professors and radical militias for a few Oklahoma and Texas right wingers. They tried to bury the provenance of the money distributed by their lawyers through a string of shell companies, letting them take the tax deductions spent every year on nutjobs like the AFPM. But, as I think I've indicated before, I'm persistent and have access to a lot of data and was able to track the Victory Fund's backers.

Born as billionaires whose riches came from their fathers and grandfathers who extracted wealth from the planet and the poor, they dug oil wells and coal mines and hired goons to keep workers in line and bribed politicians to withhold services to those in need, traditions the Victory Fund families maintain to this day. The oil-rich Mayfields of West Texas, the Oklahoma City Tock miners, and the Dukan-Basel clan with their riches coming from both oil and minerals, poured millions in support of Second Amendment extremists like the AFPM.

These men and women also backed Laskey and the ARI in more public ways, showing up at events and co-writing ARI OpEds condemning any effort to introduce even the most modest gun control in communities across the country. But as radical as the ARI is, even it has not pushed the envelope of gun rights far enough; certainly not as far as the backers of the Victory Fund seek. The AFPM, on the other hand, was right up its alley.

What the group prodigiously produced for their fans, when it wasn't moronic, was vile. The AFPM glorified killing, talked it up, extolled it, even though they didn't actually kill. The AFPM never went that far. But they sanctioned it. And they inured viewers to the horror of it. They didn't kill others themselves, but like some twisted version of Voltaire, the AFPM would defend your right to kill to their death.

Effigies made from department store manikins were the AFPM's preferred enemies. They slaughtered them in the hundreds with prepubescent joy. They mocked anyone who might have even whispered the slightest objection to the frightening policies of giving people like them the right to own and use mass-killing weapons. The guns these boys revered were designed for the specific task of killing as many soldiers as possible as quickly as possible on the battlefield.

Repeat.

On the battlefield.

They are not designed for hunting or for target practice. They are designed and built for human slaughter. Yet, in tiny minds like the AFPM members', for them to be denied the God-given right to own such a weapon was as unfair as society not recognizing the superiority of their white skin and tiny penises. If people of color and women could only see the truth, the world would be a lot better place.

Okay, I know. I'm ranting and repeating myself. Still, it bears repeating. These guys are losers.

It was not difficult to choose this lot as my second mass-killing target. Few would miss them as individuals or their pathetic AFPM. The world will be a better place without them.

Finally. I found the key to the pickup among the huge ring. I took another few seconds to listen and look. Nothing. Cranked the engine to life with a loud cough and dropped the transmission into reverse. I backed out carefully onto W. Tayler and drove north.

I had a few hours to kill before I had a few people to kill. I drove over to Granger Lake and staked out a picnic table at the water's edge on the south side. I was the only one there. It was quiet, except for the birds and the rare rolling of tires miles away. Sunday morning hereabouts meant church for most, sleeping-in for the many. Death for some.

II

For the umpteenth time I visualized each step of my plan as I drove Pine's truck along County Road 424. As with any thorny database integration project, success depended on the first moves. If they went right, everything else followed.

My first steps went perfectly.

I drove the two-rut road from 424 to Flynn's property, bumping along at a good clip in the Dodge for about five minutes, kicking up a fantail of dry red Texas dirt behind me. Pine's Confederate flags billowed embarrassingly from the rear. Never understood the appeal of the Rebel Cause. People call it tradition. A tradition of traitors and losers? Sure. What's the attraction? Has to be racism, though few flag flyers would own up to it.

Glancing in the rear-view mirror I saw my Denali bouncing in the truck bed with each lurch of the truck's suspension. I imagined the guns in my bike's bag bouncing around and was glad I had painted the fully-loaded one with pink paint to identify it.

While I had passed time at the isolated and empty Granger Lake, I checked out the Glocks for the third time with live fire. Then I cleaned the weapons and changed clothes. I swapped my cycling outfit for an official $17.95 mail order AFPM t-shirt that I matched with tight-fit black Levi's, the preferred uniform of my targets. I'd also donned a black baseball cap with "AFPM" hand-stitched, by me, in thick red thread on its crown. I wore black Sig Sauer tactical shooting gloves. My black New Balance sport shoes, the official footwear for faux storm troopers everywhere, completed my attire. I had strapped a GoPro camera, cop-like, to my chest, which didn't exactly mesh with my disguise, so I made certain that the straps that held the camera were printed with the Confederate flag.

My arrival would both flatter and reassure them with my AFPM fanboy attire and Rebel regalia. But it would also confuse, even threaten them; a stranger in Pine's truck uninvited on Flynn's property.

I wouldn't give them time to work out the contradictions. Thanks to many hours of company sales training, I would plow instantly into a stellar fanboy performance that would suck up to them such that by the time I brought out the sought-after Glock 60-ecs, the entire AFPM army would be distracted to the point of its annihilation.

It went as planned. As I skidded the pickup to a dusty stop about fifteen yards from the group, they ceased midway in their weekly video series, "Sunday Service Shoot-a-thon," published for three straight years on one of their social media outlets, gunsRgod.com. In a typical broadcast they hung effigies on a fifteen foot metal scaffold fashioned from water pipes they had stolen years ago from a construction site. When they originally started their bit of blasphemy, they had built a wooden scaffold, which they quickly blew apart by the sheer volume and velocity of bullets they fired. After rebuilding it twice, they decided to construct a metal one and heisted the pipe, though now even it was seriously dinged and chipped.

The AFPM shot at images of prominent American Muslims, particularly African Americans. Famous progressives in Hollywood and the media, Wall Street capitalists, especially Jews, and, occasionally, the Catholic Pope were popular AFPM props.

On Sundays, with the raising of a religious target, one of the boys would mumble fake words in a lousy accent as if it were a prayer. Then they'd all yell "Fuck your god. Only ours is great." They'd hoot and holler while they danced around the effigies. In the end, they'd obliterate every one with overwhelming firepower. Then they'd shout "Guns are god!" and pop open more Bud Lite. Ceremony complete. Services over. This week it was mostly the very reliable money-sucking, anti-gun Jews who were primarily being executed in absentia. Soros. Bloomberg. Cohen.

"Line 'em up!" they shouted just before unloading one magazine after another.

"Line 'em up!" was the new cry of the Republican hard right at political rallies for their candidates. The slogan was catching on.

When I brought the pickup to a halt, I did not hesitate. I opened the driver's side door and leapt from the cab.

"Hey, hey," I called loudly and cheerily, waving casually as if I had been expected. "Hello! Hello! I'm @readyfireaim. You remember me? @readyfireaim? We communicate all the time online. I'm so pleased to finally meet you guys! This is special. So special. You guys are rockin' rad, man!"

I pumped my fist in emphasis, then I turned my back to them. This was my most vulnerable moment. If they shot me now, or even challenged me, the whole massacre might be averted. But they didn't.

"Hey," a few voices replied feebly.

I retrieved my bike from the bed of the truck. I pushed the Denali forward toward the men. It elicited curious, confused looks. I smiled widely and kept my hands visible as I got closer. All six men held weapons, two had semi-automatics with illegal bumpstocks. All packed handguns. One carried a sawed-off 12-gauge shotgun. Lots of firepower on their side. They were wary. Their weapons were half pointed at me, which made them feel safe.

"Hey," I said. "I heard you fellas would like to play with the new Glock 60-ec. Am I right?" I yelled the question like a cheerleader at football game. "Am I right?"

They all grinned. Two yelped back the affirmative.

"I've got one right here."

"Whoa! Rad!"

"No shit!"

"Awesome! Awesome!"

I set the bike upright against a scraggly locust tree that marked a vague boundary between the AFPM shooting range and the rest of the property. Most of the lower limbs on the forty-foot tree had been shot off and the upper limbs were rotted with beetles. I reached into the handlebar bag and grabbed one of the guns by the barrel, twisted it so I could see the bottom of the magazine. No paint. I pulled it out.

I walked forward casually, fingers only on the barrel, unthreatening, gun swinging back and forth at my side.

I came up next to Lucas Pine, presenting him with the 60-ec. He took it reverently like priest would a saint's bones. After he fingered it for a while, I carefully took it back from him and pointed to a switch on the side.

"I know you guys are familiar with the slide safety on the Glock 40," I said, as if speaking to fellow aficionados, "but this puppy uses a push-click safety. It's a completely different feel. Let me show you."

I gave the safety a push and swung the gun toward the closest target, a poster of a long-retired California congresswoman. She had already been shot to pieces before their mock religious ritual. I fired off two quick rounds that hit what was left of her between the eyes.

"Holy fuck," Elam shouted. "Nice shooting!"

"Yeah, man," Pine said.

"Push the safety one more time and it goes into automatic mode," I said, stretching out my hands, bearing the gun back to Lucas.

He took it. His eyes fixated on the weapon. Happy, like that kid in the Christmas movie who gets his BB gun.

I stepped away. Pine's AFPM buddies gathered around the Glock 60-ec, heads bent, studying it, commenting on this and that aspect of the hardware.

Pine held it close to his chest and, echoing his favorite politician, said to his friends, "Its grip feels like a chick's pussy when you meet her for the first time."

They laughed as if knowingly.

He turned to the target. Everyone else followed his gaze. Like me, he took two shots at the poster, hitting it square, though not as showy as my bullseyes. Then he pushed the safety once more to put it in automatic firing mode. The group held its collective breath as he pointed the 60-ec toward the image of the retired Jewish California congresswoman, malign smiles creeping up the ends of their lips.

All the while, I was stepping back to my bike. No one watched me. I withdrew the other Glock from the bag and took careful aim. Jimmy TJ and Flynn had holstered their weapons, which meant I'd shoot them last. Timbo had his AR-15 with its cumbersome bumpstock under his crossed arms, making it impossible for him to unwind and shoot in any reasonable time. I would shoot him third. Elam and Billy J continued to hold their weapons in their hands, though down at their sides. I decided to shoot Elam first because he had the shotgun and he had the better angle at me.

I did not have to wait long for my signal. Pine fired off a burst of blanks, hitting no target, kicking up no dust. At first, the men laughed thinking it a matter of Pine's poor shooting.

Until.

Pop. Elam in the head. Pop. Pop. Down goes Billy J. Next Timbo flails against gravity when I nail him. Pop. Pop. Pop. Jimmy TJ and Flynn are reaching for their holsters when I release a burst of six Pops. I've got five bodies and eight bullets left. You can't fault Glock for its product. It kills as advertised.

By this time Pine had turned to me and started shooting the blanks from the 60-ec I had given him. After about ten rounds he finally understood the situation and dropped the Glock and reached for his own AR-15, which he'd left at his feet. Before his hand got there I shot him in the right knee. He fell howling to the ground, twisting away from his rifle.

I marched over to him, picked up the semi-automatic by its bumpstock, tossed it aside, and frisked him roughly as he shouted in agony. I pulled out a .22 Beretta from his ankle holster and switchblade from his left forearm; weapons he'd bragged about carrying in more than one online screed. I stripped off his GoPro camera and pushed him back hard on the ground. I made sure he was facing my direction when I put a kill shot into each of his buddies' heads. Three bullets left in my Glock.

He continued to howl in pain as I retrieved the weapons, video gear, smartphones, and other hardware from the dead. I put everything into a large canvas bag I had previously soaked in lighter fluid. I tossed the sack into the cab of Pine's truck.

His painful mewling quieted for a moment into a whimper. I moved close to him, making sure the camera on my chest captured Lucas Pine during my interview with him.

"Lucas? Lucas? I need your attention. Your full attention."

"I'm dying here, man. Help me!"

"Help you? Lucas, I'm the guy who shot you. I just murdered your buddies. Why do you think I want to help you? I am not your friend, you dumb fuck."

His crying kicked up a notch.

I squatted down on my haunches about seven feet away from him. Perfect distance for the camera.

"Lucas, I want your attention. Look at me. You're not dying. I promise you. Not from that wound. You'll be fucked up for life, I won't lie to you. Your patella is shattered. You'll need an artificial knee if you're ever going to use that leg again. Do you know how much an artificial knee costs, Lucas? Tens of thousands of dollars. Guess who didn't sign up for Obamacare because it crimped your freedom? That'd be you, asshole."

He bellowed pathetically. His face shimmered from tears.

"It hurts! Oh, god, it hurts! Oh, god!"

"Shouldn't that be, 'oh, gun, oh gun,' Lucas? Don't you worship guns? Aren't they your god?"

He continued crying, but his hollering lessened again.

"Sweet Jesus. Oh, sweet Jesus," he whimpered.

"Okay, Lucas, look at me. Look at me!" I ordered him.

He hoisted himself onto his elbows, grunting in his agony. He craned his neck up.

"Yes, sir," he said. His in-bred Texan politeness kicked in along with his teary fear.

"Good," I said soothingly. "I just want to chat with you a bit. I am probably not going to kill you. Probably. I want to have a simple conversation with you first. But it has to be an honest one, Lucas. I don't have time nor tolerance for any lies. You have to tell me the truth. And I'll know if you're lying. I'll know because I already know a lot about you. I know about your favorite porn site, galsdoguns.ru, isn't that right? And I've read your dirty texts to your cousin's daughter, Lisa. Sixteen years old, right? So, don't try to lie because I already know so much about you. If you lie to me, Lucas, I will shoot your other knee and leave you a complete cripple. Do you understand, Lucas? Lucas!"

He nodded hard, snot seeping from his nostrils.

"Yes! I understand. Yes!"

"Good. The sooner we conclude our chat, the sooner medical help will get here."

He managed a grin at the possibility of help.

I said, "Listen carefully, Lucas. And tell the absolute truth."

"Yes, sir."

"What is your full and complete legal name?"

"Lucas Pine," he said without hesitation.

I stood up, took two quick strides over to him and gave his wounded knee a prod with the still warm Glock's barrel. He screamed in pain as if I had set him on fire. His elbows gave way and his face hit the dirt.

"You're not listening or you're lying on the very first question. The easiest one. That's so disappointing, Lucas. Tell me: your full and legal name."

I brought the gun closer to his knee. He said something into the dirt.

"What was that, Lucas? I didn't understand. Full legal name," my voice impatient, angry like a parent berating a sulking tween.

He pushed himself back up on his elbows.

"Marion Lucas Fine, Junior," he said, each word punctuated by a sob.

"Very good," I stepped back and resumed my squat a few feet away from him. "Now, why did you lie about your name, Lucas? Be careful. Tell me the truth."

His eyes got wide. He went quiet. I waited.

Finally, he said, "Marion's a girl's name. Got me picked on in school because of it. Hate it."

"Good, anything else?"

"Yeah, Marion Lucas Fine Senior, my dad, is in jail in Oklahoma."

"What for?"

Only a slight hesitation. "Molesting little boys at the church where he worked as a deacon.

"How old were you when he went to jail?"

"Thirteen."

"Had he molested you before, Lucas?"

He started to shake his head. I started to rise.

He burst out, "Yeah, yes, fucking, yes, yes."

"For how long?"

"I can't honestly remember when it began. Honestly. Early, though. It stopped when I was seven or so. Older than that, my old man wasn't interested. 'I like my meat raw,' he told me the first time. I remember that. I remember that. I'll always remember that."

He was crying again, but not about his knee pain. I waited.

"When do you remember starting to fantasize about killing your father?"

"Before he stopped fucking me," he yelled, angrier at me for dredging up his past than for shooting him. "I dreamed of shooting him every goddamn night."

"I would, too," I said, nodding sympathetically. "I would, too."

"I changed Fine to Pine," he added unprompted as if in a confessional. "It was easy. Even on official documents like driver's licenses. No one really noticed. I just said Pine. So that's what people called me. That's what I became."

"Well done, Lucas," I said easily. "Now I'm going to ask you another question you must answer honestly."

"Yes, sir."

"Why do you love automatic guns, Lucas? Remember, be careful, be honest; think before you speak."

His eyes narrowed as if he were confused. He knew it was a trick question because the obvious answer was a lie, even he knew that. If he started blabbing about America and freedom and what the gun represents to keep America strong, his knee would have another encounter with the Glock's barrel. He kept mum for more than a minute as if weighing his options.

"I want to shoot people, a lot of people," he finally answered in a low voice.

"Anyone in particular?"

He paused for a while, gave a slight shrug, then answered, "No. Not really. Just a lot. A lot of people."

"Why?"

"Numbers matter. People keep score. If you're gonna do it, you gotta be in the game, you know?"

"So, you don't really care if they're Jews or Muslims or Catholics or liberals."

Again, the shrug.

"Honestly?"

"Yes, Lucas."

"It'd be nice but not necessary. Church. Concert. School. Don't care. Just so long as there are a lot of them."

"That's what you're thinking about when you're firing weapons?"

"Not all the time. Usually, but not always."

"Why haven't you actually gone out and killed a lot people?"

"Scared, I guess."

"Would it make you proud to know that your videos inspired other mass killers?"

He looked at me warily.

"It's true," I continued. "Of course, mass murderers often watch a lot of shooting videos online. It inspires them. It's amazing how many people like you broadcast their pretend carnage, and everyone, very much like you, wishing it could become real. In fact, I did a little analysis on which websites mass shooters followed. The AFPM showed up in more than a few mass killers' browser histories. So, even if you and your dead buddies here could not do it yourselves, you helped push others to take the fatal step. Does that make you proud, Lucas?"

"I'm not sure."

I started to rise.

'No, Jesus, no. Honest. I don't know. Maybe before…"

"Before what?"

"You. Before you."

"Are you saying, as long as there were no consequences to your being an inspiration to mass killers, it would have been a point of pride for you? It's only the consequences for what you did, the responsibility you bear at this very moment, that upsets you."

"Huh?" His eyes glazed over, confused, but he gamely agreed. "Yeah, I guess. I don't know," he said. "Maybe. Maybe not."

"You understand what a consequence is, don't you, Lucas?"

"Yeah, something that happens because of something else that happened earlier."

"Exactly. Consequences can really change your perspective about life, Lucas. I'm glad I've been able to give you that insight."

He actually thanked me.

"I only have one more question for you, Lucas. Ready?"

He nodded vigorously, anxious to have his interrogation done.

"Do you know who Walter Riggs is?"

He thought for a good ten seconds before saying with perfect honesty that he did not.

"He knew you, though, and the AFPM. Followed you guys for a couple of years. Unlike you, he wasn't a wannabe mass shooter, he was the real deal. His killing field was a Catholic church in Pennsylvania. Killed seventeen people."

Pine's eyes were wide.

"He murdered my daughter there."

"Oh, Jesus, no. I'm sorry."

"Hold your sympathy, Lucas. I'm not looking for that. I'm here, obviously, for revenge," I gestured to the cluster of his dead friends. "And I've almost got it, Lucas. I'm almost there."

I stood. His eyes grew even wider. But relaxed when he saw me get my bike and roll it over to his truck. I opened the gas cap and tossed it on the ground. I took small incendiary tied to wire and lowered into the tank. Hanging on the end of the wire was a cellphone.

I put the Glock 60-ec with the blanks back in my bike bag and held the loaded one across the handlebars. I pushed the Denali back to where Pine laid.

"You'll have to say goodbye to your truck, Lucas. It's part of my revenge."

He visibly relaxed.

Until I said, "Oh, and your left knee."

I aimed the Glock and fired one 10mm round into his remaining healthy patella. I heard him screaming for at least a quarter of mile before his wailing disappeared in the wind. After a mile of pedaling I stopped, retrieved a phone from my pocket, and dialed the device hanging from the truck's gas tank. On the third ring I heard the explosion. Black smoke billowed skyward from Flynn's property. I admired my handiwork for a moment before continuing my escape.

Chapter Eight
Saving Angela Merkel

```
Celeste Youngblood
```

I

The fizz in her Shasta ginger ale had settled to perfection as she opened her team's digital log on JFB. She'd gotten a notice on her phone that two new comments from field interviews had been entered into the file. She put her phone in its charger and took a seat at a workstation hardwired to the offline server.

Youngblood, as was her wont, started at the beginning of the file so that when she got to the new entries they were understood in a temporal context. Something she'd picked up from Lakes. "It's not always what you learn but when you learn it that matters," he'd said.

Plus, even though she had the digital logbook practically memorized, it never hurt to review the evidence and status of the hunt from the perspective of multiple agents. A philosophy professor she once had in Heidelberg told the class to read a passage, then read it again. If anything new occurred, anything at all, read it again, even if it was simply the punctuation that caught your eye, read and re-read, she had said, until not just the words and their meanings are clear and complete, but the typography itself, every serif, every comma. Everything matters, she'd lectured the undergraduates, even if it doesn't. Lakes and her would have gotten along, Youngblood said to herself more than once.

So she read the file again from the top. It began with a description of the mass shooting at the Duckett Watershed in Maryland, including excruciating forensic details of the mortal wounds in the victims in both words and images. There were complex equations that charted the angle the shooter fired from with each kill. Even the weather at the time of the killings had its own section in the file. Comprehensive and growing biographies covered the victims lives as well as everyone connected to the murders blossomed every hour.

Information overload was an understatement. But Youngblood liked it that way. You never knew what tantalizing tidbit of trivia would set her off in the right direction. Everything mattered, even if, in the end, it didn't mean shit.

The first item recently added to the file was from a third former colleague of JFB, who answered a question AD Lakes had added to all interviews. Mostly, he wanted to know about JFB's political biases and whether he ever showed any animosity toward the President. Most people who had known him said that no such remarks had been made in their presence. His ex-wife had been adamant in her reply. She'd told an agent, "Jeff only cared about two things, Jessica and his job. If it didn't involve his daughter or work, he didn't give a fuck."

Youngblood had doubted the wisdom of Lakes's insistence on adding the political question to agents interviews. It probably planted ideas into people's heads instead of real recollections. She had mounted a desultory argument against the question, which her boss jumped on.

"Killing Laskey's family is essentially a political murder, an assassination of sorts," he'd retorted. "A man like that thinks about the significance of who he kills. That's political thinking. And what's more political than shooting the President of the United States?"

"Why didn't he just go do it then?" she'd countered. "Why take out Laskey's kid and the others?"

"Revenge, of course," Lakes had replied. "Plus, it was easy killing the Laskeys. Shooting the President is much more difficult."

"Which is why he'll probably go after another, softer target, sir," she concluded.

"Maybe, and we won't ignore anything that will point us in a different direction, but we cannot overlook even the remotest possibility he has the President in his sights."

She didn't fight it. Until now, Lakes's question had yielded two coworkers to remember that JFB "like most sane people," as one said, found the President crude and unlikable. Worse was said every day in the OpEd pages of the *New York Times*.

But the latest accusation had a little more bite to it, she admitted. It came from a former employee named Bill. He had left the company a few months before JFB had quit. When he was finally contacted, the man recalled an instance at a going-away party for another coworker. The President's name had come up. Or, more precisely his nickname, the Boss, did; one the President had carried over from his days as a real estate wheeler dealer. Bill said that he was sitting next to JFB at a large table packed with loud people. Well into the celebratory evening someone across the table, Bill did not remember who, had said that the President alienated so many Americans that the Secret Service had to be working overtime to keep the President safe.

Bill remembered JFB saying, "Oh, I hate the Boss as much as anyone, but I wouldn't waste a bullet on him." Then, according to Bill's recollection, JFB said softly, "I'd waste two."

While JFB's enmity toward the President did interest her, she still doubted that it was inevitable his next act would be try to assassinate the President. If he was going to kill again, and that was not yet a foregone conclusion, Youngblood believed JFB would choose someone easier to shoot than the Boss.

As intriguing as the first item was, the second new entry grabbed more of her attention. It was culled from Laskey's daughter's calendar app. She had set up a lunch with her mother "at a K Street eatery joint" for two weeks after the shooting. Nothing unusual about that, except that the agent reviewing the victims' digital lives had noted that the mother did not have the same engagement with her daughter. Instead, the older woman had set up a meeting with a reporter from the *Washington Post* at its headquarters, on K Street.

Naturally the agent checked in with the *Post*, and, as expected, learned nothing from the reporter listed in the mother-in-law's calendar. But from the journalist's beat, it was clear the subject was gun control. The writer had published a dozen or more pieces in the past year about celebrities coming out against the broad protections granted to Second Amendment proponents.

Was Laskey's daughter going to betray his cause in the media? Or were mother and daughter going to grab a bite at one of the many "eatery joints" on K Street? Questions, she knew, needed to be pursued rather delicately.

II

She was about to ring AD Lakes when he stepped into her office. She spun her wobbly government-issue chair around to face him. His expression told her something big had happened.

"Okay, spill it," she said. "What's up?"

"Have you seen the FOMM report from Austin?"

She had not looked at the latest FBI field office mass murder report. They arrived almost every day from one FO or another. Most were immediately cleared as murder-suicides, quickly resolved as family disputes or gang shootings; or they were the work of the classic lone gunman taking out mostly strangers then himself. Very few mass shootings were unresolved in the first twenty-four hours, reducing the urgency to solve the crime, to find and stop the killer; the very purpose of Lakes and Youngblood and the agents they led at headquarters. That's why most HQ agents didn't read FOMM reports until a day or so after they were updated because ninety-nine times out of one hundred, little or no action was required beyond field office coordination and statistics gathering. Paper pushing.

"No, haven't gotten to it yet."

Lakes smiled and said, "Shooter outside Thrall, Texas killed five members of the American Free Patriot Movement…"

"The open-carry group."

"...and left one witness, whom he shot in both knees."

"Oh, that's harsh."

"Witness was in shock, but initially revealed that the killer asked if he knew a Walter Riggs. The victim distinctly remembered the shooter asking him about Walter Riggs before he got shot in the second knee."

"JFB's daughter's killer."

"Riggs had subscribed to the AFPM's weekly video stream cheerleading guns and shooting holes, literally, into religious leaders' effigies."

"It's gotta be JFB," she said. "We need to get down there."

"I've got a Gulfstream warming on the tarmac and the perfect driver to get us to Dulles and beyond."

He turned and left. She grabbed her purse and her overnight bag. Once again, it seemed, she was about to fly in another Bureau jet. Privilege was beginning to sour on her.

She shut down her computer, snagged the iPhone from its charger, donned her jacket, and met Lakes at the elevator bank as an empty car going down opened its doors. They hopped in. She was about to ask what he meant by "perfect driver" to Dulles, but the elevator made an immediate stop at the next and final four floors to ground level. By the time it reached the lobby, Lakes and Youngblood had been pushed to the rear of the car by oncoming passengers. When the doors finally opened, they shoved their way through the milling group in the lobby. He led them to a waiting black Ford Expedition. She buckled in up front in the passenger seat. Lakes tucked himself in the rear behind the driver. He leaned forward and tapped the man on the shoulder.

"Malone here," he said, "has volunteered to join us *ex officio* on our investigation."

Youngblood looked at the driver. Not thirty-five years old with all of his hair, most of it black, kept FBI short. He had a prominent forehead bearing three thick furrows of worry or concentration or both. His ears stuck out and he had a ready smile, which made him unthreatening. That was good because the rest of him was a definite potential threat: six-five, at least, broad across the chest, not an ounce of fat. His big, scarred hands and a roughly repaired broken nose added to his intimidating presence. His light gray eyes could go either way, she decided, gentle or cruel, depending on what was needed.

"Volunteered, sure, by AD Lakes, not exactly the definition of the term," the driver said good-naturedly, glancing at Lakes in the rear-view mirror.

He pointed his elbow in her direction. She tapped him back.

"Agent Malone Wicks, volunteer. Call me Wicks."

"SAC Celeste Youngblood. I'm Celeste," she replied, pulling down her mask, knowing every agent was up on all their latest Covid vaccinations. "And what possessed you to be volunteered or, in truth, shanghaied for this investigation?"

Lakes said, "He had the good fortune…"

"Misfortune," Wicks interjected.

"…to be raised in Thrall, Texas, our very destination."

"Lucky you," she said.

"Lucky me," he said with a broad smile and a glint in his eyes that could have been a twinkle or bitterness. "I am here for debriefing purposes," holding his right hand palm down over his heart.

"Malone here is going to give us context, history, and deep background on this case," Lakes said.

"As best I can."

"So help you God, yes?"

"Sure. Whatever. But first off, SAC Youngblood…," he began, pulling away from the Hoover Building on E Street.

"Celeste."

"Right. Sorry. First off, Celeste, what AD Lakes here didn't mention," he thumbed in the direction of the backseat, where her boss now was tranquilly gazing out the window at the sights along Pennsylvania Avenue, "is that I am officially disqualified from being involved in your investigation."

"Why is that?" she asked, though had a suspicion.

"Based on the initial reports, I know, or knew, at least three of the dead and the lone survivor, too. Thrall is a small place, so that's no big surprise."

"Agreed," she said. "I can see that might create the appearance of bias on your part in any such investigation. Certainly if the case ever came to trial and you had gathered evidence or offered counsel for the investigation or prosecution, defense lawyers might question the objectivity of that evidence or advice. Your objectivity will be a liability."

"You got that right." he said in an even voice. "If we ever catch the killer, I'll be first in line to pin a medal on him."

Youngblood turned and arched an eyebrow in Lakes's direction, but he didn't return her gaze, seemingly more interested in the tourists taking photographs along the Mall than the front-seat conversation. She swiveled back to Wicks and he started to tell a long story.

"It's long because it happened in Texas. And everything is big in Texas," he said.

"Especially the bullshit," she said.

"That's a dollar, Celeste," came Lakes's voice from the backseat.

Wicks laughed and began to talk.

Thirty-three years ago Wicks—all nine pounds, nineteen inches of him—was born in a battered mobile home along the Union Pacific railroad tracks, not that far from Thrall's Main Street. Being a black baby was never the best lot in American life. Being a black mother even worse. His mom hemorrhaged after birth and, even though they were not so far away from town, they were black, so by the time help got to her and transported her and the newborn to the hospital in Georgetown, she was dead. Bled out. He was an orphan.

Wicks's father was unknown. The mother's kin scattered to the winds. The baby was about to be handed over to a state adoption agency when a nearby Christian agency arranged to have an African-American family in Thrall adopt him. Having been born near the small town practically made him a citizen, the thinking went. Texas being Texas, the deal was done quickly and Wicks ended up born and bred in Thrall.

"Malone Wicks is from my adoptive parents. I don't know what my biological parents would have called me."

She couldn't help asking whether he had tried to learn more about his birth mother or father. He shook his head and continued his story.

His adoptive parents worked hard and were firm, but fair. They were strong on Jesus, but just as strong on getting their adopted boy an education, particularly because neither of them had much of one. They could read Scripture, which they did every night instead of watching television. He was reading the Bible by age four. Innately they knew there was something more for their child and they pushed him to read and study. He didn't need much prodding.

When Wicks reached first grade at Thrall Elementary it was so small that first through third grades shared one room and one teacher. The class of fourteen children consisted of seven white kids, five latinos, and two blacks. Everyone picked on the blacks. But being as big as he was, Wicks taught his classmates quickly that no classmate, not even a third grader, was going to push him around and peace on the playground quickly reigned.

Until Ed Flynn learned that his little brother, a third grader, was kowtowing to a black first grader. That shamed the entire family. Flynn attended the same school. He was in the class of fourth through sixth grades, though he and his three best buddies, Jimmy TJ Polton, Billy J., and Lucas Pine, later all members of the AFPM, had each been held back for at least one year. Three of the boys were already teenagers.

One day after school Flynn, Polton, and Pine bushwhacked Wicks while he walked along Main Street. They pulled him behind one of the abandoned store fronts and held him down while Flynn instructed his little brother to "beat the nigger to death." His scrawny little brother bloodied his nose and knocked a loose tooth down his throat, but he failed to inflict serious damage on Wicks. A couple Latino adults stepped into the alley and watched the attack for a minute before breaking it up and chasing away the white kids.

The next day on the playground Wicks jumped on the older Flynn boy. He pounded him hard, bloodied his nose and made him cry. In time the smaller boy was pulled off and beaten by Billy J and Pine. A teacher eventually broke up the brawl. This went on regularly until the older boys finally graduated to middle school and took a school bus to another town.

"I have to say, most everyone else in town was cool, you know," Wicks said as he guided the SUV through the government's private security gates to an unmarked hangar beyond the bustle and delays of the rest of the airport. "But they were also very uncool because they let shit…"

"That's a dollar in the swear jar, Malone," Lakes said from the back.

"…from the likes of Flynn and the rest persist, to fester, just because their families had scratched out a living there for a half dozen generations. They accepted not just prejudice, but violence fed by utter ignorance. The locals gave them cover to be brutal assholes."

"That's another buck, Malone."

"'Asshole' isn't a swear word, AD. It's a plain and simple noun." he said, bringing the car to a stop.

They all grabbed their gear and exited the SUV at the foot of the jet's stairway.

"So, Wicks," Youngblood asked as they ducked into the jet's cabin. "How'd you go from Thrall to the Hoover Building?"

"The Texas way," he replied, flipping the back of his right hand toward her, only his index and pinky fingers raised. "Hook 'em horns. Second string tackle, University of Texas football. ROTC scholarship. Army. Middle East. Rice law school. Hoover Building."

"Next stop? Congress? White House…?"

"No. I like it here. Nine years now. I fit in. I do good work. I catch bad guys trying to shaft the United States. Might be my final destination, career-wise."

"What's your specialty, Wicks, when you're not volunteering *ex officio* for AD Lakes?"

"Financial crime. Money laundering. Stock fraud. A skill, I'm guessing, that won't be in high demand while investigating the good ol' boys in the AFPM."

She laughed. A smile tipped the lips of Lakes's placid expression.

Wicks asked, "How'd you get to Hoover, Celeste?"

"The Indian way," she replied. "Piscataway nation heritage meant nothing in Baltimore when I was growing up. For a while we weren't even considered Native American. It took until 2012 to be recognized by the state. Before then, when I was a kid, we were like the Untouchables in India, a caste too far down the ladder to think about. Even blacks looked down on somebody in Baltimore. We were that somebody."

"'Thank God for the Piscataway', was a cry heard in the poorest sections of Mobtown," Lakes quipped sarcastically as they strapped themselves into their seats for the flight to Texas. "There has to be a bottom in every strata of society. You both grew up at the bottom, but at different depths, in different places."

Wicks looked at Lakes.

"Much poverty where you were raised?" he asked.

"In Woodside, California? Hardly. For a while growing up I had Steve Jobs as one neighbor and Larry Ellison as another. Billionaire's both."

"Your daddy a billionaire?"

"Nah. He only had a few tens of millions in the bank. A relative pauper. But he had inherited the estate, so that's why we lived there. No mortgage."

"I love comparing hardship stories while growing up," Youngblood cracked.

Wicks turned to her.

"Did you stay in Baltimore? Go to Johns Hopkins, maybe?"

"I left," she said. "Ran away in the early nineteen nineties. Ended up in Germany. Went to school there. Long story."

"Come on! Tell him about Merkel," Lakes said. "Angela Merkel. The German."

"What?" Wicks said, eyeing her curiously.

"She saved Chancellor Merkel's life."

"You're kidding?" Wicks said, his expression shifting to awe.

"Maybe," she admitted. "She wasn't chancellor then."

"What happened?"

"It was 1995," she said. "My German was good enough by then to get me a job as a *Kellnerin* at a *Bierstube* in the *Altstadt* in Heidelberg. Back then Merkel was the minister for women and youth, being kept in check by her boss, the then chancellor of Germany, Helmut Kohl. He knew a threat when he saw one, so he sidelined her. But Merkel didn't complain. She just did the heavy lifting of giving speech after speech, in town after town convincing people the right-wing CDU actually cared about women or youth compared to the SPD. Mostly a lie, of course. But she passionately believed it, or so it seemed. Quite the performance."

Youngblood glanced down at her phone, hoping something had come up to turn attention away from her story. Nothing.

"And…"Wicks prodded.

"Anyway," she continued. "One night late, near midnight, Merkel and her entourage arrived and took a U-shaped banquet that had been reserved across from the bar. When I served them the first round I'd overheard enough to know they'd just come from a debate with an SPD opponent held in the *Heiligegeistkirche,* the big church across the square. Merkel sat at the end, the consummate politician, ready to meet and greet anyone crossing her path. Her security guy, a classic handsome

Aryan type, scooted to the back of the U, braced by two young local CDU hotties, who had his full attention. Opposite Merkel was her minder, who never looked up from his thick binder of notes. When Merkel wasn't being recognized and glad-handing passersby, I overheard her and him talking about her travel schedule and upcoming cabinet meetings. Mundane stuff.

"When I served Merkel's table, I'd noticed a sad-looking scrawny dude at the bar nursing the same *kleines pils* he'd been sipping since he'd arrived shortly after Merkel. He had a canvas satchel that he kept between his two feet. He'd rub the bag with his left foot regularly, obsessively. Also, he took sideways looks at Merkel.

"As I was approaching her table to cash it out after a couple rounds, I saw the scrawny guy reach into his bag and pull out a big fuckin'…"

"Swear jar, Celeste," Lakes said merrily.

"…knife, a Puma *Hirschfanger* Stag Horn, if you know what that is."

"I do not," Wick answered.

"Nine-inch blade, practically a f'…sword," she said, pausing, saving herself a buck. "He came charging at Merkel, screaming her name. Her flirtatious guard was pinned between two screaming gals as the scrawny guy made a beeline for his boss. I had an angle so I took off running and slammed into the attacker a step or two before he reached his target. I had him down to the ground and for good measure I slammed his head on the floor, knocking him unconscious. I kicked his knife away. The German security dude finally made it over the table and fell on top of the scrawny guy. He said to me something like: thank you *Fraulein,* I'll take it from here.

"Merkel came over to me immediately after I stood up. She looked me over like a mother checking out her kid who had just fallen off a bicycle. She asked me if I was okay over and over. Then hugged me and said thanks. I said something in German.

She sussed out my accent and replied in English, 'Oh, my gosh, you're American.' I pleaded guilty and she gave me another hug. About then a couple of police, who'd been called, arrived. Merkel grabbed my arm and led me away, shot a look at the bar's owner and shook her head. The guy gave her a thumb's up in return. Next she ordered her aide, in a thick idiomatic North German accent I could barely understand, to bury the event. She did not want to be considered a victim, she said. Finally she ordered that the scrawny murderous dude get some psychiatric help. And we left together.

"She led me into a Mercedes waiting in the rain outside the pub. We sat in the back and talked. Or, rather, I did. She asked a bunch of questions about who I was and how I got to Germany and how I managed. As woman, I mean. She knew that a broad-faced, broad-shouldered, broad-hipped dark-skinned girl like me had it a little more difficult than a lot of women slumming across Europe. She knew because that's who she was to outside eyes; a plain, dumpy *Hausfrau* that no man ever fantasized about while jerking off. That I was the color of the wet cobblestones and she pale as printer paper made no difference to her. That didn't matter to either of us. We were impervious to playground politics. She knew that way better than me, obviously. But we bonded, instantly and infinitely like women do. Nothing that ever happened would change our singular moment together.

"After about fifteen minutes her minder joined us in the backseat. Merkel instructed me to give him my contact information. 'Someone will get back to you,' she told me, gave me a last hug, and then sent me back to my job."

"Did 'someone' ever contact you?"

"Yeah, about a month later while I was at work, I served a solo guy at a table. He asked if I was Celeste Youngblood. I said yes. He pulled out a thick envelope and laid it on the table. He said that he was happy to tell me that I had won the Joachim Sauer four-year scholarship to the German university of my choice. I told him he must be confusing me with someone else. I had never applied to any such scholarship. But he opened his envelope and brought out a new passport with a new student visa stamp, which made me legal in the country for the first time in more than a year, residence documents, and a Deutsche Bank account that included scholarship funds in my name. All I needed to do was choose a place to study and sign."

"And did you?"

"You bet your ass," she said.

Lakes started to talk, but she cut him off.

"'Ass' is not swear-jar worthy, sir."

"What school did you choose?"

"Heidelberg. I was already there. Great town. Great school."

"What'd you study?"

"Philosophy, of course. Made me a perfect candidate for a law degree after I got back to the States."

"Where was that?"

"Washington and Lee."

Wicks nodded. Story complete.

"I love that story," Lake said enthusiastically. "It says so much about Celeste's bravery, intelligence, and discretion."

She asked, "How so?"

"Well, bravery is obvious. You tackled a crazy guy with a nine-inch blade. We stipulate that fact. Your getting a philosophy degree from Heidelberg University and a law degree. Not something dolts do. We stipulate you're smart. As for discretion, the fact that a month after your heroism nothing had changed. Neither you nor Merkel had your photos splashed across *Bild Zeitung* with some lurid details and comments on the incompetence of her security detail or, worse, how the CDU failed to help the mentally ill. Nothing. As if it hadn't happened. Just the way Merkel wanted it. In other words, she knew you, the only person who could profit from making it news, said nothing, did nothing. Kept your mouth shut. Discretion, I believe it's called. Powerful people appreciate that trait as much as bravery and intelligence."

The pilot announced over the intercom that they were getting ready to land. Before securing their seatbelts, they each turned their attention to their electronic devices, checking e-mail, phone messages, news stories, and anything else that happened since they left headquarters. Soon enough she felt the engines shift power and the descent to the Austin airport begin.

"Say, Celeste," Wicks said as they hurtled down the runway. "Who the hell is the guy that gave you the scholarship; who's Joachim Sauer?"

"Ah, he's *Herr* Angela Merkel, as it were, her second husband."

"He thought his wife's life was worth a scholarship," Lakes added. "Very romantic for a physicist, don't you think?"

"Really?" Wicks asked her.

She nodded, unclicking her belt before the jet came to a complete stop.

"Well, fuck me," he said jokingly. "The Piscataway Way into the Bureau is way more interesting than the Texas Way."

"That's a dollar for the swear jar, Malone."

"I'll get myself a bank loan," he said as they clambered down the jetway to the tarmac and their trip to Thrall.

II

The helicopter set them down more than a hundred yards clear of the crime scene's wide perimeter. They hoofed the rest of the way along an unpaved farm road. The air was pungent from the scorched husk of a pickup smoldering at the end of the road near an open area where the AFPM took target practice and practiced their rituals.

The property straddled a meandering seasonal creek that fed the groves of trees stalking the water's path. On one side of the creek bed was the shambles of a shooting range; opposite, a tidy modern manufactured home stood with a well-tended garden, where five-foot marijuana plants stood tall and abundant under a mesh screen.

Between the verdant trees and blackened truck the ground was paved with sparkling shell casings. Empty bullet boxes were strewn everywhere and blue cans of Bud Lite and Red Bull littered the area. Cast among them were torn packages of jerky, chips, candy, and hundreds of cigarette butts.

Shooting stands of stacked cinder blocks ran irregularly like a drunken Maginot Line separating the targets from the shooters. Some walls were shoulder high, others required the shooter to be on his belly; the rest, in between. A bong, a baggie of weed, and a case of warm beer sat in the shade of the tallest wall.

Atop a few of the cinder block walls boxes of ammunition were stacked ready for use. In the field, beyond the block walls, countless targets sat in various blown-apart states at different distances; some as close as thirty feet, others more than a couple hundred yards away. A lot of targets were as small as beer cans, a few as big as old tractors. Most were hard to recognize from all of the gunfire they'd sustained.

Parked on the periphery were a score of emergency vehicles, crime-lab trucks, marked and unmarked police cruisers. She recognized another trio of black FBI Ford Expeditions and GMC Yukons parked nearby. A string of field agents in stark white forensic suits canvased the target practice field. Two others similarly dressed poked around the truck's carcass. A couple agents, dressed in suits, debriefed first responders in isolated pockets, getting down fresh impressions before witnesses began to talk about their experience and fogged their own memories with the retelling.

The bodies were gone to the morgue, but their blood and viscera still glistened thick around a cinder block wall. Weapons lay where the dead left them.

"So, the bodies were all shot and found right here," she said. The photos of the murders she'd seen on the flight showed the five men practically in a pile. "Wonder how JFB got them all to stand in one place for their execution?"

"Report says the survivor was found just a few feet away," Lakes added before sauntering over to a clutch of sheriffs and state police, introducing himself and cozying up with the locals.

Wicks stood with his back to the crime scene, staring through the trees at the spiffy new double-wide mobile home and the pair of recent model year Dodge 1500 and 2500 pickups. He looked down at his smartphone.

"Says here, so far, sheriffs, who are executing the search warrant, have found in the house two hundred and twelve weapons believed to be in working order, plus thousands of rounds of ammunition, another room of tactical gear, including everything from pricey scopes and silencers to a crate of bullet-proof vests. Sheriff's initial report says the double-wide's master bedroom was given to the guns."

"Appropriate. Your old pals prepping for Armageddon?" Youngblood needled him.

"I don't know about that, but I know one thing, my old pals, as you call them, were too fucking stupid and poor to afford everything we see here."

"Report says that one of them…"

"Flynn."

"…inherited this place."

"Yeah, I'm not sure from whom. The Flynn's were multi-generational white trash. Hillbilly stupid and proud of it. That anyone in that family had owned land, good land, this close to Thrall and hadn't already pissed it away is shocking enough. But Ed Flynn living here for more than a decade without selling or losing it? Not fucking likely. Add in the armory and nice trucks and it boggles my mind. It doesn't scan. These boys can't walk and chew gum simultaneously. How'd they get and keep all this? Where'd the money come from?"

"The internet? Their Google ads and online sales? Analysts haven't yet chased down AFPM online revenue completely."

"Come on!" Wicks dismissed the idea with a wave of his hand. "Six thousand followers on YouTube and a crappy website aren't exactly gold mines. These boys' bucks are coming from somewhere else."

"What about the ARI? Laskey's group underwrote the AFPM for a while."

"Possible. But Laskey cut them off quick enough after the AFPM pissed off even conservatives around here with their open-carry antics," Wicks said, head shaking. "There's another source. Has to be."

She said, "Are you sure you're not just a financial-fraud hammer looking for money-laundering nails?"

"What do you mean?"

"I mean, a financial crimes agent is going to look for financial crimes."

"Guilty as charged," he said, holding his hands up in mock surrender. "I always follow the money first and foremost. Foolish not to. It gets you answers quicker. But believe me, that bias is not nearly as strong as my bias about Flynn and his dead buddies. And that bias tells me that unless one of them won the lottery, which they didn't, or inherited cash along with the land, which they didn't, there's no way any of them or all of them together could have earned the money necessary to pay for all this," Wicks spread his arms to encompass his surroundings. "It's not in their DNA, literally and figuratively, to have either the imagination or the drive to fund everything we see here. The cost of the spent ammunition alone is staggering. There's something else at play."

"With that many guns in his master bedroom, maybe Flynn and the AFPM ran illegal gun sales."

"That makes some sense. We will need to chase down the provenance for the weapons and gear to clear up that possibility," he acknowledged. "Again, unlikely. It would mean one of the AFPM members would have had to have enough business acumen to manage the deals. Can't see it. Equally important, they would have all had to keep their mouths shut. Once again, I doubt they could all keep mum for long. It's inconsistent with their characters. ATF would have heard about these clowns and shut them down. In fact, they were investigated by them, after their stunt in Austin, and came up clean just last year."

"My reading of our files on the AFPM doesn't dispute that. They're a not-very-dangerous small group of gun-rights yahoos. No mention of illegal gun sales. No criminal records other than multiple charges of harassment and intimidation, but no convictions."

"They're just tiny-brained dickheads."

"Assholes with guns."

"Fucking assholes with guns," he said, laughing.

"It's fucking great to swear and not have to pay Lakes's swear-jar piper," she said with a wide smile.

"Agreed," he turned back and pointed to the tight circle where the bodies had been found. "Now let me add one more piece of evidence that these fucking assholes are too stupid to have managed to earn enough to live here with all these goodies. Initial forensics say all the men were shot by one man. The initial testimony of the survivor says there was only one perp. So, how did one guy kill five armed men? Because they are dumber and less useful than a sack of hammers. They fell for something. Something stupid, I bet. Anyway, there's clearly under the table money being funneled to these boys. Or was being funneled. Find the source of that money and you'll find a lot of answers to a lot of questions."

"I'll grant you all that, Wicks," she said. "But our primary objective here to is to apprehend Jefferson Fitzgerald Black, whom we now suspect of two mass shootings. While I grant you, your old pals do not appear to be brainiac enough to put together such a profitable sweet gig for gun nuts like themselves, but, unless their sugar daddy can lead us to JFB, let's keep our eyes on the prize: capturing the killer."

At that point an agent who had been inside one of the black SUVs monitoring communications opened the car door. He stepped out, holding the door open, a smartphone in his hand.

Youngblood's eyes drifted from that movement to her boss. She could see him politely separating from the sheriff honchos, gazing down at his phone as he marched toward the SUV's open door. She nudged Wicks and they followed him into the vehicle's wide open rear passenger sliding door.

Inside, instead of forward-facing seats was a bank of computer displays that formed an L-shape console inside the car. The three agents squeezed together around the comms technician. He shut the door behind them with the press of a button and bent to his knees to access a keyboard and mouse that were set on the car floor.

"Gordon Fry, Agent Fry. I'm the tech out of the Fort Worth office," he said, introducing himself, adding deferentially, "I know all of you."

"What's up, Gordon?" Lakes asked amiably.

"Something just got posted to the AFPM website, gunsRgod.com. Something you'll want to see."

Without further preamble, Fry clicked on an icon and a video of the members of the AFPM filled the screen. They were all staring toward the camera, which appeared to be worn on someone's chest like a cop's body cam. Their expressions ranged from stupefied to curious. Each man held a lethal, automatic weapon.

A voice, distinctive, clear, a hint of a flat Midwest accent, spoke to the armed men.

"Hey! Hello! Hello! I'm @readyfireaim. You remember me? @readyfireaim? We communicate all the time online. I'm so pleased to finally meet you guys! This is special. You guys are rockin' rad, man!"

The voice pattered along for a few minutes and offered to let the men use a new high-capacity revolver from Glock not yet approved for sale in most of the country. The voice chatted away while calmly removing a mountain bike from the pickup's bed rolling it next to the tree near the shooting range. The voice removed a gun from a bag hanging on the handlebars, brought it to the men. He huddled with the men for a minute, showed them the gun, fired it, showed them a feature on it, gave it to one of the men, then he backed away, retrieved another identical weapon. Within six seconds the voice had shot down five men. He then wounded the sole survivor, disarmed him, and began a most curious interrogation.

"Lucas? Lucas? I need your attention. Your full attention," the voice said.

"I'm dying here, man. Help me!" Lucas Pine yelled.

"Help you? Lucas, I'm the guy who shot you. I just murdered your buddies. Why do you think I want to help you? I am not your friend."

On it went until the voice ended the interview and shot Pine in his other knee. The recording stopped. By the end there was no doubt who had killed again.

"Play it again, Gordon," Lakes ordered. "Let's watch it one more time. Let's see what more we can learn about JFB."

Chapter Nine
Magic Ball

Excerpt from the memoir of Jefferson Fitzgerald
Black
Q-Level Access
Eyes Only

I

I forget which obscure Shakespearian character gleefully suggested that once his clan took power, "The first thing we do, let's kill all the lawyers;" a sentiment so many of us share. And, yes, I know, the speaker is actually a bad guy talking about good lawyers, if you can imagine such a thing. But the quote transcends the play like so many of the Bard's quips. It makes you wonder. Hope, even.

That's why I was tucked away in the deep rough between two holes on a private golf course outside Ft. Worth. Waiting around to kill some lawyers. What better place to find lawyers than on the links?

My second slaughter today would be more meaningful than my first. Perhaps even the start of something big. Think about it.

A pogrom against lawyers definitely has its upside. As a start, without lawyers, burying corporate and government guilt in thick rhetorical cushions of plausible deniability would not be possible. People would need to speak the plain truth when they made deals; when they wrote contracts; when they brought charges; when they testified; when they wrote laws. Everything a shrewd lawyer abhors. Lawyers make common sense insensible. They obfuscate when clarity is critical. They fix what isn't broken in order to break it so they can fix it and start the cycle again. Whichever side you're on, flushing their bullshit from the system has to be a plus.

Pick an issue. Any important issue. There're so many. Let's start with mine: guns. Troughs of lawyerly bullshit permit guns designed to slaughter soldiers on the battlefield be kept legally in your unmarried, twenty-six-year-old, spooky next-door neighbor's closet. That guy can buy military-grade ammunition over the internet at night and on weekends he can pay cash for high-capacity magazines during gun shows at your local fairgrounds. Makes you feel safe and free, no? No. Then get your own arsenal. Join the armed camp. Lawyers in their natural guise of lobbyists and legislators made such dangerous nonsense conceivable. Logical. The American Way.

Our gun epidemic captures only part of the absurd evil lawyers begat. They infect our lives top to bottom in the worst ways. Because of their creative legal loopholes the rich get richer, naturally, and the natural world, of course, gets sicker. The poor get piled on and thrown in jail because the laws lawyers devise command it. Lawyers concoct the rationale for presidents to wage bloody war without abiding by the Constitution. Lawyers protect property over people because there is little profit in people. They provide the intellectual bedrock for society's laws that perpetuate inequality, injustice, invasion of privacy, and environmental catastrophe.

All of that and more, you can lay at the feet of lawyers. They are at the root of everything that is wrong with this modern world, especially when it comes to guns. I bet if you studied lawyers long enough you'd learn they are the cause of urban bedbug infestations, poor posture, migraines, pimples, and halitosis as well as the slaughter of today's urban youth. They're that bad.

Still, Shakespeare's admonishment aside, I don't think we need to kill them all. That seems extreme. But a select few? With pleasure.

Personally, I'm starting with the white shoe firm of Wythe, Braxton, Wolcott, Rutledge, & Adams, or, as they're known around various country clubs, Wythe, Braxton. To say you have hired Wythe, Braxton is a form of bragging in certain circles. It means you don't blink at fees north of two thousand dollars per billable hour. It means you're determined, desperate even, in your current legal predicament. It means you intend to win by any legal means possible; if that fails, any means will do. Wythe,

Braxton will arrange for it inside or outside of the courtroom. It's what they do.

No partner at Wythe, Braxton had a yearly salary less than seven figures nor a net worth south of thirty million dollars. Rich they were. But making partner there meant making money for the other partners first. For years and years. A law firm is like Amway and other Ponzi schemes. The majority of legal staff on the bottom prop up the few on the top. Moving from intern to staff to associate to non-equity partner to full partner, with your name on the firm's letterhead, was a long slog, generally involving a divorce or two for the truly ambitious. Like many prestigious firms, at Wythe, Braxton people had to retire or, more likely die before a full partner slot opened up. Few lawyers made it all the way to the letterhead, just like most Amway distributors fail to reach the mythical diamond level.

Unless, of course, your name happened already to be on a law firm's letterhead. Nepotism counted. Branch Rutledge was the fifth generation of his family to claim full partner status at Wythe, Braxton, going back to the immediate post-Civil War years, when a few newly minted lawyers from the Ivy Leagues, including his great, great, great grandfather banded together into what became a limited liability corporation, a legal entity designed to remove fiduciary responsibility while maximizing financial reward for the LLC partners. With the legal veneer of a corporation protecting individuals from their own actions, a very few people got very rich and never went to jail for the crimes they committed along the way. Wasn't them who done it, your honor. It was the business. Can't put a business in jail, can ya?

It was a radical concept. Branch's ancestors were true trendsetters, bending American law to their will in new and profitable ways. Pioneers, each and every one, though not for the general good by any conceivable measurement. Once courts began recognizing the validity of erecting fictive legal barriers between the owners of the business and their responsibility for its actions, all hell broke loose. Exploitation of the economy and society ran rampant from the Gilded Age to our own equal Era of Avarice. All those years, Wythe, Braxton had smoothed the way for nineteenth century Robber Barons to twenty-first century hedge fund managers.

Corporations are bought and sold; the rich are born, some made, but all die. Wythe, Braxton, though, endures.

The firm was dug deep into Branch's DNA, so it's surprising, by what I could discern, that like so many of us, his destiny teetered in youth. He almost became a rebel. Almost. Admirably, for a time he deserted his blue blood Virginia haunts after his Yale law school graduation; bummed around the planet for the better part of a year; flew coach, even hitchhiked; got himself arrested in Dubai for drunkenness and quickly released; fell in and out of love; chased women, then men for a while, settled on women before capitulating comfortably in Houston. He liked its rough and tumble machismo. It suited him better than the bone china correctness of his genteel Tidewater upbringing. Still, like almost all of us, he eventually conformed to his ancestor's ilk.

It so happened Wythe, Braxton had a branch office in Houston with a small pod of thirty lawyers and a hundred or so support staff. They catered to the legal inconveniences of the city's old money which, compared to most of the firm's East Coast clientele, was decidedly *nouveau riche*. With his Rutledge pedigree, Branch slipped in as an associate and immediately recognized that the city's richest monied class was not the old millionaires; it was the modern scorched-earth, resource-extraction billionaires in oil, gas, and minerals, crass as they may be. They outnumbered and outspent Houston's old money by a lot. A real lot. Like their potentate buddies in the Third World, their pharaonic wealth was gleaned by despoiling the planet or poisoning the poor and unsuspecting. That kind of money needed the services of Wythe, Braxton.

Branch Rutledge's refined manners, smooth talk, worldliness, and open-minded gregariousness won over deep-pocketed Houstonians, particularly those being sued by do-gooder community groups and the rare, oddball crusading government agency. Houston produced plenty of clients. Branch's smooth, good-old-boy personality, handsomeness, personal charm, not to mention his family's oceanic connections to the rich and powerful ratcheted up Wythe, Braxton's Texas outpost's revenue plenty, especially because his team won for their clients way more often than they lost.

Rutledge's success quickly spread beyond Houston, then outside Texas, then all geographies and became the most sought after corporate criminal defense team in the U.S. In no time, Houston's thirty-lawyer outpost swelled into a five hundred-and-sixty-three lawyer township of cupidity and power.

That's why because of some long-ago childhood slight he suffered at his father's hands, Branch could scratch out his old man's name from the letterhead of Wythe, Braxton, Wolcott, J. Rutledge, & Adams and replace it with his own letter, B. He had forced his father to resign, humiliatingly in a partners meeting seven years ago, not long after he had won *Conway v. the Commonwealth of Pennsylvania*, the decision that led to my daughter's murder.

I would have loved to have been a fly on the wall when young Rutledge executed the coup that deposed his *pater* as a partner and sent the old man, a mere fifty-nine years old though the worse for wear from decades of the world's best single malt whiskeys, to pasture. The young Rutledge had threatened to mutiny, taking most of the Houston branch's business with him if he didn't replaced his unloved papa.

It didn't take the other partners long to decide. Branch's dad's days as a major rainmaker were behind him, everyone knew that. Even white shoe lawyers can count. So the elder Rutledge was sent packing with a priceless retirement parachute, of course, to tame the old shark's retaliatory instincts, numb as they were.

Branch never claimed to be a great lawyer. But with the unlimited money his clients dumped on him, he could find the best minds in any situation and crush the opposition. His motto, rumored to be tattooed in Latin on his back, was: "*Victoria non est secundum quid nosti melius nosti vel quis, illud per quod estis vos es solvere voluit;*" roughly translated by Google: "Success is not measured by what you know or even who you know, it's by what are you willing to pay." Seems rather wordy for a tattoo, but these days, who knows?

Deals came aplenty to Wythe, Braxton's Houston office and the partners never regretted their decision to axe Branch's dad. Numbers don't lie. As law firm rainmakers went, Branch was a typhoon. Whenever he texted, talked, e-mailed, voice mailed, read, Skyped, Tweeted, or ate lunch, his minutes were charged to someone somewhere for something. If Branch Rutledge took a call while taking a crap, Wythe, Braxton billed for the turd.

More than a decade ago, the ARI hired Branch and his team to fight a new Pennsylvania gun registration law. Actually, it was a fee devised by the state legislature to collect extra revenue on ammunition, a recycling fee for every one hundred rounds of ammunition. The fee was a quarter. Twenty-five cents.

To the ARI you'd think the British redcoats were enforcing the tea tax. Of course, it wasn't the money that bothered the ARI it was the provision that if you chose not to pay the tax, you could register with the state to recycle your shell casings. It was totally voluntary. But Branch Rutledge argued, on behest of the ARI and its straw-man plaintive Bob Conway, that by permitting some people to avoid taxes through a registration system the law was unconstitutional.

What the ARI most vehemently objected to were two questions on the tax-avoidance registration form. The first asked if the person had ever been charged with domestic violence. The second asked whether the registrant had ever been diagnosed with a mental disorder. Despite the fact that it was self-reporting information, the ARI fought it tooth and nail. They won three years later.

Sixteen months after that, Walter Riggs, a two-time convicted wife abuser and once involuntarily committed to a state mental ward in Harrisburg, legally bought a semi-automatic gun and shot up a Catholic Church where my daughter was attending Mass. That made Branch and his team my enemies.

They didn't know, of course, which was why they were enjoying their annual bonus meeting on the links, where historically Branch handed out seven-figure checks to his top seven lieutenants. No one left poor after the match. As always, Branch held off delivering the bonus news until the proverbial Nineteenth Hole, when everyone was well lubricated, the steaks and lobster digesting in their guts, cigars smoldering, only then were the checks handed out. Tradition. Branch loved it. Despite his embrace of all things Texas, his innate East Coast breeding craved hoary ritual, proper deference, and a clear expression of his pure power. Actually, native Texans like that, too.

Admittedly, I'm engaging in literary license based on the voluminous messages I've snooped in on with Branch and his subordinates. All the lawyers playing golf that day had been there before to kiss the ring and snag the check. They knew what was coming. They were practically giddy with greed.

II

I peeled off my camo jumpsuit and its matching tarp from the Clicgear three-wheeled golf caddy I now pulled behind me. I'd been sitting in the rough between the 15th green and 16th tee waiting for Branch and his golf buddies. While hanging out I used my iPhone to upload a slightly edited version of the killing of the AFPM's members to its gunsRgod.com website. It wouldn't take long for membership to spread the word about the slaughter. It was already local news, but I wanted major publicity. Shooting a gaggle of lawyers the same day would generate a ton more. I'd make sure of it.

The Wythe, Braxton foursomes were the final ones on the course that day, so I had plenty of time to get here from Thrall. Took about four hours to reach Shady Oaks from the late Ed Flynn's place. I had pedaled back into town to Lucas and Jimmy TJ's place and stole the latter's truck, a beat up but reliable Ford 150. Drove the speed limit to Fort Worth. Parked on Leonard Tri Drive, waded through King's Branch Creek, and settled down with an hour to kill until my targets arrived. The night before I

had driven to the course and stashed my golf cart and
weaponry into the thick copse barrier near the 15th green.

Shady Oaks Country Club is barely outside Fort Worth. Wythe,
Braxton's Houston office was holding its annual tournament for
the top eight rainmakers, including Branch. Each year they
chose some well-known, exclusive course in Texas. They made
two foursomes, always booked for the end of the day, played
slow and celebrated their previous year's success with
expensive booze, Cuban cigars, and, for most in attendance,
well-sourced cocaine. With hefty checks burning a hole in
Branch's golf bag, it was a party.

One I planned to crash.

A handful of foursomes came and went while I was in the
brush. Luckily no one shanked a ball far into the rough where I
had hunkered down. When the Wythe, Braxton team finally
arrived I remained patiently observing until they had all
gathered on the 15th green, but before the last of them had
putted out for the hole. Like the best jokes, serial mass murder
depends on impeccable timing.

I emerged suddenly and loudly from the surrounding
woodland in mufti—pastel pink RLX golf shirt with matching
long-fingered gloves, blue and white checked knee-length
shorts, white socks, and pale green cap with "Calloway GBB
Epic Star" stitched in gold on the bill. White Nike logoed golf
spikes finished my disguise. I intentionally bent my head and
cast my eyes down at the ground while holding up a golf ball
like a prize as I approached my targets.

"Found it! Found it!" I shouted repeatedly. For greater effect, I
affected a Brooklyn accent. "Found it!"

I looked up and gazed about, obviously confused.

"Where's my foursome? Where's my guys? Where'd they go?" I
said, voice laced with chagrin, and turned to look at the
lawyers. "Geez, I'm sorry, fellas. Didn't mean to butt in. Guess
my guys left without me. I was looking forever in the woods for

this ball, I guess. But for cryin' out loud, I parred nine straight holes with this particular ball."

I held it aloft, its distinctive Taylormade TP5X trademark visible. It was a favorite ball of Branch's, I knew. Cost about four bucks each when the young Rutledge bought them in bulk on Amazon with his Prime membership. But he'd paid more than six dollars a piece for them in clubhouses around the country. I knew those details and so much more about him and his colleagues. I had spent enough time in recent months reading their correspondence, monitoring their online selves, tracking their spending habits just as I had done for the poor saps in the now defunct American Free Patriots Movement. I had more than a general sense how to push their buttons.

I stood on the green a bit stooped, watching the lawyers arrayed before me. I shook my head and added a sarcastic tone to my voice.

"I'd give my left ball if this ball kept me at par for the rest of my life."

My audience laughed. One snarked about "magic balls" and another good humoredly questioned how anyone could possibly hit par on the eighth hole.

"I don't know how I did it either," I said agreeably. "That's why I spent a lifetime in the woods looking for my magic ball."

Laughter erupted again from the group. Everyone was enjoying themselves as I got closer, hauling my caddy and bag behind me, heading in the direction of the next hole. A few of the lawyers turned back to their smartphones, heads bent, not paying attention to me any longer. Alcohol and a hint of cannabis wafted from them to me, five or six yards away. They were a happy, distracted bunch.

I stopped and made an exaggerated gesture to put my precious ball into a bulky pocket on the bag. Once my hand was in the pocket my fingers curled around a 12-shot magazine for my Glock. Simultaneously I reached into the bag and grabbed the gun. In a motion I had practiced more than one hundred times, I smoothly pulled the weapon and its ammunition from the golf bag, slapped the magazine into the weapon, and began to fire.

First, I put two bullets into the chest of Lorunce Riordan, the only black man in the group and I knew from monitoring his emails, texts, and credit card data that he owned and carried licensed concealed weapons. He toted .38 and .25 calibre handguns wherever he went. He bragged about it more than once on Twitter. He was a smart guy with a hardness built in. Came from Compton, California and had what it took to not merely survive but to thrive. He was probably the only dangerous man there besides me. So I killed him first.

Next I hit Lucien Hernandez right between the eyes. He was standing closest to me. It was an easy shot. He, too, had a conceal carry permit. I doubted whether he ever packed a gun. Still, I'm cautious.

Two of the lawyers, including the only woman, Charlene Pears, sensing doom rushed at me in desperation, but they were not close enough to reach me before I downed them each with a pair of two shot bursts. Another lawyer, Starch, I think, fell to his knees, wetting himself, dropping his big screen Android phone, putting his hands in front of his lowered head, whimpering. I shot him, through his palms and into his brain. One more guy started to run, but had not gotten three steps before I put a 10mm round in his back. He fell like a tossed sack of potatoes.

Two lawyers remained. Branch Rutledge and his number two, Denver Wicks. At best, only one of them would cash his bonus check.

I pointed the gun in their direction.

"On your knees, gentlemen," I commanded severely.

As they were lowering themselves I swapped out magazines in the Glock. I could feel the weapon was running hot. Still, I walked around the bodies, putting in the kill shot to six heads as I had done earlier in the day. Can't be too careful or too dramatic. After all, it was all on film.

Attached to my golf bag was the most current model GoPro camera. I had aimed it low at the six dead golfers and the two survivors on their knees so my face did not appear in any of the frames. If it did get shown accidentally, I'd edit it out later.

I pointed the Glock at Wicks.

"Tell me about yourself, Denver Wicks. How did you end up here? Working for Wythe, Braxton, that is."

The man sputtered nonsense for a minute as if he were in an employee interview scheming for a promotion. He talked about his education, work experience, his victories in court. He mentioned his strengths as a manager and legal analyst that appealed to the law firm in their hiring of him.

His nerves made it impossible for him to stop talking once he got going. So I fired a shot a good four inches from his left ear. He collapsed, crying.

I was disappointed in Denver Wicks. He was supposed to be a larger-than-life Man of the West. Raised in the Bitterroot Mountains; son of a good Mormon dad, but a better Evangelical mom, who raised their son to love the flag, the family, and God, in no particular order. They were proud of their son, saw him in a heroic light, though they were not seeing him at the moment, failing to live up to their expectations; though real lives lived seldom delivered on the parental dream.

"Come on, Wicks. I'm not looking for a résumé, I'm looking for a reason. Was it your religion that turned you into a lawyer? Was it your God who told you to defend guns like the one in my hand over the lives of innocents? I mean, Wicks, you don't even own a gun, yet you've spent years of your life advocating for them in the courts."

I waited.

He looked up and said, "I was defending a principle. A Constitutional right."

"Slavery was a Constitutional right. So you'd be in favor of, say, the Dred Scot decision. Send free men back into their shackles and whippings. Right?"

"No, of course not, but there was a constitutional amendment and…"

"Yeah, I know. But it took the Civil War and keeping the Southern states out of the amendment process to make it happen. Things change, but it shouldn't take a civil war to acknowledge that change. Like muskets of our Founding Fathers time versus today's Glock. If I had attacked you people, eight of you, alone with a musket I would have killed just one of you, maybe, they're not very accurate weapons; from then on out it's hand to hand combat, seven to one against me. Even lawyers like you might win with those odds. Or, maybe being the cowards that you are, you'd just run like hell and live to tell about it. Not now. Not today. Point is, technology, like civil rights, changes. Don't you think the law should maybe, just maybe reflect reality?"

Wicks started to cry in response.

"And you, Rutledge," I looked his way.

Branch threw up. Twice. That, from him, I expected.

I sighed exaggeratedly.

"Gentlemen, seems neither of you are up for lengthy conversation. I understand. But I don't have time for bullshit. So, I will get to the point. Before we part ways this splendid late afternoon, I will be honest with you, I'm not gonna lie to you; I will kill one of you; the other I will kneecap."

Wicks and Rutledge exchanged horrified looks. I thought Branch would barf again.

"You know what kneecapping is, fellas?" I asked.

They nodded; Branch's eyes wide, Denver's closed tight.

"Death? What about death? Your firm has argued a lot of cases that have resulted in death. Many deaths. You say you know what kneecapping is. Do you know what death is? Do you know how it affects people? Do you know what violent, inexplicable slaughter does to families, to communities, to the nation? Well, your work, your careers, your legacies mean we will always need to ask those questions. Why can't we stop the slaughter? What can we do to stop it? Well, Branch, Denver, do you have answers to any of my questions?"

They shook their heads.

"I didn't think so," I said, angry. "I have an answer. Some of it you see lying before you. Part of the solutions starts with eliminating mercenary scum like you."

They cried.

I softened my voice with sarcasm. "Granted, it's a small step, but a meaningful one. Don't you think? So, who wants what? I might actually give you a vote. What do you say, Branch, want to die or be kneecapped."

He retched again.

"See? It's a tough choice for me, too," I went on. "Die. Or live. Sure, live as a cripple for the rest of your life ain't gonna be easy. But the key word there is 'life,' right, guys? For me it's an academic problem about which of you survives. But, I suspect, suddenly it looms larger for you both. For the first time, you are truly comprehending the arbitrary power this gun in my hand bestows upon me. In this situation I am the unelected, unappointed judge and jury, the all-powerful poobah, the gun god. I am the logical conclusion to all of your efforts in court. You two and the rest," I gestured to the field of dead attorneys, "in courtroom after courtroom spent your careers dismantling common sense views about gun rights. You've made it not just possible but legal and proper that I stand here before you with a semi-automatic Glock with silencer and a 12-round magazine, a combination that you successfully argued was the right of every American to own and use. Well, sirs, I am an American and thanks to you I own this weapon and plenty of ammunition to use as I see fit."

Wicks's crying worsened into uncontrolled sobbing.

He muttered, "I have children. Oh, good lord, my children."

I took four quick steps over to him and slapped him hard. I couldn't help myself, but I quickly returned to a safer distance. But I was still angry.

"For Christ's sake, Wicks!" I shouted barely maintaining control of myself. "How many children have been shot dead because of your bullshit in the courts? How many daddys and mommys ate lead because you successfully argued that the right to own weapons of war was a goddamn fucking right for everyone? You made each and every one of those killings possible. You better believe it, Wicks, there will be children crying tonight. They're crying every fucking night. Because of you their mommys or daddys or sisters or brothers are shot dead and they cry their eyes out. Every day. Every night. Every state. Everywhere in this country, which you have turned into a battlefield. America is at perpetual war with itself because of shitheads like you, Wicks. You and Rutledge."

The volume of his sobbing rose. I really wanted to shoot him dead to shut him up. But in that moment I realized Rutledge deserved the bullet in the brain, Wicks the knees.

I took a deep breath to calm myself. Fired two quick shots into Rutledge's forehead. He fell sideways toward Wicks, who instinctively jumped up and backwards getting off his knees. His new position made for a cleaner shot. Before he could take his eyes of his dead colleague I put a single 10mm round through his left knee. It shattered into a pink spray of blood and bone. He collapsed screaming. Wordlessly I walked over, put another round in Rutledge's skull and fired one more into

Wicks's right knee. I took the Glock, its magazine, and the
GoPro camera, leaving my cart behind. I retraced my steps to
Jimmy TJ's pickup and heard Wicks's wailing almost all the way
there.

Chapter Ten
Not As Bad As A Bus Crash With Kids

```
Celeste Youngblood
```

I

A gent Fry pressed his fingertips to the earbud in his left ear. Without hesitation he told Lakes to take an incoming call. Youngblood's boss told him to put it on the speakerphone. Fry did so without hesitation.

He said, "Sheriff Morrow, you're on the speakerphone with Assistant Director Richard Lakes and Special Agent in Charge Celeste Youngblood."

"Well, ain't that rootie-tootie," came an aged sarcastic drawl. "An assistant director and a special agent, in charge, no less. Ain't that special?"

Lakes didn't respond. No one else did either. The agents had encountered many local lawmen who resented the FBI for not only its jurisdiction over such things as mass murders, but also its expertise. And, perhaps, their wordy job titles.

Lakes thought that most of the local sheriffs were self-serving yokels, always primping for the next election by being rougher, meaner, and stupider than the next candidate. They knew themselves to be inferior to the FBI but resisted help. Everything about the relationship between the Bureau and local law enforcement was a pissing match; one the locals could never hope to win and so they resorted to insults. That's why he sent subordinates like Youngblood to work with them.

After a long silence, Morrow said, less sarcasm, a bit more professionalism in his drawl, "What I got here is seven dead lawyers. And that's not the start of a joke, AD Lakes and friends. Six men and one woman shot dead on the fifteenth green of Shady Oaks Country Club. An eighth lawyer, a man, has been taken to Texas Methodist hospital with serious, but not life-threatening wounds. Sweet Jesus, the killer…"

"He shot the survivor in both knees," Lakes finished for Morrow. "The witness was kneecapped, Sheriff."

Morrow let that sit for a second before saying, "I suppose you also know who did this, then?"

"We believe we do, yes."

"Well I know this is above my pay grade, Special Agent in Charge Youngblood and Assistant Director Lakes," he said, all the twanging sarcasm back in his voice as if he were role playing for an audience of his deputies. "But since you know who did this, I'd suggest you drive over to the fella's house and arrest him. Or, if that's too much trouble, give me the damn address and I'll do it for you. Maybe if you had done it already I wouldn't have seven dead lawyers in my jurisdiction."

"You have no jurisdiction, Sheriff Morrow," Lakes replied cooly in a low voice. "We have your coordinates. I'm sending Agents Youngblood and Wicks and a contingent of my staff to take control of the crime scene. They will be there in a half an hour or less. Agent Youngblood will expect that you will have secured a perimeter around the crime scene, but have not disturbed the evidence in any way whatsoever. And Sheriff," his voice fell to barely above a whisper, "if you or your deputies so much as crush a blade of grass or breath in the direction of the crime scene, I will have Agent Youngblood arrest you personally for obstruction of justice for altering a federal crime scene."

Lakes clicked off not waiting for an answer.

"Get going," he said to her. "I'll call in more resources from Dallas and Houston. I'll manage the situation here. Nail down anything new you find at the golf course. We need to get a handle on where JFB is or, more importantly, will be. We need to know who he's got it in for next. And we need to know that information fast. Two mass shootings in a single day by a single shooter. We can't discount that he may have a third planned."

Youngblood left Agent Fry with Lakes, but she and Wicks grabbed a trio of agents who had been interviewing first responders. She got a text on her cell that the Dallas office had confirmed a forensic unit was in transit since Fort Worth's was busy in Thrall. But the closer office had already sent a half dozen agents to oversee Sheriff Morrow's perimeter, per Lake's order. Per her request, he commanded an FBI copter secure the air space around the golf course and instruct air traffic control in the region to make the area off limits to aircraft. Drones could be a problem, but she gave orders for agents on the ground to shoot down any on sight.

Youngblood's squad of dark-suited Feds jogged to the waiting copter. Its rotors were spinning, warming up for them. They donned helmets and were wheels up in two minutes, racing toward JFB's astonishing and horrifying second mass murder in a single day.

Before the copter jerked into the air, she started reading about Wythe, Braxton on her smartphone. All the lawyers attacked on the golf course had worked there. It didn't take long to figure out why JFB targeted the firm. They were ARI allies and had been engaged in almost every major judicial action that protected gun rights, especially in Pennsylvania where his daughter had been murdered. The firm was a fierce advocate for gun owners. In one story she read, Branch Rutledge, the head of Wythe, Braxton's Houston office, was quoted as saying, "Gun control is simple code for mind control. Give up your guns? Might as well give up your will to live."

Incoming texts from agents already at the Wythe, Braxton office in Houston reported that no one there, including the five security staff, had heard of any threat from a person named Jefferson Fitzgerald Black. Social media accounts were being scoured for clues. There was absolutely no credible threat directed at the firm's annual golf tournament. Attached to one text was the list of the lawyers in the tournament and the name of the survivor, Denver Wicks.

She nudged Agent Wicks next to her. She pointed to the same last name.

He replied on his open mic.

"What the fuck kind of name is Denver?"

Nervous relief laughter filtered through the headsets from the others in the copter.

Lakes voice came in clear over the same channel.

"That'll be a dollar for the swear jar, Agent Wicks."

The laughter in the copter was briefer, though louder and less nervous. Then everyone went back to work.

Reports arrived on her phone that a 1997 Ford 150 pickup of one of the victims in Thrall, Jimmy TJ, Lucas Pine's roommate, was missing. She immediately directed an all-points bulletin be issued for the vehicle.

"That's how JFB got to Shady Oaks in time to kill the lawyers," she said flatly into her helmet's microphone.

They landed on the 16th tee minutes later. Thick glades of trees blew like in a thunderstorm without the messy downpour as the helicopter descended onto the lush golf course. Noticing all the green amidst the brown of the rest of Texas this time of year, she ordered that the course's automatic sprinkler system be shut off before they had disembarked. Two deputies stood at the edge of the circling rotors, unnecessarily bent, neither tall enough to be decapitated if they happened to get close enough, which they didn't.

Youngblood led the team to the edge of the tee to meet Morrow's men. She shook both deputies' hands. Looked them in the eyes. Smiled. Lakes was the bad Fed in this scenario; she, the good.

"Thank you for meeting us, officers," she said, hoping to strike a conciliatory note after Lakes's threat, which probably made the rounds. Not much else to do while patrolling a crime scene except swap gossip, Youngblood knew from experience. "Lead the way, please. Tell me what you know. Your first impressions are critical."

They weren't, but it helped to get the men on her side and to ease the tension between agencies.

One said quickly, "Never saw anything like it my life. Bodies and blood. It was awful. Not as bad as a bus crash with kids. I saw that once. But worst murder scene for me."

"Me, too," the other said eagerly, keeping up with the Youngblood's quick, purposeful strides toward the sprawled dead. "They's were ambushed and massacred pure and simple."

They stepped onto the fifteenth green. The murder scene appearing as they climbed the low rise to the listless flag poking out of the hole. Two balls sat on the green waiting to be putted.

"Thank you, officers," she said. "Your observations are critical. Please give us a complete statement."

She nodded to one of the agents she'd gathered from Thrall. He waved over the deputies and took out his smartphone, ready to interview the men. She turned back to the seven dead bodies, keeping her distance from them for now.

The setting for the massacre was much different than the one in Thrall. The bucolic, perfectly green golf course of the lawyers' slaughter contrasted starkly with the tattered brown and burnt landscape where the AFMP members had died. She and Wicks took slow careful steps toward the carnage on the fifteenth green.

II

She'd slept twenty-three minutes in the past thirty-seven hours. She could use another cat nap, Youngblood admitted to herself. She felt her senses dulling as she relentlessly processed data from the killings. Information sloshed in from all directions. But she wouldn't let sleep deprivation be an excuse for missing a clue in the deluge of forensics data and the foot-leather reports investigators gushed her way.

She popped open a can of Red Bull, which she hated the taste of and, worse, she knew the amount she drank threatened to harm her kidneys, leach calcium from her bones, and give her high blood pressure. In short, given time, it'd kill her. She should stop drinking it. Nothing revved her up more, though, so down the hatch went the evil swill. If only the FBI permitted her to use benzedrine, she wished one more time. It had fewer side effects. But it was a Schedule I drug and Red Bull a dollar ninety-nine at the corner Seven-Eleven. An easy decision.

Following his precedent after the morning's AFPM slaughter, JFB had posted a video of the attorneys' killings on the Wythe, Braxton's website that evening. It was gruesome to behold, particularly the kill shots. The killer's second mass shooting that day was in better focus and the victims closer to the camera than his earlier murders. The carnage churned her stomach. Traffic to the site skyrocketed until the firm shut it off.

That took a while. Someone, JFB presumably, had hacked the system and changed authentication credentials of the site's IT staff. They had to get their service provider to bring down an entire server farm, and many other sites with it, to turn it off. Lawyers fretted in texts and emails about liabilities either way, delaying the ultimate decision. By the time the plug was literally pulled, the global press had gotten hold of the video and was pairing edited versions of it along with clips showing the demise of the AFPM. Both videos had been mirrored on dozens of sites. Youngblood heard repeatedly that awful phrase, "The videos went viral."

It was all inevitable. The internet kept no secrets. No one at the Bureau was taken off-guard by the media frenzy, particularly with the eyeball-grabbing, made-for-TV gruesome images, all lacking copyright, an incentive to the big bucks broadcasters as well as to the small bore webcasters to play the videos as often as possible. Fill air time royalty-free and brace the gory stories with silly car insurance ads and embarrassing commercials about better bowl movements. A tried-and-true formula for financial success.

"We warn our viewers, these scenes are disturbing," network news anchors somberly intoned behind their sleek desks, as they had for countless other bloody scenes broadcast night after night at dinner time. Disturbing or not, show them they did.

Depicting our murderousness goes back to Bible stories about Cain and Able, Youngblood understood. Telling stories about our cruelty to each other is as human as it gets. Every culture tells cautionary tales about the pain people cause other people. The telling of the story usually includes at least context, possibly even wisdom. Depiction of the event is only part of what's important.

Technology changed that. Endlessly recorded violence was something new, a twenty-first century thing. No imagination, no storytelling required. Perpetual live action destruction of people and property was a simple click away. No middleman. Neither journalist nor prophet nor poet need describe the mayhem of the moment. Everyone had their pick of the latest and most arresting carnage of the day from CCTV footage, witness's smartphone recordings, community journalists, home security cameras, drone videos, cop body cams, local news crews, and more. Never a slow news night in the world.

But two mass murders recorded by the killer himself? In a single day? That was news gold, something rare and horrible to feed the public's insatiable maw for tragedy. One could not fault the networks for swarming to it like helicopters over OJ's Bronco. JFB's actions put even Simpson's antics in the back seat as far as media frenzy. More bodies meant more coverage. The pressure on the Bureau was singular from journalists real and fake. She'd never seen anything like it. The unpredictable, vast pack of reporters ran en masse from government building to government building, crime scene to crime scene, desperate for sound bites. They were everywhere like dandelion puff balls in early summer.

Director LeBlair, at the center of press coverage, seemed fine in the limelight. Unruffled, as if he was ready to pounce on "the Second Amendment Killer," borrowing the phrase from his friend Laskey.

Despite the ongoing bloodlust reporting, it was more of a nuisance to Youngblood than a burden. Ignoring the press was not as difficult as journalists would have you to believe. Lakes sometimes got in front of a reporter, rarely a camera, to correct a fact that had been published or to deny a rumor. Hardly ever on the record or for attribution. Higher-ups higher than Lakes liked to gaze into the glass eye of the media and declaim one reassuring storyline or another.

The FBI Director, "God bless his camera-loving ass," Wicks muttered, happily took on all the major media events about what the right-wing and tabloid press were calling the Second Amendment Killer, shortened to SAK in their screaming headlines.

"Second Amendment Killer Slaughters America's Heroes," ran a typical crawl on Sinclair News Network TV stations across the nation. FOX News went with "POTUS: FBI Will Nail SAK or I Will." The President had criticized the Bureau's inability to bring in the SAK killer. JFB's name had not been released to the public or even the President for fear he'd leak it.

The President's finger-pointing at the Bureau did not stop its machinery from turning out one media event after another. If it worked for J. Edgar Hoover, so thought every one of his successors, it would work for them. As such, Assistant Directors and Department of Justice lawyers stacked the dais behind the FBI Director for the daily press conferences. By design that left Lakes, Youngblood, Wicks, and four hundred other agents solely dedicated to finding JFB. They were quickly elbowed out of the spotlight to their immense satisfaction.

Given the sensational scope of the two mass murders, their connection to the Maryland killings, and overt political connotations, combined with the raw video JFB had posted, news briefings were constant. It was not a surprise to Youngblood when for the third time that day an agent in the mobile Secure Compartmented Information Facility nudged her to get her attention inside the crammed in-the-field war room.

There were large and small SCIFs. Her model was the smallest, a hulking cab with barely enough room inside for her and a couple of agents. It sat on the back of a black Ford 350 pickup, with enough antenna poking out the top to make it look like a giant angry porcupine. Its innards were stuffed with a slew of gear that let her communicate in utter security with anyone or anything, anywhere anytime and get the information she needed. Except, of course, the current whereabouts of JFB.

The agent who nudged her angled his iPad so she could see a live stream video. A few of the broadcast networks had interrupted their regularly scheduled programs to run a feed of the FBI Director addressing the country again about JFB's murders.

"They cut into *Jeopardy*, so it must be important," she said sarcastically.

"Nah," the agent replied seriously. "They just want an excuse to broadcast the murder videos again. I'll bet ten bucks they show them after the press conference."

Youngblood did not take the bet.

The Director did a fantastic job. He spoke intelligently, calmly, and at god-awful length, telling the public nothing more than what was already in the public domain because of the videos. He was respectful as he voiced the names of the dead. His terse, precise words about tracking down and bringing to judgment the killer had a fine Old Testament ring to them. He stuck to the provable facts while skating through every reporter's question, revealing to the audience only what he wanted them to hear not what a particular journalist wanted to know. He was confident, polished, and the streak of gray at his temples inspiring.

"That's why he gets the big bucks," she said aloud at the end of the press conference and, like the agent predicted, the networks began reprising JFB's videos.

"Don't need to see those again," he said, sliding his finger over to a stop button.

"Wait!" she shouted, the Red Bull kicking in. "Go there!"

Her finger landed on another video that had been running in the iPad's background.

He opened it to full screen.

There was JFB's white, clean-cut, brown-haired, brown-eyed, clean-shaven face filling the entire screen.

"Audio!"

The agent clicked the speaker icon.

"...leased just seconds ago is a company badge photo from the former employer of the suspect in the Second Amendment Killings," a dime-a-dozen square-jawed, sensationally-coiffed middle-aged man looking straight into the camera spoke with the rich baritone of the Final Judgment. He said, "This photo shows the suspect, a mister Jefferson Fitzgerald Black's workplace ID card. KKLL Channel Six has also learned that the Texas Rangers, whose jurisdiction was where SAK's alleged latest crimes were committed, have issued an all points bulletin for the man seen here. If you know him or have seen him, you need to contact either the Texas Rangers or an FBI office in your area. He is considered armed and dangerous and should not be approached by the general public. The Second Amendment Killer allegedly has callously murdered more than a dozen men and women that we know of. Study this man's face and if you see him, call the authorities and tell them what you know. Repeat: he is armed and dangerous."

She imagined something similar being played out on hundreds of broadcast stations and online news outlets around the world. JFB was a marked man.

"Not good," Lakes's voice piped into her earbuds. He'd been watching the same news report as she had from his own much larger SCIF outside Thrall.

"Who released his name and photo?" she asked aloud, angry. "The Director? Sheriff Morrow? We didn't and we run the investigation. It was an advantage for us someone just took away. He's been trying to hide his identity in the videos!"

She realized she'd raised her voice to a shout by the end of her rant.

"It was bound to happen," he said soothingly. "Can't fret about it now."

Seething still, she switched her attention to her own iPad in hopes of tracking down who leaked the photo. She thumbed through news stories featuring JFB's company ID. Every story used the same image. The Agency had gathered another half dozen official photos of the man. Only one was out. But savvy reporters would uncover other pictures of JFB and flood the planet with his likeness. In addition, his face was now tops on law enforcement's Most Wanted lists in all fifty states. He was more than a murderer. He was a star.

She scanned the software used to manage all the shared data with other police departments and government agencies working on JFB's killing spree. She could not find a file that shared JFB's photo with any other law enforcement or media organizations. It was behind a firewall waiting for her or Lakes to approve its release. The "Do Not Share" lock feature prevented her from sending it to herself, so she was confident the program worked and that the photo did not come from within the FBI. She spent another hour mousing around communications between agencies to see if anyone else had another source for JFB's picture and came up empty.

Youngblood threw in the towel and gave up looking for the leak, assuming the media finagled it from an insider who knew how to hide their steps.

She shifted gears. Lakes was right: too late worrying about the source now. Spilt milk. Water under the bridge. Etcetera. Etcetera.

She accepted that she had a new, though unreliable ocean of data coming in from coast to coast. Most of it would be crap. But it could not be ignored. While she was furiously searching for who threw a spanner into the investigation by releasing the photo, Lakes had put together an ad hoc team of agents to cull through the crush of incoming calls and emails and texts claiming to have seen JFB or to have known him. Thousands, it seems. Before she was ready she had been thrown into the deep end of the public data stream with her usual low expectations.

She set strict parameters: only reviewing messages that had been vetted as not completely crazy, as so many were, pointing to conspiracy theories that could be traced back to the Kennedys or even the Pharaohs. Some poor sap with a badge, though, would check out each and every one.

Each message was tagged with loads of data; everything from sightings specifics to old schoolmates' memories. Sightings were the least reliable. Contacts from former friends and colleagues occasionally could be useful.

Youngblood wrote a SQL string on her iPad to search through the massive number of public messages being added by the second to the database. She wasn't the best at devising Structured Query Language scans of the database, but it was faster than waiting for an overworked DBA to do it for her. She narrowed her query on a hunch to any JFB acquaintance in the past three years and who lived in Oregon. She feared her search was too broad and would inundate her with possibilities. To her immense relief only two files from the public met her criteria: an email and a voicemail.

She read the email first.

"To whom it may concern:

I know this sounds weird, but I knew Jeff pretty well two years ago. And the photo I just saw on TV isn't him. It looks sort of like him, but not really. Maybe it's been altered a bit for your investigation. I don't know. But it doesn't look like the Jeff Black I knew. And my Jeff certainly doesn't seem like the guy who would do this terrible thing. I thought I should tell you.

Sincerely,

Deborah Stave
Turner, Oregon
debstave@turnertown.com"

The second message was a brief voicemail.

"Hey, I don't know what you are trying to do there, but it's all wrong. Two things: one, Jeff would never do what you say he did and, two, that's not him in the photo, assholes. It's not him."

Tagged with the voicemail was data on the smartphone it came from, including the photo of its owner, her name, and location. The image showed an Asian American woman, Youngblood assumed was of Vietnamese descent, possibly Laotian. She was pretty with serious eyes. Her name was Lily Thornton. Forty-two. Divorced. No kids. Lives in Salem, Oregon.

Immediately, Youngblood ordered up the Gulfstream at the Fort Worth Airport like some people would an Uber. She logged in the destination as McNary Field in Salem. Then she called Lakes to get his authorization.

"You still mad about the photo release?" he asked before she made the request. "Could be anyone released the photo."

"We didn't authorize it. We haven't fully staffed up the call-in centers to chase down all the bullshit leads."

"That's a buck, Celeste," he said. "Doesn't matter. If it helps. APB. Most Wanted List. Whatever works. That's what some people say. People above our pay grade, Celeste. Too late for us to do anything about it."

"What if it doesn't help?" she said. "What if it's a mirage? What if it was JFB who sent out the image? What if it's not him? This guy's proven he can hack systems at will. What if he released the fake photo to the media?"

"Why would he do it?"

"Probably because it's not him?" she offered. "It's not his face. We're all looking for the wrong guy."

"Doubtful," Lakes said reasonably. "It's the same photo we have from his company ID card, Celeste. It's also the same face on his driver's license and passport. All official and all slightly different per the time, place, and technology used to take the photo. But they're all him. We ran all the photos we have of JFB through facial recognition software and they all come up positive. They're all the same man. We know who he is. We know what he looks like. We just have to find him."

"If you say so, boss."

"For now, Celeste, I do."

"Maybe not after you see this."

She sent to his screen the email and a transcription of the voicemail from the two women in Oregon.

"One more thing," she added, "I sent an agent out to his ex-wife's home to show her the official photos we have of JFB. She told the agent, 'Close, but no cigar.' It's not him, boss. The picture. It's not him. We've been looking for the wrong guy and now the entire world is, too. We've been set up. And I'm taking the plane to prove it."

"Holy shit," he said under his breath; then, "Have a good flight."

"That's a buck, boss."

"Yes it is, Celeste. Yes it is."

Chapter Eleven
Invisible, Anonymous, Armed, Dangerous

```
Excerpt from the memoir of Jefferson Fitzgerald
Black
Q-Level Access
Eyes Only
```

I

As I mentioned earlier, my experience with database integration projects taught me that exquisite timing and meticulous preparation lead to inevitable success. Starting a project was always simple; finishing it was another matter. In between it was difficult, thorny, utter hell, full of pissing matches and indelicate emails.

Then glory. Everything worked and perfection became commonplace.

Same was true in getting away with mass murder. Doing it was easy. Getting away with it was not. But it was glorious when I did.

Disguising facts about me from the FBI, such as my true appearance, probable location, and intended targets kept me a few steps ahead of its pursuit. However, I never believed I would always have control of that kind of data. I knew the Bureau would eventually discover that not everyone agreed on what I looked like. Official records showed me one way, the way I wanted them to see me; that some people's recollections and personal photos conflicted with my false trail was inevitable. But my digital antics gave me a good head start.

It's natural for law enforcement to accept as true the data received from other official agencies. After all, when multiple DMVs, the State Department's passport office, my old company, and two security clearances showed a consistent image of me, the one I had planted, there was no reason to doubt its veracity. That picture went into dozens, then hundreds of documents and files among agents and the state and local police involved in chasing me. It was plastered on conference room walls where investigators met. The serial mass murderer was the guy in the photo. Had to be. We have his driver's license. It's him.

Except it wasn't. I wore a different face entirely, and was still on the loose and on a mission to shoot even more important people who love guns more than their country, their flag, their community, their family, even common sense itself. I remained for now invisible and anonymous, not to mention armed and dangerous.

But, as I said, eventually the FBI or someone would figure out what I looked like. They'd discover the metadata I couldn't erase that was attached to the fake image of me in the various databases, proving each picture I'd planted was not what it purported to be. The face of the enemy they were chasing was not a real face at all.

Once someone sussed out my deception, a new face would quickly replace the fake ones in the official paper trail and in time it would show up on media everywhere. Eventually, they'd find a photo from an old friend or from a former business associate, even a dubious one from a high school yearbook I hadn't thoroughly hacked and expunged online. But I couldn't hit the Delete key on prints of my face. They existed. Plenty, in fact. Living in twenty-first century America meant having your image captured and stored hundreds of thousands of times, whether you liked it or not. My plan was to delay not deter the law from tracking me down. The doctor gave me only so many months to live, so I worked against her clock, not the law's.

Certain things were in my favor in keeping the FBI at bay. First, I did not seek to be in the camera lens and, in my brief time as a family man, I was the primary photographer and almost always out of the frame. Needless to say, I wasn't a selfie guy. Pix of me were few and far between, so I was able to mess around with some of the few photos people had of me that I knew about. Not everyone, but some of my obvious friends and contacts who had known me and had documented our relationship with images of my plain face.

Eliminating images of me was easier than you'd think. Starting with my ex-wife, who had burned every printed photo of her life with me, keeping in her wallet only one third-grade shot of our daughter, the work was quick. I'm not proud for having hacked into friends' PCs, smartphones, and tablets and messing with their photo libraries. Ashamed, in fact. But I needed to sow confusion for as long as possible.

I spent about a week logging into my few friends' home WiFi networks, sniffing out passwords without much trouble. I had been given most of them during visits to their homes. I'd scour their networks with image-detection software, find matches and swap them with someone who looked similar to me. That gave me a second advantage over the men and women hunting me down. I was usually in group shots, making it a snap to alter my looks. Those few closeups that I found I deleted.

To confound matters for my pursuers further, I slipped the second fake image of me into professional organizations' photo ID files where I had been a member. Was I the first image in government and other files, now being displayed far and wide; or was I the face in the second photo? Or neither? Confusion was my co-conspirator.

The second fake picture of me was a Photo Shopped version of the first one, which I had taken from a 1959 stock image catalog. The guy reminded me of me, while clearly not being me. My not-quite *doppelgänger*. Just close enough, but not enough to pick me out of a police line-up.

The catalog's copyright was still active, so I was able to pay for a high-resolution version, which made it easy with software to tweak the guy to look slightly more like me. Had I chosen a fellow who did not resemble me at all would have meant everyone who had known me would have noticed the difference immediately. With Adobe's help, the guy from 1959 looked enough like me to fool co-workers, who hadn't seen me in months, and relatives, who hadn't seen me in years; it might even convince my ex-wife, after all, we hadn't seen each other in a dog's age, either.

I was especially glad there weren't many shots of me as a husband or dad on other people's systems. Not, in retrospect, to remain hidden from the law, but because I did not want to be reminded that there was once a time when I breathed happiness day in and day out, not the smoldering asphalt that has filled my lungs since she was murdered. Happy memories are the greatest burden the parent of a dead child bears.

I had gone to significant lengths to hide my face for good reason. Facial recognition software was improving daily and security cameras were everywhere. They would be combined on a huge scale to find the Second Amendment Killer, a sobriquet bestowed on me that I embrace proudly. The best way for the SAK to hide was to have computers look for someone else.

Yes, I am thorough, clever, careful, and a bit devious. Despite the egotism in those words, I am not, however, cocky. I expect someone chasing me to find out what I look like one day and inform authorities.

And I will know when that happens. I had hacked into the FBI's dedicated server used by the agents who were chasing me. The Feds had installed a tightly secured computer after the Texas killings, isolating it immediately from anyone but the team working to locate and neutralize me. The most sensitive information was stored there and there alone. They understood my background and so kept the system off the internet and even away from the FBI's internal network as an extra and wise precaution. Wise, had I been anybody else.

The building that housed the server, like all Bureau buildings, used an uninterruptible power source, a UPS, which is a huge box of gear that filled its own shed and sat between the power company's lines and the building's electrical wiring. The UPS assured that the electricity flowing into the building was stable, constant without voltage variances. It smoothed out electricity's naturally unstable sparky flow. As a bonus, if the utility lost power, the UPS would continue to generate power for the building's needs over an extended time with its large battery backup system.

It was also my Trojan horse into the government investigators' isolated server. The UPS vendor maintained and monitored their installations remotely, via the internet. I didn't need to break through the FBI's digital defense. I slipped in via the UPS.

The walled-off computer contained everything the Bureau had on me. Facts, timelines, profiler analyses, worried memos from higher-ups, all the leads they had to track me down. Everything. I got to see it all. To get to it, I piggybacked data packets onto the steady flow of voltage from the UPS going into the server's internal power supply. The power supply massaged electrical flow inside the server while constantly communicating with the computer's operating system.

That was my ticket. I quickly inserted myself as part of the power supply's endless conversation with the operating system. Once I had established a path into the server's OS remotely, I was able to create a ghost administrator account and siphon off information about the investigation. I'd know when the FBI truly knew whom they were looking for. Keeping my looks secret was paramount to my plans. I needed to work in the open like any Tom, Dick, and Harry to complete my mission.

Until the Bureau figured out what I really looked like, my true face was my best disguise. I had diverted everyone's eyes into looking for someone else with my leak to the press of my official photo. Subsequent calls to the FBI hotline claiming to have seen "me" would waste resources in a vain search. Simple, but effective.

Before the FBI had enough faith in a new image of what I truly look like, once they'd found it, I'd have ample time to accomplish at least one more killing spree. After my next targets were dispatched, I'd change my looks and go into hiding for a while. If I was successful, I'd have earned the break.

My intended victims would be more newsworthy than gun nuts and lawyers. The targets I had in mind would make more than headlines. If I killed them, their elimination might actually make a real difference in hurting the power of the gun lobby. I had to believe that. Not just symbolically like the pathetic boys of the AFPM and the moral criminals from Wythe, Braxton. Killing my next victims would matter. I would be removing their sickness from the body politic. Things would change afterward. The world would be a better place with them dead. I had to believe that.

My targets were among the most protected in the world. They slipped into a snug, bullet-proof cocoon of security each morning like the rest of us put on underwear. My plan had to be flawless.

Timing the release of my false image, then, was critical. Like the pause between a great comic's set up and her punchline, I nailed it. Killed it, they say backstage at comedy clubs. At the moment the FBI was learning I was not who they thought I was, the world was hearing that I was exactly that person. Because the FBI didn't know what I looked like, only that I probably wasn't who their investigation had just said I was, they were hamstrung and could not immediately put out a counter-narrative to what I looked like.

I had better than a get-out-of-jail card. I had a get-away-with-murder card for at least one more roll of the dice.

II

Before I shot my first victim, that unlucky equestrian on the Maryland horse path, I was already planning future killings in the back of my mind; shifting from murdering the innocent for my personal revenge, to executing the guilty for everyone else's. My next act, though, was my dream plan of retribution, killing the heartless core of gun industry leaders. I conceived of it from the very beginning. It never strayed far from my thoughts, even during my bloody spree in Texas, I knew my true targets lie ahead.

Of all my life's obsessions, and I've had my share, my next mass murder was at the top. Beyond consuming my thinking, I had literal dreams about it. Key word there is dreams, not nightmares. In my sleep, I never failed.

If I fulfilled my quest—rather, when I nailed it—my righteous retaliation campaign would be an unqualified success, an epic slaughter of the guiltiest of American criminals, the accessories to murder on a apocalyptic scale. Success will define my legacy; failure, too, I suppose. Either way, as I see it, I win. It may sound delusional, but my upcoming victims' bullet-ridden karma will make me a hero to many, many people. They will embrace the justice of my action. It's for them I pull the trigger.

Of course, like all the best heroes, after my most selfless act I'll end up dead, too. That is the only drawback of my long studied plan. Among all the scenarios in designing the attack that I've modeled, I end up dead with a high probability, 92% in the most optimistic model. Every iteration in every model, odds are, I die. I can't conceive of how to get away with my most important killings alive. With the prior murders I estimated reasonable possibilities for escape and survival; better than 68% in each of the previous three killings. This time, no real chance. I had no options but to die trying. Granted, that's what all of us do in life, so I'm not looking for sympathy, but I sincerely am not seeking to be a dead hero. The cancer will kill me soon enough. I'd rather die on its schedule than at the scene of even my greatest crime.

Don't confuse me for a terrorist, someone who wants to die by his deeds, though there will be brainless, knee-jerk pigeon-holing by the media, law enforcement, and other talking heads who will call me one: Jefferson Fitzgerald Black, domestic terrorist. They're wrong. My victims are not random. They are purposeful. I'm a murderer. And, don't forget, I consider myself a serial killer as well as a mass murderer. Key word is "serial." It means I live to do it again. Terrorists are one-time jerk-offs trying to instill fear in everyone by killing anyone at hand. I'm far more dangerous. I want to frighten specific people, well-defined targets who deserve to die, not the general public. Joe Schmo has nothing to worry about from me; gun profiteers and fanatics, on the other hand, should be truly frightened.

The group I'm most obsessed with killing deserves death by gunfire more than even the guilty Texans I've just shot. My next victims are not amoral hired help like the lawyers in Ft. Worth or Thrall's perverted gun fetishists. They're certainly not the innocents I shot down in Maryland. These are powerful people who not only encourage the carnage happening around us daily, they profit from it. The more mayhem and bloodshed the better for their bank accounts. They buy politicians, generals, cops, lawyers, judges, and journalists to see things their way. Those who are bought are made to feel like freedom fighters, true believers in a sacred and bloody cause: Liberate the Holy Gun.

For this crowd, owning a gun has become the essence of what it means to be an American; what it means to be free. If you don't own a gun, you're a tool of the liberal elites who seek to emasculate and enslave God-fearing citizens of the USA. They've boiled the Constitution down to protecting a murder weapon.

It'd be simply silly political philosophy, if it were not so demented. Fewer than one-third of Americans own a gun and a mere three percent own more than half of all guns in the country. The unbalanced influence gun crazies have in this country is absurd. If we lived in a real democracy, the majority would vote time after time to reduce the privileges of gun ownership. Gun control would not be something to fight for, it would be the law of the land.

The arguments that such restrictions inhibit freedom wouldn't carry the day in a real democracy because they're bullshit and everyone with common sense knows it. Nothing inhibit's a person's freedom more than being shot to death. More U.S. lives are taken by firearms annually than Americans killed during the entire four-year Korean War. Every fucking year the gun industry hands us another Korean War. No wonder today's average American feels such dread. Each year we have to emotionally absorb the casualties of an unspoken war that we are encouraged to wage internally by making guns not just legal but ubiquitous. More people die in America from gun violence each year than U.S. soldiers have died in all the wars this country has waged since Vietnam. It's far more dangerous to be an American citizen than a military grunt. It's sick. And those who perpetuate it are evil, plain and simple.

So I'm going to kill them. My next victims are the theologians and priests, the American Curia who peddle the perverse religion of the Holy Gun. They let loose the dogs of war inside our borders, barking at us incessantly from within their gated communities and secured headquarters, enticing us to buy more guns to protect ourselves from each other. Their few fervent followers dutifully make pilgrimages to gun shows and gunsmiths as public expressions of their faith. It's a minority religion, but a powerful one.

Not surprisingly, just as the deity of Judaism, Christianity, and Islam surrounded himself with sword-wielding archangels like Azrael and Michael, the cynical people behind the false god of the Holy Gun are well-protected by their own Glock-packing trained security staffs. Such purveyors of death rightfully worry about their own safety. People hate them.

It's not surprising these corporate killers attract violent opponents like me. Executives get eggs thrown at them and sometimes they're even booed at shareholder meetings by activists. They feel threatened. That means they move in impregnable bubbles of protection. That will be especially true where I intend to execute them.

Security where my new killings are planned should be world-class. I will be inside of a locked-down compound where comings and goings are strictly controlled. I'll face Secret Service agents, who will be teaming with Capitol Hill security services to protect my targets because guests will include the Senate Majority Leader and a slew of House members. But the real protection will come from the horde of private security guards hired to guard the corporate CEOs and other hosts of the party I was about to crash. In short, it's with little exaggeration to claim that I'll be standing alone against a hostile army.

Oh, well. We all gotta go sometime.

Once I do crash the party and start shooting, I will become a lonely fish in a narrow barrel. Based on what I know about the venue and, per usual, I know just about everything there is to know, I will have two minutes eighteen seconds until I, too, am gunned down. But I'll die with a smile on my face because more than two minutes with the right weapon lets me kill a lot of big fish in my barrel before they get to me.

Despite the formidable odds, I am committed to the task. With three bloody successes under my belt, my confidence, while not oozing, is stoked. Still, I prepared more diligently than ever to succeed and maybe, maybe miraculously survive, despite all the modeling of the data that say otherwise.

First I had to get myself into the most exclusive and lavish gathering the gun industry organized for itself every year: the Second Amendment Party, or SAP, as they called it, hosted for twelve straight years by Ned Sargent.

Yes, that same Ned Sargent, the has-been front man for the thankfully defunct Randy Jacks rock and roll band, famous for a loud, unmelodic, crappy sound loved by 1990s thirteen year old boys. Apparently, they were a large enough demographic to make him a rich man. Sargent decided to spend a large part of his fortune on guns. He owned hundreds of weapons. Another part of his wealth he spent lobbying politicians to espouse extreme positions on gun rights. Right-wing radio hosts, Fox News, OAN, internet bloggers and kooks all loved to publish his audacious interviews, advocating fringe ideas about gun rights. Conceal carry permits. Automatics. Bump stocks. Silencers. No waiting time. No background checks. No mental health checks. No centralized weapons database. Stand your ground. There wasn't a gun-rights view too dangerous for Neddy, as he liked to be called by intimates.

"I love my fucking guns more than I fuck my loving wife," he proclaimed more than once as if it were a witty rallying cry.

His deviant affection of weaponry was why he hosted the Second Amendment Party every year at his Idaho ranch. He gathered his powerful friends at his rugged nine hundred acres an hour east of Coeur d' Alene in Shoshone county. What had started as a small gathering of like-minded, narcissistic, wealthy gun advocates exploded into a full-blown political convention, including attendee straw votes for conservative candidates, seminars on the purity of the Second Amendment, awards ceremonies for guns' most rabid defenders, and, of course, morning hunts and lots and lots of target practice in the afternoon. There was always a cover story about the event in the glossy American Rifle Institute's magazine and on its website. Fox News slavishly covered the event year after year as if it were something more than fake news.

The SAP has become a be-there-or-be-square gathering for deep-pocket gun nuts. Minor celebrities and major politicians who regularly attended always attracted a scrum of local reporters; who could be counted on to deliver docile, if not supportive stories in regional media for the evening news. Even legitimate national journalists showed up now and again, enticed by the marquee arch-conservative attendees and the beautiful country. Plus, shooting guns was fun, even for the fake news media elite.

American media are central to America's gun violence. They all but ignore the havoc guns wreak on the country. Oh, a newscast will report on this celebrity suicide or that mass murder involving guns, and local newspapers always lead with what bleeds on their beats, but they hardly ever deliver the daily news of hard truth. If they did, the lead story every night's news would be: "Today, another one hundred and six people were killed by guns." Granted, they're not Covid-19 numbers, but they've been happening much, much longer, and will continue long after the pandemic slips into history.

Imagine the effect those undisputed facts would have on people, if they simply were reminded about the carnage that guns do to our country every single day—in every newscast, in every newspaper, on every website. A planeload of people dies every damn day by gunfire and it's never the "top story tonight," even though it should be, every night.

The fact that Neddy and his ilk come together to mark such tragedy with festivities made me sick. Carrying out my mission at his perverse celebration would demonstrate the horror these people represent in the most iconic and ironic way possible.

Killing high-profile assholes meant instant headlines. The more corpses, the bigger the sans-serif type. I planned to deliver on the body count. No news organization could afford not to cover it. The more famous the bodies I racked up, the better the coverage, plain and simple. Once my own body is found and identified and my reasons revealed, the media will be forced to give at least some attention to my belief that all of these so-called victims are guilty of conspiracy to kill Americans, day in and day out.

My motivation, once known, will resonate widely not just because some will agree enthusiastically that my murders are a form of cosmic justice, but also, some will say, the hypocrisy involved. I use guns as blunt instruments against gun nuts. If it weren't for guns, my message to denounce them would never be heard. Guns are the essential, though completely absurd tools necessary to eliminate guns from society. People like me give new meaning to the right-wing phrase, a good man with a gun will stop a bad man with a gun. It's perfectly pretzelian logic, but precisely true in my case.

Accepting that more guns is the only solution to any gun problem was the professed belief of Second Amendment Party goers. I am the apotheosis of that viewpoint. Their single-mindedness was anathema to me. I believe in irony, subtlety. And I believe in payback. But those beliefs didn't get me into the SAP shindig.

The credentials committee, as it was called, weeded out every known gun-control opponent they knew from being admitted to their soirée'. They limited admission to profligate donors to the Republican Party and the ARI. To be an audience member you needed at least two recommendations from previous attendees and then be willing to pay three thousand dollars for the dubious privilege of seeing and hearing mostly old white men brag about their guns. If they weren't so dangerous to America, they'd simply be the pathetic limp-dick losers they appear to be.

But just to prove they weren't the limp dicks they are, they provided all attendees with coronavirus testing. And SAP organizers checked everyone's vaccination records to make sure they were up to date with latest virus variant surging through the nation. They made certain people would feel comfortable at a large event where masks, by Neddy's decree, were forbidden.

"Freedom-loving, gun-proud Americans don't hide behind flimsy masks like a bandit. We won't have them at the SAP," he'd declared, making certain only the most devoted of gun-rights believers would be there. Luckily for the SAP organizers, there was a large pool of deluded folks clamoring for each of the three hundred and seventy-five paid tickets.

Despite the SAP's system for sussing solely sycophants for the audience, I managed to snag an invitation to Neddy's three-day do. Well, not exactly an invitation, but entrée all the same. I paid for it like any other vendor. My slightly convoluted deception got me into the party. Even better. It put me on the dais with some of the most egregious accessories to mass murder in the country. And I planned to be the only person armed on stage.

Let me explain.

As with any conference, the costs of putting it on are only slightly offset by the credentials individuals buy to attend. Even the most high-minded and high-priced of events need underwriters. Most of the money comes from corporate sponsors, who erect pricey booths, host fancy dinners, give drunken parties, buy lavish breakfasts, and happily pick up the tabs for anyone in power.

Sponsors trip over themselves with their fistfuls of cash to get a spot on stage during the luncheon when the Second Amendment Party awards are handed out. That's when the politically powerful show up, ready to collect hardware for their offices and hard cash for their campaigns. That's why I am going there. I'm a hardware guy.

Neddy and his conference crew are way too cheap to pay for the trophies, plaques, and other bric-a-brac they bestow on their fellow gun nuts, so they always get a vendor to foot the bill. This year they took bids from six companies to create the special awards for the greatest defenders of gun rights. I'd read Neddy's and other conference organizers internal communications about what they wanted to see in this year's awards. Through a regular sponsor, I snuck in my ideas for on-the-spot, unique array of awards designed uniquely for each winner. Ideas that matched Neddy and his minions.

To ice the cake, I submitted sample trophies printed exactly like collector-class revolvers Neddy obsessed over. My newly leased, state-of-the-art 3-D printer mimicked the wood varnish on rifle butts and the pearl handles of six-shooters. In addition, I could make the printer etch anything on the faux weapon, the winner's name and particulars, the reason for winning, and a sponsor's marque.

Anything at all was possible, I claimed as the Director of Product Development for a Canadian trophy maker, Trophée Gaspé, who was venturing into custom 3-D printed trophies. Among my samples, I included a custom-built plastic AK-47 celebrating Neddy and the twelfth-annual Second Amendment Party. "The Freest Weekend On Earth," a genuine quote from the event's marketing material, whorled along the barrel in the same Hickory Jack cursive font used by the conference. The fake automatic rifle also came with black onyx-looking stock, which I knew the thankfully retired singer would appreciate because it referenced lyrics from one of his most popular tunes: "I love my dark lady lots/Like my onyx gun shoots hot." Trust me, the music's even worse.

True Bore, the ammunition maker, backed my submission. I had pitched True Bore's vice president of marketing, Ed Kervasion, who glommed on to the idea like honey from a sticky bun on a mustache. My idea appealed to Kervasion at two levels. First, he wanted to be on stage with Second Amendment heroes and give them awards. He was sincere in his fealty to the cause. Reading his emails and texts I realized that it meant a lot to him to be considered a player in the Second Amendment business. In his mind, nothing proved that more than handing out one-of-a-kind trophies to the rich and powerful, after enjoying an afternoon round of drinks, rich food, and circle-the-wagon speeches devoted to the almighty gun. He'd dreamed of this since his

Eagle Scout days. I knew, too, because I'd read his childhood diary that he'd kept, still kept, on his PC.

Second, and possibly more persuasive, Kervasion had recently converted to his wife's Mormonism and had dutifully given his DNA to ancestry.com and learned that his ancestors were Quebecois French from the Gaspé Peninsula. Three months before I'd contacted him, he'd taken his family to the region on a week-long vacation, driving in and out of the places Kervasions before him had haunted. By everything I'd read of his, he was genuinely moved by the experience and primed for my proposal.

The owner of Trophée Gaspé, which was a real company in Montreal, Quebec, with a modest business, mostly making bronzy awards for the city's high school hockey teams, didn't know me from Adam. The proprietor, M. LeBeque, who had run Trophée Gaspé by himself for forty-two years didn't even have a Web page. So it would have surprised him to see the elaborate online presence I had created for his small firm. It depicted Trophée Gaspé as on the leading edge awards design and technology. It included a state-of-the-art backend ecommerce system that was designed to deflect not accept business. In reality, M. LeBeque took his orders by landline or in person and wrote everything on paper as evidence by a pair of crammed-full four-drawer file cabinets in his office, I had surveyed on a visit to the place weeks earlier.

As expected, Kervasion had his newly hired personal assistant run a cursory review of Trophée Gaspé, including its longstanding high marks from the Canadian Better Business Association, which were real. He enthusiastically endorsed my submissions to the SAP and we won the bid.

I successfully pushed both of his current emotional buttons. He even admitted in an email to his wife that he believed the Director of Product Development of Trophée Gaspé, me, was sent to him by Archangel Moroni to help him lead True Bore to even greater profits so that he could increase his tithe to the Church. Flakey as her spouse, Mrs. Kervasion encouraged the notion. He suggested that he'd like to partner with Trophée

Gaspé for more events after the SAP. Not that I expected him or me to be alive after the conference to complete any future deals. But I appreciated the sentiment.

All my sample trophies were models, not functional 3D printed weapons. The center of the barrels were solid and included stunted firing pins. That's what was promised by Trophée Gaspé in its quote to the Second Amendment Party event planners. However, two of the AK-47s I printed at the show would be real. I'd also produce a high-capacity magazine packed with twenty custom ultra hard plastic cartridges that are designed to absorb the heat from the explosion of the bullets being fired nearly as well as metal guns. In short, they guaranteed that the plastic didn't immediately melt after the weapon was fired.

While not as powerful as rounds shot through a standard AK-47's chrome-lined forged steel barrel, my plastic bullets still killed. And efficiently, too. By printing my ammunition I could precisely calculate the grains of cordite I added to each shell's propellant chamber, lowering the amount as the weapon fired. It improved the precision of the impact, but also lowered the flashpoint with each successive bullet, increasing the longevity of my all polymer rifle before it jammed from the friction.

And jamming was inevitable. That's why I was printing two working rifles, in case the original failed early. Both would be loaded and ready. Despite all my time and tinkering with the printing process, the guns I produced jammed often, in one test after merely a second shot. On average, though, my faux AK-47s fired thirteen times before they quit working. The longevity of my weapons at SAP would make or break me. If both guns gave me an average shooting life, the carnage I inflict on the SAP attendees would be substantial; worth my very life, in fact. If both weapons failed me, I failed.

Making the guns was the easy part. Good ammunition stumped me at first. The trick to print functional bullets was the composition of the primer and powder that fired each cartridge. I perfected my ingredients over months of trial and error. By the time the conference was to start I was as ready as I'd ever be.

I'd rented a mobile home for six months in a shabby small RV Park outside Kalispell, Montana off LaSalle Road, old Highway 2 E. It was cheap and close enough to the SAP to use as a base. While I lived in Georgetown, I flew up there often from out of Austin to get the lay of the land and to try out out the largely untested bullets in the field with my plastic guns.

Not surprisingly, I had faith in the technology. In my hundreds of test firings, my 3D printed polymer bullets struck my handmade dummies with a killing force seventy-nine percent as effectively as 7.62x30mm metal-clad rounds shot from a standard AK-47. I used hickory branch-encased gelatin molds as accurate stand-ins for human bone and flesh. I practiced head shots mostly. I'd blown away more than a hundred gelatin-filled, used soccer and rugby balls while I practiced the executions. It took a couple months of dedicated shooting in another underused quarry on the Montana side of the border not far from Flathead Lake, less than 70 miles from Neddy's annual shooting shindig. The practice in the quarry improved my confidence in both my shooting and the 3-D printed weaponry.

The powders I needed for the ammunition looked harmless and I easily smuggled the chemicals in sandwich baggies as chili powder for True Bore's sponsored cookout the next day. Getting the 3-D printer into the conference area posed no issue either. Security guards looked it over, top to bottom, and found nothing sinister with the big glass-framed box. From their vantage point, it couldn't hurt a flea.

I set everything up in the back of True Bore's booth, which sat inside the cavernous indoor horse arena that Neddy had converted into a trade show hall. In the hall vendors gave the aging rock star even more money to rent floor space to hawk their wares to the deep-pocketed attendees. Neddy may be a crap musician, but he's a shrewd businessman.

Tucked away from the passing attendees, I was mostly left alone to print my stuff. Whenever a rare attendee showed an interest in the printer, I happily showed what it could do. Most, though, quickly lost interest when I lied and told them my 3-D printing technology only produced trophies, not real rifles. These folk were gun geeks not tech geeks.

Fewer and fewer took notice of me as the SAP progressed. Halfway through the event, no one took heed when I started printing bullets. After a mere day and half I'd become as invisible as the rent-a-cops prowling the grounds. Even Ed Kervasion was so wrapped up in his endless meetings and booth conversations that he took my constant presence at the back of his booth for granted, letting me produce gizmos without question or interruption.

The second day of the SAP was my D-Day. It was the big awards event. The big speeches. The big names. The biggest reason I was there. As I said, the bigger the death toll, the bigger the names of the dead, the bigger the headlines, the bigger my platform, the bigger my success.

My weapons were within arms reach after I took the stage with poor, gun-besotted Ed Kervasion to hand out trophies. They were under a curtain draped behind the podium. I found my mark in front of the curtain, about ten feet behind the podium. Ed had detailed an off-the-cuff script of my role before we walked out in front of the packed, well-lubricated audience. I was to be his prop man in the handing out of the evening's trophies. When a recipient's name was called out by Neddy, I would hand the appropriate trophy to Ed who would hand it to the winner. Then Neddy and Ed would brace the lucky person holding the fake gun award to the side of the podium for photos. Then the winners would move to a row of plush chairs on the other side of the podium and wait to hear a rousing speech by none other than the ARI's Wayne Laskey. Ed was the happiest person in the room being near to such greatness.

Next to me.

The presentation's format fit my purposes perfectly. Some of the nation's biggest criminal gun rights advocates became sitting ducks. Easy pickin's from short range. I was practically giddy and couldn't wait for the festivities to begin.

Chapter Twelve
Worth Every Penny

```
Celeste Youngblood
```

I

L ily Maryjane was Lily Thornton's posh pot shop on Salem's Commercial Street about four blocks from the city's police department. Tastefully painted signage with trendy *sans serif* typography advertised the enterprise. Inside, customers milled around striking cut-glass containers filled with cleanly trimmed buds of marijuana flowers. These displays were braced by attractively presented edibles and healing balms in colorful, but child-proof packages. During the busy hours, those waiting sipped teas and lemonade while lounging on the upholstered sofas and chairs amiably arranged around the softly lit polished oak floor showroom. It was way better than the corner liquor store.

Youngblood and Wicks approached the college-age, been-there, done-that, seen-it-all budtender at the counter. She flashed her ID. Wicks reached for his, but the kid raised his hand.

"She said to expect you eventually," he said smiling. "Right this way."

That surprised Youngblood. She and Wicks had left Thornton more than a half dozen voicemails, texts, and emails at various places and not heard a word back from the proprietress of *Lily Maryjane* after her angry message on the hotline. They expected a phalanx of lawyers to greet them and had discussed at length what to do when they inevitably encountered resistance in getting to talk to her, apparently for nothing.

The budtender stepped around the gleaming glass and polished wood counter and led them across the well-appointed and gleaming waiting area to a secured door. He tapped in a four digit code, pulled it open, and gestured for them to go on.

"Lily's just inside. Go right ahead."

Suspicious still, Wicks bulled on down the hallway; his hand inching toward his never-drawn, let-alone fired gun. She followed and the door closed behind her. They were in a brightly lit corridor. Security cameras loomed overhead and out of reach. At the end, about twenty feet away, a tall, broad-shouldered woman with a curvaceous figure and a wide smile waited by an open door.

"Welcome agents," she said. "I'm Lily Thornton. Thank you for telling me you were coming."

Youngblood raised an eyebrow behind Wicks back. Although the husky, cigarette-tinged voice was the same, the conciliatory tone did not match the fury in the voicemail the woman had left on the hotline.

"Thank you for meeting us, ma'am," Wicks said, moving forward.

"Well, you said you were coming, what choice did I have?"

"You could have returned our calls as we asked. We could have set an appointment."

"Wouldn't matter. I'm always here, sweetie."

Thornton turned and gestured with both hands toward the room behind the wall and then went inside. Wicks cautiously followed. Then Youngblood. By then Thornton was sitting behind the moderately cluttered desk of a busy entrepreneur. Two 27-inch iMacs, plus a tablet, were lit up like a command center. Youngblood caught sight of spreadsheets with rows of data pocked with occasional charts. Thornton tapped her smartphone and the displays all went blank.

"Now agents," she said. "May I see some identification?"

They handed over their badges. She had large smooth hands, beautifully manicured with polished nails the color of

columbine flowers. She studied each credential carefully and
gave them back with the slightest of bows. She pointed them to
chairs opposite her desk.

"What can I do for you?"

The office Youngblood and Wicks had walked into was drab,
unexceptional commercial real estate. It was a windowless
space with cheap beige painted drywall surrounding
Thornton's desk at four right angles. Scattered about the bland
walls were photographs, often with a shyly smiling Thornton
among various gatherings. Youngblood noticed Thornton had
not hung any pictures of herself alone. She was always in a
group shot.

Part of the wall behind Thornton included a recently scrubbed
white board. In addition to their chairs, another table and one
chair that matched the two she and Wicks were in, and a
standing lamp in the corner completed the room's furnishings.

Except for the safe.

It stood next to the small table and chair. Loomed was a better
word. Six and half feet tall and four feet wide, the gunmetal
gray steel hulk dominated the room.

Wicks's eyes lit up and he pointed to it.

"That's an ISM Treasury 7238 with dual locks."

"You know your safes, Agent Wicks," Thornton replied.

"It's a hobby of mine, knowing about places to keep money; lots
of money," he said with a sheepish look at Youngblood. "So
where'd the heck you get it, if I may ask, Ms. Thornton? That's a
relic." His voice was full of admiration and suspicion. He
nudged Youngblood and said, "I knew the legal pot business
was good, but this baby is rated to hold more than three million
bucks cash. *Cash*."

He repeated the word reverently. Real money, not bits rendered into numbers on a computer display, but cold, hard greenbacks, meant something to Wicks.

"If only it were so, Agent Wicks," Thornton said, offering a hesitant smile. Her dark hair outlined a round, pale, smooth face with shadow and light. She wore more makeup than her looks required.

"How's that, Ms. Thornton?"

"Like any business in its infancy, we cut corners, Agent Wicks. My aunt in Seattle gave me the safe after my uncle died. He was a diamond dealer there, on Fourth Street, if you know the Diamond District. He kept his most exclusive inventory in this safe. When he died she sold the business. Nobody wanted this old safe. I was going into a cash-only business. Family first, says Confucius, so she gave it to me. A bit of overkill for my shop, but it inspires hope for the future, don't you think?"

"Federal laws notwithstanding, Ms. Thornton," Wicks cautioned while nodding approvingly. "I hope you get to fill it with Franklins someday. All legal in your state, of course."

"Of course," she replied with a precious wink. "And thank you for the good wishes."

"Ms. Thornton?" Youngblood said, steering back the conversation. "We appreciate your entrepreneurial spirit, but you made a phone call to an FBI hotline regarding Jefferson Fitzgerald Black, the suspect in the killings in Forth Worth and Thrall, Texas, as well as a person of interest in the mass murder in Maryland's Duckett Watershed. That's a serious matter. Your call. You made serious allegations. You know that. But you did not identify yourself during your call. You did make the call, correct?"

She nodded without hesitation.

"I did."

"Why?"

"For the reasons I stated. Jeff would not do those things. And, besides, the picture you've got is not him. It's wrong. Not even close. So, there's got to be a mistake somewhere."

"Do you have a photo of Mr. Black you could show us, Ms. Thornton?" she asked.

At that she paused.

"I had a few," she said. "We were office friends. He dropped by my desk regularly. We sat next to each other for a while at an after-work party or during lunch occasionally in the break room. Not quite friends, but way better than acquaintances. Comrades. Office mates. That's what we were. Close comrades in corporate combat. There were not a lot of natural moments for picture taking, if you know what I mean. And I had a systems crash a month ago and I lost a lot of old files, especially my photos. I do have one, though. It's on the wall."

She pointed up to an eight-by-ten framed image of a group of young men and women around a table scattered with slices of pizza and drained pitchers of beer, workmates raising a toast to getting through another work week. Thornton was in the center of the image. The photo was covered in black ink, signatures of, Youngblood assumed, subjects in the picture.

"Jeff is third from the left," she said.

They both automatically stood up and approached the black and white photograph. Youngblood saw that the scrawled signatures and best wishes were part of Thornton's farewell party from when she departed the same software firm she and JFB had worked at.

She studied the picture closely. The JFB she sought was not him. Like him, but, clearly, not him.

"Do you mind if we take a picture of your photo? We can get a warrant later if we need to get the original."

"Knock yourself out," Thornton said.

She and Wicks took a slew of shots with their smartphones. Youngblood immediately sent her photo to a powerful facial recognition program the Bureau had installed. Then she turned her attention to the signatures. Like everyone else, their suspect had autographed the photo close to his face. He wrote: "You're gonna kill the future, Lily. Go get 'em. Love, Jeff."

"I hate to sound like an idiot, Ms. Thornton," Wicks said, his finger hovering millimeters over the glass frame. "But are you sure this is Jefferson Fitzgerald Black?"

"Yes. You can check with the others in the picture. They'll say it's him," she said, nodding toward Wicks' quivering finger.

"Can you give us their contact information?"

She took a glance at the photo and said, "For most, yes."

"What did Jeff do for your company, Ms. Thornton," Wicks asked.

"He was a field sales engineer, the very best, at the database company we worked at. But you know that. I was in the compliance department, making sure projects met specs and standards and whatnot. He installed our software, mostly integrating it with other databases. Complex shit. Nothing but tricky bits. He was a recognized wizard among the top graduates of Hogwarts."

"How'd you guys pal up?" Youngblood asked.

Thornton lit a Marlboro Light 100 and said, "I was coming out then. Trans. Going through changes in front of others isn't easy. They always see the difference. Always see what I was not supposed to be, not who I really was. Precious few people, especially in my department, knew how to interact with me. Then, one day, Jefferson Fitzgerald Black, the blackest tech-cred black belt in the company, comes into my cube normal-like.

Easy as can be. Moved out from HQ in Pennsylvania after that horrible tragedy where that guy killed his daughter and the others. Maybe because he was wounded in his heart he found me, another wounded soul. I don't know. It's best not to over analyze. Anyway, when he comes by he asks me serious shit questions about work. Appreciates my answers. Chats with me regular, too, you know; talks about the weather and whatnot. Not just once. Whenever he's in the office. Stops by. Business first. Simple pleasure next. Sometimes he'd just breeze by and say 'hey' on his way somewhere else. He's a company super star and, out of the blue, my friend. Pretty soon, everyone else does the same thing. Stops by. Says hi. Does business. Talks weather, sports. Simple pleasures. He made it happen and, truth be told, I don't even think he knew it. It was just him. Frankly, without Jeff I would not have survived there. Frankly, I may not have survived period."

Thornton paused.

"Describe your work relationship."

She looked at them both fiercely, and said, "We liked each other. We were good work friends. We worked in nearby offices. Well, he had an office with walls. I had a cube. But we talked every day he was in the building, which wasn't that often. He traveled a lot. Every major customer wanted a piece of him. He was that good. And nice. I mean really nice. Respected. By everyone. In every meeting he had with clients and executives he mentioned those of us behind the scenes, including me at a time when some of our customers in, say, Texas and Alabama would not necessarily appreciate working with a known transexual. He wasn't trying to prove anything. That's just who he was. The worst thing he was was a good guy." She tapped an ash off her cigarette, folded her arms across her chest, the Marlboro still shivering smoke toward the ceiling between her fingers, and leaned back a few inches. "He's not your mass murderer."

"Jury's out on that, ma'am," Wicks said.

"When was the last time you saw your friend Jeff?" Youngblood asked.

Thornton turned away in silence for a few seconds.

"About three or four months after I left the company," she said, catching Youngblood's gaze. "I had just opened *Lily Maryjane* and he stopped in. He had just quit, too. That very week, I remember. He didn't even get a farewell party. Everyone did. But not him for some reason; he just took off."

"Did he tell you why he left? No one where you worked seems to have a clue as to why he up and quit."

"No one really knew. But I heard it might have been health related. He'd gotten into a car accident around Christmas."

"Health-related? Who'd you hear this from?"

She paused as if weighing loyalties, then said, "Jameson Dece. He was one of the IT admins back east. I think he worked out of a data center in Haiti. He told me, no, he hinted at the fact that maybe Jeff was ill. Bad. So he left. I don't know how he knew."

Youngblood asked, "And no one has seen him since?"

"Not me."

"You knew his state of mind before he disappeared," Youngblood said, shiting gears. "Any light you can shed would be helpful. What did you do and talk about when he came by after you opened your pot shop?"

"He took me to lunch."

"Where?"

"South Salem. Acme Cafe. He had the special and like always I got the Reuben sandwich. Best ever."

"Really?" Wicks, interested, hungry, asked, "Best in town?"

"World. Best in the world."

"Sorry to break into the *Food Network* broadcast here," Youngblood said. "But, Ms. Thornton, what did you talk about? How were his emotions? Was he angry?"

"He was Jeff. Calm. Precise. Asked me a ton of questions about my new business. Offered off-the-cuff suggestions that were spot-on as always. And, frankly, I was caught up in my *Lily Maryjane* endeavor and didn't ask but perfunctory questions about him. But I did ask him what he was going to do after leaving the company and he said he might open a pot shop like me. He said something like you did, Agent Wicks, about filling my uncle's safe with hundred dollar bills. I remember he did say something unusual about that."

"What was it, Ms. Thornton?"

She squeezed her eyes shut dredging up the memory.

"He said, 'Cash is king to the frugal and the fugitive. I'm a bit of both now.'"

"What did he mean?"

"At the time I guessed he meant now that he was free from his job he was a fugitive worker or something and he needed to be money smart."

Youngblood took a breath and continued.

"Could you explain to me the various possibilities of how you have a photograph showing who you say is Jefferson Fitzgerald Black and we have multiple official documents showing a completely different image of the man?"

"Sure, I can tell you. He didn't do what you say. This other guy, the guy in your photo, he did it. But not my Jeff. You just attached the wrong name to the right picture. Or vice versa, if you prefer."

"And if that possibility isn't correct, Ms. Thornton. What else might you suggest?"

It took her a moment.

"He changed the official files."

"Could he do such a thing?"

"Probably. I think so. He knew everything about our code. And our code was embedded everywhere," she said before shaking her head slowly and stabbing out her cigarette in an ashtray, adding, "Not that he would."

"Of course not," Youngblood said, shaking her head in sync with Thornton's.

II

They snaked their way out of the building to the parking lot. When they reached the car her phone beeped the arrival of a new text. She glanced at it while slipping into the driver's seat. It was an automated response from the facial recognition software she'd sent her image to analyze. It shocked her. She showed the message to Wicks and started the engine.

"Holy shit," he said.

"That's one dollar," she said, accurately mimicking Lakes's hint of a faux Ivy League accent.

"Good imitation, but the A.D. ain't here," he laughed. "But really, holy shit. This guy, our guy, or someone with his face, the guy on Lily Thornton's wall is really fucking inside the annual Second Amendment Party jerk-off festival."

"That's what our fancy facial recognition system tells us."

"Well, it did cost the Bureau a billion dollars."

"Worth every penny if it stops JFB."

"Agreed."

She called a number Lakes had given her that was answered on the second ring.

"Youngblood."

"Yes, ma'am," came the response.

"Who do we have at the Second Amendment Party in Idaho, Ned Sargent's hullaballoo?"

There was a pause while voice recognition verified her. It prompted her with a ring tone. She punched in a six digit PIN in response. If you worked for AD Lakes, you knew what number to call about such sensitive things. Like who the Bureau was spying on.

It was *verboten* for agents to attend any of the endless right-wing gun-nut gatherings in the USA, unless there was an authorized investigation against specific individuals. Still, for high-profile events like the SAP, the Bureau always snuck someone inside, usually as a paying customer from a shill organization controlled from inside the Hoover Building. Even the politically connected, refined gun nuts at the SAP were still nuts and needed discreet observation.

"Special Agent Youngblood," said the voice, "although no authorized agent is at the Second Amendment Party, Agent Derrick Witherspoon is attending as a private citizen."

Private citizen Derrick Witherspoon must have hacked into the SAP's registration system and sent the data to headquarters, or else the facial recognition software would not have caught JFB's image at the event. Purloining the data broke the law, but Youngblood gathered from that action as well as being undercover at the SAP, Agent Witherspoon was an ambitious go-getter.

"Patch me through to him," she ordered. "Give me his pre-arr."

"Yes, ma'am. Text or voice?"

"Let's start with text."

"Yes, ma'am."

She texted: "Call pre-arr in 5."

If he was an eager field agent he'd call the prearranged number in less than half the five minutes she'd asked for.

Thirty-two seconds later her phone rang. To answer she tapped in a different six-digit PIN to authenticate her phone as the secure device Witherspoon was to call in an emergency. At the same time he was affirming his voiceprint and entering a different PIN on his end. After the security protocols hashed to completion, she heard his voice.

"Witherspoon here."

"Agent Witherspoon, thanks for being so prompt," she said, putting him on speaker so Wicks could listen. "I've texted you an image of a man we think might be in attendance at the Second Amendment Party conference, which we believe you're attending as a private citizen. We seem to have acquired access to the attendees data and photo IDs. The one I'm sending is a person of extreme interest."

"Yes, ma'am," his voice sounded distracted as he waited for the photo to be transfered. "Got it. Got the picture. Yes, yes. I've seen him. He's on stage right now."

"What? On stage?"

"Yes, ma'am. There's a luncheon awards ceremony going on. Some ammo company's giving out fancy trophies to politicians and the like."

Calmly she said, "We have him registered at the conference as the Director of Product Development of Trophée Gaspé. Can you confirm?"

"Affirmative. That's him on stage now with the dignitaries."

She and Wicks exchanged long looks. Anything said on this line could never be unsaid.

"We have him as a potential suspect in the Second Amendment Killings."

She hated using the mass media tag for the killer, but knew it would save time communicating with someone outside the investigation.

"Roger that," he said. "Shall I arrest the suspect after the event or now, ma'am?"

She said, "Describe the situation Agent Witherspoon."

"Let me get closer," he said in a low voice. There was shuffling noise and in the background an amplified voice echoed a little louder. Witherspoon's voice was dropped to a whisper. "Looks to me that the awards ceremony is wrapping up. Four winners are already sitting in chairs holding their trophies, which look like plastic AK-47s. Ned Sargent is announcing the next winner. The suspect is standing about ten feet behind Sargent where a couple remaining trophies sit. From what I gather, once a winner's name is spoken the suspect hands the trophy to another guy, I think he's the fellow in charge of the ammo company, True Bore, I think. That guy, the ammo guy, gives the award to Sargent who gives it to the winner. Then someone takes a photo. They've made it into a big elaborate deal."

She was impressed with the detail Witherspoon provided. He had a future with the Bureau, if he could keep in check his cowboy approach to the Bureau's legal limits.

She said, "Can you reach the suspect without disturb…"

"Wait. Wait. I'm pretty sure, yeah, I'm sure. He's got a gun, a real one, but a plastic gun," Witherspoon's voice cut her off, rising slightly with excitement. "It's clearly different from the trophies. It's been bored out or whatever happens for plastic guns. At least the ones I've seen. The situation, as I see it is escalating."

"Agent Witherspoon you should…"

"He's pointing the thing," the agent's voice shifting from normal to a near shout. "He's going to shoot!"

Witherspoon's voice faded and garbled for a moment, then they heard him scream at the top of his lungs, "Stop! FBI. You're under arrest! FBI!"

Screaming "FBI" during the Second Amendment Party conference did not command the same clout as it might at an arborist or endodontic symposia. That was certain. Both she and Wicks knew something bigger than even their investigation had just happened at the exact moment when Witherspoon's phone went dead.

Chapter Thirteen
God and the FBI

```
Excerpt from the memoir of Jefferson Fitzgerald
Black
Q-Level Access
Eyes Only
```

I

A t first the brouhaha bubbling out of the audience didn't get my full attention. The SAP was famous for its loud drunks; one had to tune them out to concentrate. So I ignored the ruckus, my mind otherwise occupied, running through my step-by-step plan to kill the assholes arrayed before me on stage.

First, I made sure my Bluetooth remote control unit was operational. It was. With it I controlled access to the Green Room where my ultimate victims awaited their hopefully dim future. But I also found myself listening to the conversation in the Green Room. The microphones on most of the devices inside the place fed me revelations I have not yet fully digested.

Of course, when I eavesdropped on the Green Room conversation, I could not see who was talking or what they were doing or eating or drinking while they spoke. But I recognized everyone at once. Ivy Tock, her whispered scolding voice seldom heard in public, talked first; Wayne Laskey tried to interject something, but was shut down by Garland Tock, who preceded Arnold Arnoldson, the Republican majority leader in the Senate, mumbling in his unmistakable drawl.

Ivy closed the meeting with an unnerving but powerful speech. Her final words hit me like a football coach's firing up the team before the Big Game. It was inspiring.

> Ivy Tock: *Damn it, Arnold! I don't give a flying fuck what you have to do to get that lease provision back into the appropriations bill. Goddmanit we told you it was vital. Vital! And you let a junior senator from Rhode*

Island, Rhode Island for Christ's sake, not even the size of fucking proper-sized county, you let her, her!, outfox you on the committee vote. Are you too old now to be useful, Arnold? Tell me, should we find someone else to do our work? Because if that lease is not back in the bill, your grassroots support is going to wilt and die before the goddamn primaries. Am I clear here?

Wayne Laskey: *Ivy, please, Arnold's got a tremendous burden with the coming election and the president losing in the polls, dragging the party…*

Garland Laskey: *Wayne, shut up. Look, Arnold, Ivy's right.*

Ivy Tock: *Goddamn right I am!*

Garland Tock: *This lease is what everything is about. It's the last roundup before your unchained, unhinged President loses the next election.*

Arnold Arnoldson: *We are working the election process in all the key states. There's a good chance…*

Ivy Tock: *Shut up, Arnold!*

Garland Tock: *That nutcase is losing the White House and your precious Senate. You can't pull enough levers behind the scene to stop the coming slaughter, Arnold. Don't delude yourself. That's why we need to get that lease done now so we can move equipment on the land and take control of it. If we don't get there before people start calling you Minority Leader, assuming you even win your race, the new Administration can just renege on the deal. We need to move fast. Stick that rider back into the Appropriations bill and get it passed or we're done with you, Arnold. Do you understand? Done.*

Arnold Arnoldson: *I am working on it. It's my top priority. Once the lease stipulation, your stipulation, overlapped land claimed by the Acoma tribe….*

Ivy Tock: *Listen, Arnold, we don't need a history lesson on how you dropped the ball in committee because your stupid staff revealed to the other party's staff of the overlap. Don't you train your staff? Don't they know when to keep their mouths shut? Jesus fuck, Arnold, can't they lie?*

Consider this your marching order, Arnold. Get it done! Get it done now!

With her words echoing in my head, I got it done.

II

Events on stage were moving fast and I had to keep focused. Committing murder requires your unwavering attention; mass murder, more so. Sad to say, my choice of venue made that impossible.

A growing din from the audience distracted me, all the while stunning insights into American politics filled my Air Pods; I forced myself to focus and grabbed my first live plastic gun on the stage and rechecked the magazine's full allotment of polymer shells. I pumped one bullet into the chamber and, in the face of tedious distractions, I prepared to shoot.

Through my Bluetooth control unit I switched the SAP video feed inside the Green Room of the awards event from a live one to a replay of the previous ninety seconds that would run in a loop on the monitors. The fake video made certain that the guests of honor sequestered in the soundproof room would not be aware of the danger outside.

My first target. Neddy.

That's when a man's booming voice got through to my consciousness and I realized that he was yelling at me.

"FBI! FBI! Stop! This is the FBI! You're under arrest!"

I stared at the approaching man. He was young, in his late twenties, early thirties. Square-jaw blond blue-eyed handsome. Tall, too. Wide at the shoulders, narrow at the waist, of course. More impressively, his hand was pulling out a standard-issue Glock from his shoulder holster.

Thinking quickly, I looked at our master of ceremonies.

"Neddy!" I said loudly and accusingly, "The FBI? What's with the FBI? How did they get in?"

Of course he fell for the distraction. Neddy hated the FBI. More than liberals. More than gun-control advocates. More than Barack Obama and Hilary Clinton combined. When someone said the Bureau's three-letter name, he heard Waco and Ruby Ridge. He constantly fumed on right-wing radio about the FBI's control of the Deep State and his loss of rights as a private citizen who wanted to do whatever the hell he wanted to on his own goddamn property. Every year it was said he sent Janis Ian, his ideological opposite, a sizable check for her charities so he could use one stanza from her left-wing, anti-government folk song, *God and the FBI*. He had it printed on the daily schedules and even recorded a cover of the song, but he only played one verse, especially when Neddy came on stage.

They called the FBI
I had to disappear
Called the g-men, t-men, see you at the scene men
Told 'em I was hiding here
They could fingerprint my heart
Tear my world apart
Ain't no hole for a soul to hide
From god and the FBI

Not surprisingly, he began shouting obscenities at the onrushing agent, distracting him.

"Goddamnit! You asshole! I did not invite the Fucking Bureau of Incest onto my property. Get the fuck fu...fu......"

Neddy stuttered because while he was yelling I put two quick rounds into the oncoming agent's nice looking head. The man fell in a heap while his blood and bone splattered over tables crammed with diners bent over their steak and lobster lunches. An uproar from the crowd around the dead man ensued.

More curious than careful, the ex-rocker couldn't help himself and turned to face me in his confusion. I placed the first bullet in Neddy's right eye and the next went into his throat; blasting apart the back of his skull and his carotid artery, shutting up the man for good.

When Neddy collapsed with a bloody plop on the stage, the entire audience erupted like an anthill stepped on by a boot. Everyone ran for the exits, shouting and screaming with every breath. My targets, the trophy winners, were trying to escape like everyone else, except their hosts had gone the extra mile and rented big, deep, plush and low leather chairs for them to bathe in their glory on the dais.

Instead of getting away, however, I shot all four before any of them got out of their comfy seats. My anger at them was deep and abiding. They had lent PR cover and political clout to the Murder Inc. activities of the gun industry. The quartet disgusted me. Two from Congress, a man and a woman, one black, one white. One flyover state female Republican governor. One macho male NFL star from California.
Their demographics were perfect for the cameras and the evening news. Death, alas, when it comes, does not favor one demographic over another.

My final on-the-dais execution sent Reverend Jay Issac Crymal to his Maker. As the fattest man by a few dozen kilos attending the SAP, he made an appropriately sizable living being invited to Second Amendment convocations to act as the sanctimonious satrap for Our Lord's love of weaponry. He was also an easy, slow-moving target. Week after week, he traveled the nation and blessed guns, munitions, grenade launchers, cannons, and any other killing device his paymasters invented. The Lord commanded serious firepower to spread the Good News, the Reverend Crymal endlessly extolled his listeners in fervent prayer.

The cynicism of the honored recipients appalled me. They each deserved a double-tap to their heads for agreeing to accept the ARI's tainted award, which I swiftly gave them after knocking down each with a chest shot while they were struggling to leave their chairs. Reverend Crymal had the most time to flee and was frantic in his pointless huffing and puffing off the stage, but I shot him once in the buttocks and twice in the chest. They were all bathing in anything but glory when I had finished.

I marched away from the night's winners toward the Green Room door. Two shots rang out from mid-way in the dining room. One went wildly high, the second crazily low and hit Neddy's prone body, possibly saving me from a leg wound as I walked behind his corpse. The stage lights made it hard to see exactly who was shooting at me.

I swung around and fired. But the plastic gun jammed after the first shot. Another incoming round went wide. You'd think gun nuts could shoot better.

I reached down. Neddy always wore a pair of loaded long-barrel .45s on a holster during SAP. He'd yank one or both of the hand cannons out of his holster and shoot randomly throughout the conference to prove they were loaded. I'd heard his gunshots twice while I was working the booth in the trade show hall. Everyone laughed about it and said Neddy always shot things that didn't matter and besides people never got hurt. He fired at things randomly, especially ancient tree trunks that grew on his land.

"They're big. They're old. They can take it," he'd explained once.

The guns hung in a wide black leather holster. He always wore a tan thigh-length calfskin suede jacket garnished with fringe from its four front pockets. Part of his faux-cowboy motif. I pulled the smooth pricey leather aside and grabbed the weapons. I turned and fired twice in the direction of the incoming gunfire. The big bore revolvers were loud and always caused a lot of damage on the receiving end. The recoil was hugely different from the guns I'd shot lately and I almost dropped the first gun after I shot it. Then I fired a few more times, ready for the gun's fierce response.

The painful screaming told me I hit at least one Second Amendment extremist trying to escape gun violence. More importantly, I paused the firing by the person shooting in my direction.

I ducked low and ran to the Green Room door. I clicked my control unit and heard the electronic lock open. A new shot came my way and missed. Before another was fired I was inside the Green Room and facing my primary targets.

A Secret Service agent approached from my right. His job was to protect the Senate Majority Leader, there to receive a lifetime achievement award and give a speech while soliciting campaign donations. Without hesitation, I leveled Neddy's revolver and fired at near point-blank range. The agent's face disappeared in an explosion of blood and bone. A woman to my left, an ARI flack I had seen on TV passionately defending the indefensible use of automatic weapons "by regular free Americans," collapsed to her knees screaming. I kicked the Green Room's door to the stage closed behind me, locked it electronically, and then I shot her.

The remaining foursome still alive stared at me. The smell of urine hit my nostrils.

The Senate Majority Leader, who had killed dozens of common-sense gun-control bills and thereby killed thousands of Americans each and every year, jumped to his feet, a dark stain spreading at his crotch. Stumbling up next to him was Wayne Howard Laskey Jr., his mouth moving but no words tumbling out. Across from them, still seated on a cowhide Mission-style sofa were the Tocks, Ivy and her brother Garland. The two men standing looked appropriately terrified; the two people sitting seemed mildly perturbed.

With good reason.

Until recently I did not fully appreciate the importance of gun rights to the rich like the Tocks, who secretly funneled money to the ARI and other similar organizations. You'd think wealthy people would be against arming any citizen, especially poor people. But like most of us, I was wrong. Guns weren't guns to the Tocks and their ilk. They're a wedge issue, plain and simple.

When I did background checks on those around Laskey, including the Tocks, I learned the Oklahoma siblings did not have a single weapon registered in either of their names. They didn't need to, of course. They hired their protection. They didn't need some cheesy sign reading "Protected by Smith & Wesson" stabbed in their lawn. They paid ex-Navy Seals with automatic rifles to keep them safe.

Still, it seemed odd to me that secret funders of radical gun groups didn't own any guns. That's until I did a little more digging and came across an item from more than a quarter century ago. The Tocks' mother had shot herself in the bathtub of her Oklahoma City mansion with her second husband's revolver. The twins were twenty-five years old and had just completed their Masters degrees in geology at SMU in Dallas.

The police report on her death included a note their mother had written. It read in its entirety: "Ivy & Garland, I used Daddy's gun so you won't have to. Ever."

The OKC police confiscated the weapon as evidence. The family never asked for it back.

The mother's last words must have haunted the Tock twins. Their oblique meaning implicated them not in a crime, for which they had separate rock-solid alibis, but in a psychological family mess that the police and press prodded and poked at for a day or two, but never got too deep into it because that was the week Timothy McVeigh killed one hundred and sixty-eight people in the Murrah Federal Building, about six miles from the Tock estate. The Tocks's personal drama vanished into yesterday's news. Their current drama, though, was going to be tonight's news, that I knew.

"Sit down, Senator; you, too, Wayne," I commanded with gun in hand.

They sat.

"There's no way you'll escape."

Looking at Laskey, I said, "I knew someone would say the cliche. I'm not surprised it's you."

He colored a bit, then said, almost pleadingly, "We can help you get away."

I put up my hand to cut him off.

"Wayne," I said. "You know I hold you responsible for the death of my daughter. That's why I killed yours. Eye for an eye, isn't that what your Good Book says?"

"You're crazy. Who are you?" Laskey started yelling even though we were all within whispering distance.

"My name is Jefferson Fitzgerald Black, if it matters. I'm the guy who sent you the 'Hey Joe' song. And I'm the guy who's going to shoot you so you, too, can become a statistic in another of our nation's deadly plagues."

Laskey opened his mouth to speak, but before he could shout a syllable, I fired twice into his face. The .45 made a mess of it, half of it spilling over the Majority Leader's clothes and hair. He started to gag as if to vomit, but I fired the last of Neddy's .45's rounds into his chest, cracking through his ribs and splintering his cold heart.

I tossed the big handgun away. I pulled the dead Secret Service agent's Glock from my pocket and pointed it at the Tock twins.

"Garland," I said. "I want you to pull your phone out of your pocket. I want you to call your driver and have him meet you at the back door of the Green Room where he dropped you and Ivy off."

I gestured with the gun. He stared at the two dead men on the sofa opposite where he sat. The smell of cordite, pulverized bone, and fresh blood filled the room. Garland was hyperventilating.

Ivy crushed his side with her elbow.

"Garland," she hollered. "Snap out of it!"

He turned to me.

"Call your driver," I ordered again.

He pulled out his phone and tapped the screen. His voice became calm and business-like as if the natural feel of the phone in his hand made everything else seem normal.

"Yes, Syd. Thanks for answering so promptly. We'll need to be picked up now. Yes, a change in timing. Just fetch us where you left us off back of the Green Room. Two minutes? Fine. We'll meet you."

I gestured again with the revolver, time for Ivy to rise. I motioned her toward the rear door where the driver would appear. Then I turned the gun on Garland and fired nearly point blank into his heart. Not as powerful as the .45, I fired the Glock twice into the man's head to assure I'd killed him.

Ivy's eyes widened. But she did not scream nor cry. She looked away from her dead brother to the rear door. Her face frozen in maybe fear, maybe anger. Hard to tell.

I stepped forward and thrust the barrel of the Glock into the nape of her neck. I pushed her forward with the gun, shoving her to the side of the door. I looked through the peephole and saw an ornate old limousine had already pulled up to the short covered walkway outside the Green Room's back door. Along with the driver, who was standing by an open rear door, a security grunt stood nearby, his wrists X'd across his waist, yet another Glock bulging from his shoulder holster.

I grabbed Ivy Tock, pulling her close so that her buttocks pressed to my crotch. I had the gun at her throat.

"All you have to do is walk ahead of me, keep your mouth shut, and, if we're both lucky, we'll get to live another ten or fifteen minutes."

Then I shoved her out the door.

Chapter Fourteen
The Helper Guy

Celeste Youngblood

I

The Gulfstream G600 took sixty-one minutes to land at Pappy Boyington Field outside Coeur d'Alene. Before they even got on the flight from Salem, Youngblood and Wicks had worked comms on the drive to the airport, firing off texts, sending emails, leaving voicemails, barking orders in the vain hope they were not too late to nab JFB.

Once Witherspoon went offline, Youngblood called into the SAP conference center, but got no answer. She called the local sheriff's office and requested a deputy run a safety check to Sargent's property ASAP. Wicks was hitting up Spokane and Boise field offices to assemble as large a team as possible to converge fast on the sprawling Idaho panhandle ranch.

Youngblood was getting nowhere inside the SAP until she saw that the FBI had included Sargent's law firm in Chicago among his contacts. She called the number listed and got the name of the staffer who went to SAP this year. The helpful receptionist at the office even patched Youngblood through to a young lawyer named Wagner Laughlen.

The lawyer picked up on the first ring.

"Wagner here!" He pronounced his name like the German composer.

"Special Agent Celeste Youngblood of the FBI," she replied. "Mr. Laughlen, are you attending the SAP event on Mr. Ned Sargent's estate?"

"Yes, goddamnit! And all hell's broken loose. Some crazy guy started shooting from the stage. I'm lucky to be alive. He's killed Neddy and the others. Jesus! The blood. A gun guy killing us for fuck's sake! It's insane!"

"Mr. Laughlen, you say there have been casualties. You say Ned Sargent is a victim."

"Yes. He's dead. A bunch of others, too. And we don't even know what's going on in the Green Room right now. It's a goddamn bloodbath!"

The man was bellowing.

"Is there on-site security, Mr. Laughlen? Have you seen any security personnel?"

"Shit, no! They probably ran with the rest of us."

She spoke slowly, calmly, quietly.

"We're on our way, sir. We're on our way now. Help will get there as quickly as possible."

Wicks whispered to her.

"Agents on the way. Connecting with local sheriff now. We'll have support quickly on site. Deputy almost to property now."

She passed on Wicks assurances of imminent help in a soothing tone.

"You're going to be safe, I promise, Mr. Laughlen," she said.

"Okay, good. That's good," Wagner said, his voice dropping a couple notches, her words soothing him, though she heard the break in his tone. The man wanted to cry, but was holding it back.

"Mr. Laughlen, are you in a safe place now? Can you talk?"

"Yes. Yes."

The man's composure seemed to be returning.

"Can I ask you a few questions?"

"Yes. Yes."

"Think back. Where were you when the shooting started?"

"I was…."A slight pause, a deep breath, then recovering his composure, almost in full lawyerly mode, Laughlen said, "I was in the audience. A couple tables back from the right side of the stage. I was eating the dessert. Key lime pie. Neddy's favorite."

"How many people in the room?"

"There were maybe two hundred people there having lunch. Another half dozen on the stage, plus Neddy. Twenty or so worker bees floating around the room serving food and booze."

"What happened during dessert, Mr. Laughlen?"

"A guy on stage was handing out plastic replica AR-15s or AK-47s, I can never tell the difference. They were customized trophies for people who support Second Amendment rights. They were supposed to be fakes until they weren't. Another guy on stage, the helper to the guy handing the awards to Neddy, started firing."

He stopped, then started again.

"No, wait, first a guy came storming into the room shouting he was one of you guys, the FBI. Yeah, first the FBI guy came in, Neddy yelled at him for some reason, and the helper guy shot your guy dead. Pow! Pow! Right to the head. Next the guy killed Neddy while he was standing at the podium. After that me and everybody else ran for the back exits. I could hear the helper guy still firing. Pow. Pow. Not quite the same noise as a real gun, but gunshots. When I got to the exit with everyone else, I turned back. I could see the dead people on stage. All the award winners. And the helper guy exchanging shots with some idiot hero in the crowd on the other side of the room, thank Christ. I think by then the shooter was using Neddy's Colt. Sounded like it. More people got hit. Anyway, the helper guy got into the Green Room and before he closed the door I heard him fire a shot. Neddy's Colt makes a big sound."

"Mr. Laughlin, can you tell me when the shooting started or when it ended?"

"Lasted maybe two or three minutes. Ended maybe ten, no more than fifteen minutes ago."

"We are on our way, sir. Sheriffs are close and we'll be there soon, Mr. Laughlen. Trust me."

II

Despite the short flight to Idaho from Oregon and the quick seventeen-minute full-throttle helicopter trip from Boyington to Sargent's compound, a lot had happened at the crime scene since she'd given Laughlen her promise. When Youngblood arrived forensic techs from the Bureau in Spokane were already gathering evidence and a pair of county medical examiners were analyzing the five bodies on stage. A different state ME was assigned to analyze Neddy's corpse. Agent Witherspoon's remains in the audience were being examined by an FBI forensic tech. More casualties were being examined near one of the exits at the back of the room. Looked like two more bodies. Another half dozen crime-scene techs were collecting evidence from the stage where the shooter had started firing. One agent was collecting the dozens of videos shot during the shooting by the conference organizers and many witnesses.

By the end of the day everyone would be filing a report replete with details and gruesome digital photos. The place was crawling with competence, but no closer to catching their man. He was into the wind.

Within ten minutes of her arrival, the sheriff, with the help of a local metal worker, had hand-torched their way into the fully locked Green Room. They found five dead bodies.

And not just any dead bodies. She recognized the Senate Majority Leader, the head of the ARI, one of the richest men on the planet, and two others she'd learn about later. But those special three trumped the already notable body count on stage. Governor. Congress member. Sports star. A Senator. A billionaire, whose billionaire twin Youngblood knew was probably dead elsewhere, too. And, of course, a has-been rock star. Everyone in the country was watching.

Meanwhile, the shooter, JFB, was still on the loose.

She connected her iPhone to the encrypted Bluetooth VPN the Bureau had set up on the fly in the area. She spent a few minutes observing what data was being collected by the techs. She assured herself everything was being processed properly. The forensic work, she believed passionately, needed to be done first, foremost, and flawlessly. Best to leave the pros at their job.

She led Wicks, the Sheriff, two field agents, and a handful of deputies toward the back exit. The Sheriff's men kept streaming into the compound like seagulls on a beach after high tide. She assumed it was so they could a glimpse at the famous man's digs and his bloody demise. They'd dine on this crime for a good long time.

The Green Room's rear door opened to a covered walkway that ran to a gravel road. Another body sprawled at the end of the walkway. It was being protected by a nervous deputy, waiting for an available tech or ME to examine it.

Beyond that scene, a hundred feet or so up and across the road, was a group of eight men clustered between a pair of black wannabe police Jeeps complete with Falken Wildpeak mud tires and Arsenal 40-inch LED light bars on the roof. A similar looking official county sheriff Jeep was parked in the middle of the road, blue lights flashing.

The sheriff explained that one was a real cop, the rest were security wannabes. She learned the solo deputy, who had arrived first to the scene, had taken off with a posse of Sargent's security personnel to chase down the car the killer used to escape. The deputy reported that when they reached "fancy old limo," the posse found a dead woman inside and a live Indian, the driver, standing outside it. Unhurt, unlike anyone else in the shooter's path, the deputy had editorialized in his verbal debriefing. But the killer had escaped, on what the Indian had told them was a red Honda dirt bike, with a twenty minute head start. The Indian had said he was deaf.

Once she had ID'd Garland Tock inside the Green Room, Youngblood already knew who the Indian limo driver was. As they got closer to the Jeeps, she saw what the men had gathered around: Syd Peltry. He sat on the ground between the Jeeps, his arms twisted behind him, locked in zip-tie handcuffs. His face looked like someone had punched him once or twice. The clutch of security guards smirked and whispered to each other, a couple of them smoked cigarettes, as they stood over Peltry like big game hunters posing for a photo.

She led her entourage over to the gathering with quick, angry steps.

"What happened to this man?" she demanded when she reached the group, pushing up close to the biggest man there. "Help him up and remove those handcuffs now. And put those cigarettes out now, you fucking idiots, this is a crime scene not behind the backstop on the high school baseball field. Not on the ground, you nitwits."

The two smokers, confused about what to do, but sensing a quick response was in order, pulled out their revolvers and dropped the butts into their holsters as if they were experienced at hiding their habit.

Other men helped Peltry up and cut off the zip ties on his wrists. When he was freed she stepped over and gently took his cheek in her hand and inspected the bruising.

"I thought you said he was unhurt," she spat at the deputy. She turned to Peltry and said softly, "How'd this happen?"

One of the security men joked, "Got hurt getting into the Jeep."

"Shut up!," she said. "I was not talking to you."

Peltry nodded toward the two guards on the end.

"They slammed my face into the car door before it was even opened."

A chorus of shouts from the guards.

"Liar!"

"Fucking Indian liar!"

She said, "Mr. Peltry, would you like to press charges against these two men?"

"You know," he said without hesitation, "I would. There will be some of my blood on the outside of the driver's side rear door and its window to make this more than he said-she said kind of thing. Plus, I think the outside cameras on the limo might have caught some of the action. So, yeah, I'd like to press charges."

"Come on, lady, this Indian helped the killer escape. He's the only guy who met the killer who ain't dead. He's got to be an accomplice. How else could the killer have gotten inside?"

She turned to the group, making sure Peltry could still read her lips.

"Your incompetence comes to mind. Did Mr. Peltry here vet the killer for the conference? No. Did he approve the gear the killer brought on stage? No, that would be you guys. I'd see you as a more reasonable vector as possible accomplices. What would you say, Agent Wicks?"

"Indeed, ma'am, I would."

"No! No! We did nothing wrong," one guard pleaded.

Another ranted for a few seconds about his time in Afghanistan and his unwavering patriotism to the flag and his leaders.

The biggest guy said, "Come on lady, we got...we got somebody who's guilty of something, or why else is he alive?"

"No, you're wrong, gentlemen. If you did your homework about who was on the property, which is likely to be unlikely, you'd know that this man worked for two of the victims. More important than that, he's a witness. Do you know how important a witness is in a case like this? Do you? I suspect not since you don't know how to do your basic job of securing the site you're paid to secure otherwise we would not be here cleaning up a mess that should never have happened. I will want a full investigation into just what, if any, security you provided Mr. Sargent and his guests."

She switched her gaze to the Sheriff and his small crowd of deputies who had followed her out of the Green Room and were silently watching the scene.

"Sheriff, would you please have one the county techs here gather evidence on the Jeep in question and arrest those two?" She pointed to a pair of indignant guards.

"My pleasure," he said. He nodded for his deputies to carry out the order. "Take their guns."

With that, one of the security men reached into his holster, "No one takes my gun and lives...."

Before he finished Wicks took two swift strides while pulling out a .32 Beretta from nowhere, which looked like a small toy in his hand. He stuffed the gun under the guard's jaw, pressing hard.

Wicks said, "Now I don't know if this little gun will kill you, sir. But I can guarantee that you will have a nightmare of dental work ahead."

The guard's hand froze an inch from his holster. Wicks relieved him of his weapon and the deputies handled the second man's arrest without incident.

Peltry laughed aloud.

"Mr. Peltry," Youngblood said, offering him a little smile. "There's nothing humorous about crime."

"Sorry, ma'am. Must be nerves."

"Yes, well, understandable," she said. "Now, how far away from here is the car and the body of, presumably, Ms. Ivy Tock."

"Yes, it's Ms. Tock. It's about a mile up the road. There's a deputy standing watch."

"Are you up for walking?" she asked. "You could tell us what happened on the way."

"That would be excellent."

"Sheriff? Agent Wicks? Up for a stroll?"

They ambled off in a foursome. Peltry took the rear so it would be easier for him to read lips. The Sheriff walked to his right. Youngblood and Wicks were in front and turned when they wanted to ask a question. Mostly, everyone listened while Peltry described his encounter with JFB.

"Garland Tock called me at 1:36 to come get him and Ms. Tock where I had dropped them next to the covered breezeway that leads to the Green Room. Where I had just left them at 12:53. I had been told to retrieve the Tocks at 2:30, but was ready when she called."

Even though Peltry walked behind the agents, he set their pace with the careful cadence of his words.

"You noted the exact time?" Wicks asked, his head twisted backward.

"If I see it, I note it," Peltry replied.

"Sorry, go on."

"When I got back to the Green Room entrance, I parked the limo exactly where I had dropped them off. The Tocks don't like unnecessary complexity, Garland's told me in the past. They appreciate not having to find me in a new location. I think that's why they fly me and the Chrysler to places like this. Familiarity comforts…comforted them. Sorry, I'm rambling."

Youngblood gave an exaggerated shrug of her shoulders and he continued.

"Anyway, I parked the car, got out, and opened the rear passenger side door. Tom got out of the passenger front seat and stood there like security guys do."

She turned, "Tom?"

"Oh, yeah, sorry. The dead guy on the way out of the Green Room. He was the Tocks personal security guard. Tom Dender. The killer shot him right away."

She turned to face him.

"Why not you, you think?"

"He sized us up. He was walking directly behind Ms. Tock. It took a second to realize he was holding a gun up against her back. The killer pushed her to the ground. Tom went for his gun, but was distracted just long enough by the falling Ms. Tock that the shooter nailed him before he even drew his weapon. He was hit twice. Once in the neck and the other in the chest. Tom was a good enough kid, a little cocky. Not fast enough when it counted, though. I wasn't carrying, so I didn't draw."

"What happened then?"

"That's when the shooter pointed his weapon at me and asked if I was armed. I said no. He asked if I was the driver. I said yes. He asked my name. I gave it. He nodded, kept his gun on me, and told me to help Ms. Tock into the back of the limo. He went around to the driver's seat and felt underneath all the while keeping his eye on me as I helped Ms. Tock. He found my .38 Special and put it in his pocket. He never mentioned it. It was as if he knew it was there, but didn't care so long as I had nothing else. I didn't.

"Once Ms. Tock was in the backseat, he told me to get in and drive. He watched us both put on our seat belts as he'd ordered. He got into the front passenger seat. Ms. Tock was alone in the back. He told me to lower the glass partition between the front and back and he turned to face Ms. Tock. He kept the gun on her and told me to follow the gravel driveway for a few hundred yards and turn into a narrow gap. He'd marked it with a white ribbon."

Peltry pointed between Youngblood's and Wicks's shoulders.

"It's just right up there, where we'll turn. It's a bit wider than an ATV path. The Chrysler doesn't really fit, but I did it anyway. There's a lot of scratches on the paint on both sides from the brush. It hurts me to have done it. I know, it's the least sad thing on a deeply tragic day. But still sad.

"Anyway, I drove about three quarters of a mile and the land cleared a bit as we approached a six-foot tall concrete-reinforced chainlink fence with two feet of razor wire strung across the top. I stopped. He said, 'Run through it.' I told him that he was crazy, but he told me that he'd read in an FBI file that I had bragged that the car could crash through a wall like that no problem. He turned the gun on me and asked me if I had been lying. I said no. I was not lying to the FBI. He pointed the barrel toward the fence, 'Then go,' he said and strapped himself in with a seat belt. So I floored it and banged right on through the fence like it was a spider web. He had me stop the car about two hundred feet into the bush. It was then he told me I did not have to stay. 'It's not like you can do anything,' he said. But I did stay and I was able to read most of what he and Ms. Tock discussed until just before he killed her."

By now the quartet had made the turn down the narrow path between the thick growth of hemlock, juniper, bitter cherry, and chokeberry. They each avoided walking directly in the

Chrysler's tire tracks, which were clearly visible. The scrub
brush along the path was shredded from the passing of the
limo. Bits of branches and twigs littered the ground. A bird's
nest had been ripped from a bush and fell near the center of the
path, heads from a pair of dead hatchlings poked out. They
stepped carefully around it.

"What did they talk about?" Youngblood asked.

"Well, first, he asked her why she wasn't more upset about her
brother's death. She said that she was comforted by the fact that
he was now in the arms of Jesus. He laughed and said that Jesus
must hug a lot of people day in and day out because of killers
like himself; killers Ms. Tock made possible. If not for her and
her dead brother, the killer said he would not exist. The man
was adamant, but calm."

They trudged in silence for a moment. The Sheriff was
breathing hard. Peltry pointed.

"You can just see the broken fence and the car ahead. Not far."

Youngblood and Wicks stared for a second or two before the
wreckage stood out amongst the sage and scrub pine.

Peltry continued.

"Then he accused Ms. Tock and her dead brother of destroying
not just individual lives, but entire cultures. He said, 'You go
into virgin land, run by fragile governments, and tear it apart
metric ton by metric ton, all the while annihilating villages and
ways of life that stretch back time immemorial, leaving death
and disease in your wake.'

"She said, kindly-like, like a teacher, 'We save savages from
themselves. That's what the ruling class has always done; what
we always will do. We bring civilization to the unwashed. If not
for us, these shithole villages that you fantasize about would
inhibit the march of progress toward a well-run world that
adheres to the rule of natural law.'"

"Not to be disrespectful, Mr. Peltry, but are you telling us exactly what was being said or summarizing the conversation," the Sheriff said.

"It's pretty close word-for word, Sheriff. My memory's pretty good. And I've got a Voice Memo on my phone that recorded it. I haven't listened to it. But I'm sure it's there close to verbatim the way I'm telling it." He pulled a new iPhone from his pocket and passed it forward to Youngblood. "Looks like I'll have to get yet another one."

She laughed and took it.

Wicks shot her an inquisitive look.

"Oh, this is the second phone I've taken from Mr. Peltry as evidence in the case."

"That's right," Wicks said with a nod and a smile. "I read that in your OKC report."

"Well, I'll be. As a witness goes, you're pretty frickin' good," the Sheriff said, clearly impressed. "Please go on, sir."

"As I was saying, Ms. Tock raised the issue of natural law and, frankly, the killer almost lost his cool when she did. He raised his voice like a barely under control parent does for a totally out of control teenager. He said, 'Look, Tock, your natural law, your Great Chain of Being, or whatever the fuck rationalizations you rich guys invent, is just paternalistic bullshit. It lumps the weak and stupid masses on the bottom and puts at the top a few brilliant, God-blessed men; men, Ivy, my gal, not women. You should be ashamed to be a mouthpiece for such misogynistic drivel.' She shook her head, I remember, rather fiercely, then said, 'God the Father set the rules, I didn't.'"

They walked in a silence for a minute. Peltry was collecting his thoughts. The steady percussion of the quartet's stride in the thin sandy soil mixed rhythmically with the melodic psithurism from the low woodland. When they reached the shattered chainlink fence Peltry finished recounting his story.

"I thought the killer was going to blow her head off right then when she talked about God setting the rules. His face turned red. His grip tightened on the big gun. I thought Ms. Tock was a gonner right then and there. But the guy held back. Instead, he quoted Proverbs, 'To fear the Lord is to hate evil; I hate pride and arrogance, evil behavior and perverse speech.' The killer went on, 'You Tocks and your ilk are nothing but proud, arrogant, perverse, and evil through and through. It's easy to hate you.'

"I have to say, she was undaunted, truly unafraid of the killer. She said, 'Of course, any devil like you can quote scripture. But hate is the key, I'll grant you that. Hate is fundamental to natural law. Hating others is how people define themselves. You hate what you are not. Hate releases you from respecting anyone else; you deny their importance if not their right to exist. Hate abdicates the individual from the consequences of his condition. Hate is the emotion of loneliness. And there's so much loneliness in the world. Without direction, hate flails and flounders without purpose. It devolves into random violence. It's useless. That's all Garland and I ever did; that's all anyone in power tries to do, focus the hate and the violence that comes with it. Make it useful. Give it purpose. Get all those lonely people to hate in one direction. That's what we do. That's the true art, the true magic of power. If you can focus the innate human hate where you want, your will prevails. Today, the hate is building throughout United States and even in prissy Europe. We're managing it. We're giving it direction. We're giving it purpose. We always have. We always will.'

"The killer said, 'You won't really know will you? Oh, wait, you'll be watching with Jesus and Garland on a big screen TV in heaven.' She said nice as can be, 'Blasphemy won't help you. You can't stop the Plan with your petty little vendetta. It only helps us.'"

They had reached the car. The late afternoon sun bent low shadows across the ground from the tall brush and scrub pines.

Peltry continued, "By now the killer had regained his composure. He pointed the gun at me and told me to get out. He promised he'd shoot me if I didn't exit the car in five seconds. And he started counting. I believed him. I got out. Closed the door. He turned back to Ms. Tock. I could read his lips through the windshield but the sun's glare on the rear passenger window didn't let me see what she'd said. At first."

The Sheriff said, "Was it recorded?"

"No. I had the iPhone in my pocket. Didn't think it wise to try and slip it onto the seat."

"What did you see him say?" Youngblood asked.

"The first thing I saw him say, after Ms. Tock spoke for a while, was, 'My health is no concern of yours.' I thought that a strange response," Peltry offered.

"It is odd," she agreed. "What else did Black say?"

"Well, he was quiet for a bit while she was talking. Then he shrugged casually and said, 'None of that matters because your so-called Plan is an epic failure. Your precious brother is dead. You'll be dead soon. Whatever you want to do to the country will not happen. I'm putting a bullet in your Plan.'"

Peltry cleared his throat before finishing, "At that point she leaned forward as far the seatbelt allowed and I could see her lips. She said, 'Dear boy, the mere fact of your being here proves the Plan is an epic success.'"

Youngblood and Wicks exchanged glances.

Peltry said, "I didn't hear the gunshot. But I felt it. Or thought I did. The killer got out on the passenger side, left the door open, and walked beyond the front of the car into the bush without even looking my way. I went to the front passenger door which he'd left open. I looked inside into the backseat. Half of Ms. Tock's skull was blown off. I turned away and thought I was going to puke, but immediately got distracted by the roar of a dirt bike. The killer came out of the bush riding it and skidded up next to me. He had a helmet on with the vizor up. He'd replaced the Glock in his left hand with my .38, but was still pointing a gun at me.

"Then he said the strangest shit. He said, 'You want me to shoot you in the leg?' My look must have told him something because he said, 'Look, if I don't shoot you the Feds or the local cops, more likely both, are going to think you're in on the massacre. They need someone to chase down because they can't catch me. You're the closest prey. If I shoot you in the leg, you become a victim, not a person of interest.' I told him no thanks and that I'd take my chances with law enforcement. He said 'Suit yourself.' He pocketed my gun and took off on the bike like he knew how to ride one. I tried to call someone immediately, but couldn't get 9-1-1 because the cell signal was weak out here. I was to distant to reach the conference wifi either, so I walked about a quarter the way back before I connected with 9-1-1. They said a deputy was already on his way. I walked back here to stay with the body." He pointed to the limo. "Fifteen or so minutes later I was being manhandled by those security boys and the Sheriff's deputy and starting to wonder whether I should have taken up the guy's offer and got shot in the leg."

Wicks laughed.

"Probably by the end of the day, sir, after endless interviews with the likes of us, you might think that their manhandling was the best part of your day," he said.

Chapter Fifteen
Escape Artist

Excerpt from the memoir of Jefferson Fitzgerald
Black
Q-Level Access
Eyes Only

My brother was the better dirt bike rider when we were growing up in Carson City. But I was good enough to almost keep up with him. He invariably raced ahead with unbridled abandon in the sagebrush hills and pine tree mountains surrounding Nevada's desolate capital. I chased him doggedly, but never got close when he didn't want me to. Nonetheless, because he was great I got to be pretty good following him.

What I'd learned from trailing him for miles over the slopes of McClellan Peak, across the flats near Fort Churchill, up the Sierra Nevada canyons of Clear Creek, Job's canyon, and so much other empty territory, was that a dirt bike in open country with less than a two hours head start, no matter how fast the bike, no matter how skilled the rider, was no match for search planes, much less real-time satellite image scanning and heat-seeking drones the Feds would use to find me. Don't even seriously bother, I thought. Outrunning the good guys was not my shot in the dark to escape.

I had stashed the red Honda outside Sargent's property as part of my slim chance to make a getaway after my killings. Odds had put me dead before I even finished my on-stage slaughter, but the arrival of the FBI agent in the audience somehow turned the table; the unexpected element that tilted events in my favor. Maybe he interfered with armed security reaching me somehow. Maybe I unconsciously changed my shooting angle because of him. I don't know.

If not him, perhaps divine intervention helped me survive. How else to explain my persistent luck in killing groups of people in public and then getting away? Of course, I'd like to think so;

that God was on my side more than simply random luck and my detailed plans shepherding my actions to success. It would mean what I did was not wrong, not sinful, not evil in God's eyes. That it was, in fact, goodness that I spread with my gunfire.

Bouncing on the dirt bike through the mountain scrubland, I wondered if I was the other side of karma; was I the universe's reaction to the gun nuts whose political power directly leads to tens of thousands of murders and suicides every goddamn year. How else could I have succeeded time after time with such a bloody and audacious scheme? A higher power at work? Who knows? But if there was a saint for serial mass murderers, and religions have saints for every possible avocation, he or she was surely in my corner.

But for how long? Good luck, even for the most righteous, capitulates to the odds. It has to. That's what I always planned for.

I realized before I had arrived in Idaho, that my only escape route was going to be back at the scene of the crime. After I left Syd Peltry, the Tock's driver, at the car with his dead client, I rode the bike hard into the National Forest land that bordered Neddy's property. I kicked up a brown fantail of dirt for more than a mile. I hoped to give the impression I was escaping into deep country. But after about five minutes I turned onto a deer trail that connected to a wider path that ran thirty meters below the crest of the hill on Sargent's property on the ridge. I rode up the trail for a few meters, got off the bike, busted a limb off a small pine and covered up my tracks. I returned to my bike and rode back to where the conference had been held, so that I ended up nearly 180 degrees and three miles as the crow flies from where I'd left the chauffeur.

It was a rugged ride so it took nearly thirteen minutes to reach the back of a fenced-in, gated parking lot with a postage stamp guardhouse. A few dozen upscale rentals used by VIP attendees nearly filled the lot. It was surrounded with faux Western slotted resin fenceposts and rails made in China. I cut the engine to the Honda and humped it up the remainder of the hill to the fence. I quietly disconnected a pair of rails from their slots on the posts and pushed the dirt bike through onto the pavement, then I reattached the rails to the posts. Took three minutes. Tops.

On the far end of the lot a security guard was talking excitedly with one of the valets outside the small gatehouse. The valet was wearing a Covid-19 mask, even though Neddy made it a requirement that attendees and workers not wear them. Now that he was dead, I guess people could choose to wear them or not.

The two young men faced the direction of the conference hall, their backs to me. Sirens approaching the main building were getting louder. Shouting could be heard. A thick copse of tall birch, scraggily hemlock, and impenetrable manzanita cut off the view from the parking area gate to the conference building. The guard and the valet each had a walkie-talkie at one ear and their phones over the other. They were chattering a mile a minute with one listener or the other or to each other. It had been less than forty-give minutes since I had started shooting on stage. Time enough for rumors and gory details to be flying around the compound.

There was a shed in the middle of the lot where Neddy kept a trio of identical motorcycles to mine. He'd loan them to guests to ride his well-tended trails and shoot borrowed guns. I planned to deposit my bike with his so it would disappear in plain sight.

I kept to the back of the lot, held the bike at an awkward angle to keep it from view as I pushed it behind the last row of cars. I almost dropped it twice. But the guard and the valet were fully absorbed in the play-by-play reports coming into their ears and did not notice me, a mere twenty-five meters behind them. Granted a few dozen SUVs, Jeeps, and a slew of comfy sedans partially blocked the view between us, but they remained fully focused on what they could not see beyond the trees. I was safe.

Carefully, I raised the bike's kickstand and stood it in line with the rest of the bikes in the hut. I grabbed a satchel with gear I'd need, and ducked down between the low wall of upscale vehicles. I crab-walked my way past a few black SUVs, a green Acura TL, and a white Lexus GS until I reached my destination: a brand new cobalt blue Audi A8 from one of the premium car rental companies that had survived the Covid-19 Depression. My getaway.

It was leased to Swan Talmadge at the Coeur d' Alene airport yesterday for a return today. Swan had the good fortune to be born into a wealthy family that had long ties with the gun industry, something to do with shell casings, and felt it his duty to support every aspect of Second Amendment culture, hence his attendance. Swan also had the misfortune to be the person at the SAP who most looked like me.

When I hacked into the SAP internal conference database, I ran a facial-recognition comparison between me and everyone who would be at the event. I got sixteen matches from the software, most did not resemble me that much, though a handful did. There are only so many human characteristics and most people only take passing notice of the differences. We all look for the similarities to confirm who someone is, not to question if they might be someone else. It made being another person easier than you'd think.

I narrowed my look-a-likes to three men before I had arrived the conference. After studying my possible doppelgängers face-to-face during various moments of the event, I chose Swan. Poor him.

Back in the parking lot, I pulled a pirate key fob from my backpack. I had it set to the exact 315 MHz frequency Audi had keyed into the original fob. The company stored unique keylock frequencies in a database I knew well. Those frequencies were linked to vehicle ID numbers in each country where the cars were sold. It was a snap to download the one for the rental A8 to my counterfeit fob. I pushed the button and unlatched the trunk.

It opened silently, as you'd expect from a pricey sedan. I touched the hood to keep it low. I took one last look at the guard and the valet, their attention still otherwise engaged, before raising the hood high enough to slip inside, then closed it. It took a moment to adjust to the absolute darkness.

As expected, the A8's trunk was empty and ample. Even at near six-feet tall, I curled up my knees slightly and fit with ease inside the well. I reached into my bag and pulled out a Beretta M9A3 9mm with a noise suppressor attached. Luckily for me the ARI fought to make it legal to own handgun silencers in most states. If I had to shoot someone again, I'd rather not attract a lot of attention, if I didn't need to, at least at first. I checked the safety and set it between my legs.

Next I retrieved my modified iPad that connected to leased satellite bandwidth from SpaceX's commercial spectrum. It also worked with less exotic comm systems like 5G and WiFi. For the moment, though, I was scanning the walkie-talkie traffic that the conference officials, security staff, valets, and sheriff deputies were using to communicate. I stuffed a pair of Bluetooth pods in my ears.

What the valet, security guard, myself, and everyone else were hearing over the local bands sounded outrageous: Twenty killed! Maybe thirty! The entire Congressional Second Amendment caucus slaughtered! Children and pregnant women among the dead! A government crackdown on the Second Amendment had begun! Worst of all, Neddy Sargent had been assassinated by an FBI agent!

Exaggerations, misinformation, rumors, and lies, of course, were already making their way to the world at large as attendees called their loved ones and favorite journalists. The Second Amendment Killer strikes again!

Voice traffic on a different frequency promised all available EMTs were on the way to Neddy's place from nearby towns. The sheriff and the Feds would be there soon. Managed chaos was coming. Valets were told to report to the car pick up spot. Security guards were told to secure their areas immediately and conduct hourly checks. No one was to enter or leave the compound except for EMTs and law enforcement until further notice.

It did not take long before I heard the security guard approach the Audi. He rapped his fingers hard along the trunks of the Lexus and Acura before reaching my hideout, where he did the same. Three sharp strums of his four fingers and a loud thwack with his thumb across the hood as he passed. He did the same on the cars further along. When he finished this exercise he updated an online log I could access, certifying the cars were empty. I gather he looked through the cars' windows while aurally checking locked trunks, the keys to which he did not posses. He did this like clockwork for the first six hours, then another guard took his place and the tapping on the cars and the log updates stopped. But security continued to certify the parking lot was safe.

At 5:23 a.m., about fifteen hours after the shooting began, the security supervisor sent a message to the parking lot guard that the FBI had finally cleared most of the conference attendees to leave. They would depart one at a time from the main entrance. Valets would begin retrieving cars immediately. Cars would be checked by each valet one final time while handing over the keys to the attendee. Within fifteen minutes I heard the first engines turn over as the valets started getting the cars. At 6:21 a.m., the A8's driver's door opened and I felt the slight shift in the car's suspension as the valet jumped in.

My body tensed as if an electric shock shot through me. The car was moving, crunching its way through the estate's gravel roads toward Swan Talmadge, waiting under the covered driveway outside the main hall. I was either making my escape against all odds or committing suicide.

Curled up and quiet in the Audi's trunk for more than fifteen hours I could hardly sleep and had a lot of time to think. About myself, of course. What else does anyone think about but themselves? Their children, of course. But mine was dead, so it was all about me. I had accepted the fact that I was destined to be remembered, if at all, as a cold-blooded killer. I won't argue with that. I felt nothing but a sense of accomplishment for my actions. So, yes, cold-blooded and proud.

That said, I should also be remembered for being an escape artist, especially if I succeed in making my way out of the SAP and Idaho alive. Despite all my killings happening in broad daylight, I had gotten away every time. Most mass shooters die at the scene or in the next twenty-four hours. I had just finished my fourth mass killing and was on the verge of getting away, again. Houdini, the greatest escape artist, did not accomplish his feats after massacring people then vanishing while being chased by the police and FBI. I did.

I hope I get remembered for that, too.

It took less than three minutes for the valet to bring the car to a stop. As I expected, the valet popped the trunk. I was lying on my right side. I stopped its silent rise with my left foot hooked under a smooth bend in the metal. In my left hand was the Berreta with its silencer.

The driver left the engine running. My GPS app showed we were under the awning. An indistinguishable hum of mostly men talking buzzed excitedly outside. Engines were running nearby. Trunk lids and car doors slammed in the background. People shouted goodbyes. It sounded politely chaotic.

Finally, I heard Swan Talmadge's voice. He was hovering nearby.

"I'll call when I get to Salt Lake," he said to someone over the background chatter.

"Okay, we'll get this done then," an unfamiliar man's voice replied. "Safe flight, Swan."

"You, too, Bob."

If Swan Talmadge or the valet had insisted on putting luggage in the trunk, I'd start shooting. Take as many others down with me as I could. I figured the silencer would let me get quite a few more kills before someone shot me dead.

That was the end of my plan. Hopeless? Probably. But the only winning strategy I had left was hope against hope.

I had a theory that Swan Talmadge would not need the trunk, another reason why I chose him. He had brought only a carry-on bag on his flight to Coeur 'd Alene. I also knew he had some sensitive papers in his bag. He was divorcing his wife who was trying to stick it to him, in his mind. He had sent emails during the conference to his lawyers that I had read by hacking into the SAP's laughably insecure wifi. In his messages, he said he planned to go through the final settlement "line-by-line, word-by-word, dollar by dollar, penny by penny" while on the trip. I bet that Swan Talmadge did not want those papers far from his sight even on the drive back to airport. But all that didn't mean no one would check the trunk.

"Here're the keys, sir," I heard the valet say crisply. "Shall I take your bag, sir?"

"No, thanks. I'll keep it."

Someone's hand pressed down on the trunk's lid and closed it. A few seconds later, the car took off.

Hope won.

Chapter Sixteen
Just Another Anyone

```
Celeste Youngblood
```

Rough, huh?"

Wicks's quiet question jolted her awake. She lurched forward in her hard, armless, black plastic chair. Her eyes popped open but the overhead fluorescent lighting blurred her vision and she blinked a half dozen times to clear her sight. She looked at her watch: 9:27 a.m. She'd been asleep for eighteen minutes, the last time she'd checked her watch.

After a long day and night and morning of interrogation, at 8:41 a.m., right at dawn, two stone faced agents had escorted her into the windowless, empty room, save the lone plastic chair leaning against the stark white wall. One of them told her to wait; then they left and closed the door. She thought she heard the lock fall into place, but in the hours they made her wait she never checked. Wicks's appearance meant it probably had never been locked.

"Rough, repetitious, and long," she answered. "Now I know how criminals feel. No wonder they hate us."

He laughed. "Who braced you?"

"Everyone."

She had been grilled by a trio of SAC hardasses from D.C., one after the other, each with their own companion and not taker. All the while she should have been studying the crime scene. She kept that notion to herself, knowing her days involved with the JFB investigation were over. One after the other the agents fired the same set of questions at her, mostly about her relationship with Syd Peltry and his connection to Jefferson Fitzgerald Black. Bureau higher-ups had decided that the two men had to be connected. And, perhaps, she, too.

As one SAC had barked at her during her third or fourth grilling, "Peltry's got some angle here. He's the only witness to your so-called Plan."

"If he has an angle, I don't know what it is," she'd answered. "Besides, it's not just him. You've got Ivy Tock recorded using the term."

"Maybe. Forensics will determine if it's real of not," her colleague practically snarled at her. "We'll dig into every relationship. You know that. If you're involved, we'll find that too. So, if you've got anything to say, now's the time."

She shook her head. Stupified.

Once the SACs were done with her, came a pair of ADs, one after the other, accompanied by an unnecessary stenographer who also recorded the sessions on his smartphone. Each AD went over the same material, repeating the same questions in a slightly different order as if it might trip up Youngblood. When they finished at 3:12 in the morning, for less than two minutes, shockingly, the Director Otis LeBlair himself appeared.

The only thing she remembered him saying was how disappointed he was in her. "We had hopes for you, Agent Youngblood. We truly did. But you're a real let down, you know, a real letdown," he had told her, behind his coronavirus mask. She had been given a fresh one to wear before he came into the room. He was now on the record that he met with Youngblood to further the investigation before he threw her under the bad press bus roaring down on the Bureau.

After meeting the Director, she knew the only real question was whether she had any future with the Bureau and, if she did, was it even worth having. It didn't take long to learn she did, but it wasn't.

Her last debriefing was the one she couldn't get out of her head. The one where she had learned her fate.

After the Director walked out of the room, a standard pair of stoic agents escorted Youngblood to her final meeting. Neither of her minders touched her, but given their size, the clear implication was they could do more than point her in the right direction if necessary. They guided her through the dark crush of black SUVs clogging the small parking area. A white haze from a dozen portable LED light towers turned mountain night into a desert afternoon. She squinted and raised her hand over her eyes like a salute to shade the glare as they marched along. The agents stopped at one of the SUVs and opened the side door, let her in, and shut it, remaining outside the vehicle with their wrists crossed in front of their crotches.

There was no driver; only a sleek black woman sitting alone in the back seat. She reminded Youngblood of an elegant bird of prey. She wore a gray suit with touches of red in the piping of her jacket and matching pants. Her emotionless eyes watched Youngblood's every move as she got in the car. The woman was gorgeous, with perfect skin and hair and cheekbones that could cut Minneapolis ice in January. Her bright white smile was as fake as the diamonds on her wrist and ears. She gestured to the flip-down bench that popped out of the front seat's back. Youngblood sat.

All her earlier grillings had centered on the killings, Peltry, JFB's whereabouts, and her failure to stop him, a topic that came came up in every interrogation. This chat was different.

"My name doesn't matter," the woman had begun. "But people like to attach names to things, so think of me as Grace. I predict the future for people; in this case, your future."

"Do I have a future?"

"Everyone has a future, Agent Youngblood, even if it's only death, a future we all share," Grace said with a shrug. "But in your case I am going to outline a very particular future. It will last indefinitely. During that time you'll be at your desk in Washington, which will be relocated somewhere out of the way from working agents. What you will do is provide distance support to the team that will locate and neutralize JFB.

Whatever they ask of you, you will fulfill. They want you to order search warrants or extra coffee, you do it. When they accomplish the task that you failed at, you will do nothing. You will come to the office. Collect your check. And do nothing. You will never talk to the media about your situation. You will never be a source, a confidant, an off-the-record quote. We will know, trust me.

"The next time we meet, you and I, you will resign freely from the Bureau on your own. Your government service will be reflected in the pension you will be given upon your retirement. You will receive a standard letter of recommendation from Human Resources, stating your years with the Bureau, your title, and your exit date. You'll find another job, likely in law enforcement and, if you're lucky, you'll never encounter the Federal Bureau of Investigation for the rest of your life. That is your future, Agent Youngblood."

"What if I quit first?"

"No pension, no letter from HR, and, likely, an investigation into your time as an agent with the Bureau. And everything before. Should there be a scintilla of scandal, we will find it and use it to prosecute you. Even if we don't find anything, we will prosecute you. We have lawyers coming out of our ears ready to file charges against anyone anywhere for anything. You're just another anyone to us now, Agent Youngblood."

That's the thought that rang loudly in her head more than anything else. She was just another anyone to the FBI now.

Wicks continued to hold open the door. He said, "I've been asked to gather you up and get us the hell out of here."

She asked, "Did you meet the lady in the SUV?"

"Grace?"

"Yeah, her. She told me my future. Did you get yours?"

"Yep. I'm going back to full time financial fraud computer work. No more out in the field, not that I really wanted the work, remember. But I'm getting punished, too. Being moved out of headquarters and redeployed to some nothing office building in Crystal City or somewhere else in the suburban Virginia sticks. Might as well move back to Thrall."

"Hardly," she smiled. "I've seen Thrall. D.C. suburbs, dull as they are, aren't your old hometown by a long ways."

"Maybe so. Still. Fucking Crystal City."

"Speaking of swearing, did you hear what happened to AD Lakes? I've sent him a couple of texts and left v-mail. Nothing from him yet. One of my AD interrogators let out that he was being put out to pasture; sent to some field office in the middle of nowhere."

"Close. He's being sent to Abu Dhabi. He'll be in charge of the office in the United Arab Emirates, which oversees the work of the Bureau for the entire Middle East."

That stopped her.

"What? No shit?"

"You heard me."

"Shit," she said. "That sounds like a promotion."

"Damn right," Wicks said. "I know. I saw the office's salary sheet a couple year's ago when I was working on an internal IG budget proctology report. Saw every dollar that went through the UAE. So, yeah, I know. Lakes's new job comes with a tidy salary bump."

"What's with that?"

"Wish I knew."

She pushed the chair back against the wall where she found it and followed Wicks out of the room. Each step behind him required an enormous effort in self-control. Angry, she wanted to scream questions at Wicks. She didn't. She calmed herself with each footfall. Never show that you're riled was one of her mottos.

He led her across the courtyard where morning light washed out the artificial glow from the portable LED towers. Many of the Bureau's unmarked black SUVs had disappeared, including Grace's; now replaced by a clutch of logoed state and county law enforcement vehicles.

"This way," Wicks said with a nod beyond the fancy driveway to the distant parking lot. "We're returning the lately departed Agent Witherspoon's rental to the airport. One more indignity we're intended to resent. And I do."

Wicks strode with purpose, even anger, and she upped her pace to keep up.

"Why? What does it matter?"

Wicks was quiet for a long time as they fast-walked their way into the parking lot. He waved his ID and a set of keys at a security guard who numbly nodded them through.

Finally, Wicks said, "Derrick Witherspoon, in his effort to suck up to the bean counters rented a bottom feeder."

"Compact?"

"Sub."

"Poor you," she said, glancing up and down at his nearly six and a half feet, head to toe. "It'll be a tight fit."

"Worse."

"What?"

"It's a KIA Soul," he handed her the keys. "An ugly, tiny box with windows and wheels. It's got no soul. An over-engineered car for our under-engineered world. Wouldn't be seen driving one in the neighborhood let alone for work like Witherspoon."

"I like the Soul."

They had stopped next to an iridescent lime green car.

"And look what happened to his and your careers," he deadpanned.

Youngblood bent over laughing for a long minute, tears coming from her eyes.

When she stopped, Wicks added, "You know the name of the color of the KIA Soul that Agent Witherspoon chose to drive to his surreptitious status at the SAP?"

"No, I don't," she said carefully, wiping her cheeks.

"This is the god's truth," he said, then stretching out each syllable, "Undercover Green."

With that, she shook again with laughter, turning her back to Wicks, leaning against the car door, facing the guardhouse and a shed. The guard was looking at them curiously, which sobered her up, after a couple more gulping laughs. The hilarity replenished her. Her exhaustion and resignation suddenly gone.

She looked away from the guard, somewhat embarrassed as to what he might be thinking. She glanced at the shed. It was open. Back in the shadows some undefined equipment lurked; up front were four motorcycles propped on their kickstands next to one another. A number flashed in her mind.

"Say, Wicks."

"Yeah." He was still smiling, happy to have lightened the moment.

"You remember the stuff we read about Sargent's Second Amendment Party, the marketing material used to entice paying attendees."

"Yeah." His smile fading, memory kicking into gear.

"One sales pitch was something like, 'And conference goers have access to a quartet of Jeep Wranglers, a trio of Honda CFR250 dirt bikes, and a dozen Gary Fisher mountain bikes to explore and shoot up the wild country surrounding the conference center.'"

"Yeah. Sounds familiar. That might even be word-for-word."

"It is. And I count four motorcycles."

"Me, too," his eyes looking beyond Youngblood into the shed.

The bike parked furthest from the shed's plank wall had been the only one that looked used. It was covered in the same reddish dirt from Sargent's property. Sage twigs poked out from the chain guard. Fenders were sprinkled with dust from a recent ride.

"I think one of them is the one Peltry saw JFB ride away on," she pointed to the shed.

Wicks produced his phone and began typing quickly.

He said, "There's no record of anyone signing up to ride the dirt bikes on the SAP activity list."

She said, "He never left. He hid here, waiting to escape. Taking his chances. He may still be here in one of those cars over there. I doubt it. My guess is not. Not just because of the odds but because this guy thinks things through."

"Still, how'd he do it?"

"Most likely, he hid in the trunk of a car and was chauffeured out the gate by some unsuspecting driver. Not every vehicle parked here was a KIA Soul. As I recall, when we got here this lot was packed with mostly upscale rentals, many with big trunks. But, just guessing again, that whoever took JFB out of here is probably no longer alive. Probably somewhere on the road between here and Coeur d'Alene."

"Fuck, yeah," Wicks said, nodding. "He's long gone now. But with who? Most of the wits are outta here. On their way back to hearth and home."

"One of them, maybe not destined for home, though the hearth, maybe" she said mordantly. "How could they let it happen? Did they care more about finding who they can blame; wasting time grilling me and you for not doing something perfectly rather than finding the one person who did something wrong? Come on!"

There was a long silence between them.

Finally, Wicks said, "Facts that I know are: one of the ADs started letting people leave one at a time a few hours ago. They're important people, too, sure. At least in their own minds. Gave statements multiple times. Started getting pissed off. Dropped names. Called in favors. You'd have probably done the same thing, letting them leave. Can't fault letting witnesses wanting to go after being interviewed by the Feds, state, and county officials. I'd be whining to get out, too."

"True. But I can fault someone who lets witnesses leave the scene without triple checking every vehicle that left the property."

She started walking over to the shed and pulled out her phone. She tapped on the name of one of the ADs who had grilled her hours ago. He was the most unfriendly and accusatory about her handling of the investigation. She figured he'd be the most likely to answer her call.

When he picked up, she spoke immediately.

"AD, the killer never left the property after his phony escape on the motorcycle. He didn't ride off into the sunset; he returned to the main campus. I have the evidence right in front of me. He could still be on premises. But, most likely, given the current empty state of the visitor's parking lot where the evidence is, he's gone; probably stowed away in a big shot's car, which was not thoroughly checked before it left. You might want your people to start reviewing witness departure videos from earlier this morning. Someone forgot to inspect a car trunk. Or maybe more than one. My guess, JFB's out of state by now."

After the briefest of pauses, he said, "You say you have evidence. It better be fucking signed off by God Himself."

"I'm not sure if *She* actually signed off on it or not, sir," Youngblood answered. "But it will convince even you. Bring a forensic team and a few agents, in case JFB happens to be in one of the two possible cars remaining in the lot."

She ended the call without waiting for a reply.

Chapter Seventeen
The Plan Is an Epic Success

Excerpt from the memoir of Jefferson Fitzgerald
Black
Q-Level Access
Eyes Only

I

L ike someone accustomed to driving fine automobiles, Swan Talmadge navigated the A8 smoothly through the curves of Freedom Lane. Sargent's private four-mile-long, one-lane blacktop road ran through the Kaniksu National Forest to Highway 95, the nationally funded multi-lane public highway that cut hundreds of miles south to north through the Famous Potatoes state. Freedom Lane weaves back and forth, up and down the steep wooded mountains, a nauseating ride for some, especially tucked in the dark confines of a trunk. But I was fine because my next victim knew how to handle a fine car. I didn't get the slightest bit car sick in the trunk. In other circumstances, such impressive driving skill might have earned the man a reprieve from his fate. Sadly for him, not this time.

Every so often on one of Freedom Lane's steep inclines there was a pullout so slower cars could get out of the way of passing traffic, usually Neddy driving like a bat out of hell in one of his twenty-two, for the .22 bullet, of course, American-made muscle cars. I had each pull-off location programmed into my iPad's mapping system. As we approached one of the turnouts halfway down the road, I pushed the button on my Audi's fob that opened the trunk. It popped up wildly. I had to be careful not to get bonked by the unhinged trunk lid flopping up and down.

As expected, Swan Talmadge swerved into the next pullout, responding to the noise, the alarms on the dashboard, and the unsettling sight of the bouncing lid in the rearview mirror. He skidded to a jerking stop and jumped out, leaving the driver's door open. I had grabbed the bobbing trunk lid and was holding it a few inches above its closed position. Through the opening, I heard his lizard skin Stetson boots drag over the gravel and dirt. I saw his gray crushed velour slacks appear before me while his fingers curled under the trunk's lip to raise it. I held it down slightly to give him some minor resistance. He gave it a little extra tug. I let it go. His eyes widened. I fired twice into his chest. He collapsed. I scrambled out of the trunk. Put the hot muzzle to his forehead and heard a hiss of burning flesh before I fired one more time.

I dragged his body into the thick brush that pressed up the canyon on the right side of the road. It left a glistening trail of blood. A car was rapidly making its way down the curves toward me. The dead weight of the late Swan Talmadge was in no hurry to move, but eventually I was able to get him out of sight into the bramble moments before the car whizzed by. But I could hear a slower one coming behind it.

I pulled off the dead man's boots easily enough. They fit fine, only a half size larger, which I already knew. As one more distinguishing fashion guise, they were essential for my borrowing his identity. I also grabbed the dead man's glasses, his pierced ruby ear stud, his conference lanyard, and the rest of the contents from his pockets. I had prepped my ear by piercing my lobe two nights earlier in the wild chance that I would need it. I slipped his earring in with no trouble, draped the lanyard over my neck, and donned his glasses. I knew from my research that he'd had cataract surgery the year before and his distance vision was, 20/20, a bit under my 20/15, but still the upper lenses were clear plastic. As long as I didn't look through the 2.25 reader magnification in the bifocal, I was fine.

With barely a moment to spare, I plunged out of the bushes as the second car arrived, gingerly pulling into the turnout. The A8's trunk was up along with the open driver's door, so it was reasonable for the second car's driver to be concerned. I could see that it was a single man behind the wheel. I vaguely recognized him from a mob of attendees that came to the vendor booth I'd worked at during the SAP.

I ostentatiously pulled up my zipper and glanced sheepishly at my crotch while catching the driver's eye afterwards. I could see him laugh. He stuck his hand out the window, waving goodbye. I waved back. He never noticed the bloodstained ground. Good. I wasn't in the mood to kill someone else.

It didn't take long to reach Coeur d'Alene's airport from there. Traffic was non-existent on the roads. The Audi ran smooth and crisp like it was motoring on one of those closed tracks you see on TV ads. In no time, I had returned the car to a contactless kiosk that processed everything on Swan Talmadge's credit card, which I had inserted into the narrow slit that would determine whether I was or was not him. One six-digit PIN number later, I was.

I hopped on the shuttle to the terminal. Like everyone else ready to fly, passengers and crew, I was wearing a Covid mask. With Swan Talmadge's identification, glasses, PIN numbers, and everything else I knew about the man, I was on the first flight to Salt Lake City from the Idaho Panhandle. Every computer checkpoint gave my version of Swan Talmadge a thumbs up as I sauntered my way through our contemporary automated identification authentication maze. The two humans I encountered along the way, at TSA security and the boarding area, merely affirmed with a polite "Safe flight, Mr. Talmadge."

Yet, throughout the entire boarding process, all the while in flight, and even after touch down, part of me expected armed FBI agents to swarm in from the corners of my imagination and take me prisoner or take me down; one way or the other, end it all. Never happened. The real and digital documents I used, including his Utah-issued REAL-ID driver's license that I took from his dead body, held up to scrutiny, such as it was. My perfect virtual him and my close-enough real appearance to the man got me through safe and sound. Maybe that and the boots.

After I had landed and glided through Arrivals like any other anonymous schmo, I snagged a ride on a city bus into downtown SLC. Grabbed a cab at the depot to a swank hotel and walked through the lobby and immediately out a side door. Bought a pair of navy blue and white adidas Gazelle shoes and an array of sports clothes at TopShelf SLC off West Temple. Walked a circuitous path to Temple Square. From there I hailed another Yellow cab to different upscale hotel in the tony suburbs.

These hotels thrive on white businessmen attending conferences and walking around like they own the joint. That's what I did. I donned Swan Talmadge's lanyard again, wearing it backwards. I studied the hotel map next to the concierge's podium, found a distant conference room, noted the medical instrument sales event being held there. I asked the concierge, who looked clean cut and Mormon, about bus tours to Temple Square from the hotel. He smiled back and offered a pamphlet with the Temple shuttle schedule and returned to his paperwork.

The place was big, so it took a few minutes before I reached the back conference area. It was mostly deserted. A man and a woman sat behind a table scattered with unclaimed conference badges that looked nothing like the lanyard that dangled from my neck. They ignored me as I strolled by to the bathrooms around the corner toward the rear of the hotel. Inside the men's room I changed out of my clothes into my new casual outfit. I put everything into the empty plastic trashcan liner and took it with me from the bathroom and out the hotel's backdoor to the rear parking lot, every suburban hotel had one.

I crossed the lot to the interstate's frontage road at the back of the property. It was getting dark as I walked the two miles east to a Motel 6 on the other side of an I-80 interchange. Under the freeway overpass, where homeless men pushed grocery carts to and fro, I found one without its owner nearby. I dropped the plastic bag inside without breaking my stride. I hoped the clothes and boots would fit. I removed the ruby stud and stuck it on the top.

Across the street from the Motel 6 was a dumpier joint that took cash. I circled the block, shopped for junk food and drinks at a 7-11, and watched for any signs that I was not alone. Nothing. No one had followed me.

At the dumpy motel I paid for three nights up front. I gave a name, Blake Crossler, with identification to the motel clerk, along with a handful of twenties. I had plenty of cash on me. I had emptied Swan Talmadge's fat wallet as well as hit up his ATM accounts for the maximum withdrawal amounts in both airports.

Once in the room, a dank place, but with bright fluorescent lights throughout, I hung out the scummy Do Not Disturb placard on the outside door knob, locked up, turned out the lights, and flopped onto the too soft bed. There was no TV, not even an alarm clock radio; only the bed, a battered chair, and a chipped formica table. A narrow door led to a bathroom designed to torture claustrophobics. Basic to the bone. It was the perfect place to stay. No one bothered me. I closed my eyes, exhausted. I went out like a light.

All my adrenaline drained away like water emptying from a basin. I felt spent. I crashed through the night and the entire next day, getting up only to pee, poop, and drink bottled water. I slept dead to the world until, finally, I woke up panicked after a wild dream about being chased by dog-like creatures around a racetrack to the cheers of a massive, gesturing crowd. In the dream I ran slowly, as if gravity worked harder on me than the creatures pursuing me. They tore at my shoes, Swan Talmadge's boots. The calves of my legs were bloody. Although I felt no pain, my fear was overwhelming. It jolted me awake. I had never had such a dream before and woke wet with sweat, more anxious than I can remember feeling since being a child.

Quickly, though, the hum of traffic and the murmuring of other guests through the thin walls reassured me. No one was chasing me here. I was safe. The dogs of the law were, indeed, after me, but they were not nipping at my heels. For now, I had escaped. Certainly, I was still in danger, but it felt distant like a whiff of wildfire you smell from faraway.

Soon, my anxiety drained into the impersonal room; my feelings absorbed into the dull fabric of the place where so many others before me drank and cried and fucked and slept away their fears, their pursuers, inside this cheap room. And most of them came out alive, I bet. It was that kind of place. The motel felt to me like a Four Seasons for the desperate. I'd give it five stars on Yelp!: "Great location. Almost quiet. Clean(ish). Well-lit place. Perfect for a serial mass murderer on the lam."

I slipped away early the second morning and ended up at Kneaders Cafe for an early meal of eggs, hash browns, and bacon. After breakfast I sauntered east to State Street. I eyed a string of car lots until I found one that suited my needs. Instead of paying cash, which I had on hand, I pleaded for credit. Cash transactions so soon after my SAP spree would be fodder for databases to flag. One more desperate loan would be overlooked along with the thousands of others filed for each and every day. The place I chose, Vangard Motors, specialized in selling claptraps on dubious credit to people hanging by a thread; only to send the Repo Man hours after the poor sap missed the first payment. It was a heartless virtuous circle that made Vangard highly profitable.

Blake Crossler, the man who bought the metallic gray 2015 Chevy Sonic LS four-door with the tattered black interior, didn't really exist. Technically I didn't steal his identity. I invented it; complete with a sketchy credit and employment history, one that appealed to Vangard's sales team. Crossler had a local address, living with his mom, and even worked part-time loading trucks at Harvest Foods off the 201 freeway in the city. It all checked out. Online, of course. The crack sales team didn't bother to call anyone. They used my phony Social Security number and my fake driver's license number to verify that I was someone who never existed.

The signing costs were, considering the establishment, modest, only a couple hundred dollars. However, because the state required insurance for all motor vehicles, Vangard made a tidy sum brokering the only insurance a person like Blake Crossler could obtain. The sales staff firmly believed that the Chevy would be back on the lot soon, repo'd in a month or two, available for the next hard-luck mark to start the cycle again.

Surprisingly, the Sonic ran well. It took me all the way to Lexington, Kentucky, where I set up shop to plan my final slaughter. Blake Crossler arranged to wire transfer funds to cover the outstanding debt on the car loan. Vangard Motors ceased to be interested in my fake self.

Even if I survived, which, again, I doubted wholeheartedly, I knew I would quit. Killing the Boss would end my mission. But to be true to it, to be a serial mass killer to the very end, I had to be able to take down at least three additional people. Not just the Boss of the East Lawn. I needed to murder enough of those around him to complete my mission, my statement, my fuck you to the gun industry and all their gun-loving psychos: Put the Second Amendment Up. Your. Ass.

Sorry, I said I'd largely refrain from polemics. Won't happen again. Just the facts from here on out. My facts, yes, but facts all the same.

II

Part of my conversation with Ivy Tock haunted me all the way to the Bluegrass. It disturbed me still.

After I had tossed Peltry from the limo back in Idaho, out of the blue, Ivy said, in that real friendly center-of-America accent of hers, that she and Garland's health had not been so good of late. The Good Lord is preparing a place for us, she actually had said. She smiled at me knowingly like a wicked stepmother who caught her husband's kid failing a test. Did I know they were seriously ill, she wondered?

I didn't.

Cancer, she said. Dead soon, the both of them. Most expensive doctors available all say so. Treatments had already begun. They were awful. By killing them now I was saving them weeks, maybe months of agony.

A quicker way to your place in heaven? My mocking question. She ignored me, then asked about my heart cancer. Angiosarcoma, isn't it? She smiled in a strained, sad way. Was I feeling any symptoms?

That pissed me off. I told her my health wasn't her concern.

She tut-tutted and said in that warm and false voice that my health had been hers and Garland's utmost concern for a few years. Long before even I knew about it. It was part of the Plan.

All that bullshit pissed me off even more.

I said to her, "'None of that matters because your so-called Plan is an epic failure. Your precious brother is dead. You'll be dead soon. Whatever you want to do to the country will not happen. I'm putting a bullet in your Plan.'"

But her final words frightened me even more.

She sat forward and said, "Dear boy, the mere fact of your being here proves rather the opposite. The Plan is an epic success."

I should have asked her more questions. I should have gotten more information about the Plan. What was its goal? Who was behind it beside the Tocks? How was I involved?

Certainly she aroused my curiosity, but pressing emotions prevailed. My life being in jeopardy the primary motivator. It stoked my anger toward Ivy Tock. Shooting her was nearly anticlimactic; my final act before escape. No more time for Q&A. I had to run for it.

I shot her in the head without feeling an iota of regret.

But the notion that I was a pawn, acting in ways that were congruent with the will of others and not my own, sent shivers across my shoulders. Had I been groomed to be the Second Amendment Killer? How? Had I been assisted behind the scenes throughout my killing spree?

Or was the old woman messing with my head?

That seemed the most likely. She knew she was going to die and, as a person who had ruined others' lives at so many levels in so many places during her lifetime, it probably pleased her to stab one more individual in the psychological back as a parting gift to the world before St. Peter ushered her into her just reward.

On the other hand, I had to consider that she did know about my angiosarcoma. It's possible that the Tocks had contacts in the FBI who might have told her what they had discovered during my encounter with Doctor Reese. I had never sniffed out any collusion between the billionaire twins and the Bureau. My eavesdropping on the FBI's server did not indicate that the agents had fixated on my health, so why would it come to the Tocks' attention? The Tocks themselves appeared in the Bureau's files tangentially and only after Peltry had reported to Agent Youngblood about driving by their mansion with Laskey. I did not see a solid link there. Still, it was possible.

On the other hand, the twins could have hired their own investigators to dig up everything on my background, including my health records; but that too seemed improbable. Certainly they could afford it, but why bother? I had not become a direct threat to them until Neddy's Second Amendment Party when they happened to be there.

Which raises another question: Why were they really at the SAP? Did they know I would be there? Was I their version of suicide by cop: suicide by serial killer?

My mind spun with even more questions as I drove across country.

Did I even have angiocarcinoma? Of course I had Googled my way to practically earning an M.D. in cardiology to see if there was anything I could do more than Dr. Reese had prescribed. Not much, it seems. Don't smoke. Don't drink. Eat right. Exercise. Same regimen given for every ailment known.

Still, just because the disease was real, didn't mean I had it. Did I get a second opinion with new tests? No, because I thought Reese was the second opinion. And neither Reese nor Charcot suggested I see any specialists. Doctors always recommend seeing more specialists, spreading the blame. Why didn't they?

Yet, I failed even to consider getting more medical opinions. Never occurred to me. Sure, I was, to put it mildly, in shock; was not myself. My always lucid mind began disintegrating after two brief conversations with the doctors. Emotions took over. By the time I saw that headline about the mass murder of seventeen people, rational thought vanished completely.

Did that mass shooting even happen? Did I thoroughly check it out? Not really. Was it mere fake news funneled into my online feed? Could the Tocks have arranged to hack Smoking Lauren? That was definitely possible. I never bothered to look. But why? Could they have set up my visit to the doctors? Were Dr. Reese and Dr. Charcot actors in their Plan? Again, possible. But why?

I had skipped my due diligence about everything about my health. I was lazy because I was furious and my sudden fate and of the killing of my daughter all those years ago. My impending death had liberated me and revenge meant more to me than my mere life.

But were those thoughts, that anger, truly mine? Were my actions driven by personal reprisal against those who conspired to kill Jessica or were they somehow part of someone else's scheme?

The further east I drove the more disturbing my thoughts became. Was anything that day back in Salem when I was pronounced among the Walking Dead real? Memories are both clear and vague from one moment to the next. I was unmoored, in a fog, a basketcase. Not thinking clearly. Shame, too, because I had made some pretty consequential choices back then without a complete, validated data set. Things that can never be undone. That was so unlike me. If I knew at the beginning what I know now, would I have acted the same?

You might think these questions, these doubts might have put a stop or at least a pause to my mission. You'd be wrong.

III

The reason for settling into Lexington was its proximity to every venue the Boss would need to hold one of his famous raucous reactionary rallies. Hand-wringing liberals compared his gatherings to mid-20th century authoritarians. Not so. His were less like the Nazi party's stadium events in Nuremberg or Mussolini's operatic balcony scenes, and more like the Russian Roulette crowd scene in the *Deer Hunter* movie. The Boss eschewed the goose-stepping discipline of other fascist get-togethers, but he fanned the mob's same unrequited bloodlust. It was his comfort zone.

The Boss required a stage, one where an audience undaunted by the continuing pandemic, could be assembled on short notice. That meant, for certain, he'd show up somewhere within one hundred miles of Fayette County at least once before the next election. There were only a certain number of places in the country where the campaign could generate big enough audiences and cram them inside a medium-size auditorium to please the Boss. They loved him in the Bluegrass. And while he didn't love them, he loved that they loved him, so he would show up to let them kiss his feet.

With the information I had, which included the campaign's own internal polling data, my analytic software ran hundreds of scenarios about where he could still put butts in seats. It settled on Rupp Arena as the most likely place for the Boss to hold one of his superspreader spectacles. Even if he couldn't fill the entire place, its well-designed Theater Seating mode could make the place look positively packed, while taking up as little as one third of the arena, satisfying the old man's precious ego.

"I have the biggest crowds ever. Ever. No one comes close. No one. I'm the biggest," he told the press regularly.

The one negative for Rupp was that it cost more than other regional arenas. And no matter how many times he was told otherwise, the Boss thought of campaign dollars as part of his personal fortune. Woe betide staffers who dipped too deeply into what he thought of as his own pockets.

Still, it was my analytics program's leading candidate for a venue, so I had leased a cheap shotgun one-bedroom apartment in an old bungalow on Cramer Avenue, one of the less thriving parts of Lexington. Nonetheless, the neighborhood had excellent internet access and was only a couple miles from the arena. A local bank owned the property and was glad to rent half the place to me without much ado after I had opened a checking account with $3,200 in cash. Small bills.

Blake Crossler vanished when I reached my new Kentucky home. My equally new self, Drew Barton, was as a process control engineer, now a consultant assigned to Toyota's sprawling Georgetown manufacturing plant just north of Lexington. Drew looked different from the Most Wanted image broadcast coast-to-coast from my Idaho escapade. I added a pair of glasses, a new haircut, and, most dramatically, a bright pink birthmark splotch that ran up my neck to my cheekbone and ear. Anyone I met could not help themselves. They stared at it. Not my face. It made me almost invisible.

I chose names like Blake and Drew instead of, say, Bob or Emmet, because they shifted easily between genders, adding another thin layer of obscurity between me and anyone looking my way. Again, I stole no one's identity. The slightly nerdy citizen I became was built by me from whole cloth, perfect down to my concocted three generations of Barton family history on ancestry.com and the Colorado Real ID in my wallet. Part of my digital back story included a recent divorce that left me with only a little cash, a beat-up Sonic I bought from Blake Crossler, but a full-time fake job far away from my fictional ex. I had bogus online pay stubs to prove my employment, another plus for the bank. Drew Barton quickly and easily opened accounts with Kentucky Utilities, Spectrum Cable TV, and State Farm Insurance. He got a library card and even received a Visa account through Cumberland Valley Bank. I had slipped into the community unnoticed by being everywhere.

My Kentucky neighbors had the same friendly Southern charm as my old Texas ones, with soothing accents to match. We shared a wall and easy banter on the narrow porch facing a tree-lined street on warm muggy evenings. They told me their abbreviated life stories. I told them my current lies. We got along great.

I immediately settled into a non-routine. The Covid revival meant few professionals, like I was supposed to be, had set schedules. It gave me cover to disappear for long stretches while I visited likely venues, including nearby Rupp; also my job let me stay in my apartment for days on end, designing my last kill down to the final detail. If people asked, I talked them senseless with descriptions of virtualizing workflow to maximize process fungibility. No one ever asked twice.

In planning to shoot the Boss I used an array of standard business process techniques, including the balanced scorecard method. I had used it as a strategic planning tool for every one of my mass murders. Just as I had done for every project I worked on for my old company, I had objectives, measures, initiatives, and action items listed for each and every bloody event. In addition, I ran a SWOT analysis on the strengths, weaknesses, opportunities, and threats to my plan to assassinate the Boss, as I had with my other attacks. I gamed information-rich, data-centric scenarios. I left no digital stone unturned in planning my tasks, especially regarding the Boss. That included pilfering his campaign's emails like a savvy Russian would.

The Boss's campaign IT folks used a later, stripped down and free open source version of my old company's software. They only added a few other open-source add-on security modules to protect their computers. None of the software they used was kept up to date by the campaign's thin IT staff. It wasn't hard to slip inside the network and vacuum up all internal, private communications. There were many messages about upcoming events. Rupp was always mentioned as a possible location for a big get-out-the-vote public extravaganza.

The campaign managers liked the place because the Boss knew sports and would appreciate that he had played to a packed audience in the home of the storied University of Kentucky Wildcats, who'd won eight NCAA basketball championships in Lexington. They'd tell him seating capacity was more than

23,000, even though Theater mode would chop that number enormously, he could spout that number and be more accurate than usual. They could sell him on that. Other auditoriums in Cincinnati, Ohio, Florence, Frankfort, and Louisville, Kentucky were under consideration, primarily because they were cheaper. But only Rupp had the bragging rights the Boss craved.

In the end, just as the analytics predicted, the campaign chose Rupp. By then, I had a plan for the kill, one no less of a long shot, as it were, than any of my other shootings. Longer, actually. All of my killings so far had been short range. This would be quite a bit longer, but I'd have a better angle. I was confident I'd hit the targets, but my position would be unmistakeable and and exit not feasible. After I fired, an abundance of force would rain down on me.

Needless to say, dying was not my first choice, but in this case it appeared to be my only one. As a 47 year old man, I hadn't lived a complete life, but I've been around long enough to understand that living without purpose, simply going to work and going home, was no life at all.

For months I had been motivated in my mission to kill, in part, by my belief that my time was up. I had nothing to lose after seeing Reese and Charcot back in Salem. Now, I wasn't so sure. Maybe my cancer diagnosis was an elaborate hoax and I was healthy as an ox. But if I'm not actually dying of cancer, do I really need to complete my task and shoot the Boss? Could I not forget him, sit on my laurels as a successful serial mass murderer and disappear into my Drew Barton character, or someone else I could invent? It was tempting to think that way.

With the Boss gone, though, I didn't care if I had became another victim of gun violence. I would have made an elegant and incisive statement about the menace of unfettered gun access. Nothing made society less safe than guns. Nothing. Any fanatic, even me, can grab a gun to further any cause, though seldom with as much irony as mine.

IV

HIPPA rules notwithstanding, even if you're not the FBI, it's simple for a resourceful individual with certain skills to infiltrate medical records. Most doctors, clinics, and hospitals can't afford state of the art security. They do their best but it's not enough to stop a dedicated hacker like me who slips in through their ever-present databases. Let me toot my own horn, for a moment: if I can infiltrate an FBI server that's off the grid, I can snoop through any doctor's case files.

It took seven hours to retrieve all of the Tocks' medical records, going back to their childhood. I like to be complete in my research.

She was right. Both had late stage, terminal pancreatic cancer. They'd seen a half dozen specialists from the four corners of the world. No miracle awaited, not even for them. They were doomed like the rest of us. Twins, dying of the same thing at the same time, had it been known, would be considered a public tragedy, a heartbreaking story for the Evening News, even or maybe especially because they were so fabulously wealthy. *Schadenfreude* makes for an attentive audience.

That Ivy Tock told me the truth gave her a modicum of credibility. It spurred me to look further. Quick enough, I discovered that doctors Reese and Charcot did not exist. At least, not now. Had I gone to the trouble of checking their bonafides last year, they, too, would have had back stories like my Drew Barton. But there was nothing on them since then. They had a recent past but no present. They'd disappeared. Fakes, just like me.

Worse, I suppose, was when I learned that in the 1930s a hypnotist named Javier Charcot ran an interrogation unit for France's secretive security agency, the *Direction de la surveillance du territoire*. The DST, shuttered by the French government in 2008, used every trick in the book to debrief suspects and prisoners. Hypnosis was high on the list of its methods ever since Jean-Martin Charcot, Javier's great grandfather, introduced post-hypnotic suggestion to French security forces in the 1880s for use with high-value suspects. According to a few reports, the French and other governments currently outsource hypnotic interrogations to "third-party professionals."

My Doctor Javier Charcot either had engaged in a private joke or had laid bait for me to find. Either way, it did not bode well.

Then there was the little I found out about Reese. I managed to track down a still image from an ambulance bay's security video. It was taken in the parking lot outside the Salem Hospital's emergency department an hour after we had met. She appeared walking across a small bridge that led toward the hospital. I traced her image through a face-recognition system Amazon had offered law enforcement agencies. I found three other solid matches.

The first was at PDX the same day we'd met. Reese's image was captured in the boarding area of Concourse E. The next hit came from a security camera archive at the city centre Vancouver Hilton. She arrived the same week the hotel was hosting the annual International Guild of Hypnotists convention. The third facial link to Reese was from a doorbell camera at the *Hypnoanalsye Praxis* in Berlin a week later. I was not able to link a name to her face, but I doubted Reese was it.

All that information was enough for me to consider the possibility of a plot of some kind, a Plan, as it were. But the final straw of evidence had been in my possession long before I had fired my first shot.

When designing my personal revenge against Laskey, I had copied his entire computer's hard drive onto one of the virtual servers I rent through a bogus account in Belize on Microsoft's Azure cloud service. I had checked the drive out reasonably thoroughly at the time, but failed to look at every single person he had listed in one of his directories called Major Donors. It included a few thousand entries, most had given around one hundred dollars. I wrote a SQL script to scan each directory linked to every name. It looked at every directory's files to detect patterns in the data, ones I hoped would help me reach my targets more efficiently.

But I had failed to code the script to find anomalous files in each donors directory. It looked at the data inside the files, not the types of files they were. That's why I missed Theo Nalp. His directory lacked any of the usual donor text information, name, address, email, and the rest. Instead there was audio file. Stupid me. Had I written my query of the data differently I would have learned that Theo Nalp was Laskey's lame, but effective codeword for the Plan. Again, stupid me.

The Nalp directory contained a single encrypted audio file, nalp_1.M4A. With Laskey's login credentials and passwords at my fingertips I was able to listen to it. The file was dated months before my vendetta began. Even without context, what I heard amazed and appalled me.

Laskey was in discussion with Ivy and Garland Tock. Presumably they were in a room because of the lack of background noise other than a trio of adults in conversation. There was only the occasional shuffling noise as if the recording device was being moved. They greeted each other like old friends.

> Laskey: …can't remember how long it's been since, what, Aspen? Hotel Jerome?

> Ivy: We always stay at the St. Regis.

> Laskey: That's where it was then.

> Garland: But now….

> Laskey: Always a pleasure to be with you both.

> Garland: Thanks. Us, too. Only serious business today, Wayne. Serious as a heart attack.

> Laskey: Understoo…understood, sir.

> Garland: Time to think about the Plan, Wayne.

Ivy: Time to execute the Plan. The one we discussed in Aspen.

Laskey: Yes. Yes.

Garland: Set it in motion. Get it going. That's what we need to do now. We have the perfect choice. Ready. Skilled. We just need your okay. It's such a huge sacrifice on your part. But once we go, we go; there's no going back.

Laskey: Yes. I'm still in. Don't worry about that. I'm, well, ready for the Plan. It...it's long-term purpose is more important than whatever short-term pain I suffer. The people I offer up, well, it's personal as you know.

His voice sounded raw, heavy with sorrow. The recording fell silent for a quite a few seconds. I imagined that they were all sitting and nodding sadly at one another, until I heard the ARI's CEO speak again.

Laskey: I want both those bitches dead. Dead. I built a world for them with every possible luxury and advantage. And they want to tear it all down and tear me down with it. Dead, I say. But losing Nick, that's harsh. He's practically a friend, a buddy. We go hunting together. I met his wife. Twice. Plus, good security men are hard to come by, hard to keep. Eight years, been with me eight years. You're sure he's to be included?

Ivy: Sad to say, Wayne, he is. It would raise unnecessary suspicion if he lived.

Laskey: Okay. I get it. But you're certain this will work? You're sure he's going to be under control?

Garland: Not really control, Wayne, you know that. But his direction will be specific. He's to exact revenge on you. Killing you makes no sense under that precondition in his mind. He needs you to suffer the way he did. Exactly the way he did. Your life is not in danger. Your child and her mother are the key targets. They replicate his personal loss. The same loss he intends to inflict on you. Everyone else is collateral damage. They add up to the mass murder his subconscious demands.

Laskey: What about my granddaughter?

Ivy: Of that, we're not completely sure. But his direction is to let her live. In the heat of the moment, though, it's not a hundred percent certainty that he will.

Garland: Is that a deal breaker, Wayne? Because, if it is, we'll understand completely. Family is important.

Laskey: No. No. She's a good kid and doesn't, well....

Ivy: We understand.

Laskey: But after he goes after my family, assuming he gets it right, you really think he's going to go after the President next? Right away? You can really implant a two-fer murder in his head?

Garland: Two-fer. That's good. That's funny.

Ivy: Amusing, yes. But to your question, Wayne, yes we can bury that suggestion in his mind, especially if he follows through with his first direction. It'll mean we are successful. It'll mean he is ours for the duration.

Laskey: Duration?

Garland: Until he's killed, of course.

Laskey: And that's a certainty?

Ivy: Like the sunrise, Wayne. Like the sunrise.

The recording stopped. At this point, I'm supposed to think, to say, to believe that I'd been had, scammed, punked, deceived, led down a blood-stained primrose path. I should cry to the skies that I am not guilty of my deeds because I am the Manchurian Candidate of mass serial killers. I have been hypnotized, stripped of my free will, sent, if you will on a mission not of my own doing. I have been turned into a tool, an unwitting stooge, no longer a free person. I'd been hacked, damn it.

Except.

Except I don't care about whether my will, free or otherwise, drove my actions. My actions feel good, right down to the core of my being. I am proud of what I did. My killings speak volumes about the cynical respectability of the purveyors of death I had killed. When I take the time to think about it, whether my core self drove my actions, or whether I was ridden like a tamed animal into a prearranged corral of murder. I didn't care. Plain and simple, I didn't give a shit. What I had wrought so far has been worth every bullet; especially the ones I was yet to fire at the Boss. Whether what I had done is all part of the Plan or not didn't matter. I feel in control. I feel free. That's enough to keep me going.

That said, the Plan, whatever it is, is greater than me. I'm a part of it, certainly. Maybe even a big part. I don't know. The important point is that the Plan is more than me. That's obvious. Killing me is part of the Plan, the Tocks said so. I accept that. But who will take the blame? The media will have to find somebody to point their collective fingers at. Me.

Speaking of the media, they have hyped themselves into a frenzy about me, the Second Amendment Killer. I'm the closest thing to the American bogeyman since Communists in the government or black men dating your white daughter. Those who write the first draft of history are not always to be trusted.

You'll note that I wrote my side of the story so far without dwelling on what the media and others were saying about me in public. There was good reason. From what I had read and watched, they knew next to nothing, but reported that ignorance endlessly.

Chapter Eighteen
Our One Saving Grace

```
Celeste Youngblood
```

H ave you seen this?" was the subject line on a message that came up simultaneously on her laptop, phone, tablet, and watch. It was a team-wide question from the AD, but after she started reading, Youngblood could not help but feel that the AD's query was directed at her alone.

The "this" was an alleged memoir written by Jefferson Fitzgerald Black and posted on the internal server from a new user account, Killer_JFB@bureauSecServ.X21.1R. It had appeared in every agent's in-box connected to the offline system as if it had been sent from inside the FBI's secure server room. The memo JFB attached to his statement even mimicked the FBI's format. It was as if the man was mocking the Bureau's competence.

Global responses from agents on the group's message app ran the gamut from indignation and disbelief to curiosity and suspicion.

"Is this a sick joke?"

"Not fucking possible."

"Who posted this? Is this a prank?"

"Who got hacked?"

"IT better get on this!"

"IT better explain itself!"

Soon enough, IT did. Analysts from the Information Technology department discovered quickly that the text file had been inserted from the outside. They traced the path through system log files to the electrical system. The Uninterruptible Power

Source used to protect the building from electrical surges let JFB burrow his way bit by bit into the server. To report on its usage and performance metrics, the UPS used a recent version of database tools from JFB's former company. He was able to get access to the system's process logs and slowly insert data into the server. It was arduous, the IT gurus reckoned, not real-time, but effective. Almost admiringly, the Bureau's data experts reported that JFB could monitor messages and mail on the server using a spider program that read text-only files stored on the computer and fed the results back through the electrical grid; no internet, no Ethernet, no any net required. Just juice. Along the way, JFB was able to plant his memoir into the system and schedule it to appear at a precise moment in every agent's message queue. He'd been inside and watching them for almost the entire investigation, the IT experts said.

Youngblood raced to the end of JFB's memoir. She had immediately scrolled to the end of his story, a chapter the killer called "The Plan Is An Epic Success." A good friend of hers had once remarked that she always read the last chapter of a book first. "That way, if I don't like how a story ends, I don't have to waste my time reading the rest of it," her friend had said. She thought that was good advice now.

Youngblood plowed through JFB's self-serving prose. She picked up immediately on his confidence bordering on arrogance. Like so many serial killers, his murders became just and righteous in his twisted mind. He was not a monster, merely misunderstood. But for her the writing served as his confession as easily as his manifesto.

But the memoir might not have been so disturbing to Youngblood without the warning JFB slipped in at the very end. It threw her. Again, she considered the words directed at her personally.

> *You'll note that I wrote my side of the story so far*
> *without dwelling on what the media and others were*
> *saying about me in public at the time. There was good*
> *reason. From what I had read and watched, I knew they*

knew next to nothing, but reported that ignorance endlessly.

To be frank, I paid little attention to all that noise. Even though what I had done was big news, I did not keep some secret scrapbook of my greatest hits, as it were. I never made a point to follow the coverage of my murders. I did not subscribe to the handful of podcasts that delved into the killings or watched the overwrought drama of the evening news sensationalizing me and what I had done. Even when big name journalists tut-tutted my exploits on 48 Hours *or* 60 Minutes, *I didn't care.*

Nor, however, did I try to avoid anything. It was impossible to miss it once my work in Idaho hit the internet and airwaves. Stories of me as a ruthless killer driven by insane revenge dominated lead stories on the left and the right, with the right carrying the day as always. If you believed most conservative accounts of my crashing of the Second Amendment Party, anyone in America owning a gun was at genuine risk.

Weeks afterward, while sitting with my Kentucky neighbors on the porch, the Second Amendment Killer seeped into most conversations. I was always called the Second Amendment Killer because that's what news organizations, especially the pervasive right-wing media labeled me. My neighbors said the SAK was either part of a "liberal sickness" or part of a "liberal conspiracy," depending on which earworm commentator they'd heard that morning. Naturally, I agreed with the assessment de jure *and chastised the SAK with equal fervor.*

What's ironic, of course, is that a real conspiracy exists backed by the hard right, the same people who fund the media feeding the SAK's liberal bogeyman stories. The Plan is real. As I've acknowledged above, I accept my role in it. But I want to prove that these killings go beyond me. I am not the alpha and omega of this plot. I am the instrument by which the far right gains more power, more authority over our daily lives. Admittedly, with the Tocks and Laskey dead, my hard evidence about the conspiracy consists of Laskey's audio file and, well, me; neither would hold up well in court, I suspect.

Still, now that the Plan had been presented to the FBI as essential background to my actions, it must act. It must investigate. That's why I've made this document available to the entire task force looking for me. I've stored Laskey's audio file with the Killer_JFB@bureauSecServ.X21.1R account. Yeah, sure, I might be crazy. But what I have written and what you'll hear needs a thorough vetting, something only the FBI can do. If that doesn't happen, well, we all know what that means. A white washed final report and a fall guy or two on your end to seal the deal.

Remember in the movie The Maltese Falcon *when Sam Spade convinces Guttman to make his "son" Wilmer the fall guy for the murders? Bogart's character calls his fall guy "a victim," one that the police and media will believe to be guilty. When Sidney Greenstreet's character mildly objects, wondering what would happen if Wilmer told the authorities everything he knows, undermining Sam Spade's plan. The Bogart character simply says he'll "guarantee" no one would believe Wilmer because the story of the fall guy is so believable. Anything else has to be fake. That'll be the case here. There's gonna be a fall guy in your ranks and no one will believe a word he says. After me, the fall guy will be the next victim.*

That idea stunned Youngblood because it made complete sense. She stared up at the overhead fluorescent light panel transfixed in her own thoughts. Then she scrolled back to the top of the final section to re-read it. In the midst of her review the file froze, then closed. She flayed at the keyboard to bring the file back, but it failed to materialize.

She heard a few "what-the-fucks" from agents in nearby cubicles when a system-wide alert appeared to everyone reading JFB's memoir. It warned that the document was now under Eyes-Only, Q-Level security access. Any discussion of whatever had been read by agents without such clearance, the lawyerly boilerplate cautioned, was punishable to the fullest extent of U.S. espionage laws.

Almost all the agents who had been reading the document lacked those lofty security credentials. Now, they couldn't even legally discuss it, let alone read the complete document. That, however, did not stop instant intra-office *sotto voce* chatter about the memoir as people wandered around the office floor. From what she gleaned, everyone had read the document starting from the top. It was the natural thing to do. Youngblood was the only one who had started at the end.

About fifteen minutes after JFB's document went offline, a cascade of angry and shocked yelling rolled through the floor. Frantic internal communications from the President's Secret Service detail piped through her array of devices. Anxious voices shouted incoherently across voice, video, and data links. Streaming national news feeds opened on her computer screen. The worst possible scenario was unfolding.

Chaos inside an auditorium came through loud and clear from every possible angle. Spectators running for the exits; people diving to the ground for cover; others standing hesitantly, dumbstruck. Most of crowd was crying out loud in anguish and fear. Agents' shouts on her floor blended into the noise broadcast over everyone's computer speakers streaming throughout the building. At the bottom of the video, in the chyron, the venue, "Rupp Arena, Lexington, Kentucky," crawled by from right to left steadily every ten seconds.

Despairing words punctured through the noise.

"Shots fired! Shots fired!"

"Soaring Eagle is down! Repeat. Soaring Eagle is down!"

"Red Patriot has been hit!"

Youngblood knew JFB had struck.

Minutes later fifty-plus agents packed into the nearest large conference suite on the third floor. Over a hyper-secure video link projected on large screen, the Director shouted at them for ten minutes, spitting out marching orders to the room to get to Kentucky and "find every fucking fact known to man" about what happened.

What they knew now was simple. Both Soaring Eagle, the President's self-chosen call name for the Secret Service and other agencies tasked to protect him, and Red Patriot, the Vice President's code name, had been shot and rushed to the University of Kentucky Medical Center. The shooter had been neutralized. Presumably dead. Presumably JFB.

When the Director had finished screaming, the agents poured from the dense conference room. Most took a pause by their work areas, but everyone was quickly downstairs and piling into SUVs and small busses heading to the airport.

After a brief flash of her ID, Youngblood joined four other agents plus a driver in a GMC Tahoe. The driver checked her off a list on his iPad. Before the final passenger could fill the last open seat, an identical SUV its flashers blazing pulled next to hers, blocking oncoming traffic. The driver's side window slid down. A young, blond square-headed man stuck his head out the window, nearly protruding into her car.

"Agent Youngblood," he snapped at the driver.

The driver thumbed toward the rear of the SUV.

The young fellow turned his perfectly tanned face in her direction.

"Director wants you in his office now."

The driver lifted his curious eyes to the rear view mirror. She ignored them, got out, and entered the blond's vehicle. Sitting in the second row were two AD's who had tag-teamed leadership of the hunt for JFB after she was forced out back in Idaho. She squeezed by them and sat in the Tahoe's third row. No one spoke during the drive from the building leased for the investigation to FBI headquarters. The young agent pulled up to an E Street NW secure entrance. The three passengers filed out, each keying themselves into the building through the discrete door and passing through an armed security detail inside double-checking their IDs.

They were met by a woman who ushered them to the Director's private elevator. She typed a code into the control panel and up they went. Again, no one spoke. Once the doors opened, the silence gave way to dozens of voices talking, phones ringing, and general office chaos. The woman led the trio beyond the old, polished wooden desks between low cubicle separators to a door labeled "Otis LeBlair, Director." She opened it, and gestured for everyone to enter. Once she shut the door behind them the noise vanished.

Inside, while large, the office was not massive. It didn't even have a decent view. She could see through the windows it wasn't even on the top floor. No matter high up you were on the government food chain, the General Services Administration has strict rules limiting the luxury afforded its most powerful people.

Still, there was ample room for the eight other senior agents who had already gathered in front of LeBlair. The Director had his back turned, facing an array of photos taken from his long career, many with the Vice President, his career mentor, many signed with warm words. His head was cocked, holding a handset against his ear on his shoulder listening to someone over a secure landline. The waiting agents stood at the top of the Bureau's org chart, far, far above her little perch. She was way out of her league in this room. That couldn't be good.

On one of the room's walls a large video monitor had a split screen feed with both Agent Malone Wicks and Assistant Director Richard Lakes. It was clear she was called to the meeting because of her role in the JFB investigation. She had expected such a reckoning eventually, though not such a public one, not so soon. Were she, Wicks, and Lakes about to become the fall guys in the aftermath as JFB predicted? Or maybe only her? But, if so, wouldn't the ADs she rode with also be potential fall guys? And what about the Director himself, after Idaho hadn't he boasted live on a popular podcast that he was "directly finding the Second Amendment killer dead or alive"?

Outer noise suddenly filled the room. One more agent was rushed into the room. He took a position beside Youngblood. She recognized him as the head of the Bureau's defensive and offensive cyber operations, way up the FBI's hierarchy. The door closed and the room fell silent again.

"Goodbye," LeBlair whispered into the phone. He put the handset back into its cradle as he swiveled his chair to face the group.

"The President survived the attack. He hit the deck with the first shot. Cut his hand during the fall. But he will be fine. However, the Vice President is dead. Two headshots from a medium caliber, long-range rifle recovered at the scene. Ballistics will report soon. The shooter, tentatively identified as Jefferson Fitzgerald Black, was neutralized at the scene. No other victims." He ran the palm of his hand down his face. He continued. "We have mainstream and social media video of the assassination as well as bodycam of the neutralizing of JFB. Just as his so-called memoir has been classified, the latter video has been designated Q-level, Eyes Only. As for the former, well, it's out there. Initial field DNA testing confirms the suspected shooter from the slaughter in Idaho matches the shooter in Rupp Arena. More detailed analysis is likely to confirm."

LeBlair went silent for a few beats, then another a rub of his face with his hand before saying, "The President has survived and the Second Amendment Killer has been eradicated. That, gentlemen and ladies, is our one saving grace. In every other way, this is just shit."

No one spoke, waiting for LeBlair. He grieved for a full five seconds the Vice President, a fellow earnest evangelical, long-time friend, and his golf buddy. The Veep was also the primary reason he got his job. So the Director paused before speaking again in his natural rapid fire fashion with ever-increasing volume.

"We may not have been able to stop the diabolical Second Amendment Killer, who could?, but we will strip bare everything about him that led to his attack on America," LeBlair said, raising his voice as he spoke. "What do we know? How do we know it? When did we know it? Does anyone else know it? Who needs to know what we know? Who needs to never know what we know after we know it? I want reports coming in by the minute, people. By the minute!"

The Director rattled off his questions as if he were a football coach chewing out a crappy defense during halftime. His preferred communications style was loud. He liked to ask questions instead of giving answers. He excelled in large gatherings and press gaggles, where being big and bossy worked. His style made him look like a dynamic leader. But LeBlair's high-volume rants turned even the smallest of meetings into grudge matches. Yelling back at the man was not an option. She expected to get the first degree. Everyone in the meeting did. She was not surprised when he started.

"Youngblood!"

She stepped forward.

"Sir."

"You've been dogging this guy the longest of anyone here?"

"Yes, sir, along with AD Lakes." She nodded toward the monitor.

"Yes, Agent Youngblood, but, as AD, he had other duties. The Second Amendment Killer was your sole task from the beginning, was it not?"

LeBlair stared at her with calculating bloodshot blue eyes.

"Yes, sir."

"Good, " the Director said, his beige smile raising wobbly furrows from his cheeks to his forehead. "I'm glad we agree. What, then, do you, our most knowledgeable agent on the subject, take away from his alleged memoir left on your team's supposedly secure server?"

JFB's words began echoing in her head: *The fall guy will be the next victim.*

"Sir, I was not able to complete my reading of the document because my security rating is not Q Level. If I were given a temporary clearance, I could…"

He cut her off.

"Not going to happen," he said with finality. "So, from what you've read so far, give us your thoughts on the SAK's document."

"Is there any area in the document that I should be sensitive to, Director?"

"Well, it should be obvious. With the Second Amendment Killer neutralized, the most important part of the FBI's investigation will be whether the shooter shot dead in Kentucky is part of a broader conspiracy. Is there a wider plot going on here? Was he, indeed, the only shooter during the killing spree? In short, Agent Youngblood, the most obvious question facing us here is, is anyone else involved?"

"It's premature for me…"

"Best guess, Agent Youngblood. Not asking for wisdom coming down from the mountain top."

"Well…"

"Yes?"

"No, sir. I know of no evidence leading to anyone other than Jefferson Fitzgerald Black as the shooter behind the events in Maryland, Texas, and Idaho as well as, as you say, Kentucky."

"Are you saying Black is the sole suspect as the killer in all of the crimes under investigation? That there are no other suspects?"

"At this time, yes, sir."

"Yet, the SAK in his document quotes the FBI as knowing about something he calls the Plan. The FBI, as you know, learned about the so-called Plan from you, according to your reports, and you learned from a man named Syd Peltry, who had links to the Tocks, Laskey, and was present in Idaho and, he alleges, was kidnapped by the SAK while there. Is that about right, Agent Youngblood."

"Your facts are correct, sir."

"So, everything we know about this Plan conspiracy comes from a deaf security officer who reads lips."

"And the recordings, sir. He provided recordings from two different iPhones, which we have in our possession."

"And what do these recordings amount to in a courtroom?"

"Not much, sir. Hearsay. No serious prosecutor would use it as primary evidence."

"Then what's it worth?"

"It's a launching point for investigators, sir."

The Director's face, always a shade of pink, flushed.

"By God, Agent Youngblood, are you as crazy as the SAK? Pursue an investigation of some of the most respected people in America, victims of the SAK themselves? That's the conspiracy?"

She remained calm, keeping her voice low but firm.

"Sir, as I said, since I have been involved in the investigation there has only been one shooter. He has...had no other known associates. In every way that we can know things now, sir, JFB acted alone."

"Good. Because the way we know things now, Agent Youngblood, is the way we will always know them or until you're told otherwise. Understood?"

"Yes, sir," she answered with a slight hesitation.

"Good. Now get out," he turned to the monitor and yelled for Agent Wicks's attention as she exited.

The female aide who had greeted them upon her arrival was waiting outside the Director's office. Wordlessly she beckoned her to follow and led her to the private elevator. She reached inside and punched a code into the display.

"This will take you to the ground floor. A car will take you back to your building," she said before the doors closed.

Stunned by her scolding and dismissal by LeBlair, she met the same block-headed blond young agent outside on the E Street NW sidewalk. He drove her back to the leased building and escorted her to the elevators. After she was in one and the doors were closing he gave her a mock salute and walked away.

When the doors silently opened and she automatically walked to her cubicle. The floor was unusually quiet with most agents scattered to the winds in search of whatever crumbs JFB left behind. She could hear a couple of printers spitting out reports nearby and someone was talking on the phone across the room. She passed two admins hunched over their terminals before arriving at her desk.

She found Grace waiting for her. The woman who had put her on notice inside a black SUV in Idaho, the one who had warned her what the consequences would be when they next met. The end of her FBI career was sitting in her chair. On her lap was Youngblood's travel bag.

"Once you turn in your badge and weapon, Agent Youngblood, we have some paperwork for you to complete."

Two brawny agents appeared from nowhere and braced her from behind.

Grace rose and pointed to the chair.

"Please sit and sign the papers before you."

"Your goons don't scare me. What if I sue for wrongful dismissal?"

Grace smiled her humorless white teeth.

"Gentlemen," she said evenly.

The agents backed away well out of earshot. Grace spoke in a low, menacing voice.

"Dismissal? Heavens no, Ms. Youngblood. Administrative leave, for now. Same pay. Same health insurance. Even your dental plan is intact. Only you can't leave D.C. for now. You stay home as if we were all in a stage four Covid lockdown. We expect you will become a popular person to testify on Zoom and in-person here and there and everywhere in the coming months. No, you remain on the payroll, until further notice," Grace said, lowering her voice into an even more sinister register. "Your life is in the balance, Ms. Youngblood. Any minor misstep and you will spend it locked on the wrong side of the American judicial system, the defendant. No place worse to be, especially when the full weight of the federal government is pressing down against you."

"But I've done nothing wrong!"

"You say. But we know different, don't we? We know, Agent Youngblood, that only you have read the end of the SAK's confession. No other agent was clever enough to skip to the end. We tracked where each agent had reached in the document. You alone read the last chapter first. Why's that? What did you already know to do such a thing? Plus, you alone, among all the agents on this floor, violated the Patriot Act by reading and stealing Q-Level documentation."

"I did no such thing."

"Oh, yes you did. We found the SAK's so-called memoir in its entirety on your laptop. We found the file there."

"I did not put it there."

"Nonetheless, we found it," Grace said with a shrug, her threatening smile never wavering. "Certainly in your lawsuit you might contend that all agents had access to the SAK's document, but given that you went right to the juicy bits before anyone else, possibly it tells me you might have even known what was there. And our geeks in IT tell me that your keystrokes after the document was frozen actually downloaded it to your system. Very clever, Ms. Youngblood. Or so a jury might be inclined to believe."

The women glared at one another.

Grace said, "If we had to, there's nothing we would not do to bury you, Ms. Youngblood. Remember that. So, I suggest you sign these exit papers. Accept administrative leave. Testify when and where told. Stick close to home. Heed what the Director told you. Don't waver. The best way to do that, of course, is don't talk to anyone about anything unless you're asked to. Stay at home until we tell you can leave. This will pass. These things always do. When it does, get a job somewhere far away. Don't look back. Look ahead. It's your only realistic option."

Youngblood sat. She read the words on the papers. The Bureau's lawyers managed to make them not just deliberately vague but

transparently threatening. Defeated, she signed. The hunt for
JFB had ended along with her FBI career.

Epilogue
Our One Saving Grace

```
Syd Peltry
```

She stopped the packed-to-the-rafters U-Haul cargo van across the road from Miss Jackie's. The barbecue restaurant sat back from 23rd Street, well beyond the buckling sidewalk, on Oklahoma City's east side. She seemed to be debating getting out of the air-conditioned van and into the scorching summer day.

He watched her through the array of Montavue 4K video cameras that blended into the recesses of Miss Jackie's awnings and eaves. He flicked between wide-angle and close-up views up and down the block. He had designed the security system himself; an off-the-books project for a life-long friend. He sat alone in the basement, watching a bank of monitors and a pair of iPad Pros on adjustable stands.

She finally made her decision and paused the audio book on her iPhone's speaker. *The Signature of All Things* had kept her company often on the drive out west. She'd been on the road that day since leaving Memphis at 5:00 a.m. and was undoubtedly ready for lunch. She'd only stopped once to gas up, pee, and eat junk food from a service station counter outside Ft. Smith, Arkansas.

Syd Peltry knew all this because he had been spying on Youngblood since she'd bagged the East Coast and departed in the van. During the ride she wrapped herself in Elizabeth Gilbert's long novel, which was nearing the end, he knew, having read the book himself years earlier. She never said a word aloud, never turned on the panel van's crappy radio, and never spoke to a single soul while behind the wheel. It was either Gilbert or silence. The FBI had heard the same thing.

His bug was not as comprehensive as the FBI's technology, which was also tracking her every move. But it was good enough. He could feed the audio output into off-the-shelf voice meter software, so he could see when the story was playing. He filtered the input of the voicemeter to capture spoken words and then run them through a speech-to-text application. That's how he knew she was listening to *The Signature of All Things*.

He had built the bug himself, integrating a GPS unit with the radio transmitter into an old Air Pod case, leaving out the earbuds, believing if anyone found it, they'd assume someone lost it while wearing the buds. The RF signals were carried over Verizon's 5G network. His bug even had its own phone number. His friends who had placed the tracker in Youngblood's rental back in D.C. made sure it was not near the FBI's surveillance units also hidden on board.

It was good news to Peltry when she'd arrived in OKC. It meant two things. First, she had understood his message and, second, was interested enough to risk coming to see him.

She had been under the watchful eyes of Otis LeBlair's minions long before she had been put on administrative leave. As had he. He assumed the FBI watched Youngblood to see if she contacted the press independently or sought out other people involved with the investigation, especially him. But she never tried to reach him, nor him her.

With one exception: more than a year ago, soon after she was put on administrative leave, Peltry had staged an elaborate pantomime to communicate with her, a one-way message that would let him know when she was on her way to see him, if she ever would be. He had called a childhood friend, Richard, who, like him, had parents without health insurance and too poor to pay for the atresia surgery to correct his aural birth defect when they were young. Such an operation would have fixed their deafness, but fate put them in a different strata at birth with all its misfortune. Unlike Peltry, his friend's speech was more than slightly slurred and difficult to understand. It was hard for him to get or keep a regular job. He got by with disability payments and occasional surveillance and courier work friends threw his way.

This time Peltry asked Richard to play a false version of himself, a deaf mute, handing out little sign-language cards, and asking for "donations." His friend worked Youngblood's neighborhood for a couple of weeks, even accosting a pair of agents watching her flat, before hitting on her. Richard later approached her the same as everyone else, only this time the sign-language index card he thrust at her had "Syd Peltry says thanks for the new phone. Turn over." On the front. Simple instructions were typed on the backside: "Mr. Black left me a special app on it. You should see it. When you move, rent from the 17th St. NW U-Haul. Miss Jackie's in OKC. Lunch. Anytime. Return the card to my friend." He trusted her excellent memory to hold those simple instructions for a long time.

Peltry assumed she'd eventually have to move. The Bureau and the Administration would not be making D.C. a mecca for her career. He figured it would take a while. More than a year, it turned out. In that time, she must have gone through dozens of testimonies, depositions, and interviews, public and in camera. Some made the news. Most didn't.

His never did. He, too, had been interviewed by the FBI on multiple occasions, none pleasant. His questioners clearly believed his comments about the Plan were fabrications. They considered him JFB's accomplice. They implied that law enforcement was close to accusing him of helping Black escape in Idaho.

"You're in our sights," one agent had said to him.

Drawing any undue attention to himself or the Plan, or anything, frankly, Peltry knew was not in his best interest. Truth be damned. If he kept his mouth shut, he might disappear onto a list of names of other anonymous bystanders. In the end, it worked out that way. He was never called up to testify to any public committee or in any lawsuit. His official testimony was given via FBI agents with his assigned lawyer present. His name was never a path the public investigation took. No lawyer, no journalist came to see him about what he knew. Nor did he seek anyone out.

He followed the news about Youngblood's role in the Black investigation. From the start, she was among the many FBI names referred to or quoted by the media. She had been quoted once on a morning news show saying, "I'd stake my life on the fact that Jefferson Fitzgerald Black acted alone. There are no other shooters." In the months-long coverage she was never cast as a villain or an incompetent or even a major player, just another badge doing her thankless job. In time, her name disappeared from the diminishing news stories about the assassination of the Vice President.

Despite keeping a low profile, Youngblood had to know that she remained under continued observation; although he expected that human agents were no longer on her tail day and night. Technology was. The tracking device in the van augmented with satellite and drone surveillance was good enough. He was under the same scrutiny. He assumed the watching would continue for her and him until the Second Amendment Killer receded into fake memories, manufactured by time, the persistence of conventional wisdom, and bureaucracy.

Bureaucracy was first to lay its cornerstone to that inevitable history. The publication of the *LeBlair Commission Report on the Assassination of the Vice President* the previous month proved beyond a shadow of a doubt that Jefferson Fitzgerald Black was the Second Amendment Killer. He acted alone. There was no conspiracy. Only him. He was an evil genius whose only motivation was to kill anyone who supported the Second Amendment. Although there never would be a clear view into his sick mind, the SAK while indisputably mentally ill, was a uniquely gifted individual capable of causing the terror and havoc he did. America was lucky the President survived and that the SAK was stopped.

Of course, mistakes were made, the *Report* revealed without irony. To prevent any future Second Amendment Killer from attacking America, the *Report* argued that the President needed wider latitude to direct FBI and Homeland Security investigations into individuals thought to be engaged in acts of terror against the Second Amendment. New sedition laws should be enacted as well as additional legislation needed to curb radical actions in local communities that want to limit the rights of gun owners, faith-based organizations, local police unions, and other traditional American groups. "The unprecedented assault on America's core values needs swift and determined action by Congress to strengthen the Executive Branch to remain great and free," was the most quoted conclusion from the *Report*.

The Commission's *Report* said that law enforcement, including the FBI, missed multiple clues in tracking the Second Amendment Killer. But the terrorist's ability to alter databases used everywhere by everyone made identifying him physically or even genetically, let alone pinpointing his location, all but impossible. The *Report* suggested improvements to security software protocols to allow investigators easier access private databases. It called for increased funding for cyber defense. It further said that if technology experts like the Second Amendment Killer had unofficial backdoors into computer systems, it made complete sense for software and hardware makers to give similar access to the FBI and Homeland Security. Because of the hostility of Silicon Valley types, Congress needed to pass forceful laws to make it happen.

The *Report* also noted that had the FBI agent at the Second Amendment Party in Idaho not botched his attempt at stopping the Second Amendment Killer, the rest of the horrifying murders would not have happened. The *Report*, without specifically stating it, blamed the VP's assassination on the late Agent Derrick Witherspoon, whose mistake was to die first and not kill the SAK. The solution to such a problem, the *Report* suggested, was to change FBI policy, increase staffing for domestic operations, and allow more agents to attend any event for any purpose in order to protect citizens' Second Amendment Rights.

The *Report* went on to say that the Bureau's organizational structure had been hampered by "outdated" progressive legislation. It claimed "risk mitigation," "governance," and "transparency" laws hindered ever-shifting investigations. These laws, too, needed to be revised by Congress. However, within the limited latitude it currently retains, the LeBlair *Report* revealed a partial restructuring of its Special-Agents-in-Charge staff development process to streamline the investigative arm of the Bureau. As a result, an unspecific reduction in force already had been implemented, the *Report* concluded.

That reduction was Celeste Youngblood.

He read about it months after the assassination in the *Washington Post* online. A throw-away paragraph at the end of a story headlined "LeBlair's Struggle for a New FBI" reported that "agents steeped in pre-SAK training have been voluntarily leaving or going through retraining. For example, LeBlair points to Agent Celeste Youngblood, who along with other agents put on administrative leave after the assassination of the Vice President, opted for retirement rather than face the rigorous retraining required for what Director LeBlair calls the 'New FBI.' Sources say Youngblood has taken a position as a homicide detective in New Mexico."

The next week Peltry was notified that Celeste Youngblood had rented a one-way van from the 17th Street NW U-Haul in D.C. to be returned at the U-Haul franchise on Jaguar Drive in Santa Fe. The U-Haul-suggested GPS route she had chosen with her rental contract took her through Oklahoma City.

II

When Youngblood finally shut off the van's engine, the A/C stopped. Peltry knew the oppressive Sooner state mid-day heat bore down on the metal truck like it held a grudge against U-Haul-branded transients. Still, she sat there. Peltry figured, a victim of her training, carefully observing her new surroundings.

If she were like Peltry, she'd first look for security cameras in the area. Miss Jackie's had two obvious weatherproof cameras focused on its parking lot. They looked state of the art, but angled only on the owner's property. The others Peltry had disguised to blend into the architecture and took in a broader view of the surroundings. He doubted that she identified them. Other businesses around Miss Jackie's offered less video coverage. A new fast food joint had a line of cars out its drive-thru on the next corner, and plenty of cameras, but they encompassed the franchise's property and nothing else. The nearby 7-11 was similarly equipped. Her image was unlikely to show up on a local security camera beyond Miss Jackie's. It was as if the street's video surveillance had been installed by lawyers afraid of getting into unnecessary litigation on behalf of their neighbors. No other places along the shabby strip malls nearby sported obvious cameras.

Finally, perhaps satisfied she had the lay of the land, she checked her mirrors and hopped out of the cab. He saw that intense heat made her gasp and swear out loud.

"Jesus!"

Not only did he read her lips, but he also saw that the hypercardioid directional microphone planted in Miss Jackie's logo above the entrance had picked up her sound and graphed it with blue vertical bars running left to right on a monitor. From there it was saved as an audio file, and sent it to a speech-to-text app, so he could read it. Peltry felt a moment of pride in his work, then turned off the mic.

Lunch traffic prowled NE 23rd Street, old Highway 62, downtown looming nearby. She stood for nearly minute, waiting for a perfectly safe moment to cross in the middle of the busy road. It never came. Eventually the heat got to her and she bolted into the street, her palm out like fullback about to stiff-arm a defensive tackler, as if it might pause the flow of oncoming pickup trucks as she zig-zagged her way to Miss Jackie's. It worked well enough and she crossed with only a single red Ford 150 honking rudely at her.

Once she was inside Miss Jackie's she appeared in a different window on one of Peltry's displays. He saw the A/C hit her like a cold shower. She gasped and swore again.

"Jesus!"

He saw it took a moment for her eyes to adjust to the dimly lit waiting area, where another couple sat on a wooden bench, holding hands as if on a perfect date. He was pale white. She was shimmering black. They literally stared into each other's eyes, oblivious to anything but themselves.

Behind the cash register stood a fifty-plus year-old woman with expertly treated blond hair piled high above a smooth amber face centered by a genuine wide, white smile. Her blue eyes glittered like the imposing ring on her finger, a diamond the size to inspire F. Scott Fitzgerald.

He watched their conversation from different camera angles.

"Miss Jackie?"

"Why you *are* a detective, Agent Youngblood, just like Syd said. Welcome to Oklahoma City. You must be tired and hungry from your drive. Let me take you to go see him."

"Thank you."

"Let me show you the Ladies Room first. After such a long drive, I always gotta piss like a stepped on bull frog."

Youngblood laughed.

Miss Jackie turned and walked toward the rear of the place and Youngblood followed. At that, Peltry climbed upstairs to the main floor and into a very private room he'd designed specially for his friend years ago. Built for serious security.

Soon enough, the door opened revealing the two women.

Miss Jackie said, "Detective Youngblood, I hope you don't mind, but would you slip your phone into my little baggie here?"

She handed Youngblood a mesh gray cloth bag. With her dazzling smile at full wattage, she said, "Just a formality, honey."

She deposited her phone in the bag.

"After you, darlin'," she said, glancing down. "Watch your step."

Crossing the door's sill, a good three inches above the floor, was like stepping into a Navy ship's compartment, a stateroom or possibly the bilge. Inside, the room's stark, but bright copper walls accentuated the nautical vibe.

Miss Jackie closed the door and left.

"You've entered a Faraday cage, Detective Youngblood. I assume you're familiar with them."

She studied the room for a moment, taking in its bare shiny metal mesh walls compared with its well-appointed and pricey furniture. The side tables were all custom made from exotic woods. A full bar hand-carved from oak and embedded with crystal mirrors stretched across an entire 15-foot wall at the back. Peltry had estimated his friend's custom made twelve-foot long hewed from solid walnut must have cost his friend a thousand dollars a foot. The chairs weren't bad either. His friend's off-the-books business interests, whatever they might be, were highly profitable.

"Yeah," she said. "A Faraday cage blocks electromagnetic waves from passing in or out. No radio frequencies, cellphone, no wifi, no Bluetooth, nothing in any frequency can be transmitted or, equally important, listened to by anyone outside the room. The FBI had their share of similar ultra secure rooms. We called them SCIFs for Sensitive Compartmentalized Information Facilities."

"Exactly the same."

"Not exactly, Mr. Peltry. Ours weren't so comfortable," she said as she gestured around the room. She turned back to him, looking serious, and said, "Obviously, Mr. Peltry, you want to have a very private chat with me. Perhaps you should tell me what this about."

"Indeed, but first, feel welcome to Miss Jackie's. Join me for lunch. The food's great. You must be starved."

He was enjoying a plate of ribs while perched in a gleaming Thomas Moser Continuous Armchair, where the gorgeous wood flows from the tip of one arm to the other. He pointed to a matching chair across from him.

"How'd you know I'd be here now?"

"U-Haul puts GPS trackers on their vehicles."

"For them."

He shrugged.

Her eyes flared angrily.

He said, "Please, sit. As I said, the food is great and I'll explain."

He gestured again amiably to the table setting before the empty Thomas Moser chair, one of eight surrounding the long table. Music played softly in the background. A famously endlessly long, live version of the Grateful Dead performing "Truckin'." He couldn't hear it, but thought she might appreciate it.

She sat, succumbing to the delicious smells pulling her to the table like a hungry shark. She grabbed a handful of paper napkins with one hand while putting four ribs on her plate from the heaping mound on the table's platter. She added a pair of corn bread muffins and a generous scoop of coleslaw to her meal.

She dug in. Her eyes rolled ecstatically after her first bites. She moaned contentedly.

"Good, huh?" Peltry said.

"Good huh!" she replied, looking down at her plate, probably wondering if it was enough.

He laughed.

"There's always more," he said as if reading her thoughts.

They ate in companionable silence for a few minutes. She drank greedily from a tall glass of home brewed sweet iced tea.

"Detective Youngblood, if I may be the first to call you by your new title…."

"Miss Jackie already did."

"Well, the second person, then."

It was her turn to grin. Red barbecue sauce stained her bright smile. She took a few more bites.

Facing him, she said, "I've come because you said Mr. Black left something for you on your phone that I needed to see."

"Yes," he pulled out a Samsung Galaxy from the same kind of gray mesh bag Miss Jackie had given her. "Just so you know, Miss Jackie puts everyone's phones in one of these. Her boss insists. This," he waved the phone from his bag, "is the one I got after you took away my second iPhone. Figured a Galaxy would last longer. But I never used it, at least as a phone. After I saw the app, I, well, thought it best to buy a different phone from a different carrier for myself. Crossed my fingers and got an LG. It's already lasted me longer than my last three put together."

This prompted another smile from his guest.

She reached out her hand. "Let's see."

Youngblood turned the phone on. He told her the passcode. It only took a few seconds to display a home screen. It had a single app on the display: a rifle's icon. Underneath it in Helvetic italics read: *Killing a President.*

She slid the screen left and got the normal home startup screen and apps like Email, Texting, Settings, Photos, and Contacts. She slid back right.

"This was how you found it?"

"Yep."

"You watched it?"

"Wouldn't you?"

She hesitated a heartbeat or two, then tapped the icon, launching a video. She tilted the phone to landscape and lifted it a foot or so from her face. Her eyes went wide at the opening sequence. He remembered every scene as she watched.

It opened with JFB's voiceover, with captions, Peltry assumed inserted specifically for him. The camera scanned the surroundings unsteadily. It revealed a cramped space completely encased in sheet rock screwed to a steel frame. The space was triangular in shape, coming to a point on the ceiling. He remembered the scrolling text verbatim as the scene progressed.

> *Thank you for getting a new phone so quickly, Mr. Peltry. We met before under difficult circumstances and I apologize for any inconvenience my taking you hostage may have caused you. But fate has its way of throwing people into circumstances time and time again. If I've learned anything in the months I've been on my mission, Mr. Peltry, it's this: circumstances are always beyond your control, but the decisions you make under those circumstances are completely yours and yours alone.*

> *As you know, my name is Jefferson Fitzgerald Black. The FBI calls me JFB. The media calls me the Second Amendment Killer. If you received this, Mr. Peltry, I am dead. In this app you will find my memoir. It's not my life story, but my life on a mission to make victims of the*

> *perpetrators of gun violence in this country. My goal is not simply to kill, but to bury my victims in irony; particularly one hateful man. In addition to this introductory video, I will live stream my final murder. I'm certain the press will crawl across Covid-infested broken glass to get a copy from you once they learn about it. I hope that you will get out my side of the story about how and why I killed the President. It's all here.*

She stopped the video.

"Huh? Then why did he shoot the *Vice* President first and not the President? That makes no sense."

"Watch," he said.

She tapped the screen again.

Peltry set down a rib, wiped his fingers on a napkin, sipped his tea, then stood and walked to her side, looking down so he could see the video. Even though it was vivid in his memory, watching it still amazed him. She angled it his way to help his view.

After the killer had shown his surroundings he explained that he was holed up in an enclosed space in the rafters of Rupp Arena in Lexington, Kentucky. The steel frame he was within provided major load-bearing support for the arena's theater mode partitioning system. Mechanical arms pushed the many-ton walls to and fro to create custom-sized auditoriums. They linked to the steel truss that held everything together. The sheet rock's only purpose was to hide the unsightly cold metal frame structure from the audience.

At that point Black changed the perspective from his surroundings to himself. He looked blankly into the camera.

She looked at Peltry.

"He's had so many guises, I've actually had no clear image of the man in my mind. There he is. JFB in the flesh."

"Looks mostly like the guy I was with back in Idaho," Peltry confirmed.

Black began explaining the technical issues about how he had built a tiny camera into the bridge of a pair of clear sharpshooter eyeglasses. He laid out in detail how the glasses sent the video stream to a phone he had hidden about twenty feet outside his sniper nest. The phone had a direct line to a server Black controlled in IBM's cloud network. The server was programmed to add the video to the app and then install it on Peltry's new phone once Black had failed to deactivate the program, presumably after he'd been jailed or killed. He'd hacked Peltry's carrier's database of customers and adjusted his profile to load the app 33:33:33 hours, minutes, seconds after the feed from his sharpshooter glasses stopped transmitting. The scheme was interesting to Peltry technically, but he could see that Youngblood was tuning it out.

Then Black began to discuss his planned assassination. That got her attention.

> I sealed myself into this forgotten alcove because until I shoot the President from my perch above the podium where he will spew his lies and his hate, no one will have even thought about it as a place for an assassin to hide. It's not called out in the architectural drawings, but written in as an engineering modification during construction. Few people know about. Fewer people care. I knew this because, for one thing, I've already been sealed in here for a week with another three days to go before I get to shoot the President dead.

> You might want to know how I got in here. Easy. A week before Rupp was announced as a venue for the President's endless campaign, I had infiltrated the arena's maintenance database and inserted a critical five-year inspection into the calendar. At the same time, I put the steel-truss inspection onto the work calendar of Clyde Dolmont, Lexington's assistant chief building inspector, a man well known around the arena. Both databases

assigned Bluegrass Drywall Professionals to remove the sheet rock containing the truss; wait throughout the inspection; then replace the drywall once the inspection was complete. Bluegrass Drywall Professionals, a fake twelve-year-old company I started last month, only had one employee, me.

I met Clyde at the entrance to the massive building with my tools and slabs of sheet rock on my dolly. I let him lead the way and we took a freight elevator to the top of the structure. We located the wall among a narrow gantry way atop the arena. While Clyde patiently toyed with his smartphone, I pried off the plaster wall surrounding the unsightly truss hanging above the hardwood floor sixty feet below. The Wildcats were playing that night. The inspector ambled inside and took two and half hours measuring the support structure with laser tools and running acoustic and vibration tests on the metal. In the end, he seemed satisfied. Once Clyde signed off on the condition of the truss, he left me to complete my work putting in a new false wall, which I did. Only, instead of following Clyde after my job was completed, I sealed myself inside the enclosure and waited.

The best snipers are able to lie in wait. I'm not among the best, but I am among the most tenacious. I will be here for ten days before the President shows up for me to kill him. I have planned for this moment. I have two weeks worth of rations. I have air tight containers and zip lock bags for my shit and piss. I brought three big novels to read, including, I kid you not, Tolstoy's War and Peace, a pretty good soap opera to alleviate the long dull hours waiting for my singular moment.

So, anyway, I'll check in later, killing time until I can actually kill someone who deserves to die.

She paused the video, put the phone down, turned, and looked up at Peltry.

"I hope he's not going to walk us through his days of shitting and pissing in baggies, is he?"

He laughed.

"No. Here he stops with his intro and, well, the video cuts to the chase when he starts up again."

She eyed him skeptically, then tapped the phone's video screen.

The final segment begins from JFB's vantage point. He's lying on his stomach. He's removed a square of the sheet rock where it meets the steel floor. He scoots forward and the viewer sees his view of the ground below. A few thousand people packed into a near triangular configuration of the arena's theater mode. The podium is perfectly placed eighty feet forward and sixty below. A turkey shoot.

He knew Youngblood heard crowd noise pouring from the smartphone's speakers. He read the captions Black provided once again.

> *The President's in the building and his fans are in a frenzy. Can't wait until he takes the stage. I won't wait long. I'm not much for suspense. I'm ready to go.*
>
> *This is the big build up for the big man. Lots of people crammed inside. Loud music. A frenzy just for him. He needs these crowds like a junkie needs a fix. And the more freakish the bile he spews at them the more they love...*

Although he couldn't hear, two short explosions spewed sheet rock and bits of metal into the enclosed space. Black twisted his prone position to face up as a hail of plaster rained down on his perspective. Four hands from two different men wearing Balaclavas pushed him back to the floor. A third masked man approached, towering above Black. The man's bright blue eyes lit up. You could tell he was smiling. He pulled a gun with a long sound suppressor, bent down, brushed a few bits of plaster off Black's glasses, and stood back up.

The caption for Peltry read:

> *The Boss says "nice shot, dead man."*

The screen went blank.

He moved across the table from her to see her face.

"What the fuck!" she whispered over and over. "Jesus! What the fuck?"

"Exactly."

They were quiet for a solid minute.

"Have you read the complete memoir?" he asked.

"No."

He leaned across the table and tapped a menu bar in the app.

"Read it. Take you an hour or so," he retrieved a deck of cards from his hip pocket. "I'll play solitaire."

He dealt out the cards. She hesitated for a split second before beginning to read.

When she finished reading the memoir he saw Youngblood let out a long, exasperated sigh.

"I'll say it again, Jesus, what the fuck? JFB believes he was hypnotized, which is ridiculous. But, even if true, he's okay with it? Somehow he doesn't mind being part of the Plan, whatever the fuck that is. It's madness. He's looney. Come on. I mean, I'm not trying to call you a liar, but you're the only source for the so-called Plan. Even this app comes from you. It's just not realistic. There's no real evidence."

"Except for the memoir. Except for the video. Except for the missed shot at the President."

"Shit."

She bent her head into her arms folded on the table. She may have been talking. He saw her jaw moving. But he couldn't see what she was saying. Finally, she sat up straight and turned to him.

"You've been sitting on this for more than a year. Why?"

"Lots of reasons. Mostly having to do with staying alive and/or keeping my freedom."

"You think if you go to *CBS News* with this you'll get killed or thrown in jail?"

"Yes. For one thing, someone killed a sitting Vice President, and probably not Black like everyone thinks. How hard would it be for those guys to nail a deaf security guy in Oklahoma? And what's to say the app won't be proven to be a deep fake in the FBI lab and I'll get thrown in jail for bringing false evidence? Or, even if it's believed, doesn't it link me closer to the Second Amendment Killer, part of his conspiracy? Like you said, it comes from me, the only guy who has witnessed a discussion of the Plan. Who's gonna take my side? There's nothing but pain in it for me. No thank you."

"But what you're saying is that the Vice President should not even have been shot. If the video is accurate, JFB was dead before the assassination took place."

"I've had time to think about it, Detective Youngblood, and it's not rocket science. The men who killed Black shot the VP. They didn't want the President dead. What it looks like is that the President wanted a martyr. And he hired the guys who shot Black to give him one. Haven't you always wondered why Black missed the President, who was standing, an easier shot by far, and instead hit the VP, who was sitting stage right. Black proved he was a crack shot in all of his other killings. He wouldn't miss. The assassin, whoever it was, didn't miss either. He aimed for the Vice President. He was the target."

"I can't believe it."

"The first rule you'll need to follow as a detective in New Mexico is, who benefited the most from the crime? In this case, obviously, it's the President."

"Still, why shoot the Vice President?"

"So he could choose his son as his Vice President for the final years of a second term. He's been floating that idea since the assassination. That's why it's taken so long for him to choose a VP. He's grooming America. And, you know what his son has said, that if he ever runs for the White House on his own he'll choose his dad as his VP candidate. The President owns the Supreme Court. They'll rule it's fine for him to be VP because there is nothing specific in the Constitution preventing him. He'll continue running the show as VP."

She shook her head and looked at him again.

"And if the Supreme Court rules against him?"

"Junior will make him Secretary of State or something. It doesn't matter. He just wants Junior to get the spotlight enough to be elected. Keep the country in the family."

"That's crazy conspiracy thinking," she said. "I can't get behind it."

"Again, except for the missed shot, the memoir, and the video."

He returned to his seat, pushed his plate away.

She said, "Can you go anonymous with it?"

"You mean post it to 4chan on the internet or email it to Rachel Maddow?" He snorted. "It'll either be deemed a deep fake or, if it isn't, some sort of a elaborately staged event to discredit the President. He's a hero now. He survived a direct assassination attempt. This is only credible if someone with a role in the official investigation comes forward with the video and the app."

"So you're showing it to me thinking I might drop by the *Washington Post* with a copy?"

"Maybe. But truth is, I thought you might know of someone inside the Bureau who might."

She rose, shifted her chair so her back was to him. She put her chin in her palm, her elbow resting on the polished oak arm. She thought for a long time. When she turned back to him, tears brimmed in the corner of her eyes.

"I wish I could. I wish I could. I can't. I don't know any martyrs. No one I know is going to risk their career for this."

"Even if it's the truth?"

"Even if."

He nodded.

"Didn't think so. It's too much to ask of anyone."

"So, I ask again, why show it to me? Why lay that burden, the knowing, on me?"

"Because I can't carry it alone. It's too fantastical. I try to think of how to make people see this, to read this, to think about it, to believe it like I do," he gestured to the phone. "But I can't think of anything. It's as though our country has been stolen, but I'm the only one who saw the crook hijack it. And no one, trust me, no one will believe me or I won't live long enough if I come out with this by myself. I've thought about it, if we both went public together on this, we might just get some traction. The media might follow it up. There might be a real investigation. The truth might come out."

Her head bobbed in understanding.

"'Might.'"

"Yes, good things *might* happen."

"But probably not."

"Yep, probably not."

They were quiet for a long time. Finally, she pushed back her chair and rose.

"Thank you for the once-in-a-lifetime lunch, Mr. Peltry. Be sure to thank Miss Jackie for me."

He stood.

"I will. It's been a pleasure to have you as a guest."

He went ahead of her to the door and opened it. She took her phone out of the mesh pouch tossing the cloth to him.

"I'll keep our conversation in mind, Mr. Peltry. I will. But I wouldn't expect to hear from me right away, maybe not for a long time. A long time."

They exchanged weak smiles, shook hands, and she walked away.

Peltry went back into the room. He gathered up his playing cards and put the deck back into his hip pocket. He grabbed the Galaxy phone, stuffing into his other rear pocket. It was heavier than the cards and he felt unbalanced as he shut the door.

the end